I0825224

Also by Jamie Pacton

The Vermilion Emporium

The Absinthe Underground

Furious

Lucky Girl

The Life and (Medieval) Times of Kit Sweetly

Homegrown Magic

Praise for Jamie Pacton

"What a treat to return to this world, which is as enchanting and wondrous as it is deadly! I never wanted to leave it behind. Like a faerie spell, *The Hyacinth Labyrinth* will ensorcell readers with its lush atmosphere; swashbuckling heroines; and sweet, slow-burn romance."

—Allison Saft, #1 *New York Times* bestselling author of *Wings of Starlight* (on *The Hyacinth Labyrinth*)

"A thrilling magical romp with an enchanting mixture of whimsy and adventure. There's nothing more perfect than stories about girls with swords and tiny dragons and Jamie Pacton delivers the most delightful tale imaginable!"

—CG Drews, *New York Times* bestselling author of *Don't Let The Forest In* and *Hazelthorn* (on *The Hyacinth Labyrinth*)

"*The Hyacinth Labyrinth* soars with warmth and whimsy! Equal parts cozy fable and magical DnD adventure, readers will be utterly charmed by Hyacinth's and Chloe's story."

—Erin Cotter, author of *By Any Other Name* and *A Traitorous Heart* (on *The Hyacinth Labyrinth*)

★ "In this haunting tale . . . Pacton weaves a romantic and thrilling story of ambition, magic, and peril. Sybil and Esme's chemistry is palpable, and Pacton's lush portrayal of Severon as a city filled with art and beauty reminiscent of fin de siècle Paris adds additional layers of enchantment."

—*Publishers Weekly*, **Starred Review (on** ***The Absinthe Underground*****)**

"An enchanting romantasy brimming with glittering, intoxicating prose and wild Fae magic. These quick-handed thieves will steal your heart from your first meeting."

—Elizabeth Kilcoyne, author of William C. Morris Award finalist ***Wake the Bones*** **(on** ***The Absinthe Underground*****)**

✦

★ "[A] unique examination of class inequality and exploitation set against a provocative landscape . . . a hauntingly romantic fantasy adventure."

—*Publishers Weekly*, **Starred Review (on** ***The Vermillion Emporium*****)**

★ "A fantasy novel clothed in romance and adventure, *The Vermilion Emporium* weaves together themes of loyalty and destiny, delivering a heartfelt and dazzling triumph."

—*Foreword Reviews*, **Starred Review (on** ***The Vermillion Emporium*****)**

Moonshadow Kingdom

to Starlight Kingdom

Queen Mab's Palaces

Crescent Atheneum

Meadow Lands

Keldale

to Solstice Kingdom

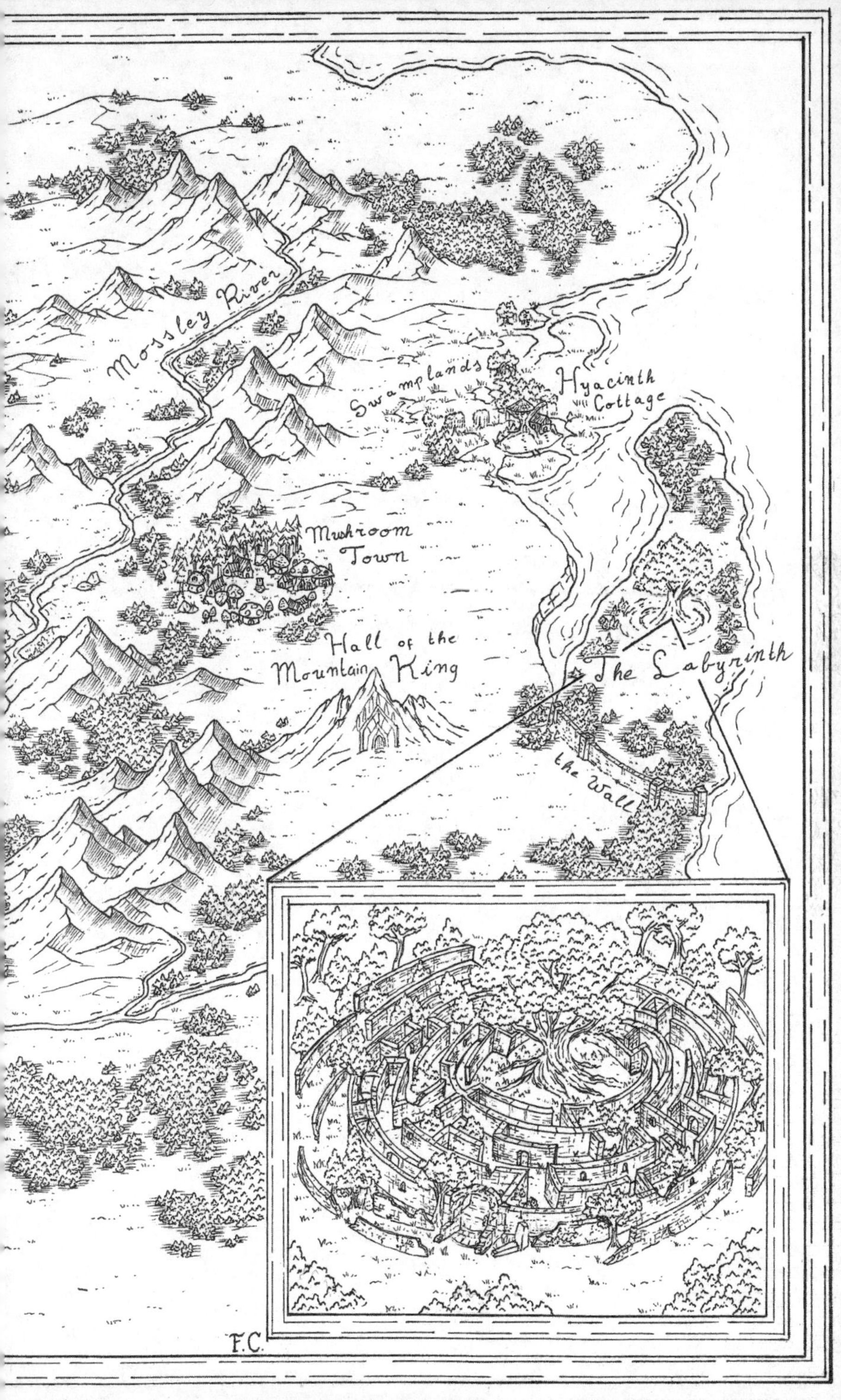
Mossley River
Swamplands
Hyacinth Cottage
Mushroom Town
Hall of the Mountain King
The Labyrinth
the Wall
F.C.

THE HYACINTH LABYRINTH
JAMIE PACTON
PEACHTREE
Teen

Published by Peachtree Teen
An imprint of Peachtree Publishing Company Inc.

Map illustration by Feycompass Cartography

Printed and bound in April 2026 at Sheridan, Chelsea, MI, USA.
Edited by Ashley Hearn
Book design by Lily Steele
PeachtreeBooks.com

First Edition, 2026
ISBN: 978-1-6826-3-819-4 | 1 3 5 7 9 10 8 6 4 2 (hardcover)

Library of Congress Cataloging-in-Publication Data

Names: Pacton, Jamie, 1979- author
Title: The Hyacinth labyrinth / Jamie Pacton.
Description: First hardcover edition. | Atlanta : Peachtree Publishing Company Inc, 2026. | Audience: Ages 14 and Up | Audience: Grades 10-12
Summary: "When Hyacinth and her friend Chloe, a human stable hand trapped in Fae, sneak off to a riverside market, Hyacinth discovers a magical book sent to her by her father that reveals that he is trapped inside a library at the heart of a treacherous labyrinth"— Provided by publisher.
Identifiers: LCCN 2025052923 | ISBN 9781682638194 hardcover
Subjects: CYAC: Fairies—Fiction | Missing persons—Fiction
Labyrinths—Fiction | Lesbians—Fiction | Fantasy | Romance stories
LCGFT: Fantasy fiction | Romance fiction | Lesbian fiction | Novels
Classification: LCC PZ7.1.P3 Hy 2026
LC record available at https://lccn.loc.gov/2025052923

EU Authorized Representative: HackettFlynn Ltd, 36 Cloch Choirneal, Balrothery, Co. Dublin, K32 C942, Ireland. EU@walkerpublishinggroup.com

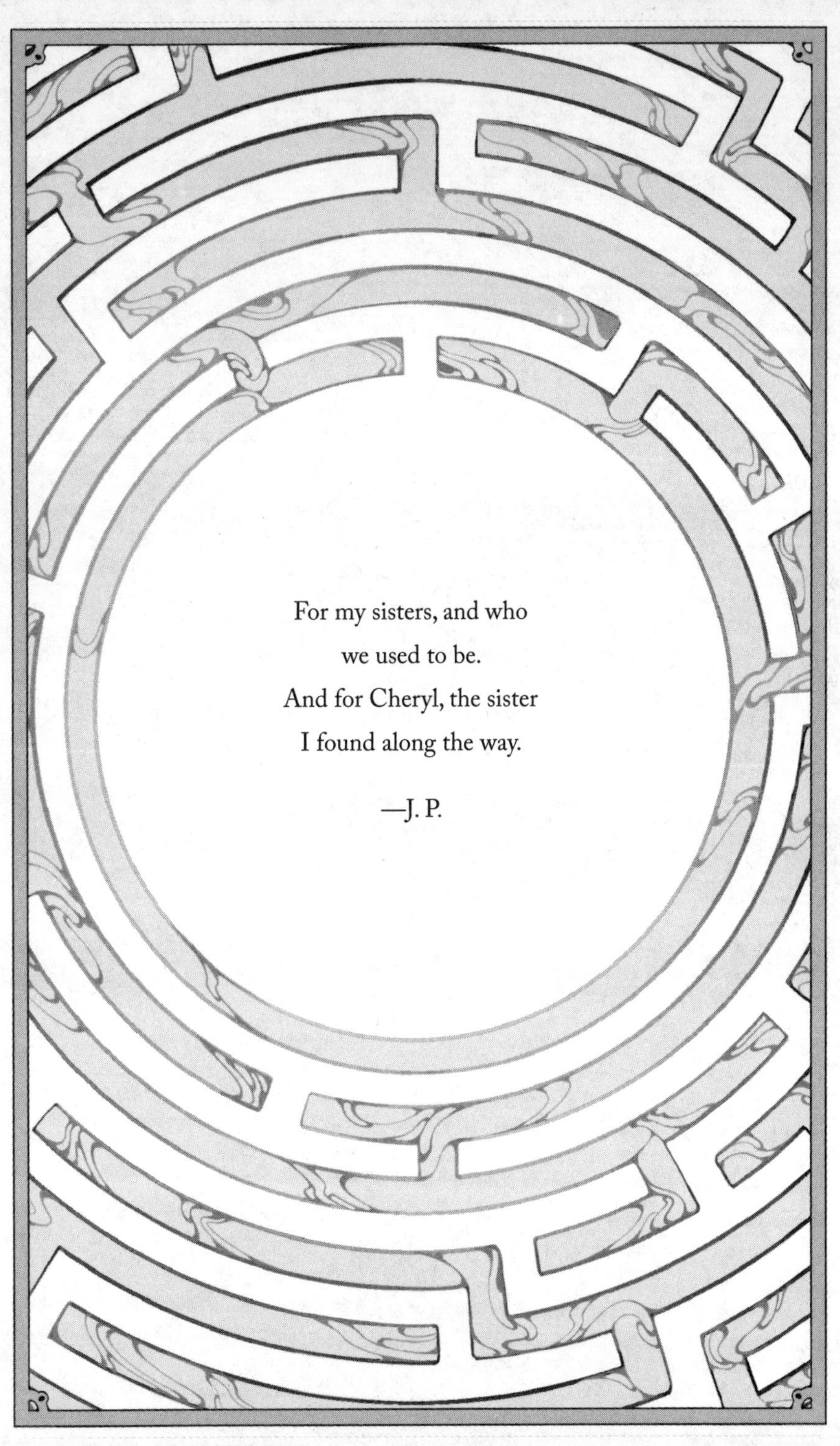

For my sisters, and who
we used to be.
And for Cheryl, the sister
I found along the way.

—J. P.

Author's Note

Although *The Hyacinth Labyrinth* is a standalone, it's set in the world of *The Vermilion Emporium*—where we first meet Chloe and her sister Anya. More specifically, it's set in the Fae world from *The Absinthe Underground*, where we encounter Chloe again and first meet Princess Hyacinth. You don't have to read these books in order, but if you have, then it's helpful to know the events of this story take place several months after what happened in *The Absinthe Underground*.

Chapter One
Hyacinth

The Solstice Ball was in full swing, and Princess Hyacinth Bramblefen, the youngest of Queen Mab's daughters, couldn't wait to leave.

"Bramble and marsh," she grumbled under her breath as she stood on the dais at the front of the ballroom. "You'd think the High Fae had never seen a party in their near-eternal lives."

Hyacinth scowled and her full-moon eyes tracked dozens of High Fae nobles swirling around the queen's dance floor. The dancers moved in a kaleidoscope—no, *landslide* was a better word for it—of feathers, silks, mosses, berries, and sparkling dew-spun dresses and suits. Elaborate masks hid the dancers' faces, and jewels glittered in their hair, on their horns and clothing, and across their rainbowed complexions. A pixie string quartet played a lively melody in one corner of the ballroom, and raucous laughter filled the space. Silvery-blue starlight knifed across the polished floor. Summertime perfumes floated on the air, a heady rush of honeysuckle, sweat, endless moonlit nights, fireflies, and fresh grass.

It was *awful.*

Hyacinth anxiously folded and unfolded a scrap of paper in her pocket. Written on it was the most important clue about her missing father that she'd ever found. Not that she could do anything about it while she was trapped at the ball.

What absolute misery.

A pair of High Fae lords twirled past Hyacinth, their lips meeting for a moment as they danced. Hyacinth's mind immediately wrenched away from the scrap of paper and the party, landing firmly on a kiss of her own that she was trying to forget.

It'd been a sloppy kiss. A secret one. All warm lips, summer-wine-scented breath, and the dizzy laughter of the common Fae girl feathering against her throat.

Chloe.

Just thinking about the red-haired stablehand made Hyacinth's insides twist.

Did Chloe regret kissing her?

Hyacinth flung the question away like a stone skipped across a deep pool. Absolutely not to be considered. To distract herself from more thoughts of kissing, she moved her hand from the scrap of paper to the six small potion bottles on the leather alchemist's belt around her waist. Mentally she recited their contents and effects, hoping that would help her *not* think about Chloe.

Juniper heart for illusion. A moon-drenched secret for levitation. Bitterroot berry for healing. Gray tendrils of fog for vanishing. Wraith tears for compulsion. Dragonheart ashes for fire and ruin.

Chloe always asked what the potions were for, and Hyacinth always deflected.

Stop thinking about Chloe.

Impossible.

Hyacinth's fingers flitted from the wax-stoppered potion bottles to the enchanted compass attached to her belt. It was supposed to help her find exactly three locations, according to the tinkerer she'd bought it from. Which might be true. Or not. In the last few months, Hyacinth had bought dozens of ultimately useless magical items. She ran the compass's chain through her fingers, loving its slithery, slippery feel.

Chloe's hair had felt just as smooth when Hyacinth had run her finger through it last night.

Hyacinth sighed, surrendering and letting her thoughts dwell on the stablehand.

They'd been circling each other for months: flirting, chatting, sneaking off into the woods for walks, but when the solstice parties had started at midnight yesterday and the torches burned low in the castle, Hyacinth found Chloe in the garden. She'd brought a bottle of starred-berry wine. They drank, and laughed, and danced—then, all at once, they stumbled against one of the garden walls. Their bodies tangled, their hands caught in each other's hair, their breaths came in ragged gasps. . . .

Hyacinth leaned forward, or perhaps Chloe did, and the distance between them evaporated. There had been only lips and hands and—

"Hyacinth Bramblefen! Stand up straighter," Queen Mab, the ever-glorious monarch of the Moonshadow Kingdom, snapped. "Unknit your brows, let go of that wretched belt you insist on wearing, and smile, for bramble's sake. It's a *party*. You don't have to look so gloomy."

Hyacinth rolled her eyes at her mother.

She wasn't gloomy. Not really. She was remembering a kiss that never should've happened. High Fae princesses didn't talk to the common Fae, unless it was to give them orders. They certainly didn't befriend them. And they most definitely didn't spend an evening kissing the taste of starred-berries off their lips.

Hyacinth's fingers moved from her enchanted compass back to the scrap of paper in her pocket. *If* she could ever escape this party, she might be able to learn more about the book it had come from and how it connected to her father.

Unlikely on both fronts if my mother has anything to say about it.

Hyacinth looked over at the queen.

Tonight, Mab presided on a carved amethyst throne, appraising her guests. Jewels glittered in her cerulean hair, and her sharp teeth gleamed in the slant of moonlight streaming through the glass dome above them. The queen's most trusted advisor and bodyguard—Maurelle, a High Fae knight with a thatch of white hair, a foxtail, and pointed ears—stood beside the queen, scrutinizing the crowd. She twirled a knife carelessly through her fingers, a habit that made Hyacinth's skin crawl.

How was she ever going to get past her mother and Maurelle?

First, stand up straighter, so the queen stops fussing.

Hyacinth shoved her shoulders and the phony wings attached to them backward. Pain spiked down her spine, chasing all memories of last night's kiss and her missing father away.

Bramble and marsh, her fake wings were *heavy*.

It wasn't bad enough that Hyacinth didn't have magic like her half sisters and every other Fae in the kingdom. No. She *also* lacked a beautiful set of jewel-toned wings she could manifest with a whispered word. Her true wings were supposed to have appeared months ago on her seventeenth birthday, along with her High Fae magic. Without the potions and other trinkets on her belt, though, she couldn't even pretend to do common Fae magic like warming a cup of tea (not that she'd ever had cause to warm tea, since the palace kitchens provided all her meals, but she'd heard it was something the common Fae could do). She certainly couldn't do any of the higher Fae magics like shifting a flower into a flying bird, painting a glamour over herself, crafting complex potions, convincing rivers to abandon their beds, or opening doors to other realms.

She was broken.

The secretly unmagical princess of the Moonshadow Kingdom. It was miserable most of the time, but some nights were particularly bad. And the solstice revelry season was the absolute worst.

The queen glanced over and raised an eyebrow at Hyacinth.

Hyacinth forced a pleasant smile and fought not to itch the spot on her shoulder blade where the fake wings irritated her pale purple skin.

Seemingly satisfied, her mother turned her attention from Hyacinth. The queen was the only other person who knew about Hyacinth's lack of magic. *Don't worry, darling*, the queen often said, a frown between her eyebrows betraying her true thoughts. *I'm sure your High Fae gifts will arrive soon. No need to tell your sisters or anyone else about this.*

Hyacinth wasn't so sure, and that's why she kept swiping potions from her mother's alchemists and buying enchanted trinkets from every trader who visited the palace.

The queen had made her favorite jeweler craft Hyacinth's fake wings in secret, and earlier that day, she'd secured them to Hyacinth's back with a spell that would hold for at least a fortnight. It wasn't perfect, and it'd make sleeping awkward, but it'd get Hyacinth through the next few balls. Which was something. At least she'd seem normal for those weeks. After that, who knew.

Stop thinking about your ridiculous wings and get moving!

How was she going to leave, though? Hyacinth considered the ballroom.

Hyacinth's half sister Maeve—a green Faerie who had found herself in their mother's ill graces a few months ago after she'd snuck into the human world and then tried to snatch Queen Mab's throne—had taken over planning the solstice celebration in her latest effort to make amends. She'd magicked the ballroom to look like, in her words, *a glittering nightclub in the human world*, complete with stained glass lamps, marble arches, flowing absinthe fountains, and sumptuous flower sculptures. Now Maeve stood beneath an arbor of wisteria, laughing with Clover and Tansy, two of the other Moonshadow princesses. The three princesses' mossy-green, pale gold, and pink-hued skin tones all matched their *real* wings.

How they would laugh if they knew Hyacinth had no magic. That she kissed stablehands and enjoyed it. That she wanted nothing more than to flee the party so she could uncover more about her long-lost father.

"How much longer do I have to stand here, Mother?" Hyacinth asked as evenly as possible.

"As long as I say," Queen Mab shot back. "We want people to see your *quality*, child. So they don't have any . . . suspicions about you." Like Hyacinth was a prize-winning racing salamander. Some creature to be warred over among the gentry. No one would want her if they knew how broken she actually was.

Would Chloe still want her if she found out Hyacinth had no magic?

A silly question.

One you certainly don't have time for.

Hyacinth glanced at the clock above the ballroom door—9:43. She had to go! She was meeting Chloe in the largest dragon paddock at ten. Tonight, party be damned, they were sneaking away to the Solstice Market in Keldale: a magical market with goods from all over the Fae realms that only appeared once a year and disappeared at midnight. It was nearly ten already!

If Hyacinth didn't get moving, she'd be late. Then she'd have to wait a full year to find the bookshop she was searching for tonight.

Making sure her mother wasn't watching, Hyacinth slipped the paper from her pocket and yet again studied its handwritten words.

Property of Evan Bramblefen.

Then, in blocky, worn letters below those five words was a bookshop stamp:

PURCHASED AT THE WILTING SPARROW BOOKSHOP, KELDALE.
SHOP HOURS DURING THE SOLSTICE MARKET ONLY.
IF LOST, PLEASE RETURN—

It wasn't much, but it was a clue—no matter how small—about her father. Evan Bramblefen. It was more valuable than any crumb she'd ever forced from her mother. After Hyacinth had found the scrap of paper tucked into a history book a few weeks ago, she and Chloe had devised their plan to visit the market. To learn anything more about her father tonight, though, Hyacinth had to leave the party. Now.

"Mother," Hyacinth said sweetly. "May I get some refreshments and have a dance? I'm certain my 'quality' will be much better shown among the other revelers, don't you think?"

Maurelle stopped twirling her knife and raised an eyebrow, but Queen Mab sighed. "Perhaps you're right. Very well then. Go on."

"Can I get you or Maurelle anything?"

Queen Mab's stern royal countenance relented just a bit. "No, nothing for me. Please enjoy yourself, Hyacinth. Find someone to dance with, and celebrate the solstice. I'll be giving my speech soon, and then I plan on doing the same."

"As you wish, Mother," Hyacinth said, curtsying as gracefully as she could with her wretched wings.

Queen Mab rested a hand on Hyacinth's shoulder, her silver nails biting into Hyacinth's skin. "You're such a good daughter. It's a relief on my nerves, really."

Hyacinth fought to maintain her own smile. She tried to be a good daughter. She really did. She was polite, pliable, obedient. Always striving to do the right thing, be the right thing, make her mother happy and proud. That version of herself should want nothing to do with Chloe and summer wine and dragons and bookshops in magical markets, but she *had* to sneak away tonight. She couldn't miss the chance to uncover the truth of where her father was and what had happened to him!

Hyacinth knew almost nothing about him. Her half sisters were the children of the old Moonshadow King, who'd passed away before Queen Mab met Evan Bramblefen. Then, Evan had disappeared when Hyacinth was barely two. Her mother always dismissed Hyacinth's questions, maintaining that talking about him would bring more heartbreak than hope.

Still, Hyacinth wondered. What kind of High Fae was he? Who were his parents? How had he met Queen Mab? What parts of him lived on in her? Was he still alive? Where had he disappeared to? What sort of magic did he have?

The questions had been haunting her for years.

The Wilting Sparrow Bookshop could have the answers. As long as she returned before the Solstice Ball ended, which would be hours after midnight, her mother wouldn't catch her. And, *if* Hyacinth did find out more about her father, then perhaps her mother would finally talk about him and help Hyacinth understand herself better.

A vision of Hyacinth and her mother bonding over memories of the missing Evan Bramblefen filled Hyacinth's mind. She'd felt different from her mother and half sisters long before her magic failed to materialize. Perhaps, if she knew more about her father, she'd finally feel like she belonged in her family.

It was enough to lend speed to her steps.

Fleeing the royal dais, she hurried toward an enormous gnarled weeping willow tree growing from the floor in one corner of the ballroom. It'd rooted there long before the castle was built, and it slept most of the time. When it was awake, the tree was known for declaiming melancholic poetry, so most of the High Fae gentry avoided getting too close, which suited Hyacinth's purposes. She ducked under the branches. Hidden in the wall behind the tree was a door—one of many secret passages in the castle—that led from the ballroom to the garden.

Hyacinth turned the doorknob, but it was locked.

She swore to herself, and her stomach sunk.

Why was it locked? It'd been open this afternoon when she tested it. Who could've locked it? Was she going to have to sneak out through the ballroom entrance under Maurelle's gaze?

Before Hyacinth could figure out what to do, the weeping willow stirred, shaking its green tresses. The branches slithered across Hyacinth's fake wings. A rough whisper, like the wind rattling dried leaves, emerged from a horizontal crack across the tree trunk that might've been its mouth.

"What a calamity, this merriment.
So fleeting, so fickle.
Echoes of joy lost in the frenzy of time. . . ."

Hyacinth waited for more verses, but the willow fell silent. Poor thing had suffered through thousands of parties in its lifetime. Hyacinth would write subpar brooding poetry too if she were stuck eternally in this ballroom.

A boisterous cheer pulled Hyacinth's attention from the tree. The pixies stopped playing, and golden goblets of summer wine were passed around the dance floor. Queen Mab raised her glass.

"All magic begins in stories!" the queen declared.

"All magic begins in stories!" The crowd echoed back one of the most well-worn phrases in the Fae world. Hyacinth wasn't sure if it signified anything or if people simply threw it about.

Queen Mab went on: "Tonight, we celebrate the solstice, the day our world began, and the three sisters who built it! Tonight, we honor them. To Celestine! To Millicent! To Aria!"

She gave this speech every year. Hyacinth could recite the story of the three Celestial Sisters from memory.

The three Celestial Sisters—Celestine of beginnings, Millicent of middles, and Aria of endings, goddesses of fate and fortune—were weary of the human world, where magic was fading and only a few could practice it. Riding their great dragon, Ora, to the end of the horizon, the Sisters spun a country of their own from magic, erecting a wall between their world and the human realm. Their children—the Fae—were many and varied, all of them gifted with some affinity for magic—be it glamours, or shape-shifting, vanishing, moving things, flying, and many more tricks. The High Fae were the Sisters' favored children, and they were blessed with the most magic. They could do it with spells, bargains, or potions. But magic was in their bodies and in the land itself. All Fae could enjoy it.

All Fae except for Hyacinth, of course.

She sighed as Queen Mab droned on. After three more toasts and a final rousing shout of "all magic begins in stories!" Queen Mab called out, "Let us dance through the night!" Then she pushed into the crowd. Maurelle hurried alongside her protectively.

Hyacinth had to go now, while they were distracted!

She crept away from the willow, headed in the direction of a table piled high with fruits and cakes. At the same moment, a pair of nobles—one a frog prince and the other a High Fae elf—twirled to a stop beside the table. The frog prince, Lord Helston from the Swamplands, popped a strawberry into his mouth.

The other gentleman, whose name she couldn't remember, drunkenly crashed into the table, sending a waterfall of food *and* Hyacinth tumbling to the floor. Off-balance from her dreadful wings, she got to her feet, brushing off her skirt and checking that her potion bottles hadn't broken.

"Apologies, apologies, Princess Hyacinth," Lord Helston said. He bowed low.

The elf also bowed, his hand over his heart. "Would you care to dance with us, Princess?"

Absolutely not. But could she really turn down two High Fae lords? What would her mother say to that?

She glanced up at the clock. Five minutes until ten. She had to get to the stables!

Hyacinth peered across the ballroom. Her mother was whispering with a plum-haired duchess. The two of them looked utterly absorbed in each other, and Maurelle stood nearby, her attention on the queen. Hyacinth decided to risk the scandal of refusing a dance.

"I cannot, my lords," Hyacinth said with a dip of her head. "Please, though, continue your revelries. I insist."

The two of them were back in each other's arms and dancing away from her before the sentence was out of her mouth. A few more drinks, and they'd surely forget they saw her.

Hyacinth pushed into the crowd. Hands grabbed her, laughter battered her ears, bodies grazed her wings, and the churning unruliness of the Solstice Ball drew her toward its center like a whirlpool.

She pushed harder, fighting against the dancers.

Someone stepped on her skirt, tearing part of it. Fingers raked down her arm as two women pulled her toward them for a waltz.

A gauzy bit of someone else's dress snagged on the chain of her enchanted compass, but she yanked it away. Step by forced step, Hyacinth struggled through the partygoers like someone shoving out of a dense hedge.

Then, suddenly, the swirl of dancers spit her out. Hyacinth's back ached from her wings being beaten about in the fray, but as she stumbled into the wide palace entry hall, her pounding heart slowed. She'd made it! She was free at last.

But the party was too close for comfort. The queen's guards farther down the hall too near at hand.

Hurry away now. Before someone misses you.

Her spider-silk slippers whispered over the marble floor as she ran out a back door of the palace, desperate to reach the stables and meet Chloe.

Chapter Two
Chloe

Chloe Wreckersfind tore through a maze of cobblestone alleys and muddy straw paths, racing toward the dragon barns in the center of Queen Mab's stable complex.

Her watch showed it was 9:48. Already? She should've left to meet Hyacinth twenty minutes ago, but she'd been finishing a letter to her twin sister, Anya, who was quite literally a world away. Anya might never read the words, but still, Chloe wasn't going to leave a letter unfinished.

A ridiculous thought.

Chloe didn't do anything by halves.

Besides, if she sprinted, she'd make it to the dragon barns before ten.

She pushed herself to go faster. Always lean, she'd become strong from months of shoveling shit in the stables. Learning to use a sword in her off hours had made her light on her feet as well. Her sheathed blade banged against her thigh as she ran, and her mind moved almost as fast as her legs.

Had Hyacinth left the Solstice Ball yet? Would they really have time to make it to the market in Keldale? What would they find there? Why did Hyacinth want to go anyway? Chloe had been to the small river town a few times, but never to the Solstice Market. Would tonight be the night Chloe found a door back to her own world?

Would she return home if she did?

Another ridiculous thought. Of course she would.

There was nothing she'd really miss in the Fae world, right?

That wasn't entirely true, but she didn't dwell on the thought. She was a human marooned in Faerie. She *had* to get home. That was all she'd wanted for months. Nothing had changed—had it?

Things with Hyacinth changed last night, whispered the hopeful part of her that wanted impossible things. Chloe ignored it.

One kiss—excellent though it had been—was hardly a reason to never return to her own world.

But a kiss from Hyacinth....

Chloe spared a glance at Queen Mab's castle. The palace was tucked against a mountain that towered over the stables. Velvety blue light poured from the windows, casting long shadows across the lawns and gardens. Drunken snatches of song and lilting laughter floated on the summer breeze around Chloe as she ran. There was a waywardness on the wind that excited her. Supposedly, the veil between the Fae world and the spirit world thinned during the solstice.

Chloe didn't know if that was true, but the night air hummed with wildness, and she loved it.

Stop thinking about the blasted night air and keep moving!

Chloe grinned at her own fanciful thoughts and sped up her pace.

She ran past the barns where the queen's guests' coaches and the beasts that drew them—gryphons, fire salamanders, giant boars, and a host of other creatures—were kept. Taking a left at the horse enclosure, she sped onward. The stables were like a small city in themselves, and hundreds of common Fae lived and worked in them. There were grooms, coachmen, messengers, blacksmiths, healers, squires, and many others.

As far as Chloe knew, she was the only human employed there. If there were others, they were hidden like she was, and she had no way of—

"Chloe! There you are!" someone shouted, their voice loud, and tipsy with drink.

Skidding to a stop, Chloe turned to see her fellow stablehands Hester and Fellmi stumbling toward her. Hester was a silver-haired wood nymph. Tall, boxy, and "strong as my grandmother, a fine old oak," she liked to say. She loved a bottle of summer wine, a dip in the lake behind the castle, and riding horses more than anything else in this world. Well, more than anything except for Fellmi. The bookish dwarf was Hester's opposite, which was probably why they were so smitten. Fellmi's parents were professors at the Crescent Atheneum, a magical college on the western border of the Moonshadow Kingdom, but Fellmi wanted a life full of adventure. How that had landed them cleaning up after Queen Mab's dragons, Chloe didn't know. But Fellmi seemed quite happy with the arrangement, and they were working on a book about dragons in their off time.

"Hester, Fellmi, I didn't expect to see you tonight," Chloe said. As she spoke, she shifted the leather wristwatch on her arm. Beneath it was the glamour token that disguised her human appearance. What her friends saw when they looked at her, she wasn't quite sure. But Hester liked to compliment her ears—"Such nice points!"—and Fellmi was always asking her if she was from the mountain elf clans, so it seemed to be working.

"Where are you off to?" Hester asked, raising one mossy eyebrow.

Fellmi peered at her. "Are you . . . running?" Their tone made it clear running was the worst sort of idea. "After the day we had?"

The three of them had spent hours stabling guests' mounts, brushing them down, feeding them, and being yelled at by the overwhelmed stablemaster, Plod, who had let them leave only an hour ago, when the night shift came in. Chloe had barely had time to go home, wash, and change clothing. (There hadn't really been time to write her sister that letter. But when missing her sister snuck up on her, she had to sit down and write to her immediately, or she'd start crying. Never an acceptable option.)

"I'm not running for *fun*," Chloe hastily assured Fellmi, before they could launch into a lecture on the benefits of slow living.

"I should hope not." Fellmi took a long swig from the bottle in their hand. "You're sweating, though."

Chloe swiped at the thin sheen of sweat on her forehead with her sleeve. So much for the clean shirt she'd changed into for her night out with Hyacinth. "It's nothing."

Hester slung an arm over Chloe's shoulder. A boozy smell wafted off her along with something that smelled like burnt kindling, likely from the fire salamander Hester had been wrangling earlier. "Where are you headed?"

"Sword practice . . ."

Hester snorted. "On the solstice? Not even Wendell will be training you tonight."

Wendell was the retired stablemaster and former captain of the king's guard who Chloe lived with. Hester was absolutely correct; he wouldn't be training anyone tonight since he was deep in his cups with old pals.

"I am! Or, well, I was going to practice some sword drills, but first I'm meeting someone—"

"Someone?" Fellmi's voice quirked with interest.

"A girl?" Hester poked Chloe in the side.

Heat rose in Chloe's cheeks, and she ran a hand through her short red hair. "I'm not telling you anything."

"It *is* a girl!" Fellmi crowed. "Who is she? Do we know her? Does she work in the stables?"

"Or in the palace?" Hester clapped a hand over her mouth in mock scandal. "Chloe, you naughty thing, are you kissing one of the palace maids?"

Words abandoned Chloe. If only they knew who she'd been kissing from the palace.

"I have to go," she said, pulling away from her friends.

"Stay! Bring your girl and let's join the party in the garden." Hester pulled an apple from her pocket and took a bite. "Lots of trouble we can get into over there."

Chloe shook her head. "Much as I'd love to find some trouble with you, I'm promised elsewhere."

"We'll miss you!" Fellmi pouted, taking another long swig from the bottle they held.

"Say hello to your girl from us!" Hester added.

"Not my girl," Chloe said.

"Not yet!" Hester waggled her eyebrows again.

"Not ever. Now, really, I must go."

"At least eat something—you're going to need your energy for meeting this mysterious someone!" With a laugh, Hester tossed the apple in Chloe's direction. Without thinking, Chloe drew her sword and split the apple in half in a well-practiced maneuver.

The halves fell at Hester's feet.

"Well, you're certainly still quick," Hester said. "Even if you are sweaty." She picked up the apple halves and offered one to Chloe.

Chloe took it with a grin. "See you tomorrow at work."

"Not if we drink enough tonight and have to stay in bed all day!" Fellmi said cheerfully. They passed their bottle to Hester.

Chloe hurriedly wiped her sword and sheathed it. Then she took a bite of apple, waved to her friends, and hurried onward to the dragon barn.

The apple's sweetness filled her mouth with the tingling Fae food offered her.

Everything Chloe had read about eating Fae food before she got stuck in this world a year ago, when she'd just been an apprentice realm mapper, had been wrong. She'd thought that no human could eat Fae food without feeling immediately, overwhelmingly disoriented or intoxicated, but that was wrong. As far as she could tell, the rules for humans consuming Fae food centered around hospitality.

According to Wendell, this was how it worked:

She could eat Wendell's food with no enchanted effects at all because she was a guest in his home. That's why she had a packet of homemade cookies, some dried meat he'd prepared, and a few apples from his backyard tree in her bag. If she were to grow or prepare her own food, that would also be fine for eating.

She could also enjoy food or drink that was offered in friendship with some minor effervescent effects—a tingling in her hands and lightness in her head, almost like drinking fizzy alcohol—but it would pass after a few glowing minutes. That's why the apple from her friends was relatively harmless. And why the wine she'd drunk with Hyacinth last night made her feel giddy and reckless, but the effects faded once she'd gotten home.

Was that the wine or Hyacinth's lips?

Chloe wasn't entirely sure. Perhaps they'd revisit the question later.

The dragon barns were in view, and she slowed her pace, not wanting to dash up to Hyacinth like she was too eager.

As she caught her breath, Chloe considered whether she could buy some food at the market in Keldale. Hyacinth had mentioned food stalls with delicacies from all over the kingdom. Wendell had assured her purchased food would have minimal effects, since there was a bargain implied, but Chloe hadn't risked this yet because she rarely had enough money or the opportunity to purchase anything. Plus, she didn't want to chance eating Fae food that might make her forget who she was.

One thing Wendell had made very clear was this: Fae food she took without being offered and food or drink forced upon her were always dangerous. Too much of this sort of food could supposedly captivate a human, forcing them to do whatever the Fae they'd taken it from willed.

Chloe shuddered at that thought.

As she approached the dragon barn, more unsettling things she'd learned about humans in the Fae world wormed through her head.

Some humans were stolen into Fae, others found their way through Fae doors by accident, like she'd done, and still others had families who had been here for centuries. For the most part, humans were ignored by the High Fae. They had no social mobility. No real organization. There were loose collections scattered throughout the Moonshadow Kingdom, holding menial jobs and scraping by. Even the common Fae looked down on them.

Chloe also knew that some humans were seduced by Fae magic. Thinking to move up in the world, they'd bargain with the Fae, spending years of their lives, their beauty, or their health for trinkets and small boons. Fae magic was like a drug. They wanted more. They needed more. They craved it until it ruined them.

Sometimes she wondered if she'd end up like them if she stayed here long enough.

No. She was always careful, never got caught off guard, and she had her sword if anyone tried to force food on her.

She touched the pommel of her blade and glanced upward. Above her, a silver coin of a moon sat among the scattered stars. Were those the same stars that shone in Anya's world?

A pang went through Chloe as she thought about her twin sister. Would she wonder why Chloe had been gone so long, or was she so happy in her new life, she didn't miss Chloe at all?

Chloe cleared her throat and buried that thought. She could *not* be worrying about her sister when she was supposed to be meeting Hyacinth.

Where was Hyacinth?

Chloe checked her watch—9:55. If Hyacinth showed up soon and they managed to convince a dragon to fly them to Keldale—at least a half-hour flight!—they still wouldn't have much time to shop.

Perhaps Hyacinth was waiting on the other side of the barn?

Chloe circled the largest dragon barn, a grand structure that looked like a museum in Chloe's world. It had a vast entrance lit by torches, tall carved columns, and arched wooden doors towering above Chloe.

No Hyacinth.

Chloe leaned against a tower of hay bales, waiting. Straw prickled her back, and her mind whirled with the wildness of the night, her encounter with Hester and Fellmi, and all her thoughts of her sister.

Restless, she drew her blade and faced the straw bales. Sword fighting would calm her thoughts.

Lunge—

Her thoughts turned to kissing Hyacinth last night anyway.

Thrust—

Kissing Hyacinth had been a mistake.

Stab—

But what a delicious mistake indeed.

Chloe swore. This was not clearing her thoughts. Chloe redoubled her sword drills. Straw flew through the air, the golden filaments dancing in the torchlight.

Lunge—

Chloe *was* quite good at delicious mistakes.

Stab—

But she'd known it was a bad idea to drink the Fae summer wine with Hyacinth.

Reset and lunge again—

She'd known she should've pulled away instead of leaning forward.

Thrust—

She'd known High Fae princesses weren't supposed to kiss girls they thought were common Fae.

Stab—

If Hyacinth found out Chloe was a human, and therefore far worse to be kissing . . . well. That would only bring trouble.

Chloe stabbed again and again into the pile of straw.

What was she even doing worrying about kissing princesses? And where was Hyacinth?

Chloe lowered her sword and drew in a heaving breath. Her heart thumped furiously, and her thoughts raged onward.

She was *supposed* to be a realm mapper's apprentice, but she'd gotten trapped in the Fae world. She was *supposed* to be finding a way home so she could see Anya again. She was *not* supposed to be thinking about Princess Hyacinth like they had any future together.

If that's the case, why are you so excited to see her tonight?

Chloe scowled at the thought and picked up her sword again.

Lunge—

She would go with Hyacinth tonight. Fine.

Thrust—

Hyacinth wanted to find a shop, and Chloe would see if she could discover any new information about portals back to the human world. Fine.

Stab—

She would *not* make a big deal of their time together.

Chloe repeated the sword-fighting sequence she'd been trying to perfect again and again. Her arms ached, but she needed to drive thoughts of Hyacinth from her head.

Lunge—

Still, Princess Hyacinth filled her mind.

Stab—

Last night the princess had stepped into the garden, all soft curves and wide eyes, her skin painted with moonlight. How could Chloe have said no to a drink together? A dance? Hyacinth had cupped her cheek gently, whispering her name. They'd said goodbye too soon, hazy and sweet and promising something more.

The stable clocktower chimed ten, pulling Chloe out of her reverie.

"Where are you, Hyacinth?" she muttered.

Maybe she was inside already?

Worth a look.

Nerves tingling with anticipation—Chloe had been in the dragon barn before, but she wasn't supposed to be here at night, since that was a good way to get eaten or at least in trouble with the dragon keepers—she pushed open the doors of the dragon barn and stepped into the cavernous main enclosure. She breathed deeply as she took in the space. It smelled of moss, straw, metal, and smoky heat. Torches flickering with magical blue flame lined the walls, making azure shadows dance. Limned in their glow was a dragon paddock as wide as a city block. The queen's favorite dragon, Runa, curled up in the middle of it, snoring contentedly on a vast bed of moss. Her scales—each larger than Chloe's entire body—glittered blue-black. There was a saddle on Runa's back, as if the queen might go for a ride at any time. Even asleep, the dragon felt unfathomably mysterious and ancient.

Far above Runa, an enormous round window looked down from the barn's roof. The window was open, the night sky visible through it.

Feeling both brave and curious, Chloe tiptoed closer to the enclosure.

Hello, whispered a silky voice in her head.

Chloe brandished her sword. "Who's there?"

She spun around, but saw no one.

You really can't miss me, the voice said.

Chloe turned to see Runa staring back at her.

"You?" she squeaked. According to Wendell, dragons spoke only to their riders, and only if they felt like it.

Runa inclined her head. Her ancient eyes held Chloe's.

"How are you talking to me? I'm not . . ."

Oh, I know you're not magical. Nor are you Fae, despite that little trinket in your arm. I know you're a human, Chloe Wreckersfind. What I don't know is why you're here tonight.

Chloe's hand shook as she held her sword. "I'm meeting Princess Hyacinth."

Runa scoffed, smoke puffing from her nose. *Try again.*

"I'm here—well, we're here, or she's going to be here, to see if we can get a ride to the Solstice Market . . . if you'd be inclined to take us." Chloe hadn't even considered that she'd have to talk to the dragon before she borrowed it.

Aaah. Very well then. Perhaps I will grant that wish. I'd love to stretch my wings. But first you must tell me a story. Dragons really are quite fond of stories, you know.

Chloe fought to find the right words. "If I tell you a story, you're going to let us ride you?"

Runa smirked—did dragons smirk? *Yes. Tell me the story of how you met Hyacinth, please. And put that sword away. It's thinner than my smallest claw. Don't insult me by waving it about.*

Chloe put her sword away. Runa's neck snaked over the edge of the paddock. Her eyes glittered in the torchlight. Chloe had a very good view of her teeth.

She swallowed hard. The story of how she'd met Hyacinth was neither all that exciting nor interesting, but it would have to do. "It was the end of my first week in Fae, when I was sitting in a hidden corner of the garden, writing my sister a letter. Hyacinth popped out of a secret passage in the garden wall with a book, and she quite literally ran into me. I think we surprised each other so much, there was nothing to do but start talking. I thought she was the loveliest girl I'd ever seen, though I have no idea what she must've thought of me."

It was the same hidden spot in the garden where they'd met last night. The same place where Chloe had spent so much time over the last year, daydreaming about kissing Hyacinth. The same place they'd finally—

A satisfied rumbling left Runa's lips, along with a puff of smoke. *A romance from the first moments, very enchanting.*

"Not a romance," Chloe insisted, though the words sounded hollow even to her.

Go on then, tell me more. You may climb into my saddle to wait for the princess. You'll have a better view of her there as she walks in.

Spinning more of the story of the first day she'd met Hyacinth—the conversation they'd had, the way it had made her feel—Chloe climbed into Runa's saddle.

"What do we do now?" Chloe asked Runa.

Wait for your girl, I suppose.

"She's not my girl," Chloe said, echoing what she'd told Hester and Fellmi not so long ago.

As you insist. That was a lovely story. Thank you.

"Chloe?" Hyacinth called out, interrupting her conversation with the dragon. A loud clanking filled the room, signaling Hyacinth's approach as the trinkets on her belt clattered with each step. Why she always carried so many things, Chloe didn't know, but she'd gotten used to the noise.

"I'm up here! On Runa!"

Hyacinth strode toward the paddock, and Chloe's breath caught in her throat. Tonight Hyacinth's curly hair was piled in a waterfall of ringlets. She wore a diaphanous dress with an enormous tulip-shaped skirt. Lantern light glinted over her light-purple skin and the tips of her pointed ears. She also had wings on her back. Where had those come from?

Chloe exhaled slowly to calm her ridiculous racing heart as Hyacinth climbed the ladder to Runa's saddle. They were just friends. Nothing unusual about two friends who'd kissed each other last night borrowing a dragon for an illicit nighttime flight.

Certainly not.

Despite her dress and wings, in a matter of seconds, Hyacinth had settled in behind Chloe. "Hi," she whispered, her voice warm in Chloe's ear. "Sorry I'm late."

A shiver went through Chloe at the words. At Hyacinth's closeness. At the honeyed scent of her skin. Chloe swallowed hard. "You're not that late, and I've been telling Runa stories."

"She spoke to you? She speaks only to my mother!"

Before Chloe could say anything else. Runa got to her feet, stretching.

If you're ready, we'll be flying now. Hang on.

Chloe had never ridden a dragon—stablehands didn't get that privilege—and she nearly slipped out of the saddle with Runa's first step. It was only her grip on the saddle horn that saved her. How embarrassing to nearly fall off in front of Hyacinth! Chloe gritted her teeth. They hadn't even left the building, and already she was in trouble. She squeezed her thighs against the saddle. Hopefully, this wasn't too different than riding a horse.

In front of her, Runa snorted, almost as if she could hear the thought.

It's much better than riding a horse, Chloe amended in her mind.

With one graceful move, Runa jumped to a perch on a ledge a bit higher up. Once there, she opened her wings, which spanned the length of the barn. With three flaps, she soared through the round window and landed on the roof. She chuffed happily as the wind hit her face. Chloe grinned as well.

They were really doing this! Chloe Wreckersfind, former "worst orphan in the entire city" according to the headmistress of the orphanage she'd grown up in, former miserable seamstress, and current lost human in the Fae world, was riding the queen's dragon.

Anya would never believe her. She could barely believe it herself.

"Let's fly, please." Chloe's heart pounded in her chest so loudly, she was certain Hyacinth could hear it.

With pleasure.

Runa strode toward the edge of the stable roof and launched herself into the sky. Chloe whooped as they climbed. All worries were driven from her head, replaced by the feel of the warm air against her skin, the dragon spiriting them toward the Solstice Market, and Hyacinth's arms around her waist.

Chapter Three
Hyacinth

The stables and palace grew smaller below them, soon replaced by a vast expanse of forest.

"Isn't this marvelous?" Chloe called out, her words nearly whipped away by the wind. The stablehand was all sharp angles, and she smelled like hay, cinnamon, and a rich, woody fragrance. Hyacinth inhaled sharply, savoring their closeness. For the first time all night, she felt the sparkling headiness of intoxication.

"It's not terrible," Hyacinth admitted, swallowing a lump of nervousness. She was risking so much leaving the party and riding Runa, but it had to be worth it. She *had* to find the Wilting Sparrow Bookshop. She *would* find out more about her father tonight!

Memories of her father rose in her mind as Runa raced toward Keldale. He had dark hair like hers, kind eyes, and a laugh big as the glittering night sky all around her. He'd read Hyacinth stories, doing voices of the three Celestial Sisters, or giggling with her through the tale of bold imps who tailored a dress of invisible water lilies for a hag. At least Hyacinth *thought* those were memories. They were foggy with the fifteen years that had passed. Maybe she'd made them up after seeing the portrait of her family hanging in her mother's library. Maybe her father had done none of those things. Maybe he'd been a terrible father.

She really had no idea.

She desperately wanted to find out.

"You alright back there?" Chloe called out.

Hyacinth squeezed Chloe's waist once in affirmation. Even if she didn't remember her father at all, she had to try to discover more.

Runa flew fast, and the miles whipped by. Hyacinth's dreadful fake wings caught the wind, but they stayed affixed to her back. Her enchanted compass rattled against the tiny potion bottles, and some of her curls tumbled loose from her bun, but she wasn't going to release Chloe's waist to brush them out of her eyes. Instead, she looked to the left, where the stars shone like pieces of glass flung across the moonshadow-dark marble floors of the palace. It really was lovely to be out of the palace. Sometimes she forgot how big the world was outside her mother's walls.

In what felt like no time, the lights of Keldale came into view. It was a walled town hugging the Mossley River on two sides. Runa descended in a controlled fall that tore a scream out of Chloe and Hyacinth. She landed on the edge of town. There was a stable there with room for Queen Mab's dragons, because the queen often traveled this way when meeting with official delegates. Still, the groom looked surprised to see them land. He jumped to attention as Hyacinth and Chloe clambered off Runa's back.

"My ladies," he said, bowing. Chloe snorted at the formal address, and Hyacinth elbowed her. The groom bowed again, nearly falling over. "We weren't expecting anyone from the court. You are from the court, yes? I just assumed because you're on the queen's dragon. She's not here too, is she? Bramble and fern, I don't have her usual carriage prepared." He looked around nervously.

Hyacinth took pity on the groom. "The queen isn't here. But, please, don't worry yourself on her account. My friend and I have some shopping to do. We won't be terribly long, but see that Runa is comfortable, please."

The groom's face relaxed. "Of course, of course. We always have Runa's favorite meals and paddock ready."

He bowed a half dozen more times as they strode out onto a wide cobblestone street.

"Put this on." Chloe pulled a simple gray wool cloak out of the bag strapped across her chest. "Your dress is outrageous."

"It's not *outrageous*. It's High Fae fashion." Even as she said it, Hyacinth felt ridiculous. She ran her hands over her glittering gold honeysuckle bodice and tulip skirt. Some part of her had hoped Chloe liked her in this dress. That she'd thought it was pretty. Her fingers slipped through the silvery compass chain, and she touched the slip of paper in her pocket again to ground herself.

They weren't here so Hyacinth could preen for Chloe in her Solstice Ball dress. What a revolting thought.

Wasn't it?

Yes. It absolutely was. Chloe probably didn't give an enchanted mulberry about what Hyacinth was wearing.

"Also," Chloe continued, interrupting Hyacinth's spiraling thoughts, "since when do you have wings? Those weren't there last night."

Called out, Hyacinth glared at Chloe. It was a fair question, but Chloe couldn't learn Hyacinth lacked magic. That wasn't a secret for sharing. What would Chloe think of her if she knew the truth? Hyacinth didn't even want to know.

So she raised a shoulder, flicking one of the wings, and lied. "These wings are my magical inheritance. I call them up for special occasions."

"Can you make them disappear now?"

If only she could.

"Absolutely not." She searched her mind for any excuse. "That's a very intimate piece of High Fae magic. Not one I can do on the *street* of all places."

She spoke haughtily, hoping Chloe had no idea about magic the High Fae might use behind closed doors. Her fingers flitted again over the potion bottles on her belt.

Juniper heart for illusion. A moon-drenched secret for levitation. Bitterroot berry for healing. Gray tendrils of fog for vanishing. Wraith tears for compulsion. Dragonheart ashes for fire and ruin.

Chloe rolled her eyes and shoved the cloak into Hyacinth's chest. "Whatever. Far be it for me to question the High Fae and their many magics. But you're going to get robbed. Wear the cloak, please. Maybe we can't hide the wings, but you can *try* to blend in, Princess."

"Fine," Hyacinth huffed. She wrapped the cloak around her shoulders and covered her dress. It was itchy and smelled of horses, but it did make her feel less conspicuous.

"Ready now?" Chloe asked, looking around. She glanced at her watch. "It's ten forty-five. The market closes at midnight, right?"

Hyacinth nodded grimly. They really didn't have much time to find the bookshop and the truths she hoped it held. "Let's get moving."

They walked quickly into Keldale. Although Hyacinth had been in the city before with her mother, she'd never been here at night, let alone secretly. It was exhilarating.

The town always bustled with diplomats, royalty, and merchants. The Solstice Market, however, brought traders eager to bargain their wares and lured tourists from all over the kingdoms.

Hyacinth's heart thrummed as they turned onto a wide cobbled street. The houses in this part of Keldale were smashed together like crooked teeth, and many had roofs and balconies hanging over their neighbors.

The market bustled with common Fae—pixies, gnomes, wood and mountain elves, dwarfs, horned redcaps, fauns, goblins, and many others. There were also groups of fox-tailed High Fae, and some winged members of the gentry, whom Hyacinth hid from by pulling her cloak over her head. Surprisingly, there were even a few humans carrying packages for the Fae or sweeping the streets. Hyacinth didn't see them at Queen Mab's court often, and her eyes lingered on a thin, stoop-shouldered woman with brown hair that hung in a braid down her back. The woman's hand rested on an emerald-green moss cloak set out on a table a few feet away from where Hyacinth and Chloe stood. Behind the table, a swamp hag with teeth like pebbles bargained with the woman.

Moss cloaks were good for healing broken hearts. Hyacinth knew that from the trader who'd tried to sell her one last month.

Who broke your heart? Hyacinth wondered as she overheard the human woman beg the hag for the cloak. The hag shook her head once, and then the woman leaned in and made another suggestion Hyacinth couldn't hear. The hag must've agreed to that offer, because she shook the woman's hand. There was a flash of green light, and the human woman cried out. Her dark hair turned bone white in a breath.

Beside Hyacinth, Chloe sucked in a quick breath. Hyacinth's own blood ran fast in her veins. She'd never seen a human bargain happen before, and she was vaguely sick to her stomach, though she couldn't put her finger on why.

As the woman turned, her hard gaze met Hyacinth's for a moment. What had she traded for that moss cloak? Years? Beauty?

"C'mon," Chloe said beside Hyacinth. Her eyes narrowed on the woman and then she turned away abruptly. "Let's cross the bridge."

Hyacinth pushed the human woman and her moss cloak from her mind as she took in the wide stone bridge in front of them. It spanned the Mossley River, crowded with shops, tents, and vendors. Long barges floated along the waterway, each advertising different wares. Jaunty music, haggling, laughter, and the hum of conversation filled the air alongside the smells of roasting meats, pastries, and ale. Golden torchlight flickered off the water and along the streets. If Hyacinth had more time, she'd love to get lost among the stalls and see what sorts of magical items, spell scrolls, and other helpful trinkets might be on offer. Instead, she studied dozens of wooden signs as they fought their way across the packed bridge, hoping desperately that she'd spot the Wilting Sparrow.

There were so many booksellers! Lost in a Book, the Page Keeper, Tatiana's Tomes, Will-o'-the-Wisps, but not the Wilting Sparrow.

A long, frustrated sigh left her lips.

"Are you alright?" Chloe asked. She pulled Hyacinth out of the crowd's path, toward a narrow ledge along the river.

Hyacinth touched her potion bottles for comfort, her chest tight with worry. "No! It's already getting late—"

"It's not that late." Chloe looked at her watch. "Only eleven; we still have an hour."

"That's not enough time! Soon, the vendors will go home or shut up shop, and then we'll have to wait a full year, and I'll never find—"

Chloe's finger tapped the end of Hyacinth's nose, startling her out of her rant. "Princess?"

"Yes?" Hyacinth didn't know whether to laugh, rage at being bopped on the nose like a puppy, or cry in frustration.

"Breathe, please."

"How am I supposed to do that when I'm *never* going to find it!?"

A smirk pulled at Chloe's lips, which made Hyacinth want to shake her.

"What are you *never* going to find?" Chloe asked.

"A specific shop. One that I've heard about . . ."

"What's it called?"

"The Wilting Sparrow. Oh!" Hyacinth's fingers shot to the compass chain on her belt. "I suppose I can use my compass!"

What good was hauling around all these magical items if she forgot to use them? Hyacinth flipped open the lid of the compass.

Chloe scoffed. "You don't need a compass."

"It's a magical one, I'll have you know."

"You don't need magic either. We'll ask someone." She strode over to a nearby stall to talk to the gnomish woman behind the counter. The woman started nodding and pointing.

Why hadn't Hyacinth thought to ask someone? She snapped her compass shut, shame at her own foolishness heating her cheeks.

She hadn't thought to ask because she was a princess and often had other people anticipate her every need. But here, she needed to ask for what she wanted. It was a refreshing, delicious thought. One that whispered of freedom and much more. *If you want something, ask for it.*

She wanted to kiss Chloe again.

"Bramble and marsh, not that again," she muttered to herself. "Focus, Princess. You are here to learn more about your father, not—"

Hyacinth closed her lips over the rest of her self-chastisement as Chloe walked back toward her. A smile lit her face, and she brandished a piece of paper. "According to Tulip, the shop owner I spoke to, the Wilting Sparrow is one of the oldest shops in the market. It's on a barge. Extremely magical, and very hard to miss once you're deep enough in there. She drew me a map!"

Relief and a touch of wonder filled Hyacinth. Chloe really was magnificent. Smart, capable, the best sort—

"Are you coming, Princess?" Chloe took off through the warren of boats, stalls, alleys, and walkways, adeptly stepping around customers and over each small bridge they encountered.

All Hyacinth could do was keep up.

Before long, they reached the center of the market—and there it was: the Wilting Sparrow. It was a long barge painted bright purple.

Lanterns hung outside its arched door, their light bouncing off the water. Hyacinth eagerly clasped the scrap of paper with her father's name on it. Her heart raced.

This was it! If she was going to learn more about where her father had been all these years, maybe it would be here.

"Let's go." She started off.

"Ermmmmm . . ." Chloe was fixating on something farther down the market. She glanced quickly between the bookshop and the rest of the nearby stalls. Hyacinth could see tables of swords, a key shop, some animals under a tent, and much more.

"Go on," Hyacinth said, grateful for the opportunity to enter the bookshop alone. "I'll be fine. Books aren't dangerous."

Chloe bit her lower lip. "Are you sure, Princess?"

Hyacinth pointedly did not look at Chloe's lips. "I am. Now go, see the market."

"Be careful, okay?" Chloe pulled Hyacinth into a hug before she could say anything else.

Hyacinth exhaled sharply. Instead of doing what she wanted—pulling Chloe's lips to hers—Hyacinth patted Chloe on the back twice because she didn't know what else to do with her hands.

Really, was she the most awkward girl to ever live? What was wrong with her? Couldn't she hug a friend to say, *Thanks for coming with me to this wild market*?

She could. It's just that being this close to Chloe was making Hyacinth think about last night. Her gaze returned to Chloe's annoyingly perfect lips.

"I'll be back soon," Chloe promised. "Don't go anywhere else without me."

"I'll be right here," Hyacinth murmured as Chloe released her from the hug and hurried down the street.

Chloe's red hair was soon lost in the crowd. Still reeling from the embrace—or maybe that was the leftover excitement of the dragon ride and the energy of the market?—Hyacinth strode into the bookshop.

✦

The Wilting Sparrow was bigger on the inside than it seemed from the outside. The narrow barge somehow magically expanded into a room that stretched in several directions. Bookshelves rose along every wall, stretching far higher than they should have given the dimensions of the barge's roof. Books of all shapes, sizes, and descriptions crowded the shelves, and many were stacked on the floor. A painted sign above the door declared, ALL MAGIC BEGINS IN STORIES! As far as Hyacinth could see, there was no one else in the shop.

"Hello?" she called out.

No answer. She walked past a yellow velvet sofa piled high with books. The barge rocked on the water with her every step, but Hyacinth paid it no mind. Gently, she ran her fingers along the closest shelf, grazing the books. She moved deeper into the shop. How would she find what she needed in this muddle?

She pulled the slip of paper from her pocket. "Is anyone here?"

A clattering noise from somewhere near the ceiling answered her. "I'll be right down!" someone cheerfully replied.

A book tumbled off a shelf, but before it could hit the ground, an enormous spider caught it. Hyacinth's eyes widened as she took the spider in. He wore four pairs of spectacles over his eight eyes and an embroidered waistcoat covered his round belly. The spider lovingly placed the fallen book back on the shelf and then scrambled down from a nook in the ceiling.

"Hello there!" the spider called out. "Apologies for missing your entrance, but welcome to the Wilting Sparrow! I'm Dalton B. Wordstartle, proprietor, reader, story spinner, and book lover. What can I help you find?" The spider blinked at her from behind the spectacles.

Surprise overwhelmed Hyacinth. She'd never seen a spider as large or as dapper as Dalton B. Wordstartle.

Momentarily speechless, Hyacinth pulled the scrap of paper from her pocket and offered it to him.

The spider's eyebrows—did spiders have eyebrows?—shot upward. "Where did you get this?"

"I found it in a history book in my mother's library. Do you know what book it's from?" Hyacinth didn't dare to hope. There were so many here, and she wasn't even sure of the title this torn page came from.

Dalton, however, was undaunted. "Of course! I know every book that's been here and every one that will find its way back to the Sparrow. Part of how my magic works. All magic begins in stories and so on."

The familiar words struck Hyacinth as strange, though she'd heard her mother declare them in the ballroom not long ago and they were written on the bookshop's wall. But here in this floating, enchanted space, they felt imbued with more heft.

She couldn't linger on the thought, however, because Dalton moved over to the desk in the center of the shop and started tossing aside books with every one of his eight legs. He flung them over his shoulder with alarming zeal.

"Has to be here somewhere. I recall seeing it earlier this evening, but with the trip to the market, it might've gotten shuffled, and then who knows. . . ." He moved away from the desk and scuttled back up a bookshelf.

"Do you need any help?" Hyacinth called out, dodging a pair of books that sailed past her head.

"Absolutely not. I know what I'm looking for, just need to—Ah-ha! Here we go!" Dalton stopped flinging books and held up an emerald-green one with a triumphant flourish. He hurried down the bookshelf and handed it to Hyacinth.

A pattern of diamonds and thick double lines decorated the outside of the tome. There was no title on the spine or the front, and a large piece of malachite sat in the center of the book's cover. A dark vein split the mossy-green gem, making it look almost like an eye. Although the book wasn't very large, it had weight. It seemed to grow heavier each second Hyacinth held it. The deckled edges were rough cut, and silver clasps lined them.

Anticipation shivered through Hyacinth as she caressed the clasps. "Are you sure this is the one?"

Dalton returned the scrap of paper. "Undoubtedly. Open it."

Nerves tingling in anticipation, Hyacinth undid the clasps and opened the book. The first page was torn, and she fit the scrap into the space.

A gasp left her lips as she read:

Property of Evan Bramblefen.

Purchased at the Wilting Sparrow Bookshop, Keldale.
Shop hours during the Solstice Market only.
If lost, please return
to Dalton B. Wordstartle,
who will make sure it finds its way back to its owner.

Hyacinth hugged it to her chest, happiness, worry, and delight surging through her. "This belonged to my father! I can't believe I found it."

Dalton goggled at her. "Your father is Evan Bramblefen?"

Hyacinth nodded and Dalton stepped closer.

"I suppose that means you—well, no it can't be! Are you little Hyacinth? Grown so big already?"

"I am Hyacinth."

Dalton beamed at her.

Hyacinth felt like she should say something to address Dalton's astonishment that she'd managed to grow up, but her head was full of desperate questions. "What is this book? How do you have it? Where is my father? Can you really make sure this gets back to him like it says here?"

She stabbed a finger at the note on the paper:

If lost, please return
to Dalton B. Wordstartle,
who will make sure it finds its way back to its owner.

"A fantastic bunch of questions!" Dalton replied. "But I'm afraid I can't be too much help. I haven't seen Evan in fifteen years. Last time

I saw him, we met at the Wild Root Inn, and he was on his way to the Labyrinth. There was no—"

"The Labyrinth?" Hyacinth interrupted, excitement about clues regarding her father overtaking her manners. "What was he doing in a maze?"

"Not a maze, child. *The* Labyrinth. An ancient, dangerous place at the edge of the map."

Hyacinth had never heard of such a place, and she'd gone through a passionate geography phase when she was ten. At the time, she'd known every map in her mother's library like she knew the potions at her belt and the names of her many half sisters.

So why wasn't *the* Labyrinth ringing a bell?

But there was a better question that she put forward first, in order to hide her ignorance of something she'd apparently missed.

"What would my father want with a—I mean *the* Labyrinth on the edge of the map?"

Dalton shrugged two of his shoulders. "He was a bit cagey on the details. There have always been rumors of a magical library there—something your father had such a weakness for—and I've heard whispers of a portal to another world. But I'm not sure. Lots of people whisper about the place, but none return."

Hyacinth held up the green book. "How did you get my father's book?"

"When we crossed paths at the Wild Root Inn, Evan and I drank the night away, talking of our travels, and then he departed early the next morning. It wasn't until he was long gone that I realized he'd left this book. He must've forgotten it."

Disappointment knotted in Hyacinth's belly. "Is that really all you know? Can't you tell me anything more? Please?"

All of Dalton's eight eyes flew open in surprise. "Do you know nothing about him at all, child?" he said, in a heartbreakingly gentle voice.

"Very little," Hyacinth ground out, not wanting his pity. "My mother doesn't speak of him."

Dalton sighed. "I suppose she wouldn't. I don't know much of their story, but Evan and I were friends long before he met Queen Mab. He was the finest scholar I've ever known. He spoke so fondly of Mab and of you that night at the Wild Root Inn. Said you were the brightest toddler he'd ever seen. Even showed me a little picture he'd drawn of you."

The idea of her father flashing a hand-drawn picture of her to his drinking buddy melted any resolve Hyacinth had to be mad at Dalton for pitying her.

Hyacinth managed a watery smile. "If that's true, why did he leave me?"

"He said he desperately needed to get into the Labyrinth to help his sister. . . ."

"His sister?"

Who was her father's sister? That would be Hyacinth's aunt. How many other people were on her father's side of the family? Suddenly, the canyon of things she didn't know opened at Hyacinth's feet. She hated it. She wanted clear answers about her father, not more questions!

Dalton shrugged. "I don't know much more. He promised to tell me all about it when he got back, but he was in a hurry. That's probably why he forgot this book. He was distracted the last time I saw him. Head even more in the clouds than usual."

Hyacinth ran her fingers along the edge of the green book again. Perhaps there was some clue inside that would help her better understand her father. She turned to the first page, and her stomach plummeted.

"*The Traveler's Guide to the Moonshadow Kingdom*?" she said flatly. It was so ordinary. Her mother had several similar books about famous places throughout the kingdom.

Dalton nodded. "A very useful book indeed. Your father was curious about everything and working on his own guide—one much more detailed and full of history—to the Moonshadow Kingdom. His notes are scattered throughout the margins."

Hyacinth gaped at him for a moment, frustration sharpening her words. "Well, what do I do with it?"

She'd waited so long to uncover more about her father, and here was his book—but it was just a travel guide of the Moonshadow Kingdom. That was useless!

"There's a map too," Dalton offered, as if sensing her disappointment. He flipped to the front of the book and unfolded it.

It showed the Moonshadow Kingdom, and there were some familiar places on it, including Queen Mab's castle, Keldale, and the Crescent Athenium to the east. But there, on the far western side of the map, was a labyrinth with a great tree at its center. Why wasn't that on any of her mother's maps? Why had none of her tutors mentioned it in their geography lessons? There were also a few other unfamiliar places drawn onto the map including the Wild Root Inn, a mountain marked as *Hall of the Mountain King*, and a cottage near the Swamplands.

She flipped through the pages of the book, noting the scrawl in the margins. "These are my father's notes?"

Dalton nodded.

"And this is *the* Labyrinth he was going to?" She pointed to the maze on the edge of the map.

Dalton nodded again.

"So, if I wanted, I could follow this map there."

Dalton blinked, every one of his eyes holding her gaze. "Oh no, child. Don't go to the Labyrinth. No one returns from there. Your father wouldn't—"

"But you said my father was going there. Do you think that's where he is?"

"I think that's where he was heading, but I don't know if he made it."

Hyacinth refused to consider that.

"Suppose he did make it to the Labyrinth," she pressed. "Why hasn't he come back? Where is he now? What if—" Before Hyacinth could press further, two water nymphs and a goblin matron walked into the shop.

"Excellent questions, my dear, but ones I cannot answer. Now, please excuse me." Dalton scurried past her to greet the other customers.

"How much do I owe you for this book?" Hyacinth called out.

"You don't owe me anything, child. But I wish you—and your father—much luck. If you find Evan again, please let him know I'd love a visit. I've got several rare titles he'd be thrilled to study."

With that, Dalton hurried away.

Clutching the book to her chest, she called out a thank-you to Dalton and left the shop. Chloe wasn't among the shoppers milling about outside, so Hyacinth leaned against the canal railing and flipped the book open.

Maybe there was a clue in here that would reveal why her father went to the Labyrinth and how she might get there herself.

"Let's spend some time together, Father," she whispered, running her fingers fretfully over first her potion bottles and then along the enchanted compass's chain at her belt.

In a matter of minutes, Hyacinth was immersed in her father's world and his guide to the Moonshadow Kingdom. The noise and bustle of the market fell away.

Or it did until Chloe came barreling toward her, shouting at her to run.

Chapter Four
Chloe

As Chloe strode into the market after leaving Hyacinth at the Wilting Sparrow, she could still feel the princess standing rigid in her arms. Clearly not wanting to be hugged. Why had Chloe hugged her? It'd been an instinct. Just a quick, friendly goodbye, like she'd give to Hester and Fellmi, but plainly one Hyacinth had no interest in.

Well. Good.

Neither of them had mentioned last night's flirtation yet, which led Chloe to assume it had probably meant nothing to Hyacinth. Who was a princess, for bramble's sake. Of course, she wasn't still thinking about the taste of Chloe's lips. *Hyacinth* was on a mission to find something at a bookshop. Something that she didn't need Chloe for.

It hurt more than Chloe wanted to admit, and so she had hurried away from the bookshop, desperate to lose herself in the chaos.

She wasn't exactly sure what she was looking for tonight beyond something that would help her get home. But an old, familiar hunger for wanting to see it all, experience it all, explore new places, and see new things overtook her as she walked away from the bookshop. The Solstice Market was full of intoxicating smells, irresistible stalls, and fascinating-looking Fae. Chloe's curiosity got the best of her.

Something in her gut tugged her to the heart of the market.

Perhaps what you're looking for is out here, it seemed to whisper.

Of course, that was the problem with Chloe—what she was looking for was always out there somewhere. That's how she'd wound up an apprentice realm mapper.

As Chloe moved deeper into the market, she thought about Marcel, the time-traveling master realm mapper with whom she'd left her world.

Her first trips with Marcel were amazing. They slipped in and out of magical doors, mapping the golden and silver dragon threads that wove through time and space. Chloe didn't understand all the theory behind it, but she knew dragons were ancient powerful beings who connected different realms. Some of them left routes between worlds. Savvy travelers and realm mappers followed these to explore new places. In her time with Marcel, Chloe had gone back in time hundreds of years and seen incredible things—like the building of ancient temples and the founding of her city of Severon. She'd visited countless realms, including the Fae realm that contained the Moonshadow Kingdom.

But every time she'd done so, she had Marcel with her. She'd known where the door was to get back to her time and the city of Severon, where her sister lived.

Her first solo trip into Fae was meant to be a quick one. She didn't even tell Marcel about it. While he was away on business, she crept through the magical door he kept open and wandered into Fae. She wanted to show him she was ready to work alone, following up on a rich vein of golden dragon thread Marcel had been mapping for years. She was going to gather information on Queen Mab's dragons, nothing more, nothing less.

But the door she'd come through slammed closed. The enchantment Marcel had taught her to open a new door didn't work. Eventually, Wendell, the Fae stablemaster, found her after her third day of hiding and trying to figure out a way home. He fed her—thank goodness, since she'd refused to eat or drink anything beyond a bit of water since her arrival—gave her fresh clothes, got her a job, and offered her a place to sleep. She hadn't even known there were other doors between the human world and the Fae one until a few months ago, when two humans had come through one to steal Queen Mab's jewels. Chloe had almost made it back home with them, but she'd missed her chance, and Queen Mab had since closed all the doors between the worlds. For good. Which meant Chloe was stuck unless she found another way home.

Did she really think a clue was waiting here? At the Solstice Market?

Stranger things had happened. Maybe there was a key to a door Queen Mab had forgotten, or maybe—

"Are you looking for a new sword, fair one?"

Chloe shoved her thoughts of Marcel and doors back to her world aside and appraised her surroundings. She'd wandered into a sword-selling stall. A small creature wearing a pointed hat and a gray cloak peered up at her from behind the blade-buried table. Warts and wrinkles covered his face, and his yellow eyes sparkled. He picked up the largest broadsword on the table with surprising grace given his size. "This one will protect anyone who carries it from flying raptor attacks."

"That seems wildly specific," Chloe said. She rested her hands on her own sword.

The creature nodded. "All of these are very specific swords for very purposeful tasks." He picked up a pinkie-sized dagger with a serrated edge. "This one is enchanted to deliver the killing blow to an enemy after exactly a decade of feuding. And this one"—here he picked up a vicious-looking rapier—"is intended only for piercing through a troublesome knot of worries."

Chloe nodded gravely as she fought back a laugh. The Fae world was still so strange, but she loved that there was a sword for every purpose. "I think I'll stick to my sword, but thank you for showing them to me."

The creature bowed low, still holding the rapier. He nearly impaled himself with the movement, then let loose a stream of curses.

Hurrying away from that stall, Chloe passed cloth sellers and acorn hat makers. Game shops and taverns. Arrow fletchers and barrel smiths. Gem artists and fortune tellers. How could she possibly find what she was looking for when there was so much to see?

Pausing for a moment to get her bearings, she glimpsed a pair of humans in an alley, dancing around a purple-flamed fire with languid grace. Both of them had the hollowed-out look of those who'd been chasing Fae magic for too long, and their clothes hung from them in tatters. Chloe's stomach twisted. Should she give them some money or try to help them find a place to sleep? She had a few coppers in her bag, but would food offered in friendship help them, or were they happy as they were?

Chloe didn't know, but the question troubled her mind.

You don't have long before the market closes. Keep searching for what you need.

Wrenching her gaze away from the other humans, she strode toward a perfume stall farther down the lane.

But before she could ask about the scents, a stall at the back of a narrow alley lined with trash cans snagged her attention. Flickering torchlight illuminated an assortment of animals in wood and metal cages. A broad redcap with ram horns protruding from his forehead, arms the size of Chloe's torso, and a knit hat on his head hunched over the table. He ate a piece of meat with a gleaming serrated knife. His brows were drawn together, and with every bite, his scowl seemed to deepen.

None of that worried Chloe in the least. It was what sat on the table next to the redcap that consumed Chloe's attention.

"Tiny! Dragon!" she exclaimed, far louder than she'd intended. Ignoring the fetid-smelling puddles and the piles of trash, she hurried over to the stall, taking in the dragon. It was the size of a teacup with silvery-blue skin. One of its wings was bent at an odd angle, and it looked utterly miserable in the too-small birdcage the redcap had shoved it into.

The tiny dragon looked up at Chloe as she approached, as if she'd spoken to it. Enormous purple eyes met her own, and the creature whimpered like a kitten mewling.

Chloe's heart nearly shattered.

"Hush, worthless," the redcap snarled. He poked his knife through the cage, sending the dragon skittering backward.

"Leave him alone!" Chloe cried. A ferocious protective feeling lit her every nerve. She'd never seen a dragon so small—not even in Marcel's books—and according to Wendell, only High Fae in the Queen's employ could breed and raise dragons. This swamp-smelling redcap with the cruel-looking knife and back-alley stall was clearly not that.

"Mind your business unless you're buying," the redcap snapped back.

The other caged creatures—moonshadow snakes, diamond-ear foxes, fluffy-faced rabbits, birds with bright feathers, and a host of other magical animals Chloe couldn't identify—started rattling their cages, preening, and calling out to one another. Bits of fur and feathers rose in a cloud behind the redcap.

The redcap lifted a stick and walloped one of the cages. The tiny dragon hissed at him ferociously. Chloe's heart soared at the creature's bravery.

"How much for the tiny dragon?" she called out.

"That one's not for sale," the redcap snarled.

Chloe patted her pockets and checked her bag—in it was a book of letters to her sister, the food she'd packed from home, and a handful of copper coins. She pulled these out. "Really, I'll pay anything. Name your price."

She couldn't pay much, but perhaps she could borrow money from Hyacinth. There had to be a way to help this little dragon!

The redcap sized her up, interested. "I'll take three of your teeth, one of your fingers, and your sword. You can have a magical chicken.

Lays golden eggs every full moon." He nodded toward a scrawny hen who looked like she'd not laid a regular egg in months, much less a golden one.

Chloe liked her teeth, her fingers, and her sword. She'd be keeping them all *and* getting the dragon. Somehow. "I don't want a chicken! I want the tiny dragon."

The redcap leaned forward, and his meaty breath engulfed Chloe. "And I want your pretty teeth and fingers and that sword."

Chloe put her hand on the sword, drawing it ever so slightly. She couldn't give the redcap the sword. It belonged to Wendell, and he'd loaned it to her for sparring.

"My sword's not for sale, nor my teeth and fingers. I can get you more coins, though."

That might not be true, but the redcap didn't need to know that. Besides, Hyacinth had to have some coins. Surely she'd give them to save this creature. Or all the creatures in the stall.

"No deal," snapped the redcap. "Get out of here."

At this, the tiny dragon let out a small growling noise. The redcap brandished his knife again, smacking it against the dragon's cage. The dragon retreated to the far side of the cage.

"Don't do that! You'll hurt him!" Chloe reached for the cage, but the redcap got there first, slamming a fist on top of it.

"This one's trouble. Haven't fed him in days because he's misbehaving, and even when I do feed him, he won't grow. How am I supposed to become a dragon dealer if my only dragon won't grow?"

Chloe suspected Queen Mab would have something to say about illegal dragon dealers in her realm. Maybe that was the path to rescuing this tiny dragon. "How did you get him in the first place?"

"You ask too many questions," the redcap roared. "Now buy a cursing cat or a magical chicken, or get out of here before I take your fingers for being curious."

Anger filled Chloe. She never could stand a bully.

"I'm *not* leaving without the tiny dragon."

The redcap stood, and the thick, corded muscles in his arms bulged as he gripped his knife more tightly. "You're *not* taking the dragon."

Chloe's sword was out before her mind had time to catch up. In one quick, clean motion, she swiped at the redcap, forcing him backward.

This gave her the opening she needed. She darted behind the counter and slashed at the wooden locks of the cages holding a pair of moonshadow snakes, one with a black cat in it, and then two of the bird cages.

"Go on!" Chloe shouted to the animals. "Get out of here!"

"What are you doing?" The redcap grabbed for the locks. "These animals are mine to sell!"

The animals surged forward in a whirlwind of feathers and fur, all screeches and hisses. As one, they attacked the redcap, who swung his knife around wildly.

Chloe urgently undid the locks of the remaining cages, freeing the poor chicken and releasing two very confused-looking rabbits. She hoped they all found a safe place to flee or new homes.

"I'll kill you, girl!"

"First you have to catch me!" Chloe busted the lock on the tiny dragon's cage. She reached in, and the little creature settled on her palm. His needle-thin claws dug into her skin, drawing blood, but she didn't care. She cupped her hand around him.

"Give that dragon back!" the redcap shouted. "Stop, thief!"

Chloe didn't look back as she pushed into the market crowds. The redcap shouted, calling for others to chase after her.

Chloe ran, heart pounding, with the tiny dragon curled in her hand. She twisted through street after street, racing over small canals, and shoving through the crowds. The bookshop barge where Hyacinth was shopping had to be around here somewhere! She ducked behind a wall and then turned down another alley. Her breath stuttered in her chest as she looked around. Gods, it was a dead end. Perhaps they wouldn't find her here. She just needed a quick moment to catch her breath and get her bearings.

Chloe cradled the little dragon to her chest.

"Are you alright, Little One?" she whispered, peering at his perfect face.

As well as I can be, he answered in a small voice, sounding old and exhausted.

"Are you speaking to me?" Chloe wheezed. She hadn't really been expecting an answer. First Runa had spoken to her, and now this tiny dragon? What a magical solstice night indeed!

I'd love to chat more, the dragon said, *but trouble's already here*. The little dragon nodded toward the redcap shopkeeper at the end of the alley. He had two brutish goblins, mercenaries from the looks of their boiled leather armor and curved blades, beside him.

Bramble and marsh. Despite her months of sword lessons, Chloe was certainly not going to beat all three of them. But she'd try.

Chloe tucked the tiny dragon into her shirt pocket and drew her sword. "Stay hidden. They're not getting you back."

You're brave, aren't you? The tiny dragon sounded pleased.

Chloe grinned, hefting her sword. "Foolish more than brave maybe, but we'll see."

Before she could find a place to hide, the redcap spotted Chloe. "There you are!" he raged, storming into the alley. Feathers stuck to his cap, and a long scratch marred his cheek, dripping blood. Cheers to the cursing cat or whichever animal had attacked him.

The redcap glared at Chloe with murderous eyes. "All my animals are gone! Gone! Because of you!"

"Good!" She tightened her grip on her sword.

"I'm going to kill you and soak every drop of your blood into my cap."

Chloe swiped a shallow cut across his cheek to match the scratch. "Your own blood seems much more likely to soak into your cap at this rate."

The redcap hissed in outrage and waved his knife. "Kill her!"

One of the goblin mercenaries stepped up, his own sword drawn. Chloe met his blade. He was stronger than her, and he pushed her against the alley wall. The tiny dragon's head popped up out of her pocket.

"Don't hurt the dragon!" the shopkeeper shouted. "I can't sell it if you slice it open!"

The mercenary turned. "Why'd you ask us to help if you're not going to let us hurt her?"

"You can hurt her! Just not the tiny dragon!"

The goblin muttered a string of swears at the shopkeeper. "It's going to be more money if you want us to be tidy about it."

"I don't want you to be tidy! I just want you to bloody end her!"

"Well, if you'd let me do my job—"

Taking advantage of their bickering, Chloe pushed off the wall, shoving an elbow into the goblin. Air whooshed out of him, and his blade clattered to the ground. Not the best mercenary by a long shot. Wendell would beat him in a fight half-drunk, and he was at least a century old.

The other goblin surged toward Chloe, but in a smooth bit of evasion—hard-won from a lifetime of dodging blows and more recently from nearly being kicked every time she had to clean the gryphons' stable—Chloe ducked away from the redcap and his thugs and took off toward the entrance of the alley.

In seconds she was back in the main marketplace, running and pushing through a group of revelers who marched in a parade. They held lanterns and swayed to a lively song that filled the air. It was disorienting, and Chloe tried to get her bearings. Where was the Wilted Sparrow Bookshop? Where was Hyacinth? Chloe had to find her before the redcap and the goblins caught up. She wasn't so sure she'd be able to escape again without help.

"What's happening?" Chloe asked a mushroom-capped woman as the crowd flowed toward the bridge.

"End-of-the-market celebration!" the woman called out drunkenly. "Best time of the night!"

"Do you know where the—"

Before Chloe could finish, the revelers shoved forward, and Chloe was swept along with them. Behind her there was a loud cry as the redcap spotted her. He started pushing through the crowd. His goblin mercenaries swung their swords, parting the celebrating groups of people. Bramble and marsh, what was Chloe supposed to do now? Where was she supposed to hide?

She fought her way to the edge of the river, taking an elbow to the nose and tripping several times, before she scrambled up a low wall. Desperately, she scanned the mass of boats along the river.

And there! The Wilting Sparrow was only a bit farther down the street. Chloe nearly collapsed in relief.

Hyacinth stood outside the bookshop, clutching a green volume to her chest. Leaping from one boat to the next and then back onto the street, Chloe barreled into Hyacinth.

"Run!" she said, grabbing her hand and pulling her away from the Wilted Sparrow.

"Why?" Hyacinth asked, looking around. "What did you find? What's wrong?"

"Long story." The tiny dragon popped his head out of Chloe's pocket. "But I have a tiny dragon now."

Hyacinth let out a delighted gasp and bent to look at him. Her nose brushed against his. "Where did you get it?"

It was adorable. If Chloe weren't certain the goblins and redcap would soon be here, then she'd let herself enjoy how cute Hyacinth and the tiny dragon were together.

"I stole him from a redcap in a back alley. He was hurting him!"

"Well done." Hyacinth nuzzled the tiny dragon. "Oh, aren't you the most precious thing to ever exist in the entire world," she cooed. Chloe was nearly embarrassed for her, but she felt the same way.

"Truly, he is," Chloe agreed hastily. "But let's discuss this back at your mother's garden."

Who's this? the dragon asked into Chloe's mind. *A friend of yours? She's lovely. And she's worried about you.*

Before Chloe could answer, the redcap and his goons caught up to them.

"We're going to take you apart for making us chase you, girl." The shopkeeper's eyes gleamed with malice.

Blade ringing out as she drew it, Chloe stepped in front of Hyacinth. "Get out of here, Princess. I'll take care of this."

"No," Hyacinth said.

"No?"

Hyacinth shook her head, a fierce look in her eyes. She slipped the book she was holding into her belt pouch, and Chloe saw her fingers reach for the tiny potion bottles strapped there.

"Get out of the way, dainty," the shopkeeper snarled.

"No," Hyacinth repeated.

Chloe saw her touch a finger to her lips, and all at once, the air smelled like metal shavings and smoke, like the factories in Chloe's world.

Where had that come from? Probably something at the market. A blacksmith's booth nearby. Or a bonfire to celebrate the solstice.

Chloe's mind was wrenched away from the smell as the redcap scowled. "This one's stolen something from me. And I'll have it back."

That's rich, considering he stole me, the tiny dragon said into Chloe's mind.

"You're not going anywhere," Chloe whispered to the dragon.

Hyacinth glared at the redcap, looking every inch as ferocious as he was. Bramble and marsh, she was going to get herself killed.

Chloe pulled on her arm. "Let me take care of this, please."

Hyacinth shook off Chloe's hand and then touched her fingers to her lips again. The factory smell filled the air once more. She glared at the redcap. "You're *going* to give my friend the tiny dragon. You're *going* to leave us alone."

The redcap's eyebrows came together, and he opened and closed his mouth, like he was fighting to speak. "That's not your business," he said in a strangled tone.

A frown appeared between Hyacinth's eyebrows, and she touched her lips a third time.

"It is," she said. Then she pulled her cloak aside. Her party dress glimmered under the lantern lights, as out of place as Chloe had feared. Hyacinth stepped forward so her nose was inches from the redcap's.

"I'd say it's my mother's business as well, and I doubt very much *Queen Mab* would be happy with people selling dragons illegally in the market."

The redcap swallowed visibly, his eyes fixed on Hyacinth. "You're Queen Mab's daughter?"

"I am."

Chloe bit back a groan. It was a terrible, awful idea for Hyacinth to admit that. So much for the low profile Chloe had suggested when they left the stables.

Chloe glanced around. A crowd of merchants, customers, and Fae of all sorts had stopped to stare. Their expressions ranged from curiosity and surprise to suspicion and downright malice. Hyacinth was going to get killed. Or kidnapped. Or robbed, at the very least. Chloe wasn't sure how she could protect the princess in this case, but she gripped her sword more tightly.

Steady on, Brave One. I think your friend has this handled, the tiny dragon whispered in Chloe's mind.

Chloe wished she shared his confidence, but she didn't. "Hyacinth," she whispered. "Let's go now. I can distract them. You run for the stables."

"No," Hyacinth said, touching her lips one more time. That metallic scent overtook her again, and all at once, Chloe wanted to do only what Hyacinth said. If she wanted to stay here forever, Chloe would do it. She'd dance with the redcap if Hyacinth commanded it.

Chloe shook her head. What was going on here? Something in the solstice air was making her thoughts run wild.

Hyacinth stepped closer to the redcap. "You are *going* to leave us alone."

Much to Chloe's surprise, the redcap stepped backward. "Your Highness, my apologies. I didn't know it was you. Or that you . . . What I mean is . . ."

"You are *going* to forget about the tiny dragon, and we'll find the proper authorities—"

Chloe touched Hyacinth's shoulder. She wasn't sure what Hyacinth was playing at, but she didn't want to linger longer than necessary. "Let's get out of here," she said. "It'll be three versus two, if they change their mind."

"He won't change his mind."

"How can you be so sure?"

Hyacinth's lips curved into a half smile. "I'm sure."

Chloe looked between her and the redcap.

The redcap made an awkward bow toward Hyacinth. "Take the dragon and good riddance. I snagged it from a trader in the Swamplands. It was supposed to grow more, but it stayed the same size for months." He turned away, taking the two goblin mercenaries with him.

Chloe couldn't believe he'd left. It didn't make sense. Not after he chased her through the market, eager to kill her.

Still, she wasn't one to deny a bit of luck.

"Let's go, Princess?" Chloe let out a shaky breath and grabbed Hyacinth's elbow. "I appreciate you stopping that shopkeeper from painting his cap with my blood, but declaring yourself so boldly has brought a lot of attention we don't need."

Chloe glanced around again. The now-larger crowd was murmuring about the smell on the air, Hyacinth's expensive dress, and the way the redcap had left so suddenly.

Hyacinth looked around in surprise at the crowd, as if finally realizing they were there. Gone was the imperious princess who'd so boldly defied the redcap. Chloe watched her fidget with one of the potion bottles on her belt and then wring her hands. "Right, yes! I didn't even notice them. Leaving now seems like a very good idea indeed."

With her sword still out and her other hand clutching Hyacinth's, Chloe shoved through the suspicious crowd as they hurried toward where they'd left Runa.

Chapter Five
Hyacinth

Hyacinth's heart pounded, and her thoughts raced like the wind at their back. She was once again seated behind Chloe, with Runa soaring over the darkness of the Moonshadow Kingdom. Hyacinth couldn't believe how the night had gone. Honestly, so much better than she'd expected! She'd found a clue about her father—now she knew where he had been heading when he disappeared. She'd gotten his book and stopped those redcaps from hurting Chloe or taking the tiny dragon.

Well, the magical potion had done that.

Wraith tears for compulsion.

The smoky, metallic taste of the wraith tears still lingered on Hyacinth's lips. Not entirely unpleasant, but not something she'd make a habit of using again. Not that she'd have another opportunity. The bottle on her belt was empty, and wraith tears were nearly impossible to find. Hyacinth had been saving this bottle for months.

Had it been worth it? To compel the redcap? To force her will upon him and use up the rare magical item? To reveal herself to that crowd? Would she have been able to convince him without the compulsion charm?

She wasn't sure, and all at once doubt and exhaustion raced in, as the nerves from the evening caught up to her. Without thinking, she leaned forward, resting her forehead against the space between Chloe's shoulder blades.

Chloe turned her head slightly so she could see Hyacinth. "What are you doing, Princess? Are you napping? In the middle of a dragon flight?" Her tone was teasing, but the frown between her eyebrows told Hyacinth she actually was worried about her.

Hyacinth liked it when Chloe worried about her. A blush warmed her cheeks, but thank goodness for the darkness preventing Chloe from seeing it. Hyacinth offered Chloe a smile. "Thank you. For coming with me."

"Thank you for saving my tiny dragon. He says he's very grateful."

"He speaks to you?"

Chloe nodded. "He does."

A pang of jealousy gripped Hyacinth, but she wasn't sure if that was for the dragon talking to Chloe—the second dragon to do so tonight!—or the dragon getting to know Chloe when Hyacinth still had so many questions to ask the stablehand.

Was she jealous of a teacup-sized dragon? She really must be exhausted after all the evening's activities. And last night's in the garden.

Her blush deepened. It was on the tip of her tongue to tell Chloe how much she had enjoyed the last few days with her, but instead she blurted out, "Look how lovely my mother's palace is from up here."

"It looks like a dream," Chloe agreed, looking down. Her voice was full of wonder.

Silver and gold lanterns bobbed above the palace lawns, and the garden swayed with the moving shapes of dancers that trailed ribbons of light and song. Sapphire fountains glowed among the hedges of the garden maze, and even the torchlit stable complex looked softer from up here.

Runa flew over the palace entryway, where a handful of guests were getting into carriages—several of them gasped in alarm to see the enormous dragon above them—and then she headed toward her enclosure.

Chloe turned again to Hyacinth for a moment as Runa began to descend. "I enjoyed our night out, Princess. Do you— Oh, gods. That's not good."

Hyacinth followed Chloe's gaze. Three palace guards and the queen's bodyguard, Maurelle, waited outside the main entrance to the dragon barns. Shouts rang out as Maurelle and the guards pointed up at Runa. A sick feeling rose in Hyacinth's stomach.

She was caught.

"Bramble and marsh," Hyacinth swore under her breath.

She was going to be locked in her mother's highest tower. She'd grow old there. She'd be trotted out to attend balls and maybe to marry some dreadful lord. She'd never learn more about her father, and she'd never get to explore more of the kingdom. She'd never see Chloe again. She'd never feel as brave as she had when standing up to that redcap.

What absolute misery.

"How much trouble are we in?" Chloe's voice was tight as Runa landed on the roof of her barn.

Far below them, Hyacinth could see Maurelle and the palace guards running down a lane toward Runa's stable. Chloe's tiny dragon peeked over her shoulder to cast Hyacinth a baleful gaze.

They were in so much trouble. But there was no way she was letting Chloe get marched to the dungeons for Hyacinth's desire to go to the Solstice Market. "Let me do the talking," she said. "I'll keep you out of it. Actually, better yet, you get off once Runa's on her moss bed."

"Absolutely not. You're not facing this trouble alone."

"I am." How was Hyacinth going to make that happen, though? How could she hide Chloe from Maurelle and the others? The question spiraled through her head as Runa dropped from the roof through the open window. The dragon landed with a soft *thump*.

Chloe shook her head. "You already stood up to the redcap for me. I don't need you fighting my battles, Princess."

Hyacinth had stood up to the redcap with the help of a potion—that was it! She could use one of her potions. Quickly, she grabbed a blue glass bottle. *Gray tendrils of fog for vanishing.*

"I'm not fighting your battles," Hyacinth said as she pulled the potion out of its holder. "I'm making sure you don't end up my mother's prisoner for the rest of your life."

"Your mother wouldn't throw me in the dungeon for going to the market in Keldale."

"Do you know what she did to the last person who tried to steal one of her dragons?"

"No."

"Exactly. No one does, because my mother obliterated their memory from all the records to make sure no one ever tried that again."

Chloe scoffed. "She's not going to disappear me for going with you to a bookstore. Plus, technically, we didn't *steal* Runa. We borrowed her."

This girl was maddening. Hyacinth wanted to shake her. "Do you want to argue semantics? Now? Just take this." She thrust the bottle roiling with gray tendrils of fog toward Chloe.

"What is it?"

"Magical fog. Pour it into your hands and rub it over your skin like a lotion. It should make you vanish long enough to get away."

"Where'd you get it?" Chloe narrowed her eyes, studying the bottle.

"Does that matter?" Hyacinth snapped in desperation. Was she really supposed to tell Chloe she'd swiped it from an alchemist's bench?

"Yes! You can't just trust *random* pieces of magic." Chloe's voice strained on the words, as if something dark and terrible lurked behind them. "There could be anything in there!"

Hyacinth had no idea what Chloe meant, but maybe she'd bought a bad potion once or heard tales of someone who had. Whatever the reason, Hyacinth needed Chloe to use the potion. So she lied to Chloe for the second time that evening. "I made it with my High Fae magic, okay? Just in case we ran into trouble."

"Can't you cast an illusion over me or something?"

"No! Take the potion!"

Chloe shook her head. "I don't want—"

Footsteps sounded outside the enclosure.

"There's no time!" Hyacinth shoved the bottle into her hands. "Now go! Please!"

Chloe's eyebrows pulled together in a frown, but she nodded. "Fine, but meet me in the garden, in our spot, if you can. Just so I know you're okay. I'll wait for you until sunrise."

Hyacinth offered her the ghost of a smile. "If I survive my mother, I'll meet you there."

Chloe squeezed her knee, and the gesture was more comforting than it had a right to be. In one quick move, she slid off Runa and landed on her feet in the moss bed.

Shouts and footsteps drew closer. With a quick glance back up Hyacinth, Chloe uncorked the potion bottle and poured it into her hands.

"Please work," Hyacinth muttered, hoping the potion would be as magical as promised. Her mother's alchemists were extremely talented, but there's always a chance she'd grabbed the wrong bottle or that it was no longer potent. If that happened, she didn't know how she'd hide Chloe. "Please work."

Gray ribbons of fog poured from the bottle, encircling Chloe as she rubbed the mixture over her body. In the space between one blink and the next, she vanished into smoke and shadows.

And not a moment too soon.

"Princess Hyacinth," Maurelle called, stepping into Runa's paddock. "Get down here at once."

"Oh! Maurelle! So nice to see you. I was just out for some night air." Hyacinth called, fighting to keep her eyes away from the waft of smoke that moved along the edge of the moss bed.

"Your mother is waiting for you in her library. Go to her. *Now.*"

Hyacinth swallowed hard. "Is she . . . angry?"

The queen's bodyguard glowered. "She's not happy to be pulled away from her party, or to worry about you."

"But I didn't mean to—"

"Save it." Maurelle pulled out her knife, flipping it through her fingers. "I care even less about your excuses than Her Majesty does. Now move."

Making sure the smoke that was Chloe was fully out the door, Hyacinth hurried down the saddle ladder, dread coiling in her bones.

"Thank you, Runa," she whispered, as Maurelle grabbed her arm and dragged her out of the enclosure.

Runa inclined her head for a moment, as if to say, *You're welcome and also good luck. I hope your mother doesn't kill you.*

✦

Hyacinth wasn't actually worried her mother was going to murder her. Of course not. That would be silly. Queen Mab, ever-glorious monarch of the Moonshadow Kingdom, had a reputation for many things, but she didn't hurt her daughters.

Though . . . there had been that *incident* a few months ago.

As Hyacinth trudged along the cobblestone paths beside Maurelle—who kept shoving drunk Fae out of the way and scowling so hard, Hyacinth was sure her face would break—her thoughts flew back to what had happened during the Spring Equinox.

She still wasn't entirely sure what had occurred, but she and Chloe had met two humans, Esme and Sybil, who'd come through a door from their world into this one. They stole some of Queen Mab's jewels, and then Chloe (with Hyacinth's accidental assistance) helped them escape to their own world. When the queen discovered the theft and learned from her guards that the human girls had gotten away, she blazed with wrath. She threw things, shouted at anyone and everyone. Then, when Hyacinth let slip that she'd heard the girls mention her sister Maeve, who was supposed to be in the Swamplands, the queen left on Runa without a word. She'd come back not long after, dragging a screaming, furious Maeve with her.

Neither the queen nor Maeve had spoken since about what happened, but Hyacinth still felt bad about mentioning her sister's name. Not that she'd ever reveal she had done so.

Queen Mab's temper was something of a legend in the Moonshadow Kingdom. After she'd returned with Maeve, she locked and sealed every other door between the human world and the Fae world—Hyacinth had never known there were so many!—and she'd been icy toward Maeve for months. They were only just beginning to make up.

What would she do to Hyacinth now?

Probably nothing, right? She'd only left the Solstice Ball early, borrowed Runa, and declared herself boldly in Keldale—bramble and marsh, did her mother know she'd done that? How could she know that? Hyacinth let out a nervous laugh and then clapped a hand over her mouth.

Hyacinth glanced at Maurelle as they neared the palace steps. Should Hyacinth ask her how much the queen knew? The guard stared stonily forward, her posture a map of her anger at Hyacinth.

Nope. Hyacinth wouldn't ask. She'd just face whatever waited for her.

As they entered the palace, Maurelle shoved Hyacinth past guests kissing in the shadowy hallways. Hyacinth's frantic thoughts continued to race as they trudged up the stairs.

If her mother knew to send Maurelle to the stables, then she must've missed Hyacinth at the party. Someone else must've told her about Runa being gone, but why or how she'd connected those things . . . Unless someone had seen them leaving?

"We're at the library, *Princess*," Maurelle mocked. "Good luck. I'll be right outside in case you try to run away again."

"I wasn't trying to run away; I was just—"

The library door swung open, cutting off Hyacinth's words.

"Hyacinth!" Queen Mab strode toward her, her face a stony, regal mask.

This was it. Hyacinth braced herself for the storm, and then her mother . . . pulled her into a tight hug, nearly crushing her. What was happening here?

Gems from the queen's elaborate gown dug into Hyacinth's shoulder, and she remained stiff in the hug, just as she'd done with Chloe earlier that evening.

What was her mother doing? Where was the wrath? Her mother hadn't hugged her like this since she was three and had nearly drowned in the lake behind the castle. Hyacinth still remembered that particular hug, one of a very small number in her life.

"I'm so glad you're safe," Queen Mab said, her voice thick with emotion. How much had the queen drunk at the Solstice Ball? Had something else happened? Was this all a trick before the queen raged at her?

Hyacinth decided to play this as nonchalantly as possible in the hopes that would keep her mother calm. Best to just ride out this affection, wherever it was coming from.

"I was just book shopping in Keldale, Mother." She shrugged, as if it were quite normal to fly to Keldale at this time of night. "Why aren't you at your party?" Of all the things she wanted to ask, why had Hyacinth mentioned the party? Now Queen Mab could be angry at her for leaving *and* borrowing the dragon.

The queen finally released Hyacinth, casting a tearful gaze upon her. By the Sisters, why was her mother crying? Queen Mab, ever-glorious monarch of the Moonshadow Kingdom, *never* cried. She was notorious for casting watery lords and ladies from her court for "too much fuss."

The queen brushed a lock of hair off Hyacinth's check, tucking it behind her ear gently. "We didn't know where you were or what had happened to you! Do you know what that's like as a mother? Not knowing where your child is?"

The queen's voice broke on the last few words. The pain and worry in it made Hyacinth flinch. Had her mother really been that . . . worried? About her?

Anger, Hyacinth could understand, but this level of concern? From a High Fae ruler whose teeth were sharpened with the bones of her enemies once a fortnight if the rumors were to be believed?

Hyacinth cleared her throat, uncomfortable to the point of mortification. "Mother, I'm fine. Really, I just was . . . overwhelmed by the party and wanted a bit of night air."

"You can't disappear like that!"

A vision of the redcap threatening Chloe rose in Hyacinth's mind. She forced it away and smiled at her mother. "I assure you, I was perfectly safe."

Queen Mab scoffed. "Safe! You'll never be safe. You don't have *any* magic, Hyacinth! Don't you know how dangerous that is?"

The words were a blow. Hyacinth recoiled, stepping away from her mother. "Of course I *know*! How could I possibly forget with you moaning about it every morning over breakfast? Or with these wretched fake wings spelled to my back?"

Queen Mab's gaze was a knife. She gripped Hyacinth's shoulders. "Those wings are to keep you safe! *Everything* I do is to keep you safe!"

That was ridiculous.

"Everything? Please, Mother, don't tell me you hosted this Solstice Ball to 'keep me safe'—"

Queen Mab's nails dug deeper into Hyacinth's shoulder, sending pain spiking through her. "Don't be obtuse on purpose. You *know* what I mean. Without magic, you're . . ."

The queen's gaze flicked to the side, and Hyacinth followed it to the only portrait of her parents in the castle. It showed the queen looking regal and intimidating as always, with Hyacinth's father, Evan Bramblefen, a handsome, dark-haired Fae man, sitting in a chair in front of her. A pair of glasses perched on his nose, and baby Hyacinth sat on his lap, smiling at the painter like he'd just told her a joke. Hyacinth had spent long hours as a child staring up at this portrait, wondering what her father looked like now and what her family would've been like if he hadn't disappeared.

"What, Mother? What am I?"

"You're too much like your father sometimes, I fear," the queen finished softly.

Hyacinth's interest sparked at the words. "What do you mean? You can tell me about him, you know!"

Her mother sighed. "What could you possibly need to know about Evan?"

"Everything! Because you haven't told me anything! I've wanted to know more about him for years, and you avoid every question."

Her mother released her shoulders and waved a hand. "That's for your own good. As I told you, I'm *trying* to protect you!"

"Maybe I don't need protecting! Maybe what I *need* is to know more about my father. Is he even alive?"

Queen Mab's shoulders slumped. She clutched the silver locket around her neck. "I have no idea. I haven't heard from Evan since he left fifteen years ago."

Hyacinth thought of the book tucked into her belt pouch. Should she tell her mother about it? Did her mother know her father had been seeking out the Labyrinth?

No. Queen Mab didn't need to know. Not tonight, when she was weirdly emotional and looking at Hyacinth like she'd break. The last thing she needed to do was pour vinegar in the wound of losing him.

Still, she could offer her a bit of something, couldn't she?

"Mother," Hyacinth said, making her voice soft. "What if we could learn more about what happened to him? Wouldn't you want to know?"

Queen Mab shook her head, her posture straightening, her royal mask slipping into place. "*No*. That time is done. As I've told you, there's more heartbreak than hope to be found in looking for more information about your father."

"But, Mother, what if—"

"Enough, Hyacinth. Maurelle is going to take you to your room. Stay there. You're grounded until I come get you. I'm going back to our guests. If you leave your room, I'll send Maurelle after you. She won't be as forgiving the second time around."

The queen stormed out of the library.

Hyacinth collapsed into a chair and buried her face in her hands.

✦

Once she was safely inside her room with the door closed, Hyacinth pulled the green book from her pocket.

She ran her finger over her father's name written on the inside cover.

Evan Bramblefen.

"Where are you?" she muttered.

Hyacinth studied the map for a moment, biting her bottom lip. It was a long way to the Labyrinth, and there was so much of the kingdom between it and Queen Mab's castle: miles and miles of dense forest; a mountain range, sharp-peaked and snow-covered; the Swamplands; and then beyond it all, the Labyrinth and whatever waited inside it.

Don't go to the Labyrinth, Dalton warned ominously in Hyacinth's mind. *No one returns from there.*

But what if she did? What if her father had made it to the Labyrinth, but couldn't get home? What if he was still alive and needed her somehow? Wasn't that chance worth crossing forest, mountain, and swamp for?

She ran a finger over three more places her father had drawn onto the map: a settlement, deep in the forest, marked as *Mushroom Town*; a tall mountain labeled *Hall of the Mountain King*; and then *Hyacinth Cottage* in the Swamplands along the eastern coast.

Why had he marked those? Dalton said they'd met at the Wild Root Inn in Mushroom Town, but where had her father gone after that?

Hyacinth started pacing her room. She had so many questions, but one stood out: If she found him, could he tell her why she had no magic? Would the truths of her be revealed in finding him?

She didn't know. All she knew was that there was a chance her father was still alive, and if she found him, in addition to reuniting her family, maybe he could help her innate magic manifest.

The thought sent excitement fizzing through her, until she caught sight of herself in her mirror. Her party dress was rumpled from the flight on Runa's back; the hem was filthy from the streets of Keldale; and her fake wings looked vaguely askew. But she was still every inch a High Fae princess. An unmagical one at that. Could *she* really save her father? She hadn't even thought to ask directions in Keldale. How would she get halfway across a kingdom?

Hyacinth considered the potions she had left at her belt.

Juniper heart for illusion. A moon-drenched secret for levitation. Bitterroot berry for healing. Dragonheart ashes for fire and ruin.

Plus, she had her enchanted compass. And her father's guide to the kingdom.

What did she have to lose? She was already in trouble and grounded. What more could her mother do?

She was certain she didn't want to know the answer.

"Will you survive out there?" she asked her reflection.

The girl in the mirror blinked back at her.

Hyacinth was so tired of waiting around the castle, of being protected. It was time to actually do something in her life! She would find her father. That would make her mother happy, surely, and then Hyacinth could understand even more about herself and her family.

"You *will* survive out there," she replied to her reflection. "You'll find him and come back with answers to all your questions."

Perhaps Chloe would be up for another adventure?

With that thought, Hyacinth changed into a sensible dress and leather boots, packed a bag with as many coins and jewels as she had in her room, then tucked the book from her father back into her belt pouch along with an enchanted pen she'd swiped from her mother's library.

Hyacinth studied herself in the mirror again. She looked more ready for an adventure. She couldn't do anything about her wings, but she could move fast, while her mother was still at the party.

She glanced around her room, making sure she hadn't missed anything. The next time she returned to Queen Mab's castle, hopefully she'd have her father with her. No matter what it took.

Hyacinth opened the secret passage in her wall and fled the room, hurrying toward the garden, where she hoped Chloe was still waiting.

Chapter Six
Chloe

The solstice party raged as Chloe made her way through the towering hedges and flower-lined paths of Queen Mab's garden. Hyacinth's vanishing spell still clung to her, rendering her nearly invisible. She was a wisp of smoke and shadow as she passed unnoticed around a trio of dryads dancing in a sparkling sapphire fountain. She slunk past two fauns singing a lilting summer song beneath an arbor of wisteria that twinkled with a group of tiny pixies having their own party among the flowers. Jasmine and lemon trees perfumed the air, and the night tasted fresh as the blackberries that grew among the hedges. Chloe's stomach grumbled, and she popped a blackberry into her mouth, unable to resist its sweetness.

A rush of heady contentment filled her, easing her worries for Hyacinth, who was likely getting eviscerated by her mother's wrath.

The anger of queens is always something to fear.

Chloe popped another berry into her mouth to push that whisper from her past away. Tonight was not for thinking about queens and their wrath. The berry seeds stuck in her teeth as the taste of it danced over her tongue. The magic from consuming Fae food in the wild like this was bright and warming. It felt almost like sitting with her eyes closed in a patch of sunlight. In the midst of such delicious magic, the past, the present, and the future dropped away. There were no angry queens, or lost sisters, or brave princesses. There was only the taste of the blackberry.

Until it faded, which it always did.

Chloe picked more berries.

This forgetting was why some humans gave in to Fae food and drink. It could keep their worries and their woes at bay. It was comfort and reprieve. Even for just a few moments. But if they ate too much, they'd lose themselves entirely.

Magic is dangerous. You know this, even as you flirt with it here. You know where in humans it comes from. You know the costs, whispered a memory in Chloe's head. She closed her eyes against recalling what had happened a little over a year ago, when Chloe and her sister found out that humans had starlight in their bones. When they were forced to work for a vicious human queen who wanted to harvest it from them to make magical lace that she could use to ensure her power.

Chloe shuddered, crushing the other berries in her hands. She wanted desperately to eat all of them, but if she let Fae food enchant her, she might not remember her sister. She might forget she needed to go home.

She couldn't forget anything about herself right now. And what if Hyacinth needed her?

"What are you going to do, break her out of the palace?" she asked herself with a touch of embarrassment. She'd tested her sword skills against the redcap and his mercenaries in the market, but she wasn't ready to storm the castle.

You will if you must, Brave One, the tiny dragon whispered. Her body was becoming more visible as the vanishing spell wore off, and the tiny dragon popped his head out of her pocket.

"You're right; I will go rescue the princess if I must," she agreed. She ran a finger over the dragon's head, and he preened under her touch. "Are you doing okay, Little One?"

I'd be better with some food.

"Berries?" Chloe said, picking another few from the bramble.

The dragon scoffed.

Chloe laughed. "Fair enough. I have some dried meat in my bag. Let me get to our spot before this spell fully wears off so I don't have to talk to any of these revelers, and it's all yours."

The tiny dragon inclined his head. Chloe kept walking. After several more twists through the garden maze, Chloe slipped into the tucked-away, leafy alcove where she and Hyacinth always met.

On one side of the nook, the stone face of the mountain soared upward. The other two sides were made of tall lilac hedges, enchanted to always be in bloom. The air was thick with the lilacs' sweet perfume. This was where they'd kissed last night. Where Chloe finally let herself give in to her feelings. Kissing Hyacinth was a bit like eating one of the Fae berries—warm and lovely and it made Chloe forget her worries about being stuck in Fae or missing her sister.

Of course, kissing Hyacinth had brought its own problems, and Chloe knew it couldn't happen again.

That didn't mean she wasn't worried for her friend.

"Where are you, Hyacinth?" Chloe whispered to the wall. She ran a hand—she could see most of her fingers now as the last of the vanishing potion wore off—along the ivy there, tracing the outline of the door that led from the garden to the palace.

She'd told Hyacinth she'd wait until sunrise in the garden, so despite Chloe's desire to slip into the palace's secret tunnels and seek out Hyacinth, she settled instead on a mossy bench in the middle of the alcove.

She pulled the tiny dragon gently from her pocket and rested him beside her, then offered a dried bit of meat from Wendell's. The dragon sniffed it and then made a delighted little chirp. He gulped down the meat in one bite and then looked up at her expectantly.

Chloe grinned and tore off another piece. "What's your name? I can hardly keep calling you 'little one,' especially if you start growing more."

Can't remember, the tiny dragon said into her head.

"You can't remember your own name?"

Lots I can't remember, actually. Don't even really remember how I ended up with that dragon dealer. Just remember hating him. And that he bought me from someone else.

That was strange. According to Wendell, dragons had memories deeper than the mountain lake behind the palace. They inherited ancestral remembrances from their parents as well, so even as younglings, they should remember generations past. Perhaps this one was lying, or perhaps he truly didn't remember because of the trauma. Either way, Chloe didn't see any reason to push. The tiny dragon was hungry and exhausted. He needed care and rest, not suspicion.

"How old are you?"

Don't know. Not young, that's for sure.

"Why are you so small?"

Don't know.

"What should I call you?" Chloe repeated the question she'd started with.

Whatever you want. Name me after your favorite thing if you'd like.

Her favorite thing? What was that? Perhaps—

Before she had a chance to really consider it, Hyacinth burst into the garden nook.

"Chloe, there you are!" she said, breathless. She'd changed out of her glittering party dress and had a silk bag looped over her shoulder. She crossed to the bench and sat beside Chloe.

Gratitude filled Chloe. Somehow, Hyacinth had survived her mother's fury. She was in one piece and not trapped in the queen's dungeons. She was here and soft against Chloe's side, and all Chloe wanted to do was hug her.

Which would be embarrassing for both of them, Chloe imagined. Especially since her last hug had been so unwelcome it seemed. Instead, she shrugged and grinned at Hyacinth. "I'm where I'd said I'd be, Princess. Are you in too much trouble?"

A frown crossed Hyacinth's face, there and gone again. "Nothing worth worrying about. I'm leaving the castle, though."

Chloe's eyebrows shot upward. "When?"

"Right now."

Right now? That didn't make any sense. Why was Hyacinth leaving the castle right after getting caught doing so? Did she *want* her mother to lock her in the dungeon? Had she hit her head when getting off Runa or drunk too much summer wine between now and when Chloe last saw her?

Chloe held back on asking any of those questions. "Where are you going? Off to another bookshop?" Her voice was teasing and light, to show she understood Hyacinth had to be joking.

Hyacinth shook her head, all seriousness. "Hardly." She pulled the green book she'd gotten from the Wilting Sparrow from her belt pouch and flipped it open to a map. "I'm going to the Labyrinth." She stabbed a finger into the immense maze at the edge of the map.

What in the world?

Chloe decided to indulge Hyacinth, who was probably just overtired from all their adventures. "The Labyrinth is incredibly far from here. What are you hoping to find there?"

Hyacinth bit her lip, and a long silence stretched between them. She ran a hand over the tiny potion bottles on her belt and then traced a finger along the edge of the map.

"What is it, Princess?" Chloe prodded.

"It's . . . well. This is going to sound absolutely ridiculous."

Chloe shrugged, recalling how she'd ended up in Fae. *Ridiculous* barely captured it. "Try me."

Hyacinth flipped the pages to reveal notes scrawled in the book's margins. A breathless rush of words poured out of her: "So, believe it or not, this book is my father's. He's been missing for fifteen years and—well, I found his book tonight at the Wilting Sparrow. The bookseller, who's an old friend of my father, told me that the last time he saw him, my father was heading toward the Labyrinth. . . ."

Understanding hit Chloe like a gryphon's hoof. "And you think *you* should see if he's still there?"

Hyacinth nodded, her eyes enormous in her face.

It was a terrible idea. Surely Hyacinth knew that? Even Chloe, who ran toward most risks like they were long-lost friends, knew that.

Hyacinth talked faster, like she would lose her nerve if she didn't get it all out at once. "I don't really know what's in the Labyrinth or if my father is there. Supposedly, there's a magical library inside an oak tree, and the bookseller said there might even be portals to other worlds. Maybe my father . . ."

Chloe's racing thoughts screeched to a halt.

"A portal?" Chloe managed despite her galloping pulse. "To other worlds?"

She swallowed hard. It was what she'd been looking for all these months.

Hyacinth nodded. "Like the door we saw last spring . . . during the *incident*."

They'd never talked about the *incident*, though Chloe had wanted to bring it up a thousand times. But she didn't want to answer Hyacinth's questions about it, and then months had passed without them talking about it.

Why did they never talk about these things?

Chloe would have to get better about that.

"I thought your mother locked all the doors to other worlds," Chloe said very carefully, fighting to keep hope from her voice.

Hyacinth returned her attention to the book. "Maybe she did and the portal in the Labyrinth is locked. Maybe it's not there at all. Maybe my mother doesn't know about it. I don't know what waits for us inside the Labyrinth, but I have to go!"

This sounds like a terrible idea, the tiny dragon chimed in.

Exactly Chloe's thought, but Hyacinth looked so hopeful. How could Chloe possibly make her see how dangerous this was?

Plus, what if there was a door that could take her home and back to her sister?

A flame of hope lit in Chloe's chest, but she had to make sure Hyacinth understood what she was proposing. This was so much more than gallivanting to a market town.

"Princess," Chloe said, working to keep her tone measured. "While I understand what it is to seek someone you've lost—believe me, I do—are you sure this is what you want?"

"Of course! It's the first clue about my father I've had in years!"

"What if he's not there?"

Hyacinth bit her lip. "I've considered that, but I have to try." Pride and fear laced her words.

"Put aside not knowing what's waiting for you in the Labyrinth. What do you know about traveling through the Moonshadow Kingdom or finding people? Can your magic help with that?"

"I have no idea," Hyacinth snapped. "I just have to do it. And I could use some help. Do you want to come with me? As my bodyguard and friend?"

Chloe did.

"I'll go with or without you," Hyacinth added, being exactly the stubborn, ferocious, wretched, lovely princess that she was. The one Chloe liked so very much, even now.

Chloe sighed.

Perhaps there really was a door waiting to take her home at the center of the Labyrinth. Or maybe there wasn't. But if she didn't try to find it, she'd never know.

She had to try.

You don't have to do this, the tiny dragon whispered in her head.

She really did, though, for herself and Hyacinth. "Okay, let's go."

Hyacinth's face brightened. "Really?"

"Really."

Hyacinth flung an arm around Chloe's shoulder and squeezed her in an excited half hug. Then she hopped up from the bench. "Let's get moving. I don't want my mother to know I'm gone until we're many miles away."

"Is your mother still looking for you? Are her guards after you?" If that was the case, then Chloe wasn't so sure they should be leaving. But what were they going to do, ask Queen Mab for permission?

"Nothing to worry about there. She's back at her party, and Maurelle is guarding my door. Neither of them would believe I'd sneak out again, even if they did know about the secret passage from my room to the garden, which I'm sure they don't. By the time my mother comes to check on me, I'll be long gone. Now, come on. Let's go find our ride." Hyacinth strode off through the garden, her belt clanking and her steps sure.

Do you know what you're doing? the tiny dragon asked as he settled back in Chloe's pocket.

"I think so," Chloe murmured. "Is this a bad idea?"

The tiny dragon didn't reply as Chloe hurried to catch up with Hyacinth.

✦

"Do you want to steal a pair of horses?" Chloe asked as they snuck into the stables. They'd agreed that walking to the Labyrinth would take forever, but the stables were busy with guests coming and going and harried-looking grooms bustling about. Someone was bound to see them and start asking questions.

"I have a better idea." Hyacinth pointed to a green-skinned, frog-headed Fae in a luxurious jacket. He stood by his coach, which was an ostentatious thing, paneled in jade and gilded with golden lily pads. He was clearly very, very drunk and kept stumbling as he struggled to attach a pair of enormous boars to the carriage. "That's Lord Helston. Follow me."

Hyacinth strode over to him, a smile plastered on her face. "Lord Helston, leaving so soon?"

"Princess," he slurred, sweeping one arm out toward his carriage. "I missed you at the party. Our dance was going to be the stuff dreams are made of!" He bowed so low, he toppled over. A bottle of summer wine fell from his coat pocket, and his legs went over his head in a tumble of silks and gems.

Chloe snickered. Hyacinth elbowed her. "Our ride," Hyacinth mouthed. "Keep it together."

Chloe inclined her head ever so slightly. "As you say."

Hyacinth smiled at Lord Helston, her words all sweetness, her face a portrait of exaggerated care. "What a loss our dance was!"

Chloe held back a laugh at Hyacinth's over-the-top aspect as she helped haul the frog to his feet. "Careful there, Your Lordship."

Lord Helston started to bow his thanks again, but then he huffed, glaring at one of the boars. "Don't know where all the grooms have gotten to. . . . One said they'd be with me in a moment, but then they hurried off to help someone else. I've never seen the stable so ill-attended. Honestly!"

"Let me," Chloe said, stepping forward. Avoiding the boar's tusks with long-practiced movements, she tightened wide leather harnesses around the boars' necks and secured their collars to the lines that attached to the carriage. It was done quickly, and Lord Helston beamed at her.

"Ah, very well done . . . Lady . . . ? I'm sorry, my lady, but I don't think I know you." Lord Helston hiccupped as he peered at Chloe, trying to place her. "Were you at the ball?"

Chloe's eyes widened. Did her glamour really make her look like she belonged at the ball? Surely not.

"This is my friend, Chloe," Hyacinth said quickly. "We've both left the party on a mission from my mother. Could you give us a ride toward the Swamplands?"

"Your mother! The queen! Oh, I'd be honored!" Lord Helston bowed again. He pulled the carriage door open with a flourish and clambered inside, sprawling across a seat.

"Are you sure about this?" Chloe whispered. The tiny dragon peeked out of her shirt as well. "It's barely big enough for him in there, much less all three of us."

Hyacinth shrugged. "His Swamplands are on the edge of the Labyrinth, and I want to be gone before my mother catches us. Getting a ride with him is our best option."

Inside the carriage, Lord Helston started snoring. Loudly.

"We could always borrow another dragon?"

"Absolutely not," Hyacinth said. "The dragon paddocks are assuredly under watch after our flight earlier. Now get in, please. Before someone sees us."

Chloe clambered into the carriage, taking up half the narrow bench across from Lord Helston. A small lantern lit the space, and Hyacinth squeezed into the seat as well. She turned to close the carriage door. Her wings smashed Chloe's face, giving Chloe a close-up view of the gold veins and silvery surface along them.

"Hyacinth," Chloe managed to say through a mouthful of wings. The tiny dragon in her pocket squeaked in alarm.

"What?"

"I can't move."

"Well, there's not much room for me either." Hyacinth turned in a quick movement that nearly took out Chloe's eye. The lantern swayed as her wings brushed it.

"Can't you retract your wings now? It's cramped enough in here as it is."

Hyacinth scowled. "If you'd stop hogging the seat, then I'd have more than enough room for my wings."

Hogging the seat? Was she kidding?

"There's no room for me to go anywhere." As it was, Chloe's back was pressed against the opposite wall of the carriage.

Hyacinth huffed and Chloe caught something about "bloody awful wings . . ." Then she turned enough so the wings were smashed against the carriage door instead of smothering Chloe.

Of course, that now meant Hyacinth's face was a few inches away from Chloe's, and Chloe could see every fleck of lantern light sparkling in Hyacinth's silver eyes.

They sat very still for a long moment.

Chloe shifted uncomfortably. "What do we do now?" she whispered, pointing at Lord Helston. He snored on, his boozy breath filling the air. "Besides open a window."

Hyacinth giggled. Ever so delicately, she tapped Lord Helston's knee. He didn't move. She tapped him again.

This also did nothing.

"Oh, for goodness' sake," Chloe said. She leaned over and shook him. "Your Lordship, how do we make this bucket move?"

He startled awake. "What's that? Who's there?"

"Is there a driver? A coachman?" Chloe pressed.

"My boars know the way." Lord Helston opened the small round window above his head and addressed the boars. "Raffles and Waddles! Take us home!"

There was a jolt, and the enormous boars trundled forward, leaving the barn and moving down the road.

"That is where you were going, right?" Lord Helston asked, looking blearily at Hyacinth and Chloe. "To my home?"

"Close enough," Chloe said. "Now, you get some sleep, Your Lordship. We'll wake you if anything interesting happens."

Lord Helston nodded and then pillowed his head against the thinly padded seat. The carriage juddered as it picked up speed, sending Hyacinth into Chloe's lap.

Avoiding Hyacinth's wings, Chloe's arm snaked out to hold her there, just for a moment. The closeness sent a flare of awareness along Chloe's skin. Her heart raced and her breath whispered along Hyacinth's neck.

"Steady there, Princess." Chloe gently scooted to the side so Hyacinth could slide off her lap.

"Apologies for that," Hyacinth muttered, though her cheeks blushed pink in the lantern light. "These wings make things awkward."

"It's a very small carriage," Chloe offered. "Filled with quite a lot of Swamplands lordship."

Lord Helston shifted in his sleep and draped one arm across his forehead dramatically. A small laugh burst from Hyacinth. "He is ridiculous." She grinned at Chloe, like they were sharing a joke as well as another adventure.

"Decidedly so," Chloe said as she pushed back a velvet curtain and peered out the window. Moonlight painted the road as the boars turned toward the forest and Swamplands. In the distance, the lights of Queen Mab's castle dimmed with each passing mile. Above them, the stars flickered silver. It was so lovely. As the carriage rattled onward, Chloe's mind drifted back to nights spent with Anya and her parents. Her mother and father had been explorers, and before they'd died in a shipwreck when Chloe was six, they'd all traveled everywhere together. At the start of every adventure, they'd stop for a cup of coffee, her parents' favorite beverage. Chloe and Anya always got a cup too, with melted chocolate and warm milk because *explorers must stay awake as they start a journey!* as her father liked to say. The smell of coffee always reminded Chloe of starting out on an adventure. Of home, safety, and the love of her family.

She'd give anything to share a cup of coffee with her sister again.

The tiny dragon shifted in her pocket, pulling her from her thoughts. Chloe rested him on her lap. Already, his eyes were brighter and his movements less lethargic than they had been. Protectiveness and care filled her as she looked at him.

"I think I've figured it out," she whispered, both to the tiny dragon and Hyacinth.

"What?" Hyacinth ran a finger along the silver bumps on the tiny dragon's head. He preened under her touch.

"This dragon's name."

Hyacinth quirked an eyebrow. "What is it?"

"Coffee."

"Coffee? What's that? I've never heard of anyone named that before."

Chloe had forgotten that Hyacinth could have a rainbow assortment of beverages here—from hummingbird nectar to starred-berry wines and a hundred others—but ordinary things like coffee were missing from this world.

"Why do you want to name him that?" Hyacinth continued. "I think he looks more like a Larkspur or Milkweed."

Larkspur? Milkweed? the tiny dragon sputtered in disbelief. *Absolutely not. I may not remember who I am, but I do know I'm a gentleman dragon who will not be named after a flower!*

"Oh!" Hyacinth said, her eyebrows climbing even higher. "I heard that one too. Very well, no flower names."

Chloe giggled and looked at the dragon. "What about Coffee, little one? Does that suit you? It's one of my favorite things in the world. Before every trip with my parents and sister, we'd drink coffee and toast the adventures ahead. Years later, when my sister and I were in the orphanage, we dreamed of drinking coffee every morning in one of the shops in town."

"What does Coffee taste like?" Hyacinth asked very gently. Her eyes met Chloe's, which made Chloe realize just how much she'd revealed—and how much she'd never told Hyacinth before. "I've never had it."

"Bitter, hot, a touch sweet sometimes . . ."

I am none of those things, the tiny dragon grumbled. *Perhaps arcane, brilliant, and terrifying is what you mean, but very well. I accept this name.*

"And your sister?" Hyacinth pressed. "Where does she live now?"

Chloe swallowed hard, overwhelmed all at once by the memories of her family, the ghost of her sister's laughter, and the terrible feeling that she'd never see her again.

"Far from here," Chloe said, letting silence fall.

Coffee the dragon yawned and settled into Chloe's hand for sleep.

"I think Coffee is a wonderful name," Hyacinth said after a few long moments. She trailed her finger along Coffee's spine. "Thank you for telling me about your family."

Grateful to not answer any more questions, Chloe smiled back. "I'll tell you more some other time. We have a long drive ahead with who-knows-what waiting for us at the end. Get some sleep, Princess."

"You too. And thank you again for coming with me."

Soon, the sound of Hyacinth's and Coffee's breathing mingled with Lord Helston's snores. It made a kind of music along with the rolling of the wheels over the rutted, bumpy road, the snorting of the boars as they pulled the carriage, and the thumping of Chloe's own heart. Hyacinth's head lolled onto Chloe's shoulder. Chloe leaned in, letting sleep take her as well.

✦

Hours later, Chloe woke to the carriage shaking. Something pounded against the side.

Had they hit a tree? Was one of the boars trying to escape?

Chloe struggled to get her bearings, looking around the tiny space. Her head rested against Hyacinth's still, and her neck ached from falling asleep in that position. Coffee had moved from her lap onto Hyacinth's. Across from them, Lord Helston slept with his feet in the air, his suit coat flung across his face. He still reeked of booze and something that could generously be described as *pondish*.

"Get out of the coach!" someone with a rough voice yelled from outside the carriage door. "C'mon now, you fancy folk. We know you're in there. Get out, and give us all your valuables, or things will get messy!"

Chloe swore under her breath.

Bandits.

Gripping her sword, she pushed back a slit in the curtain. They'd stopped somewhere in the mountains. Pine trees rose on a slope to one side of them. It was sunrise. Pale pink, orange, and gold morning light filled the sky, and dense mist slunk around the base of the trees. Surrounding the carriage were three Fae—two wood elves and a goblin—in mismatched, ragged clothing. All held swords. There were probably more bandits hiding deeper in the mist too. Leaning over Hyacinth's lap, Chloe peeked out the other window. In that direction, dense woods stretched as far as she could see. How far were they from Mushroom Town? She wasn't sure how long they'd been driving through the night, and their map would do them no good if they didn't know where they were.

They had to get out of here. Chloe could certainly fight, but she couldn't take on three—or more—armed bandits on her own.

"Hyacinth," Chloe whispered, her heart racing. She shook the princess. Somehow both she and Lord Helston were still sleeping despite the pounding on the carriage. How exceedingly noble of them both.

"Hyacinth!" Chloe repeated, louder now.

"What?" Hyacinth muttered, blinking. She yawned prettily. "Is it breakfast time already?"

Chloe bit back an exasperated scream.

Someone pounded again on the carriage door, and Hyacinth looked around in terror. Chloe held one finger to her lips.

"Bandits," she whispered.

"What are we going to do?" Hyacinth sat up now, her voice laced with fear. "They can't catch me. If they do, they'll ransom me back to my mother, and then I'll never find my father!"

Chloe had to admire the princess's bravery, even if she had no idea how to get out of this. She checked out the other window again, considering the forest. If they were quick, they might be able to lose the bandits in the trees, though what would that mean for Lord Helston, Chloe had no idea.

"Wake up, Your Lordship!" Chloe shook him. She'd at least do him the courtesy of being awake for all this.

He didn't stir.

"Lord Helston! Wake up now!" Hyacinth shouted. "We're under attack!"

"What?" he said groggily, one eye opening for the barest of moments.

Before Chloe could explain anything, the carriage door opened. Rough hands grabbed Chloe and flung her to the ground. She tumbled out with a cry, landing on the road with a *thump*. Gravel and dirt bit into her palms. A grizzled-looking goblin with pointed ears and long teeth scowled at her. One of the wood elves dumped Hyacinth unceremoniously on the ground. The bandit wrenched her bag away and started pawing through the contents.

"Hey!" Hyacinth yelled.

"Give that back," Chloe commanded the goblin, gripping her sword and scrambling to her feet.

Chloe hoped Hyacinth wouldn't take it upon herself to try to stand up to all these bandits. That had worked in Keldale, with crowds around them, but out here, Chloe had no doubt the bandits would cut them down before giving in to any of Hyacinth's demands.

Glancing around quickly, Chloe counted two more bandits standing by the boars, holding their reins. The beasts snuffled loudly, nearly knocking one of the bandits over.

That meant it would be five against one, but Chloe would fight them all if she had to.

"What are we going to do?" Hyacinth hissed beside Chloe. "There are too many."

She's right, Coffee, the tiny dragon agreed, peeking out of Chloe's pocket.

It was true. There was a smart choice and a corpse-making one. Chloe nodded toward the line of trees on the other side of a narrow ditch. "We're going to run," she whispered to Hyacinth.

The bandit with Hyacinth's bag produced a small coin purse. He held it up with a triumphant noise. "Knew these were rich ones!" he called out. "I found coins, jewels, and a bag of provisions!"

Hyacinth glared at the bandit. "Where are we going to run if we have no money or food?"

Chloe glanced again at the goblin, who was now arguing over the loot with one of the bandits near the boars. "Running is our only chance."

"Search their clothing!" the goblin ordered, turning toward them. "Bet they have coins sewed into the hems! Be sure to take that one's potion belt." He took a step closer to Hyacinth.

"Don't touch me." Hyacinth scrambled backward, compass and potions clinking as she ducked behind Chloe.

Chloe was not letting them take Hyacinth. "We run in three, two . . ."

Before she or Hyacinth could flee, a loud noise arose from inside the carriage.

"Let me go at once!" Lord Helston's voice was high-pitched and imperious.

The largest bandit shoved a sword under Lord Helston's chin. "We'll cut you from toes to nose, Your Frogginess. Get out of the damn carriage."

"Do you know who I am? Or who I'm traveling with?"

Chloe swore. Lord Helston was going to blab about who Hyacinth was and get them all killed or ransomed back to the queen. She wanted to run, but she couldn't let the bandits kill Lord Helston. She stood for a moment, paralyzed by the choice between running and rescuing.

As it turns out, she need not have worried.

"Hands off me!" Lord Helston yelled. He smashed a wine bottle into the goblin's sword, knocking it away. One of the wood elves surged forward, trying to grab him around the middle, but Lord Helston planted his enormous feet on either side of the carriage door and refused to move.

Lord Helston shouted something in a language Chloe didn't know. Whatever he said must've had some magic attached to it because all at once, the boars pulling the carriage sprang to action. With a loud snort, they charged forward, trampling the two bandits who'd been standing beside them.

"Get back here!" yelled the goblin.

"Now, Hyacinth!" Chloe shouted, pulling the princess toward the trees.

"I can't believe he left us," Hyacinth said, mouth agape as she stared after the carriage.

"Doesn't matter!" Chloe yanked Hyacinth from the road. "This is our chance!"

Hyacinth stumbled, but Chloe caught her. Hand in hand, they ran from the road, leaped over a narrow ditch, and raced into the woods, the shouts of the bandits growing fainter behind them with every step.

Chapter Seven
Hyacinth

Hyacinth's boots were made for riding or a light stroll through the palace gardens, not hiking rough terrain. They slipped on the dense pine needle carpet, and she felt every stone and stick as she and Chloe dashed through the woods. Low-hanging branches slapped her legs and face, and she tripped over roots and rocks. Golden morning light filtered through the pines overhead and dappled the ground, but Hyacinth was too busy trying to stay upright to appreciate the forest's loveliness. Chloe's hand never left hers as they ran, not even as the ground sloped upward sharply.

"Are you okay?" Chloe asked, finally releasing Hyacinth's hand as they crested the top of a hill.

The shouts from the bandits were long gone, and why wouldn't they be? With her jewels and money, they'd probably gotten what they wanted.

Right?

Hyacinth certainly hoped so.

"I'm fine," Hyacinth managed, hauling in deep breaths. "I've just never considered how much work adventuring might be."

If she'd known that, she might've never left the palace. But it was too late to turn back now.

Chloe grinned. "Tiring stuff indeed, though I think we can take it a bit slower through here. No one's following us, far as I can tell, and there's a path ahead at least."

"Thank the Sisters," Hyacinth said, studying the narrow winding path in front of them. It had to lead somewhere. Didn't it?

"Can I see the map again?" Chloe adjusted the bag slung over her shoulders.

Hyacinth pulled the book from the pouch on her belt—she was so grateful the bandits hadn't taken it or her potions and the enchanted pen and compass, even if they did get her jewels and money—and opened it to the map. Her feet hurt, and she was hungry, tired, and scared. Had her mother discovered she was gone yet? Would she be looking for her? Surely not. It was morning, yes, but her mother might've gone to bed after the party and not woken yet.

Maybe they had enough time to get well and truly away. Hyacinth hoped so.

She bent her head to consider the map with Chloe.

"The road we were on with Lord Helston snaked through this pass there," Chloe said, pointing at a narrow gap between two mountains. "Which means if we follow these woods and head north and east, we should bump into Mushroom Town eventually. The Wild Root Inn would be a good place to rest for the night at least."

"Are you sure you can get us there?"

"No, but I don't have a better plan. Do you?"

Hyacinth didn't. If only she had magic of her own, then . . .

Her fingers tightened around the enchanted compass on her belt. "Well, I might. Stay here."

"What are you doing?"

"Magic! I need a quiet moment to think."

"What sort of magic are you doing? Can I see?" Curiosity laced Chloe's voice, which made Hyacinth feel sick to her stomach.

Chloe couldn't know she was unmagical. That was a secret Hyacinth had to keep. If Chloe found out Hyacinth had been lying to her all these months . . . well. She hated to think of how much that would hurt her.

Some of her worry bled into her voice as she snapped at Chloe. "No! I need to concentrate. Stay here. I'll be right back!"

Hyacinth gripped the compass and walked a few steps away until she was hidden behind a wide pine that towered over her. She held out the compass and whispered the words the tinkerer had taught her when he sold it to her. "Wayward finds a way. Wayward finds a path. Spin you needle, and show me the route to the Wild Root Inn. Please and thank you."

The *please* and *thank you* were important, and supposedly without them, the compass wouldn't function, if it worked at all.

Hyacinth watched the brass needle under the glass.

Nothing happened.

"Come on, please, please..." she muttered.

Still nothing.

Hyacinth glanced over her shoulder. Chloe sat on a fallen log, her sword resting beside her. Coffee was on the log, nosing a piece of moss. As Hyacinth watched, Chloe rolled up one of her sleeves. A long red gash stood out against her pale skin.

When had she gotten that? It looked terrible. Snapping the useless compass shut, Hyacinth strode back toward Chloe.

"What is that?" Hyacinth demanded.

Chloe tore a strip from her shirt and tied it around the wound. She shrugged. "Nothing."

"It's not nothing. You're wounded."

"Please. I've had worse in the stables. Once, a fire salamander kicked me and—"

"Let me see."

"Absolutely not." Chloe pulled her shirtsleeve over the bandage.

Hyacinth pulled out a potion bottle. *Bitterroot berry for healing*. "I can heal it."

"Doesn't need healing. I've bandaged it."

Hyacinth grabbed Chloe's wrist. "Stop being stubborn and let me help you!"

Hyacinth was suddenly very determined to heal Chloe's arm with the potion. That would show Chloe she was useful. That she could help on an adventure. That she did, indeed, have lots of magic, and then Chloe could never question that fact and Hyacinth's lies would never need to be exposed.

An excellent plan. Hyacinth just needed to sell it.

Chloe interrupted Hyacinth's spiraling thoughts with a low chuckle. "I'm fine, Princess, truly. Stop worrying. How did your secret, behind-the-tree-magic go?"

Before Hyacinth could answer, a loud whirring filled the glade. Chloe wrenched her arm away from Hyacinth's grip and snatched up her sword.

Hyacinth spun around too and then realized that the noise was coming from her. Specifically from the compass at her belt.

"It works!" she cried out, failing to keep the surprise from her voice as she clicked the compass open. She peered at the whirling needle. It spun around and then stopped between the *N* and *E*.

"Did you doubt it would?" Chloe said, glancing at the compass. "Isn't that what the magic was for?"

Sisters help her, Hyacinth opened her mouth, and another lie came tumbling out. "Of course I didn't doubt. I'm *excellent* at High Fae magic, but sometimes devices like this can be tricky. It's working now. The Wild Root Inn is that way."

She pointed in the direction the compass indicated. In which there was no path to speak of, only a dense mess of trees, undergrowth, fallen logs, and feathery ferns.

"Are you sure?"

Hyacinth nodded. It had to be that way. It had to! The compass was working, so what was there to worry about?

Chloe frowned. "We might not make it there by nightfall if we go that way."

Hyacinth was determined. This compass would get them there; she just knew it. "Let's get moving. I'd love to sleep in a real bed tonight. I dozed off in the carriage, but we've really not slept since the early hours of solstice morning—"

"As I recall, there wasn't much sleep then either." Chloe's tone was wicked. Teasing.

Heat flared on Hyacinth's cheeks. "I didn't mean that! You know what I meant! I just—"

Chloe laughed. "I do know what you mean, Princess. And it's fine. We don't need to talk about what we were doing besides sleeping in the early hours of the solstice."

Hyacinth swallowed hard, her mind wrenching back to their summer-wine-dizzy kiss. Bramble and marsh, had that been only one day ago? "No, no. I don't mind talking about it. If you want to. It's just—"

"It's just that we're in the middle of the woods and your mother is probably looking for us and we have no real idea if we'll make it to the Wild Root Inn by nightfall?"

"Exactly."

Chloe shrugged. "Let's walk, then."

Hyacinth started to say more, but then she closed her mouth. "Fine by me. But, we will talk about it eventually."

"Maybe."

"And you will let me try this healing potion on that wound."

"Not likely."

"You really should let me try!"

Hyacinth didn't know why she couldn't let this go.

"Leave it, Princess. I'm fine."

With that, Chloe started off through the woods. Hyacinth fell into step a few paces behind her, holding out the compass. As she walked, her mind moved back to when she was seven and her half sisters Maeve and Tansy, who were closest in age to her but still more than ten years older, had dared her to walk alone through the woods behind the palace at night.

Of course she'd done it, because they were her big sisters and she adored them. And because they'd promised to take her on a dragon flight, even though her mother wouldn't let her start lessons until she was twelve.

"Walk for half an hour to the moon-drenched stream," Maeve had said. "Bring me back a vial of water from it, and then I'll take you dragon riding in the morning."

Hyacinth walked through the woods, clutching her little vial, jumping at every roar and shuffling in the darkness.

After exactly 213 steps into the woods, which she counted precisely, she realized she liked being out of the castle, alone at night, with the shadows all around her. She'd liked the thrill of danger and adventure, and she'd liked doing something her mother would've never allowed.

Walking through the thickets with Chloe now made her feel like she had on that night. The world seemed big, unknown, and exciting. She was brave enough to face it, and she loved it.

Well, mostly. She could've done without the dread coiling in her belly at her mounting number of lies to Chloe.

A birch branch whipped backward, stinging Hyacinth's cheek. She cried out in surprise.

"Sorry!" Chloe called out. "I'm trying to hold them back, but they keep slipping out of my grasp."

"Because of that wound on your arm."

Bramble and marsh. Stop bothering her about the wound.

Chloe snorted. "*Not* because of that. It's a scratch, Princess. I got it when we were running from the bandits and I stumbled against a sharp branch. I beg you, stop worrying about it before I cut off my arm to cease your fussing."

"You're ridiculous."

"You love it." Chloe made a courtly bow, managing to fall over in a parody of drunk Lord Helston.

Hyacinth really did enjoy her company, not that she'd declare that so boldly. "Get up, you silly thing." Hyacinth laughed. "The compass says we need to go that direction slightly."

"Off we go, then," Chloe said, springing to her feet with a flourish.

Hyacinth grinned, and they headed deeper into the forest.

Pines rose around them, the trees standing higher than the vaulted ceilings of the palace Hyacinth had grown up in. Mist still curled along the tree roots, and the air hung sticky with sap and the heavy dampness of the deep forest. Although Hyacinth's legs ached from their long hike, she found enormous comfort in Chloe and her sword.

Chloe quirked a half smile over her shoulder at the princess. The look made Hyacinth's knees wobble. Chloe's lips were red as cherries, and all at once, Hyacinth ached to kiss them. . . .

Her cheeks flushed.

There would be no more kissing. This wasn't a romantic ballad! They were lost in the woods, and Hyacinth needed to find her father, not get swept up in thoughts of Chloe's lips. With some effort, Hyacinth wrenched her attention back to the present, which meant studying where they were.

These woods were nothing like the ones near Queen Mab's castle, where Hyacinth and Chloe went sometimes to catch moonshadow snakes or where Hyacinth enjoyed rare walks alone. These woods felt older and more sinister.

She shivered. If these woods were menacing, what would the Labyrinth be like? How in the world was she supposed to face the unknown dangers within its walls?

A spike of fear gripped Hyacinth, but she suppressed it. The only way through this was forward, so she kept walking.

And walking. And walking.

They walked up tree-covered hills and along ridges, until Hyacinth's feet ached and her stomach grumbled. The light filtering through the trees was brighter now; it had to be at least midday.

Finally, when they hit a stand of trees that were somehow even taller than the rest, they stopped in a small glade. The only sounds were birds, animals in the underbrush, and Coffee's excited gnawing on another piece of leathery meat that Chloe had given him.

"Are we close?" Hyacinth plopped onto a fallen long, a relieved noise escaping her lips as her feet got a rest.

Chloe sat down next to her. "I'm not sure. Can I see the compass and map again?"

Hyacinth pulled the compass off her belt and opened the book to the page with the map. The compass still pointed in the same direction, and she studied the map. "I know where we started and where we want to go, but I'm not sure how long we were traveling or where we are now. I suspect we're generally somewhere here." She pointed to the forest-covered mountains. On the other side of them was Lord Helston's swamp, and beyond that, the Labyrinth, but they could be anywhere within the ink-and-paper trees and mighty towering peaks.

"Well," Choe said, looking around. Her bright green eyes caught flecks of the light coming through the pines. "I guess all we can do is keep moving." On her shoulder, Coffee chirruped, and that seemed to settle it.

They kept walking.

The day passed. Blisters formed and then popped on Hyacinth's heels. She'd never walked for this long in her life, and her fond memories of a childhood night in the woods faded with the throbbing in her feet.

She took it all back. The woods were awful. She'd do anything—even sit through another ball or endure one of her mother's lectures—if it meant they could stop walking.

They kept walking. Sometime in the late afternoon, they drank from a stream, but that did little to quell the insistent rumbling of Hyacinth's stomach. Chloe found an apple and some smashed cookies in her bag, which they shared, but that wasn't enough for either of them.

Above them, the sky changed from blue to the deep pink and orange of twilight. Hyacinth kept looking over shoulder, expecting to see someone. Her mother? Maurelle, with a troop of guards? The bandits they'd left behind?

There was no one, and a wave of resentment toward her mother filled Hyacinth, nearly knocking her over. Here she was stuck in the Sisters-forsaken woods, tired to her marrow, so she could try to find her father. All her life, Hyacinth had wondered about him. She'd asked Queen Mab questions, all left unanswered. She'd made up stories that always ended with a happy father-daughter reunion.

And now that she had a chance to find him, Queen Mab grounded her, forcing her to sneak away! If her mother had talked about him, Hyacinth could've taken a royal carriage—one with cushions and cakes and fast horses—to the Labyrinth. Then she could've gone in with a troop of guards and—

"How are you doing?" Chloe asked. They'd reached a clearing atop a hill. Far below them, Hyacinth could make out a river surrounded by an endless sea of trees.

Hyacinth would very much like to not see any trees for a very long time.

It's the first full day of your adventure; you'll never find your father with that attitude, she thought. *You love trees. They're your favorite. Hopefully, you'll spend lots more time among them.*

"I'm doing fine," Hyacinth said, more sharply than intended. "Why do you ask?"

"You're stomping through the underbrush like it personally hurt you and muttering to yourself."

Hyacinth's cheeks heated. For bramble's sake. "I was . . . thinking."

"Loudly," Chloe said with a grin. "Let's stop here for the night."

That was the best idea Hyacinth had heard all day. She cheered weakly.

"You rest. I'll find us some firewood. Take this too, just in case you need a pillow." Chloe tossed Hyacinth the cloak she'd given her at the Solstice Market last night. Was that just last night? It felt like a year ago.

"I don't need a pillow," Hyacinth said, though she clutched the cloak to her chest. It was rough, but it *would* make the ground softer.

"I'll be back soon, and I'll take first watch."

Hyacinth spread the cloak out on the ground, just to see how it would feel. She'd never slept outside before and was curious about it. That was all.

She stretched out on the blanket, letting her sore body rest.

It was so very, very good to lie down. The cloak was somehow more comfortable than her bed at the palace, with its spider-silk sheets and cloud-softened pillows.

Her eyes would stay open, of course. She had to watch for Chloe.

A yawn crept up on her, and she gave in, just for a moment. She glanced at her compass. The needle still pointed to the Wild Root Inn, even if they wouldn't make it there tonight. Hyacinth rolled onto her back and settled her hands under her head, looking up at the tree branches above them. She should count her potions. See how many were left for the adventure. Yes, that's what she would do.

Juniper heart for illusion.

A moon-drenched secret for levitation.

Bitterroot berry for healing. Chloe really should let her try that potion on her cut.

Gray tendrils of fog for vanishing. Those were gone, used up by Chloe to avoid Maurelle and the palace guards. Where was Maurelle? Was she looking for Hyacinth yet? Hyacinth yawned again and kept cataloguing her potions.

Wraith tears for compulsion. Also gone, used on the redcap in the market.

Dragonheart ashes for fire and ruin. What in the world would she do with those?

Four potions left wasn't enough for a whole adventure, was it? Maybe she could find more along the way? Though she didn't have any money, so how would she buy anything?

She sighed, letting herself rest. Letting her eyes fall shut. Letting her mind sink into the darkness that tugged at her.

Hyacinth didn't hear Chloe coming back with a handful of firewood, and she didn't see her start a small fire with matches from her bag. She didn't watch Chloe settle Coffee on a pile of moss. She didn't even stir when Chloe covered her with a corner of the cloak. She did hear someone whisper, "Sweet dreams, Princess," though she might have dreamed that.

Chapter Eight
Chloe

The night deepened, and Chloe stared into the campfire, watching the flames lick upward. Hyacinth slept on Chloe's cloak a few feet away, and Coffee was curled up at the edge of the fire. They didn't really need the warmth of the fire; it was summertime, and even in the deep woods, there was only the hint of a chill in the air. The light, though, was crucial for holding the shadows of the forest at bay.

There were so many shadows in the forest.

Gods, how Chloe hated enduring the darkness alone. Keeping watch always fell to her—she made sure of it. That first night in the orphanage with Anya, she'd stayed awake, holding her sister's hand across the rusted iron beds they'd slept in. She'd spent those long hours, even at six years old, alert, ready, her eyes on the door of their room, listening to the dream whimpers and movements of all the other girls stuffed in there with them.

She'd done the same that first night they'd been whisked off to the human queen's castle, watching while her sister slept. Ensuring none of the guards bothered her.

Even with all her vigilance, Chloe hadn't been able to stop starlight from being harvested from Anya's bones. That was how she and the other girls with them in the castle made magical lace for the queen. That's what kept them alive. That's what had almost killed them.

Chloe took a long steadying breath. She hated remembering her captivity and being worked to her marrow for the sake of magic. The night was too dark, and she was too far away now to give it space in her thoughts.

She glanced at Hyacinth. The firelight smoothed the worry lines carved onto the princess's forehead by their encounter with the bandits and the long walk. She slept curled up like a snail shell, with her book and belt tucked close to her chest.

A rush of fondness filled Chloe, making a smile ghost on her lips. It was brave of Hyacinth to leave the castle and pursue her father. Even if they didn't find him, it was more than Chloe had ever thought the princess would do. Chloe liked that about Hyacinth: She was always surprising her. Going to the market in Keldale, standing up to the redcap dragon dealer, running away from the castle. Always a surprise. What would she do if she knew that Chloe was human and from another world? Would she denounce her? Rage at her for lying? Walk away from her and never look back?

Maybe she'd surprise you. . . .

No. That wasn't possible. A High Fae princess couldn't end up with a human if she knew the truth. Which was why Hyacinth could never find out the truth.

Chloe's stomach grumbled, and she dug in her bag again. There were only a few crumbs in there, plus her leather journal, with its dozens of letters to Anya. She popped the crumbs into her mouth and touched the cover of the journal. More questions about her sister filled her mind.

Who watched over Anya's sleep now? She'd had a girlfriend, Ruby, who was a lovely person, but could she keep Anya safe? That had always been Chloe's job.

She doesn't need you to keep her safe anymore. Ruby makes her happy; that's what matters.

On some level, Chloe knew that, but other parts of her weren't sure. If only she could go back to her world and check on Anya. She'd already missed their shared eighteenth birthday a few months ago, and what if time worked differently between the human and Fae worlds? What if by the time she got back, Anya was already much older? How much of Anya's life had passed without Chloe in it?

Would there really be a portal in the Labyrinth that could help her return home?

A twig snapped in the darkness, wrenching Chloe from her whirlwind of questions and memories. Her eyes flew upward from the flames, and she surged to her feet, sword ready.

Steady, Brave One, Coffee said into her mind. *It's just a mouse running in the leaf litter. I'll let you know if anything bigger is coming this way.*

Chloe let out a long breath, relaxing her vigilance.

"Thank you," she whispered.

Anytime. I'll be on watch with you all night, even if it looks like I'm sleeping.

Chloe scoffed as her eyes met the tiny dragon's. "You were snoring."

Dragons don't snore, Coffee replied haughtily. *We stoke the fires deep inside us with our eyes closed.*

That made Chloe laugh out loud, which felt good. She was exhausted from the journey, the lack of sleep, and the battering of her own memories. The cut on her arm hurt; she really could use some healing potion. But it was only a few inches above her glamour token, and Chloe didn't want to risk Hyacinth seeing that.

"How's your arm?" Hyacinth asked, sitting up and yawning.

Chloe startled at the question. It was almost like Hyacinth had been reading her thoughts—which, no. That couldn't happen, could it? Coffee seemed to be able to get glimmers of her thoughts sometimes, but High Fae couldn't do that, right? Surely Hyacinth would've told her if she had magic that involved mind reading?

Heat rose in Chloe's cheeks. Hyacinth definitely did not need to know her thoughts.

"My arm is fine," she said.

Hyacinth got up from her cloak and approached the log where Chloe sat. "Let me see it," she said.

Chloe shook her head. "It's just a scratch, really."

Hyacinth rolled her eyes. "Nonnegotiable. Just like you getting some sleep is not up for discussion."

Chloe relented. She was too tired to argue, and thinking of Anya and all they'd been through together had made her vulnerable. She held out her arm, keeping one hand over her watch and the glamour token hidden beneath it.

Hyacinth hissed to see the long cut. "This is really deep," she said with a note of accusation.

"It doesn't even hurt," Chloe lied.

Hyacinth pulled a small green bottle from her belt. "This is a healing potion. Supposed to mend any cut in no time. May I?"

Chloe inclined her head. Why not try it? Healing magic wouldn't make her forget herself like Fae food, and it wouldn't be starlight pulled from her bones, as she'd experienced back in her own world. She could benefit from magic—like her glamour token; she just didn't like to make it a habit.

Hyacinth uncorked the bottle and poured a stream of bright green liquid onto Chloe's cut. It let out a puff of white smoke, and then pain shot through Chloe's arm.

"Ouch!" She wrenched her arm backward. "Are you trying to kill me, Princess?"

Hyacinth's eyes widened. "What's wrong?"

"It's agony!" Before, the cut had just ached, but now it burned like she'd caught her arm in the fire. Chloe gripped her forearm, squeezing it to help with the pain.

"Bramble and marsh," Hyacinth muttered, glaring at the little bottle. "This was *supposed* to be a healing potion."

Coffee ran over to Chloe and nudged at her arm. *Let me see it.*

Chloe offered him her arm. He licked at her wound with his tiny tongue. All at once, the burning stopped.

That's phoenix balm, Coffee said. *Heals dragons, but terrible for anyone else.*

"Coffee says it's phoenix balm in the bottle," Chloe reported back.

Hyacinth covered her face with her hands. "I heard that too—I think he talks to both of us sometimes, but not all the time." She looked at the now-stoppered bottle in her hand. "I'm so sorry. This was supposed to help, but it only made things worse."

She sounded miserable, and Chloe took pity on her. "I'm fine, Princess. I told you I was, and now it feels better."

Which was true. Coffee's lick, strange though it was, had actually alleviated the pain from her original wound too.

Hyacinth shook her head. "I'm sorry," she muttered again.

Chloe rested a hand on Hyacinth's shoulder. "Stop apologizing. Please. But, I am wondering, if you have High Fae magic, why do you have that belt with all its potions?"

A panicked look crossed Hyacinth's face, but then she mastered it. She seemed to attempt a shrug but only grimaced. "I have High Fae magic, of course, but that doesn't cover everything. And I like being prepared—though I'm not sure I'm really prepared. What if we run into a troll or a swamp hag or—"

"Hyacinth?"

"Yes?"

"We'll figure it out. We're only at the start of this adventure. We have a long way to go."

Hyacinth slid her eyes sideways and sighed. "You're right. Of course you're right. I just . . . didn't know what I was getting myself into. I didn't think I'd be sleeping outside on night one."

"It's better than being in a carriage full of frog farts," Chloe said.

This made Hyacinth laugh, as Chloe had hoped it would. "And the trees are really quite lovely," she agreed.

"They are. What else do you like about being out here?"

Hyacinth brightened. "Easy: no Solstice Ball. My mother isn't here. I have a whole unknown ahead of me, which terrifies and excites me and . . ."

"And?" Chloe prompted.

Hyacinth bumped Chloe's shoulder gently with her own. "And I like being out here with you."

Warmth filled Chloe, as sweet as the blackberries she'd eaten in the palace garden. It was lovely to be welcome, not just for what she could do, but for who she was.

"I like that too," she admitted. "Now, you still haven't told me much about your father. Who was he?"

Hyacinth yawned, a movement so infectious, Chloe caught it too. They giggled as their enormous yawns cut off their words.

"I'll tell you about my father if you tell me more about your family," Hyacinth bargained. She yawned again.

"Perhaps tomorrow," Chloe said with a laugh. "For now, go back to sleep. I'll keep watch."

You most certainly will not, Coffee fussed into Chloe's head. *Neither of you will. I'll keep watch. Now, both of you, go to sleep!*

Hyacinth giggled again, a sound edged with exhaustion. She saluted the tiny dragon. "As you wish, Coffee. But I insist you take the cloak." She held it out to Chloe.

Who was really too tired to argue.

She should offer to share, but the princess was already curling up on a moss bed.

Chloe nuzzled Coffee for a moment. "Wake me at the first sign of trouble," she murmured. Then she dropped into sleep, letting her wearied body rest at last.

Right as she was drifting off, a thought passed through her mind: What did Wendell think had happened to her? She should've left a note. Was she always doomed to leave those she cared about for the next adventure?

She pulled the cloak over her head. That could be another night's question. For now, she let herself cease her vigilant watch for a little while.

Chapter Nine
Hyacinth

They walked for the better part of the next day, but by sunset, when Hyacinth truly thought her empty stomach couldn't roar any louder, the compass led them to a clearing in the trees. Hyacinth's mouth fell open as she walked forward

Chloe let out a little shout of happiness. "If this isn't Mushroom Town, I don't know what is."

Hyacinth had to agree.

Tucked under the boughs of enormous pines were dozens of mushrooms, nearly as tall as the trees. Some had thick white stalks that would've taken at least ten people to put their arms around. Enormous red caps with white spots topped some of the stalks, while others were feathery, with yellow or brown caps. Under the mushrooms sat a tangle of log-and-stone buildings that comprised a small village. Humans, Fae, and many other creatures moved along its cobbled road, pushing carts, lighting lamps, and calling out to friends.

"I can't believe we found it," Hyacinth whispered with relief.

Chloe grinned. "C'mon, let's go find some dinner and a place to sleep."

"We don't have any money—all my things were taken."

"I have a few coppers. We'll figure something out, I promise."

It was only then that Hyacinth noticed her own breath shuddering out of her chest. Suddenly, she was so, so tired.

"Are you alright?" Chloe asked.

"I just . . ." Tears rose in Hyacinth's eyes. "I'm not sure I can do this. Maybe I should go home? Maybe I really can't find my father or help him."

"Don't think that. You're worn out from walking and need supper. Leave that to me," Chloe said, taking her hand. "Now, please, take a deep breath, Princess."

Hyacinth did as she was told, hauling in a lungful of air. It felt good to release it slowly. It felt good to have Chloe's hand in hers.

Coffee gave a little growl of approval, and Chloe laughed.

"Exactly like that," she said. "Follow me. There's the Wild Root Inn."

She pointed toward a wide two-story building at the far end of the street. It backed up against a mushroom stalk twice its size, and its stone facade was green with moss. Colorful mullioned windows jutted from its front like large bellies, and a wooden sign over the door marked it as THE WILD ROOT INN. Laughter and people spilled out of the tavern, and the smell of baked bread and roasted meat filled the air. It was so incredibly inviting, Hyacinth wanted to weep.

"And, Princess," Chloe said, "don't give them your real name like you did in Keldale, okay? We need to keep a low profile."

"Of course," Hyacinth said. She could only imagine what the tavern folk might do if she declared herself one of Queen Mab's daughters. "I shall be Rowena Rollinglane, a normal Fae girl who's traveling with her friend for reasons of her own design and who desperately needs a room and bowl of—what do you think they have here? Pheasant? Roasted phoenix eggs?"

At Chloe's look, Hyacinth quickly amended her imaginary dinner order. "Stew. Just stew please, and perhaps some bread?"

"Sounds perfect." Chloe squeezed Hyacinth's hand and then started walking down the street. Her sword swung with every step, and Coffee scuttled from her shoulder into her shirt pocket.

Gratitude filled Hyacinth. At least she had Chloe. That had to count for something, right?

✦

The Wild Root Inn radiated warmth and light. As Hyacinth pushed through the door, a wall of smells nearly knocked her over—freshly baked bread, frothy cider, loamy herbs, the sweat of many bodies, and something savory that had been cooking for hours. It was the best thing Hyacinth had ever smelled.

The main level of the inn was a bustling tavern. A balcony ran along the second level that overlooked the central floor. A long bar occupied the back of the tavern, and a vast stone hearth sat opposite. Wooden beams spanned the ceiling, and stone arches divided the main room into smaller sections. Patrons sat at tables all around the room, and the bar was packed with Fae of all sorts. A bard played a song near the hearth, and talking, laughing, and singing along filled the room. No one spared Hyacinth or Chloe a glance as they approached the bar.

This was Hyacinth's chance. Despite her moment of doubt outside, she'd show Chloe and herself how ready she was for whatever lay ahead. She would ask for what she wanted! Pushing her way into the crowd at the bar, she called out, "Hello! Barkeep! Hello!"

"What are you doing?" Chloe pulled her backward. "You can't just belly up to the bar and start hollering. There's a way to do these things!"

"Well, how was I supposed to know?" Hyacinth's cheeks heated with embarrassment. Clearly, she was *not* ready for whatever lay ahead. She wanted to hide under one of the tables. "I've never been in a tavern," she muttered.

Chloe exhaled sharply and pointed to a table tucked into a nook near the back of the tavern. "Just follow me. Please."

Hyacinth nodded, blinking back tears of embarrassment.

They sat down at the table, and soon enough a willowy green-haired barmaid who certainly had some dryad in her lineage plopped two tankards on the table in front of them. Froth from the ales sloshed over the rim. Hyacinth frowned at the grime on the lip of the glass.

"That's the house ale," the barmaid barked. "Only thing left after the solstice parties last night. What're you having to eat?"

"Just the ale and some stew, please," Chloe said quickly.

"What's in the stew?" Hyacinth ventured.

The barmaid's look could wither the heartiest of flowers.

"Never mind that," Chloe said. "Please bring us two bowls of stew and some bread if you have it."

The barmaid left without another word.

"*Never* ask what's in the stew," Chloe advised.

"What if I want to know?"

"Trust me, you don't."

A vision of fingers, feathers, wings, toes, and all manner of other awful things thrown into a soup pot filled Hyacinth's mind. Nope. She really didn't want to know, especially because she was hungry enough to eat several bowls of it anyway. To distract herself, she looked around the tavern. A wood elf and two bearded dwarves sat at the next table, playing a game that involved a handful of mushrooms, a board with green pebbles on it, and several tankards of ale. At the start of each turn, one player drank, and then they were allowed to move their piece the number of spaces that their friends had counted out.

It was fascinating! It looked much more fun than Moonshadow Trove, a game the High Fae played that was all strategy, moving armies, and making alliances.

A loud shout rose in the air as the wood elf tipped back their tankard, and the dwarves counted enthusiastically. They got to fifteen seconds before the wood elf spit out suds all over the game board.

The dwarves pushed back from the table, laughing and protesting.

"They remind me of my friends, Hester and Fellmi," Chloe said fondly. "They're always playing Mushroom Takes the Wall after work."

"Do you know how to play?"

Chloe shrugged. "I know the rules, but I never win. Don't have the stomach to drink as much as they do." She took a small sip of her ale.

A pang of envy went through Hyacinth at the words. Of course, she knew Chloe had a whole life without her, that she had a job, and friends, and a past. Hyacinth had just never really thought about what that might look like on a daily level. There was so much about Chloe she didn't know and so much she desperately wanted to learn.

"What else do you do with your friends?"

"Mostly clean stables, saddle horses, and practice sword fighting. My teacher, Wendell, says—"

Before Chloe could finish, the barmaid was back. Brushing some of her long green tresses out of her face with her arm, she plopped two bowls of gloopy brown stew onto the table in front of them. "Need anything else?"

"No—" Hyacinth said.

"Actually, we need a room too," Chloe piped up. "Do you have one for . . ." She paused to dig in her bag and pull out some coins. "Three coppers?"

The barmaid snorted. "None left for that pittance. It's busy tonight."

"Surely you have something," Chloe pressed. "We'll sleep anywhere: the stables, the main room, at this table. . . ."

"There's *nothing* for that amount of coin."

"We'll do the dishes," Chloe offered.

That was a good idea! Not that Hyacinth had ever done a dish in her life, but she beamed at Chloe for her cleverness.

The barmaid lifted an eyebrow. "And my closing chores. Do that and you can have a corner of the attic."

"Done," Chloe said.

As soon as she was gone, Chloe grinned at Hyacinth. "Not sure what we've gotten ourselves into, but I've worked for my supper many times before."

"I haven't. . . ."

Chloe fished a piece of stringy meat from the stew and offered it to Coffee. He gulped it down in just a few bites. "Don't worry, Princess, I'll teach you how to wash a dish."

✦

Chloe kept her promise.

After they ate two bowls of stew each, which cost them an additional promise to mop the floor, the barmaid led them to the kitchen. A nearly empty pot of stew boiled above the fire, and a tired-looking cook stirred it.

"Alright then, Gemma?" the barmaid called out.

The cook nodded. "No more than a half dozen bowls left, I suppose. I'm leaving now."

"These two will serve those bowls and clean up." The barmaid nodded toward Hyacinth and Chloe.

Hyacinth started to drop into a small curtsy to show her thanks, but Chloe elbowed her hard in the side.

"Not here, *Rowena*," she muttered.

Right. Travelers who didn't have enough money for stew certainly didn't curtsy to the cook. Hyacinth had to stop thinking like a princess.

Music still poured from the common room, and Hyacinth felt full, warm, and tired. All she wanted to do was curl up in a bed, read her father's notes for a few minutes, and fall into a deep sleep.

Instead, she faced a lopsided pile of dirty bowls, plates, cups, and spoons that packed nearly an entire wooden table. Two buckets also sat on the table, filled with water and soap.

"We're supposed to do all these dishes?" she asked weakly.

The barmaid barked a laugh. "And the rest that will come in tonight. Don't suppose a winged High Fae like you has much call to do the dishes."

Did she really look that helpless? She had been on an adventure for two days; she wasn't as entirely useless as all that. Besides, perhaps she could use her levitation potion and make these dishes fly from the soapy water to the clean bucket.

"I don't suppose you know anything about me at all," Hyacinth shot back. "I'm *excellent* at doing dishes."

Chloe made a strangled noise beside her as she held back a laugh.

The barmaid raised an eyebrow, then shrugged. "As you say. No magic back here, though. The owner's put a charm on the room to ensure that. Too many dishes get broken when magic is involved."

So much for Hyacinth's plan with the levitation potion. Her mother used charms like the tavern owner's to prevent certain types of magic in certain rooms of the palace—you wouldn't want magical battles breaking out during a ball or some unsavory High Fae noble running off with the queen's silver during a feast—but Hyacinth hadn't realized they could be applied to something as mundane as a tavern kitchen. It must be a mighty powerful charm, which seemed unnecessary here, but who was she to judge?

She was just a weary traveler scrubbing for her supper tonight.

What an oddly refreshing thought.

The barmaid and cook left the kitchen, and Hyacinth walked over to one of the bowls. Brown lumps of stew crusted the side of the dish. She picked at them, but they seemed to be glued to the bowl.

"This is way too many dishes for a meal and a room," Hyacinth grumbled, not that she had any real idea of the economics of exchange when it came to labor for accommodations.

Chloe shrugged. "No more than I've seen on a day at the orphanage. And those I usually had to do alone as a punishment."

Hyacinth's interest was immediately piqued. "Tell me more about this orphanage? What did you get into trouble for?"

Chloe laughed and picked up a rag. "Everything you can imagine. Stealing food for my sister, not minding my stitches at sewing, singing too loudly in the bathroom, *not* singing in church, trying to run away, fighting with the bullies who hurt the younger girls, trying to run away again . . ." She picked up a plate, dunked it in the soapy water, and scrubbed. "My sister, Anya, always snuck in to help me with the dishes eventually, but until she could get away, it was only me against stacks of dishes taller than I was." She dipped the soapy plate in the bucket of clean water and held it out to Hyacinth.

Coffee, who'd been watching the encounter with the barmaid from Chloe's pocket, climbed out and picked up a rag as well. He met Hyacinth's gaze, and she smiled at him. If the tiny dragon could do dishes, she certainly could too.

"How long did it usually take to finish them?" Hyacinth took the plate and dried it.

Chloe grinned. "You don't want to know, but Anya and I usually sang as we worked. I'll teach you our favorite song."

Hyacinth would like that very much. Her sisters were always scheming or too busy with their own lives and plans. There was something incredibly cozy about doing simple work with someone else.

Bramble and marsh, what would her sisters say if they found out Hyacinth was not only unmagical and kissed stablehands, but also that part of her enjoyed doing dishes?

They'd never let her hear the end of it, and her mother would certainly lock her in the dungeons.

Well, they were many miles away. Hyacinth saw no reason to think more about them tonight.

"Let me hear this song," she said to Chloe.

As they scrubbed dish after dish, Chloe taught Hyacinth a ballad about a pair of sailors who wandered the world looking for a mythical treasure. The sailors argued through every verse, even when they got swallowed by a whale, were captured in an underwater palace, and fought a sea god and a sorceress to make it home.

The refrain was a delight, and by the second time Chloe sang it, Hyacinth knew the words too.

"Willow and wallow,
The sea we will follow, until we make it home!
Storm and shore,
We'll carry the oar, until we make it home!
Tarry and parry,
This tale we will carry, until we make it home!"

They sang it loudly and happily as they finished the dishes. Then Chloe taught Hyacinth two more songs as they swept the floors, scrubbed the bar, washed the tables, and finally collapsed into chairs in the now-empty tavern. "I'll sleep here if I have to," Hyacinth declared, the sailor song still running through her head. Because she couldn't possibly do another chore. Her body ached in ways she'd never known possible.

"You rest. I'll find the barmaid," Chloe said. She shot Hyacinth a quick smile and walked away, still humming the sailor song.

Warmth bloomed in Hyacinth's chest. There was so very much more to the world, and Chloe, than she'd ever imagined.

Chapter Ten
Chloe

The barmaid led them from the ground floor and up four flights of stairs that rose along the carved-out stalk of the mushroom. They stopped inside a small attic built into the eaves of the mushroom cap.

"There's only one bed." Chloe observed, considering the narrow pallet under a round window.

The barmaid shrugged. "All we got, so take it or leave it."

They would take it. But it was hardly enough space for one of them, much less both.

Chloe sighed. She'd been looking forward to a bed, but she'd live with the floor.

The barmaid shut the door, leaving Hyacinth and Chloe alone. Suddenly, the silence was overwhelming. For all that Chloe and Hyacinth had done together over the last few months, or even the last few days, they'd never been alone in a room like this. It was different from sleeping in the woods or Lord Helston's carriage.

Was Chloe nervous to be alone with Hyacinth? That was ridiculous.

Chloe let Coffee out of her pocket and set him on one of the pillows. He paced in a circle and then curled up to sleep. A yawn split Chloe's face, and she was suddenly entirely exhausted. Had it really been just two days since she left Wendell's house to go to the Solstice Market? Once again she wondered what Wendell thought had happened to her. Was the queen looking for Hyacinth already?

The thoughts were too much for tonight.

"I'll sleep on the floor," Chloe said, pulling a dusty blanket from a trunk at the foot of the bed.

Hyacinth rolled her eyes. "You're not sleeping on this filthy floor. We'll share the bed."

Chloe's heart thudded at the thought. "It's . . . smaller than the feather mattress you're used to, Princess."

"I'm highly adaptable," Hyacinth declared. "Besides, I read a book recently about the best way to sleep, and it's curled on your side, not taking up very much space. Though I suppose my wings will make that difficult."

Chloe couldn't hold back a laugh at this. "You read a book on how to sleep?"

"*Everything* is better with a book."

Chloe didn't point out that were it not for a book, they wouldn't be in a mushroom-cap attic, sharing a bed. It didn't need to be said, and besides, she wasn't sure she minded so much. Plus, if there was a portal home at the end of this journey, it would all be worth it.

Slipping off her boots and resting her sword on the floor, she lay down. The mattress was softer than she'd expected. She sighed as her head sunk into the pillow.

The bed dipped as Hyacinth settled in. A surprised exclamation left her lips as she rolled into the middle of the bed. They were so close, Hyacinth's forehead lay inches from Chloe's. She could feel Hyacinth's every breath.

Which was fine. It meant nothing, other than that there was nowhere else to sleep.

"I'll just rest for a few moments," Chloe muttered sleepily, as her tiredness washed over her.

Hyacinth's only answer was a huge yawn, and soon, her breathing settled into a steady rhythm. Chloe fell asleep with Hyacinth's jasmine smell wrapped around her. She was entirely aware of Hyacinth's body so close, feeling oddly comforted despite the very arduous day they'd had.

✦

Chloe was on a ship, with her family. It was deep into the night, and a vicious storm tossed the vessel over the sea. Chloe clung to Anya, who sobbed in fear and buried her face in Chloe's shoulder. Chloe's father ran around the ship, helping sailors secure the mast and tie down barrels. Rain pelted them and the wind howled. Chloe's mother ran to her daughters, pulling them close.

Her mother's hands gripped Chloe's shoulders as she held them.

The swells rose higher, towering walls of water that broke over the ship with salty fury. Chloe screamed, horror filling her as her father—her brave, wonderful father—was washed out to sea.

Frantic, her mother looked around. She grabbed a rope and wrapped it around Chloe's and Anya's waists, and then she secured them to a barrel.

"What are you doing?" Chloe shouted.

"Keeping you alive!" her mother screamed. "If you get washed overboard, this will help you float."

Thunder cracked overhead, and Anya wailed in fear.

"Mother! Come with us!" Chloe shouted.

Chloe's mother leaned in close so Chloe could hear her. "*Stay together. Keep her safe, always. This is your job, Chloe.*"

"Don't leave us! Mother!" Anya begged.

Before her mother could reply, another swell overtook the ship. It swept their mother into the churning sea. The ship listed dangerously, launching the girls and their barrel toward the water. They flew through the air, before landing hard on the ocean. But the barrel floated. Anya sobbed, but Chloe didn't cry.

"We're together, Anya," she said. "I'll keep you safe, always. This is my job."

Chloe sat up suddenly, staring into the dark, her heart thundering. It was the same dream she'd had so many times before. She could still smell the sea, pounding at the edge of the ship, splintering it into pieces. Where was her sister? Her parents?

She could never save them all. That's what broke her heart every time. How much of it was a memory of what had really happened and how much was an amalgamation of her nightmares over the years, she wasn't sure. But she knew the raw terror of the wrecked ship and the hollow of loss that she always woke up with were real.

A sob broke loose, and she clapped a hand over her mouth.

She'd been beaten in the orphanage if she cried, and she'd never lost the habit of covering her sorrow.

Breathe, Chloe. Breathe. She could almost hear Anya whispering it to her now as she'd done so many times before. Her hand would rub Chloe's back, and she'd repeat the words until Chloe stopped shaking. *It was just a dream.*

Chloe had never told Anya the details of her nightmare, and they didn't talk about the shipwreck.

Why hadn't they? There was no time after they'd washed up on the beach. They'd been gathered like so much flotsam by the fishwives, given the name *Wreckersfind* like the other children who washed ashore, and then sent to the orphanage. Each day there was about survival, and Chloe had never wanted to deepen Anya's suffering by bringing up the shipwreck or their parents.

They probably should've talked about such things. Chloe should get better at talking about such things.

Breathe, Chloe. Breathe.

She inhaled sharply as her eyes adjusted to the dark, and she took in unfamiliar shapes. A low ceiling made from the feathery inside of a mushroom cap. The bed with Hyacinth curled beside her under the covers. The shape of Coffee on Chloe's pillow.

Right.

They were at the Wild Root Inn. Chloe was in the attic with Hyacinth and Coffee, and she'd been dreaming of a shipwreck.

"Probably because of the sailor song," Chloe whispered.

She knew that was the likely reason, but it still felt too real. She reached out for the comforting weight of her sword. It would do nothing against the terrors of her past, but it made her feel safer.

Still, even with her blade at hand, it took her a long time to get back to sleep.

Chapter Eleven
Hyacinth

Hyacinth opened her eyes and then froze. Chloe's sword was at her throat.

"Bramble and marsh," she swore, lying very still. She shifted her eyes to the right, taking in the scene around her.

Chloe was asleep on her back, mouth open, sword hilt clutched between her hands. It was splayed outward, so the blade rested on Hyacinth's skin. Had Chloe grabbed it in the night? Did she always sleep with a sword? How close had she come to murdering Hyacinth in her sleep?

Better question, how was Hyacinth going to get out of bed without being stabbed?

She shifted ever so slightly so the sword was less of an immediate threat.

Coffee curled on Chloe's pillow, and he snored as he slept. It was early—Hyacinth could tell from the pale pink light seeping through the attic window and the quiet from the tavern below. She'd been having the strangest dream about her and Chloe riding a dragon while doing hundreds of dishes. She'd woken up only because she'd dropped a dish in her dream and the rest of them fell all at once.

She managed to slither out of bed, even with her ridiculous wings.

"Ooof," she whispered as she landed face down on the attic floor. Dust rose made a cloud around her as she got to her feet.

Carefully, she reached for Chloe's sword. With the lightest touch, Hyacinth unwrapped Chloe's fingers from the pommel, slipping her own around it.

Chloe stirred in her sleep, her eyelashes fluttering.

"Shhh," Hyacinth soothed, watching the other girl. She looked so peaceful, all the frown lines in her forehead smoothed. She was devastatingly lovely in the morning light as she rolled onto her side.

Hyacinth didn't dwell on that fact.

"Princess?" Chloe said from the bed. Her voice was sleepy. "Hyacinth?"

Hyacinth nearly dropped the sword. "Chloe?" she whispered.

Chloe laughed once and then burrowed deeper into the covers, taking Coffee with her as she pulled the blankets over her head. She muttered, "Princess," one more time, and then the sound of Coffee's snores filled the space again.

Was Chloe dreaming about Hyacinth? What were they doing in her dreams that was making her laugh?

The thought made heat rush to Hyacinth's cheeks. Before she could think more on it, she set the sword against the windowsill; picked up her belt with its potions, book, compass, and enchanted pen; and slipped on her shoes. She would find breakfast and then return. Chloe could keep sleeping without stabbing herself or anyone else in the meantime.

Hyacinth hurried down the stairs, trying not to think about Chloe or the way she'd whispered her name while sleeping. The stairs creaked under her feet, filling the quiet space of the inn more than Hyacinth would've liked. She stepped into the main room. The tables were empty, the fire down to embers. It must be very early indeed. No one stood behind the bar, though the smell of baking bread and roasting apples filled the air.

"Hello?" Hyacinth called out. Her stomach rumbled.

No one answered her, so she walked forward. There was a basket of bread left over from the night before on one of the tables. She grabbed two rolls and tucked them into her pocket. Surely they'd paid for a bit of breakfast with all their scrubbing last night.

"Hello?" she called out again.

Voices drifted in through a crack in the front door. Hyacinth walked over to it and peeked outside. The green-haired dryad barmaid from last night stood on the stoop, broom in hand. Thick gray mist curled along the street outside the tavern, obscuring who she was talking to.

"We're not open yet," the barmaid said with a hefty sweep of the broom. "I'll be getting the loaves out of the oven soon, but you can wait outside for a spell if you'd like."

"I'm not here for breakfast," a brisk, familiar voice replied.

Hyacinth swore as cold terror crept up her spine. It was Maurelle, Queen Mab's vicious bodyguard. How had she found them already? Had she checked every inn from here to the castle? Had Lord Helston sent a message to the queen, telling her what had happened?

Hyacinth supposed the how of Maurelle finding them didn't really matter. What were they going to do now?

Maurelle continued, "I'm looking for someone—"

"Not really in the business of helping people find someones," the barmaid said gruffly.

Metal clinked, and Hyacinth could imagine Maurelle rolling a pair of coins over her knuckles, as she liked to do when her knife wasn't at hand. "Be that as it may, I'm looking for a young girl—seventeen or so. Light-purple skin, curly brown hair, wings. Usually wears an outrageous belt that clanks when she walks."

Well! That was rude. Who was Maurelle to judge her belt or the way she sounded when she walked?

Hyacinth's indignation was quickly replaced by dread piling like stones in her stomach. Did Maurelle have a dragon with her? Was the queen here too? Maybe there was a whole troop of guards outside, waiting to drag her home.

Placing each footstep carefully, Hyacinth moved from the door to the tavern window, hoping to catch a better glimpse of Maurelle and who was with her.

That was good at least. There was no one aside from Queen Mab's bodyguard standing outside the inn. She was dressed in riding leathers, and her knife hung at her hip. Her mouth was set in a grim line as she pulled two more coins from her pocket. She held them out to the barmaid.

"Well," the barmaid said, reaching out for the coins. "Now that you mention it, I might've seen someone like that come in last night with another girl. We put them up in the attic. Why don't you come in, and we can see if they're ready for breakfast too."

Hyacinth didn't linger to hear more. As the door creaked open, she fled the common room. She crashed into a chair and then sent a copper tray clattering to the floor, but she didn't care. Her feet pounded up the staircase. She had to get to Chloe, and they had to get out of there!

Chapter Twelve
Chloe

Chloe rolled over. A blanket covered her head, and the bed was lumpy, but still warm. The whole thing smelled like Hyacinth—an intoxicating combination of jasmine, citrus, and old books—and Chloe allowed herself to linger in the scent. Hyacinth was probably sleeping on the other side of the covers.

Best to be still, then, and let her rest. They'd come a long way since leaving the castle and had much farther to go.

No matter what today brought, getting a bit more sleep would be a good thing.

A clattering noise from downstairs, like someone dropping a tray of dishes, caught her attention. It was probably nothing, just the normal sounds of a tavern inn waking up, but Chloe was the watchful one. She couldn't just ignore it and go back to sleep. Sighing, she peeked out from under her blankets. How strange. The bed was empty except for Coffee, who still snored. Where was Hyacinth?

Chloe sat up. Her sword leaned against the wall under the window, which wasn't where she remembered putting it. How had her sword gotten all the way over there?

Slivers of sunlight filtered through the window, and the attic room was quiet and peaceful. Chloe stretched, pulled on her boots, and strapped on her sword. Her stomach rumbled, and she rummaged through her bag. There was nothing left from Wendell's, but the tavern food from last night hadn't made her forget herself, which was a good thing. She now knew she could buy food and eat it in Fae with no ill effects, and, if the clattering from the kitchen was any indicator, the staff was up for the day and cooking. She'd make sure she and Hyacinth took something for the road, though they couldn't be stuck here all day doing dishes to pay for it. . . .

Before she could decide how they would get more food, Coffee stirred on the pillow. Chloe picked him up. "Good morning, Little One," she said. "What do dragons need to do in the morning?"

He nodded toward the window. She carried him over and opened it. Coffee preened and stretched in the sunlight. Chloe leaned out. They were halfway up the mushroom cap, and the village street stretched far below them. A gray ribbon of fog flowed through the town. The smell of the pines and freshly turned soil hit Chloe. It reminded her of working in the orphanage garden with Anya. Being in the garden without anyone watching over them, digging in the soil, watering and picking vegetables, and laughing with Anya had always made Chloe feel freer. Like there was life beyond the orphanage walls that they might get to experience someday.

Did Anya keep a garden now? Did she think of Chloe as she tended it?

Perhaps Chloe really would find a portal home in the Labyrinth and she could answer these questions soon.

Before she could linger on that thought, the door to the attic burst open. Startled, Chloe turned to see Hyacinth in the doorway.

"Go, go, go!" Hyacinth said, her breath coming in gasps.

"Go where? Why?"

Hyacinth flung Chloe's bag at her, which she caught with a surprised noise.

"My mother's bodyguard, Maurelle! She's found us! She's coming up here now! We can't take the stairs. We need another way out!" Hyacinth glanced around the room frantically.

Reality crashed down on Chloe. They'd been found! Queen Mab knew Hyacinth had run away, and now they'd be hauled back to the palace. Chloe would likely get thrown in jail and never see Hyacinth again. If she wasn't outright executed. Either way, she'd never see her sister.

They had to get out of here.

Chloe ran to the door and slammed it shut. "Help me!" she called, nodding toward the bed.

Together she and Hyacinth dragged the bed against the door.

"Hopefully, that'll hold her for a few minutes," Chloe said. "Let's go."

"Go? Where? How?" Hyacinth's voice was high-pitched, desperate. "We're trapped!"

Chloe considered the open window and the downward slope of the mushroom cap. "Only one other way out of this room."

"We can't go across the roof! In case you didn't notice, it's curved. And covered in morning dew. We'll fall to our deaths."

"Princess, we'll be fine." Chloe wasn't at all sure of it, but she smiled encouragingly. At least on the mushroom cap, they could put distance between themselves and Maurelle. If they could reach the ground, they might have a chance of escape.

Chloe picked up Coffee and tucked him into her pocket. "Stay in there, Little One," she whispered. "Promise I'll get you some breakfast soon."

A loud pounding rattled the attic door. Chloe's heart leaped in her chest. Behind her, Hyacinth's fingers dug into her shoulder. For the briefest of moments, Chloe imagined what she'd write to her sister: *Dear Anya, I hope I don't die on a giant mushroom. Wouldn't that be embarrassing?*

Silencing the thought, she stepped out the window. Her boots sunk into the mushroom's spongy surface, making her slide a bit. The roof *was* slippery and slanted, but maybe that would work to their advantage.

"Careful!" Chloe called as Hyacinth stepped onto the cap. Chloe wasn't afraid of heights, but it was at least thirty feet to the ground below. They wouldn't survive a fall from up here. Fortunately, that's where Hyacinth came in.

More banging shook the door.

"We can't just jump down from here!" Hyacinth said anxiously, looking once at the ground and then turning away. "What are we going to do?"

"You can fly us down!" It was the most sensible thing in the world. Chloe couldn't believe she had to suggest it.

Hyacinth shot her a wild look. "*Fly* us? With what?"

Unbelievable.

"Your wings! The ones on your back, Princess! Can't you get us down with those?"

"No!" Hyacinth's breath was ragged.

"Why not?" Frustration chased the fear galloping through Chloe's system. If Hyacinth wasn't using her wings because of some High Fae custom, she'd truly lose it. If she was locked in Queen Mab's dungeon because—

Someone burst through the door with a shattering noise, interrupting Chloe's thoughts.

"Is this really the time for a discussion?" Hyacinth's voice sounded desperate. "I can't use my wings, alright!? We have to find another way."

Another way? *What* was the other way besides wings? Chloe whipped around. Most of the village roofs were made of different-sized mushrooms. If she and Hyacinth timed it right, maybe, just maybe, they could jump and slide across the rooftops and then hit the ground on the far side of the village.

It wasn't a great plan, but it was the only thing she could think of if Hyacinth's wings weren't an option.

Why weren't her wings an option?

"Are you sure you can't fly us down?"

"I'm sure!"

Chloe blew out a frustrated breath. "Fine." She grabbed Hyacinth's hand. "Jump when I say so, and don't let go." Chloe laced her fingers through Hyacinth's and began to run across the Wild Root Inn's mushroom cap. Hyacinth slipped, but Chloe pulled her to her feet. The edge of the mushroom cap loomed, but, luckily, the red-and-white one next to it overlapped, making for an easy leap. A loud shout sounded behind them.

Chloe glanced over her shoulder. Maurelle, the queen's bodyguard, a Fae woman with white hair, dark eyes, a foxtail, with a knife at one hip and a long sword, stood at the window.

"Stop, Hyacinth!" Maurelle yelled. "Your mother demands you come home!"

"Jump!" Chloe pulled on Hyacinth's hand and leaped.

They landed on their knees atop the next mushroom cap. After scrambling to their feet, they ran up the slope toward the next rooftop.

"She can't catch us!" Hyacinth panted. "If she does, she'll drag us back to the castle, and then I'll never find my father!"

And Chloe would never go home or see her sister again or even spend a day outside the dungeons, not that Hyacinth seemed to care about the consequences of the stablehand getting caught as well.

That wasn't entirely fair, Chloe knew. She hadn't told Hyacinth everything she had at stake, but she was still upset. Why wouldn't she use her wings to help them? This would all be so much easier then!

Chloe glanced over her shoulder. The fox Fae woman clambered out the window and stood on the Wild Root Inn's cap, hands on her hips. "Hyacinth! I'm losing my patience! You're not a child. Stop acting like one!"

Hyacinth squeaked beside Chloe. Inside her pocket, Coffee made a similar noise.

Would Queen Mab take Coffee away from her too if they were caught? Of course she would. He'd be one more dragon in her stables, and Chloe would never see him again.

Not happening.

"Keep going!" she urged Hyacinth.

The next mushroom cap was a gigantic chanterelle, yellow with a ruffled edge, and it was farther away than the cap beside the tavern. They could still make the leap. Hopefully.

Chloe ran as fast as she could with Hyacinth's hand still in hers. "Jump!"

They raced toward the edge of the second mushroom cap and flung themselves toward the chantarelle. They fell for only a moment. A loud scream tore from Hyacinth's mouth, and Chloe's ankle twisted under her as she landed. Pain shot up her leg as she crumpled to her knees. The soft mushroom cap broke her fall a little, but it still hurt. She swore.

"What happened? Are you okay?" Hyacinth said.

"Keep going! I'm fine!" Chloe stood up, pleased to see she could put weight on the ankle. It had just been a bad landing. They had to keep moving.

Adrenaline surged through her as they dashed-slid-leaped from one mushroom cap to the next. The mushroom rooftops were a bit like stairs, though some of them had four- and five-foot drops between them. At others, they had to climb upward to pull themselves onto the roofs.

When they reached the last cap and jumped to the ground, they stopped to catch their breath. Chloe's ankle throbbed, even more sore after every landing, but it would be fine. She wasn't hurt, just tired from all the running and jumping.

"What . . . do . . . we . . . do . . . now?" Hyacinth gasped.

Chloe's heart thundered. She checked on Coffee—he grinned up at her from her pocket. Then she looked around. From where they stood, hidden under the lowest mushroom cap in the village, they couldn't see their pursuer. But she was surely still giving chase. If she reached the ground too, there was nowhere to hide.

"Maurelle's horse!" Chloe pointed to a saddled gray mare waiting outside the tavern. "Let's get it and escape!"

Hyacinth was already running toward it. Chloe started to follow, but her ankle gave way again. Pain seized her leg.

Bramble and marsh, she was more injured than she'd thought. "You get the horse," she called after Hyacinth. "I'll wait here in case she comes down!"

Anger broiled in Chloe as she hobbled painfully over to lean against the nearest house. If Hyacinth had used her wings, this would've never happened. She wouldn't have gotten hurt. When they were far from Maurelle and Mushroom Town, she was going to tell Hyacinth what she really thought of High Fae magic with all its rules and niceties.

The notion had barely crossed her mind when Maurelle landed right in front of her.

"Hyacinth!" the fox Fae bellowed, furious. She looked right past Chloe, as if she were no more than a gnat.

Chloe glanced over her shoulder. Hyacinth had reached the horse and was mounting it. If she rode over here, Chloe might be able to manage getting on the horse, but she'd have to prevent Maurelle from stopping them. Which was going to be harder than she could possibly manage with her hurt ankle, but when had that stopped her before?

Gritting her teeth against the pain, Chloe spoke up. "Leave Princess Hyacinth alone. She's not going back with you."

"Who's going to make me, girl?" Maurelle sneered, looking her over. "You?"

Chloe drew her sword. She wobbled into her fighting stance, but she held her ground. "Me."

"I see a stablehand with a sword, not a fighter."

Something in Chloe broke at the words. Rage, hot and surging, flashed through her. She was *not* just a stablehand with a sword! She was an apprentice realm mapper and someone who'd survived a shipwreck, an orphanage, a vicious human queen's cruelty, and nearly a year in the Fae world on her wits and luck alone. She was *not* someone to underestimate.

Hoofbeats clattered down the cobblestones behind her as Hyacinth rode Maurelle's horse toward them. Chloe just needed to buy them a few moments.

"I'm more than that," she shot back.

"Prove it."

With a roar, Chloe slashed out with her sword. Maurelle stepped back, as if surprised. Then she drew her own sword and grinned. Her body language as she held the blade marked the truth: She was clearly ten times the fighter Chloe was and had been training most of her life.

Well. Chloe didn't care. She would fight until she couldn't anymore. She was *not* going to Queen Mab's dungeons.

They crossed blades, Chloe barely maintaining her footing. She lurched forward in response, swinging wildly. Maurelle blocked every cut of her blade.

Chloe's bad ankle throbbed, but she kept fighting. She dodged a blow, looking for an opening. Chloe was good at sword fighting—she really was!—but Maurelle was a High Fae queen's bodyguard. She'd faced foes much worse than Chloe.

Chloe's back was against a wall, and Maurelle slashed out, gouging her cheek. Out of the corner of her eye, Chloe saw Hyacinth approaching on the horse.

Maurelle laughed. "Catch your breath, little fighter. Then we'll head back to the castle. I see the princess is bringing me my horse."

"We're not going back to the castle," Chloe said, twisting away from Maurelle.

Maurelle laughed again and launched a new attack on Chloe. All her playfulness gone, she ruthlessly barged into Chloe's defenses.

Steel clashed on steel as Chloe did her best to parry Maurelle's assault.

"Chloe! Get on the horse!" Hyacinth yelled.

"Trying!" Chloe dodged another blow, hobbling toward the horse.

I will help you, Brave One, Coffee whispered in Chloe's head.

He rose from her pocket. When had his wing fully healed? Maybe the phoenix balm he'd licked off her arm had fixed it? She'd have to ask him. Later. When she wasn't being attacked by a swordswoman ten times her superior.

Coffee flew toward Maurelle's face. Bramble and marsh, he was going to get himself killed.

Maurelle swatted at him like a fly, but he landed on her cheek, digging his claws into her skin and swiping a long scratch over her eye.

"Nice work, Little One!" Chloe shouted.

This is hardly the extent of my powers, as I seem to be remembering, Coffee answered back.

Chloe grinned at that. She loved everything about Coffee, and at least *he* was willing to use his wings to help them.

Maurelle flung the tiny dragon off her face. Chloe caught him out of the air, and tucked him back into her pocket.

It had been only a few seconds, but it was enough. Hyacinth and the horse were right in front of Chloe. She put her good leg into the stirrup and heaved herself upward, landing hard in the saddle.

"Go!" Chloe yelled.

Hyacinth dug her heels into the horse's flank. Behind them, Maurelle bellowed, "We will find you, Hyacinth! You hear me? You can't run away!"

Chloe didn't look back as they flew down the twisting forest road, putting as much distance between them and the queen's bodyguard as they could.

✦

They rode hard, leaving Mushroom Town behind them. The trail narrowed with each passing mile, and Chloe's patience wore thin. Her ankle hurt, and the cut on her cheek from Maurelle's blade stung. Hyacinth's wings kept hitting Chloe in the face as she sat on the horse behind the princess, trying to hold on.

Annoying, maddening, awful wings.

Why hadn't Hyacinth used them to help in the escape from Maurelle?

Other creatures used their wings to flee danger! Those ravens they passed on the trail flew into the trees at the sound of hoofbeats! Coffee, who'd had a wounded wing a few days ago, used his wings to fly into battle! But, Hyacinth, who had a blasted giant pair of wings, couldn't have used them to fly down from a mushroom cap? It didn't make any sense!

Be fair, whispered a voice in Chloe's head that was neither hers nor Coffee's. It sounded more like her gentler, more patient sister's voice. *She did steal the horse, which is the only reason you're not being carted back to the castle right now.*

The horse leaped over a broken log, and Hyacinth's wings smacked Chloe in the face again.

She huffed. Hyacinth had stolen the horse, yes, but that didn't fix Chloe's sprained ankle or the fact that she'd have to somehow reach the Labyrinth on it.

"I'm not sure where we're going," Hyacinth called out. "But I think if we make it to the mountains, Maurelle won't be able to find us."

The forest path curved toward a soaring, snowcapped mountain range. Chloe was fairly certain this path would take them farther from the Labyrinth, but she wasn't about to ask Hyacinth for a peek at the map. Instead, she focused on the landscape around them. The trees were smaller here than the towering giants they'd encountered yesterday. Tight clusters of pines, maples, birches, and oaks lined the road. The ground beneath the trees was covered in moss, broken logs, and leaves. The road itself was a churning mess of mud from an earlier rainstorm. The air smelled like growing things, dark places, and secrets.

Why Hyacinth thought getting to the mountains would keep Maurelle away from them was a mystery, but Chloe was too annoyed to ask for her reasons.

"Glorious. A great plan," Chloe grumbled sarcastically.

"What did you say?" Hyacinth said, over the sound of the horse's hoofbeats.

"Nothing."

They kept riding, and Chloe kept stewing on the uselessness of High Fae wings.

Eventually, Maurelle's horse began to slow. When the forest path ended at a shallow stream, he stopped altogether, whinnying his disapproval. A rocky, tree-lined slope with a path that was barely narrow enough for one of them wound up it on the other side of the stream.

Chloe slid off the horse, landing on her good leg. Hyacinth was off a moment later, but Chloe's attention was on the animal.

"You did a good job," she whispered to the horse. "Thank you."

It nuzzled her hand. She petted its nose and held its bridle, limping toward the stream.

"Are you alright?" Hyacinth called. Her voice was soft, laced with exhaustion. She bent down and splashed some of the stream water on her face.

"We should've stopped sooner; the horse is exhausted," Chloe snapped.

Hyacinth nodded, looking up. Water dripped down her neck. "I know. I just . . . well, I wanted to get far enough away that Maurelle wouldn't have a chance to catch up."

"How could she possibly catch up? We took her horse!"

Hyacinth looked at Chloe like it was a silly thing to say, and of course it was. Maurelle likely had money to hire a horse from someone in Mushroom Town. She was probably only a half hour behind them, at most.

"Here." Hyacinth undid one of Maurelle's saddlebags and pulled an apple from it, which she offered to the horse. "That should make up for some of the trouble."

She also tossed an apple to Chloe, who couldn't help but catch it and take a bite. She hadn't had breakfast that morning. "It might make the horse feel better," Chloe muttered, swallowing. "But fruit doesn't make up for what you did. Or, rather, didn't do."

Hyacinth's stare was sharp. "What didn't I do? Run upstairs and let you know Maurelle was looking for us? Grab the horse and get us out of there?"

Chloe scoffed. "You didn't use your *wings*! Why didn't you use your glorious High Fae *wings* to get us off the mushrooms? If you'd done that, we would've been way ahead of her! I wouldn't have gotten hurt!" Chloe touched her cut check in anger. As if to underscore her point, she also stumbled on her bad ankle at the same moment.

Hyacinth looked stricken, her cheeks pale. She ran her fingers over the tiny bottles on her belt. "I'm sorry, I don't have another healing potion. But maybe we could have Coffee lick that cut? That seemed to work yesterday and—"

Chloe couldn't take it any longer. Her control over her anger broke, roaring like the stream before them.

"You *never* had a healing potion! You had some phoenix balm that only made my last injury worse! Why can't you just use your High Fae magic to help us on this journey? Whatever we have ahead of us—we can't just hope you have the right potion for it!"

"Why can't *you* use your magic?" Hyacinth shot back.

That question hit Chloe like a blow. What was she supposed to say? If she'd *actually* been a common Fae girl, she would have some magic that could help them. She deflected the question, lashing out instead.

"You're a *High Fae princess*! Your smallest magic is fifty times that of even the most powerful common Fae! You should be able to heal; or cast illusions; or fly with your enormous, sisters-forsaken wings that keep whacking me in the face! Why won't you?"

The words rang out between them, and Hyacinth deflated. She slumped on a large boulder beside the stream and buried her face in her hands.

Chloe's anger quelled slightly at the curve of Hyacinth's spine. She hadn't meant to be so harsh; she was just injured and frustrated. Hyacinth was her friend. They'd been through a lot together already, and they had a long road ahead of them.

"I'm so sorry," Hyacinth said through her hands. "This is all my fault."

It was, perhaps, but saying so wouldn't do any good. Chloe blew out a breath and hobbled over to where Hyacinth sat. She nudged her to scoot over.

"This isn't entirely your fault. We knew there was risk in leaving the castle—"

"No, it *is* my fault. I didn't use my wings because they don't work."

Her wings didn't work? Had Chloe heard that right?

Chloe looked over at Hyacinth, who was staring at her like she'd just confessed a terrible secret.

"What do you mean your wings don't work?"

Hyacinth tugged at one of the gauzy sections over her shoulder. "I mean these wings are fake! That's why they don't work. That's why I couldn't fly us down from the mushrooms. They're no more than a pretty ornament, like a cloak or tiara."

Chloe's mind struggled to make sense of what Hyacinth was saying. Was this some new trend among the High Fae? To wear fake wings for who only knew what reason? "But, why would you want to wear *fake* wings? If you have High Fae magic—"

"I don't!" Hyacinth burst out, so loud that she startled the horse from its drinking. Coffee peeked out of Chloe's pocket, and the words rang out, echoing back to them off the rocky slope across the stream.

Chloe started to say something, but Hyacinth barreled on, facing her with a wild look in her eyes.

"I don't have magic! That's my terrible, pathetic secret. Unlike my half sisters or every other damn Fae in this kingdom, I don't have any High or common Fae magic! I bet you—a stablehand!—have more magic than me."

Chloe flinched at the words, but what was she supposed to do, lay her own truth at Hyacinth's feet? Besides, she was still reeling from Hyacinth's revelation. A High Fae princess without magic? That meant she'd been lying to everyone—including Chloe—for all these months.

The thought hurt more than Chloe would've liked to admit. "Have you ever been able to do magic?"

Hyacinth scoffed. "Never! I didn't get my wings when I turned seventeen. My mother had these ones crafted by sylvan smiths, and I'm stuck with them for at least another week. They're meant to trick people at her Solstice Balls. I've never been able to do any of the High Fae magics. I can't do glamours, I can't make rune lights, and I can't even do a simple illusion spell without all these potions. You want to know about those?" Hyacinth jabbed a finger at her belt. "I stole three of these from my mother's alchemists, and the other two I bought from a traveling potion maker. Allow me to tell you the extent of my skills: We have juniper heart for illusion! A moon-drenched secret for levitation—well, I suppose I could've used that for getting us off the mushroom. Apologies. My fault. See, I told you it was my fault!"

"Hyacinth—"

"What else, let's see! I used my fog tendrils for helping you escape in Runa's barn and the wraith's tears for compelling the redcap, so that just leaves dragonheart for ashes and ruin . . . oh! And the phoenix balm, which, as you pointed out, was *supposed* to be a healing potion, but I couldn't even get that right!" Hyacinth swiped at tears rolling down her face.

A mixture of sympathy and confusion filled Chloe, sitting like a lump under her ribs. She wanted to be angry at Hyacinth, to blame her for everything that had happened, but she'd just been doing her best after all. She'd already helped Chloe in many ways with her potions. That the truth of her was different than Chloe had expected wasn't Hyacinth's fault.

"Feel free to hate me now," Hyacinth finished. "Everyone else will once they find out. I don't know who I'm fooling, pretending I can actually find my father. I'm *nothing* without these potions and trinkets. Totally useless."

"Hyacinth," Chloe said again. Her ankle still hurt, but that had faded beneath the magnitude of Hyacinth's revelations.

"What?" Hyacinth snapped, crossing her arms. "I don't have more to confess. Unless you want to know about the time I broke—"

Chloe reached out and pulled her into a hug.

Hyacinth startled, then leaned into the hug.

"You're not useless," Chloe said softly. "In fact, I've never met anyone like you."

That was true on many levels, but Chloe meant it. She touched Hyacinth's back, gently rubbing the spot between the fake wings. Comforting her like Anya had used to do when Chloe had a nightmare.

"You're just being nice," Hyacinth said through a sob.

"Hardly. I'm not known for that, just ask my sister. She always told me I was 'fiercer than a bull terrier,' but that was okay with her."

"She sounds lovely." Hyacinth sniffled.

"She is. Besides her enthusiasm for cabbage. I swear she'd have a birthday cake made of cabbage if I'd let her." Chloe gave an exaggerated shudder.

Hyacinth laughed, a ragged braying sound.

Chloe pulled back a bit to wipe one of Hyacinth's tears away. "We're not going back to the palace, okay? We're going to keep looking for your father."

"But your ankle?"

Chloe pointed to a large stick on the ground. "It'll be fine. I'll use that as a walking stick, and I bet we will find someone who can heal it."

"You really believe that?" Hyacinth's tear-filled eyes were silver moons in her face.

Chloe nodded. "I do. Though we should get going so we don't run into Maurelle again."

Hyacinth hugged her. "Only the truth between us from now on."

Guilt snaked through Chloe at her own lies. She *would* tell Hyacinth the truth. When they had a quiet moment later to unpack it all. Or when she got to the portal inside the Labyrinth. It did feel good to tell Hyacinth little things about Anya, but after a lifetime of keeping her own thoughts and feelings close, Chloe wasn't in the habit of sharing them. Even if Hyacinth had been honest with her.

"Only the truth," she repeated. *Eventually.*

They left the horse on the road because the path up the mountain was too narrow for him. Either Maurelle would find him and take him home, or he'd find his way back to Queen Mab's stables. All her animals had both navigation and protection charms on them, so he'd have a long walk home, but no one would bother him.

Chloe propped the walking stick under her armpit, and then, with Hyacinth in the lead, they started up the narrow path over the mountain.

They walked until they could no longer see the forest road from Mushroom Town behind them. Chloe's ankle still hurt, and the cold mountain air bit into her lungs the higher they went. Hyacinth paused every few feet to wait for Chloe.

"How's your ankle?" she asked, turning. They were at the top of another rise, and a vast view of the mountain range spread in front of them. Two boulders stood on either side of the vista, framing it.

Before Chloe could reply, Hyacinth leaned against one of the bounders. The patch of earth beneath them opened like a trapdoor.

Chloe screamed as she and Hyacinth tumbled into the vastness of the mountain.

Chapter Thirteen
Hyacinth

A bell rang out three times as the mountain devoured them.

Hyacinth plunged downward, utterly disoriented. One moment, they were standing in the bright sunlight; the next, they were falling through darkness.

Or sliding, rather. The trapdoor plunged into a stone chute, and now Hyacinth, Chloe, and Coffee shot down it—a tangle of legs, wings, Chloe's sword, and Hyacinth's belt.

Hyacinth clapped a hand over her belt, hoping to preserve the potion bottles—by the Sisters, had she really told Chloe all about her potion bottles?—but the thought flew from her head as her elbows smashed against the sides of the chute. Pain spiked through her body, and she tried to curl in on herself to protect her limbs from worse injuries on the way down.

Another scream ripped out of her as the chute twisted to the left, and then it fell away altogether. Darkness, vast and complete, surrounded her as she dropped.

What would they land on? Stone spikes? An underground lake? Someone's home? Who lived under this mountain? Was this the end of Hyacinth's story?

As she descended, Hyacinth fought to remember her father's map or what his book said about this part of the kingdom, but her mind was scrambled by the fall, the enormity of revealing her lack of magic to Chloe, and Chloe's taking it rather well. She'd been angry, yes, but not as much as Hyacinth had expected. Which was nice. As was the hug. If they weren't plummeting through endless underground darkness, she'd let herself linger on that.

"Hyacinth!" Chloe called out somewhere near her.

"I'm still here!"

"Where's here?"

Hyacinth didn't have time to answer, because all at once, she landed on a soft, pillowy substance. It was sticky like a spider's web, but fluffy like royal swan down. She sunk into it with a *whoosh*, and it absorbed her fall, cocooning her. Before Hyacinth could sit up, Chloe dropped screaming out of the darkness and landed beside her.

"Ooof," Chloe said, sitting up slowly. A small light glowed from inside her shirt pocket, illuminating her face. "You alright?"

Hyacinth did an internal check. Nothing seemed to be broken. She was winded, but not wounded. She brushed aside some of the sticky substance. "Surprisingly not dead. You?"

"Likewise. This is not at all how I imagined this day going."

Hyacinth felt exactly the same way, but as she was learning with adventures, things usually went differently than expected. Where this descent through the mountain would lead them, she had no idea, but she found herself excited to find out.

Bramble and marsh, she did love being out of her mother's castle and in the wide world. Even with all its dangers and unknowns.

"Where are we?" Chloe called out.

"Not sure. I don't even know which way to roll out of this . . . web? Enormous pillow?"

"Spun-sugar net?"

"Possibly that too."

Coffee crawled out of Chloe's pocket and chirruped. He jumped upward and hovered in the air above a carved stone sign set into the wall near Hyacinth's head. Silver light radiated off him, making a lantern of sorts.

Hyacinth read the sign he'd illuminated. "WELCOME TO THE HALL OF THE MOUNTAIN KING."

"Who's he?" Chloe peered at the sign. "Also, since when do you glow, Coffee?"

Since always, I think, the tiny dragon said into both their minds. *I find I'm remembering more and more of myself now that I'm free of captivity. The phoenix balm has done me wonders too, and now that we're in the dark, my light streams forth.*

"Thank goodness for that," Hyacinth said, gazing around in the soft silver light. A cavern about the size of her mother's library stretched around them, with tall rock formations making shadows along the wall. Water dripped somewhere nearby, and something like music floated on the air, but that was probably just her ears playing tricks on her. The sticky substance that had caught them stretched across the entire floor, silvery and thick as she was tall. If it was a spider's web, she didn't want to see the size of the creature that had made it. Best to get moving.

"What do we do now?" She rolled toward the wall, brushing off filaments of the substance.

Chloe scooted out of the net behind Hyacinth. "First, we figure out who this Mountain King is, I suppose. Maybe he can help us get back on the road. Have you ever heard of him?"

Hyacinth hadn't, which was strange since her mother had employed all the best tutors in the kingdom from before Hyacinth was old enough to read. Her geography and politics tutor, a hedgehog Fae with a prodigious memory and a rattling cough, had made her memorize all the Moonshadow Kingdom monarchs back three hundred years. He'd never mentioned a Mountain King.

Hyacinth shook her head. "I know nothing about him. Maybe my father's book has something?"

She pulled it out of the pouch on her belt. "Coffee, come closer, please." He did, bringing his light with him. She flipped the book open, running her finger over her father's notes. The mountain range was in there, along with some cautions to travelers about avalanches in the winter, and her father had scrawled something in the margin. Before she could read them, flickering torchlight filled the chamber, and a tired female voice called out.

"Well, wouldn't you know! Thought I heard the spiral silk's trap-door bell ring out." A human woman walked into the chamber, carrying a torch. She looked more like a memory of a person than an actual one, and Hyacinth wondered how long she'd been under the mountain. She was thin as a reed, and her collarbones poked out above the top of her tattered, faded-green dress like two wooden spoons under her skin. Her long brown hair was tied back with twine, and it might have been glorious once, but now pieces of it hung in clumps around her face like straw left out in the rain too long. Her eyes were tea saucers against cheekbones that could've carved glass with their sharpness.

Still, a smile pulled at her lips as she appraised them. "More visitors for the Mountain King's Endless Ball; he'll be so happy," she rasped. It sounded like she was reading something, and the smile didn't quite reach her eyes.

Hyacinth glanced at Chloe, who had a hand on her sword.

"Endless Ball?" Chloe mouthed.

Hyacinth shrugged. She had no idea what it was, but it didn't sound promising. Perhaps it was part of the solstice celebrations? Perhaps they could just ask for directions and leave?

"There must be some mistake," Hyacinth started, with a small curtsy toward the woman. "My friend and I were walking on the mountain, when we fell into a hole—"

"The southeasterly chute that ends in the spiral silk net, indeed," the woman said, almost proudly. "I heard the bell toll for you three times! I know that route well. It's how I first found the king myself. What a happy day that was!" Her eyes were vacant as she said it, and a tear rolled down her cheek.

Hyacinth opened and closed her mouth as a reply evaded her. Who was this woman, and what was wrong with her? Should they offer comfort or ask more questions?

Chloe squeezed Hyacinth's arm as she stepped forward. Hyacinth was all too happy to let her take charge. "Please, could you help us find the way out? We've got somewhere to be tonight."

The woman shook her head. What might have been a laugh, but sounded more the dying gasp of a small reptile, fluttered out of her. "There's no way out, just an invitation to the Endless Ball. The Mountain King will be so pleased to meet you. So pleased, so pleased. And he'll be so happy with me for finding you. Happy, happy." She moved her lips, showing her teeth in a way that no longer resembled a smile.

Hyacinth shuddered. She truly had no idea what was going on, but everything in her screamed for them to leave. How were they supposed to do that? They needed more information so they could attempt to find an exit. "Do you get many visitors here?"

The woman fluttered her hands in front of her. "So many, so many. They fall through doors, like you did. Or knock on the main one. We catch them all so they can dance. Please, friends, this way, this way." She gestured out of the chamber and started walking, leading them through a stone hallway that stretched into the distance. The low ceiling brushed Hyacinth's wings.

Hyacinth glanced again at Chloe, who shrugged. What choice did they have but to follow the strange woman?

"You go first," Chloe whispered.

"What about your ankle?"

"I'll manage."

Hyacinth wasn't sure she would, but the corridor was too narrow for them to walk beside each other.

They followed the woman, who muttered to herself as she walked—"So happy, so pleased with me, I think"—until she drew up short and spun around. Her torch nearly knocked Hyacinth in the head.

"What are your names?" the woman demanded. "I must introduce you to the king, but I can't do that unless I know your names!

He won't like it if I don't know your names! Oh, silly, foolish Larissa! *Always* ask their names and their stations. You won't be put on the trapdoors again if you forget that!"

She let out the rasping, jagged laugh again. Fear coiled in Hyacinth's belly at the sound and the unspooling monologue that accompanied it. Suddenly, everything about this woman under the earth and the king she served seemed dangerous, and Hyacinth longed to flee. But where could she possibly go?

"I'm Chloe, and this is my friend Rowena," Chloe said quickly.

"A winged High Fae and a common Fae." The woman frowned, peering at them with her torchlight thrust forward. "Very well, very well. Not sure what the king will do with you. I want him to be so happy, but . . ."

"What's your name?" Hyacinth interrupted. She'd heard her say *Larissa*, but she wanted to know more in the hopes it might help them get out of here.

Impossibly, the woman's eyes grew even larger. She leaned forward and whispered like they were friends sharing a secret. "Larissa . . . well, I'm not sure of my surname any longer, but it matters not! I'm a human from above. Found the Endless Ball many years ago and know all its steps. All its steps, all its steps. I'm so good at them, the king lets me find others for his ballroom. Come! Let me show it to you! Welcome to the most magical, magnificent place in the world!"

Larissa did a grotesque twirl on her toes, like a scarecrow come to life, and then suddenly she started dancing and weaving down the corridor in front of them. Her torch bobbed along with her, sending shadows dancing as well, and they had to hurry—as much as they could with Chloe's sprained ankle—to keep up.

"I don't like this," Chloe muttered behind Hyacinth.

"There's nothing to like," Hyacinth agreed. "We'll get out of here as soon as we can."

"Hurry, this way! To the ballroom!" Larissa cried out.

They followed her through the stone hallway, turning right, then left, then right again. They went down two sets of stairs, and then back up another one. They passed an underground waterfall, and a garden of towering stalagmites. Strange, bittersweet harp music that sounded like the wind though birch leaves and reminded Hyacinth of a dream floated through the air, growing louder with each step. They could've been walking for minutes or hours, time blending together in the dark.

Hyacinth was thoroughly lost by the time Larissa called out, "We're here! We're here! Welcome to the Mountain King's ballroom and the Endless Ball! Isn't it magnificent?"

It was not.

"Bramble and marsh," Chloe said, behind Hyacinth. She limped forward to stand beside her. "What a nightmare."

Hyacinth couldn't agree more.

The Mountain King's ballroom was an enormous cavern ten times larger than Queen Mab's. Frozen waterfalls of stone held up a vast domed ceiling. Hanging from that ceiling was a massive chandelier, three times the size of Lord Helston's carriage, whose silver-blue glow painted the space with eerie light. A long thread of illumination connected the chandelier to a golden throne in the center of the room. A harp taller than Hyacinth sat a few paces away, played by a trio of pixies who flitted among the strings.

None of that was what made a rotten taste fill Hyacinth's mouth.

It was the hundreds of human dancers—all stick-thin like Larissa, in tattered clothes and worn-out shoes, with vacant expressions in their eyes—who twirled beneath the chandelier that made Hyacinth's stomach churn. Some of them wept, but kept dancing. Some of them moved like puppets on strings. Some of them just twirled with the loose, erratic grace of ribbons caught in the wind.

Little spheres of light rose from their bodies like dandelion fluff. These lights floated upward and gathered in the chandelier, hovering there for a moment before being sucked into one of the crystal globes that sat on each of many arms. Several goblin guards in rusted armor and holding long swords and pikes encircled the dancers, egging them on and occasionally poking them with weapons if they stumbled too far off the dance floor.

Something is very, very wrong here, Coffee said inside Hyacinth's mind.

"It is," Hyacinth agreed.

"I know this light," Chloe muttered. Her hand was on her sword, and her voice was a knife. "We have to go, *now*."

What did she mean, she knew this light? What was it? Where would they go? Back through the twisting way they'd come? Up the chute they'd fallen from?

Still, Hyacinth was willing to try if it took them away from the haunted frenzy of the Endless Ball.

"This way!" Larissa said, offering them another ghastly smile. "You must meet the king!" She clapped five times, and the dancers parted, still swaying in their clearly ensorcelled waltz, but now there was a path across the dance floor.

Three of the goblin guards stepped toward Hyacinth and Chloe, swords out as they blocked the way back to the tunnel behind them. "Move it!" the largest of them said. He had to be half troll, and two long tusks protruded from his mouth. He looked like he could snap them in half with one hand.

Perhaps a little diplomacy was in order.

"We'll meet the king," Hyacinth said, placing a hand over Chloe's before she could draw her sword. "Pay our respects and then ask to leave."

"Don't tell him who you are," Chloe said through gritted teeth. She glanced upward at the chandelier, her mouth set in a frown.

Hyacinth wouldn't dream of it, but she was no longer in a dreaming space. Being under the mountain, in this ballroom, was all nightmare, so who knew what she would have to do?

She slipped her hand into Chloe's as they followed Larissa toward the king's throne.

She had a terrible feeling about this, but as long as they stayed together, they could make it through. She was sure of it.

✦

Much to Hyacinth's surprise, the Mountain King was a narrow human man, spindly as the stalagmites that rose from the ground around him. She'd been expecting a winged High Fae lord or some sort of goblin or troll, not a middle-aged human with a shaved head and bright blue eyes. Amber beads, feathers, and gems were braided into his waist-length gray beard. They clanked with his every movement. A pair of rose-colored spectacles hung from a chain around his neck. His eyebrows were thick, and they drew together as he studied Chloe and Hyacinth. The king sat on a throne made of bones, each of them gilded in gold. Skulls, femurs, and hip bones all gleamed in the torchlight. The king was happily tucking into a piece of cake as they approached. Two goblin guards flanked him, hands on the pommels of their swords. The long silver filament from the chandelier led to a goblet beside the king. Liquid dripped from it into the goblet, and the king sipped from it every few moments, smacking his lips after each sip. Cake crumbs flew from the king's mouth as he ate. He swiped a bit of cake out of a golden eye socket beneath his wrist and popped it into his mouth.

"That's disgusting," Chloe muttered.

Hyacinth absolutely agreed, but she was trying to be diplomatic. "Which part?"

"All of it."

The king waved them forward. The movement sent more cake crumbs flying and made his decorated beard sway wildly.

"My king," said Larissa, bowing to him. "May I present—"

"Hush, Larissa," the king bellowed in a voice too big for his narrow chest. "Let them speak for themselves. Who are you, and how have you ended up at my party?"

Hyacinth swallowed hard. What was she supposed to say? If she gave her true name, the king might contact her mother.

Chloe spoke before Hyacinth could. "I'm Chloe, Your Majesty. Adventurer, warrior, and keeper of ancient beasts."

"Welcome, Chloe," the king said, waving a hand. "And who are you?"

Hyacinth took a steadying breath and curtsied. "I'm Rowena Bramblefen—"

Larissa hissed in a breath. Hyacinth glanced over at her quickly, to find her staring back with a glazed look that had the barest hint of a spark behind it. Why was Larissa staring at her like that?

"*Rollinglane*," Chloe muttered through her teeth. "Your last name is Rollinglane."

Bramble and marsh, Hyacinth had given the wrong name. She cast a dazzling smile at the king.

"I mean, *Rollinglane*, sire. Forgive me for being so flustered in your esteemed presence. I'm Rowena Rollinglane of the Moonshadow Kingdom," Hyacinth said quickly, giving a small bow.

"And how did you find your way to my kingdom?"

A bunch of cave tunnels and a creepy ballroom were hardly a kingdom, but Hyacinth didn't bother pointing that out. "We were passing over the mountain and found our way here. Perhaps you can tell us how we can make our way back outside?"

The Mountain King scoffed. "Back outside, oh no! Stay for my Endless Ball!" He patted his gilded throne of bones. "All my friends are here! Humans live such a short time. I have to keep them close."

Chloe made a strangled noise, and Hyacinth swallowed hard. Desperately, she pulled upon her many years of courtly etiquette lessons. "Indeed, sire. It's good to keep one's friends close."

"Especially when one's friends keep dying over the centuries!" The king frowned at his macabre throne, but only for a moment. Then he glared at Hyacinth.

She shifted from one foot to the other under his gaze.

"Wings!" the king bellowed, as if noticing Hyacinth's fake wings for the first time. "Certainly not in my court! Not at my ball! What did you say your names were again?"

Larissa slid in front of Hyacinth and Chloe and made another bow. "They are Chloe and Rowena, Your Majesty. Aren't you happy I found them? Do you think I might be able to rest for a moment since I did?" She cast a longing glance to a pile of rags in one corner of the ballroom. "Or perhaps have a measure of cake? It's been so very long since my last bite."

"Silence, Larissa!" the king thundered. "Always whining for more cake. Let me have a look at these two. Time to see the truth of them."

The king stumbled down the stairs and slid the rose-colored glasses around his neck over his eyes. He blinked a few times, his eyes huge behind the lenses, and then frowned at Hyacinth through them. She felt his scrutiny down to her bones. What was he seeing?

"A High Fae princess," he declared. "Ha! And no magic in her!"

By the Sisters, how did he know that? *Those must be enchanted glasses.* He couldn't just go shouting Hyacinth's secrets out loud, no matter that Chloe already knew them. She didn't want them to become public knowledge. The goblins closest to the king snickered as they stared at her. Hyacinth had to get control of this situation and correct the king's error.

"I don't know what you're seeing, sire, but none of that is—"

"Silence," the king boomed. "We don't need a vile little High Fae's opinion on anything here." He turned to Chloe, examining her through his glasses. "And—what's this?" He snaked a hand out and grabbed her wrist.

Chloe wrenched her wrist away, but the king pulled her closer.

What was he doing? Hyacinth racked her brain for all the many diplomacy lessons her mother and tutors had taught her. Something about hospitality would surely work. "Please, Your Majesty," Hyacinth said. "There's no need to treat your guests like that."

The king ignored Hyacinth completely.

He peered at Chloe through the glasses and then stared down at her arm, where his bony fingers encircled her wrist. Hyacinth looked at Chloe, whose face could be described as only murderous. Hyacinth truly hoped Chloe didn't kill the king. Then they'd never get out of here.

"You're hiding something, aren't you, adventurer?" The king spit the last word out with such scorn, it made Hyacinth flinch.

Hiding something? What was Chloe hiding? Hyacinth tried to meet her eye, but Chloe's gaze bored into the king.

"I'm *not* hiding anything."

"Let her go," Hyacinth called out. "You have no right to keep us here!"

The king pulled a knife from somewhere inside his beard. The blade glinted in the eerie blue light from the chandelier. "Aaah, but you're my guests. And one of you is telling lies, so I'm within my rights to do what I like. Hold them!"

Several things happened all at once. Two guards rushed forward to grab Hyacinth, and two more grabbed Chloe's shoulders. Coffee surged out of her pocket, but the king reacted with surprising quickness and plucked him from the air. "Bring me the pixie cage!" he yelled to one of the goblin soldiers, nodding toward a golden cage on the floor by the throne.

The goblin grabbed it and opened the cage's door. The king shoved Coffee inside. The tiny dragon slammed into the golden bars, whimpering.

I'm going to kill this so-called king, Coffee raged in Hyacinth's head.

Not if she got there first.

"Easy, Little One," Chloe called out. "We'll get you out of there, I promise."

"You'll do no such thing," the Mountain King taunted. "Now let's see what you're hiding." With one quick movement, the king whipped off Chloe's watch and sliced a deep cut into her forearm.

Chloe screamed in pain, a string of curses pouring from her.

"What are you doing?" Hyacinth cried out, panic rising inside her like a great beast. What was happening? Why was the king slicing Chloe open? "Stop it! You're hurting her!"

"Oh, bad manners, bad manners," Larissa mumbled, wringing her hands as she watched the king. "We should be dancing! Let's dance and eat cake!"

"Why did you do that?" Hyacinth demanded, fighting against the goblin guards who still held her. "Do you always treat your guests this way?"

The king turned to Hyacinth, his knife coated with Chloe's blood. His foul breath washed over her. "Your friend is a *liar*, did you know that?" He held up the bloody stone token he'd dug out of Chloe's skin. It was the size of a coin and carved with words. "She's a human who's been glamoured as a Fae for who knows how long. But no matter, no matter. Now the truth is revealed; she may dance with us always!"

Hyacinth's heart nearly stopped beating. Chloe was a human? She'd been hiding that from Hyacinth? Confusion chased by a sharp sting of betrayal overcame her. Hadn't they promised to tell the truth? Did that even matter now?

Hyacinth again tried to meet Chloe's gaze, but the stablehand had eyes only for the king.

"I'll kill you!" she shouted, struggling against her captors. "I'm going to put my sword through your heart!"

"You're not," the king said with an unhinged low chuckle that sounded like the bone chimes that rattled in the wind near Queen Mab's solarium. "*You're* going to help me live even longer." The king dropped his bloody knife and picked up the piece of cake he'd been eating. He walked back over to Chloe with the cake in his blood-covered hand. "Eat, human. The cook has put an extra helping of willow-winged whimsy into the batter. A bit of a spell for dreaming in there too." He leaned in and whispered loudly, "Everyone here loves it, and they keep coming back for more!"

Larissa whimpered slightly, her eyes on the cake. Hyacinth fought against her guards, trying to pull away. What was this madness?

"Don't let him feed you anything, Chloe!" Hyacinth called out.

At last, Chloe's gaze met Hyacinth's, but only for a moment. She looked frantic and sorry all at once. Before she could say anything, the Mountain King wrenched her lips open and shoved cake into her mouth with his disgusting fingers. Hyacinth shuddered, utterly repulsed and consumed by helplessness.

Chloe choked on the cake, sputtering while the Mountain King cackled.

Bramble and marsh, what was in the cake? How could Hyacinth possibly hope to get them out of here now? She could deal with her feelings about Chloe's lies later. For now, she had to stop this.

"Let us go!" she yelled. "Stop hurting her! My mother will give you anything you want!"

Hyacinth didn't know if that was true, but she had to try.

The king seemed to remember she was there all at once. "Oh yes, the High Fae princess," he said almost as an afterthought. "I have no interest in what your mother might offer me." He turned to his guards. "Throw her in the deepest dungeon until she is no more than dust. We have a dance to continue."

With that, he wrenched Chloe into a spin. Her eyes met Hyacinth's for one more moment, wide and wild, as the king shoved her onto the dance floor with the other humans.

"Chloe!" Hyacinth screamed.

Rough hands grabbed Hyacinth, pulling her away from the ballroom. She bucked and fought the guards as they forced her down three flights of stairs and along a hallway lit with flickering smoky torches. The Mountain King's dungeons smelled of death, fear, and rot. Iron doors were set into the walls at intervals, and she glimpsed a pile of bones through one of the doors—the blue-green wings over the skeleton still glowed faintly. Fear ran like ice through her blood. She was going to die here. All they'd find of her, if anyone found her, would be her bones and these wretched fake wings.

"Let me go! There's been a mistake!" she screamed, struggling to her feet.

"No mistake," the largest of the goblins said. "This is where we bring High Fae to die."

"And common Fae," his companion added. "Lots of them down here too."

"Aren't you common Fae?" Hyacinth cried out. "Why are you serving the Mountain King?"

The largest goblin stepped closer. "We're serving him because he lets us have a measure of starlight every month."

"And he killed our last king four centuries ago—"

The larger goblin elbowed the one who'd spoken. "She doesn't need to know that. Shut up!"

Hyacinth was consumed by fear, both of the violence the goblins would visit upon her and the thought of being locked in the cell. She had to get out of here. "Please!" she begged. "I have money! Or my family does! I can—"

"Save it," the larger goblin said, shoving her backward through an open cell door. She landed hard on the stone floor. "No one is coming to help you. Don't take your time dying. More of a hassle for us."

Then, with a cruel laugh, he slammed the door shut and turned the key. Darkness fell around Hyacinth.

A sob rose in her throat, and despair swept through her. She was sealed in a dungeon far below the mountain. No one knew she was here, she didn't know what was happening with Chloe, and she'd never be able to find her father. Hope abandoned Hyacinth.

She buried her head in her hands and wept.

Chapter Fourteen
Chloe

Chloe's thoughts spun. Her body and mind were dizzy like she'd been whirled around in a child's game of Spin the Kitten. What had been in that cake?

Fae food offered in malice is the most dangerous. . . . Wendell's warning whispered through her head.

"Eat more, eat more!" the king said. He wrenched Chloe's lips open again, shoving more cake past her teeth. She chomped down on his fingers, biting him. A foul taste filled her mouth, and she gagged. The king laughed. "Keep that up, ferocious human, and I'll take all your teeth. You don't need them for the Endless Ball!"

Horrified, Chloe released his fingers and swallowed the cake. Sweetness filled her mouth, even as she fought against the urge to spit it out. At least she still had her teeth. For now.

Even as she had the thought, a frothy lightness, bright and soft like a spring breeze, drifted through her head. It replaced her dark thoughts, chasing the cake's sweetness.

What a lovely treat.

Why would she spit the cake out? It was delicious. She wanted more. If she had more cake, she could forget the pain radiating from where the king had sliced open her arm and the spot where Maurelle had cut her face and even her sprained ankle. If she ate more cake, she could forget the hurt look on Hyacinth's face when the king had ripped away her glamour token and declared her secret. She could forget how far she was from home, forget every mistake she'd ever made.

What a pleasure that would be. Yes. More cake would be nice.

Chloe reached out and accepted the rest of the cake from the king. He grinned with rotten teeth.

What a generous king he was, sharing his cake with her. She was so happy they'd found his ballroom.

The lilting harp music got louder, and the dancers whirled around Chloe. Didn't they look charming and happy? Chloe wanted to dance. Her ankle didn't hurt so much anymore. She wanted to join them. She wanted more cake. Yes, she definitely wanted more cake and then to join in the dance.

No.

The clever, dangerous, razor-edged part of her mind that had kept its wits on a churning sea after the shipwreck, the part that had fought orphanage bullies, the part that had managed to help her stay alive and hidden in the Fae world for so long screamed at her.

No more cake! No dancing! You don't want those things.

Chloe glanced at the dancers again, this time seeing their exhausted faces and blistered feet.

She had to fight this. She had to think. Bramble and marsh, her head was fuzzy. Her internal battle raged.

You want more cake.

I do not *want more cake.*

The king's hand gripped hers, and he pulled her into the stream of dancers and spun her around. As they twirled, Chloe didn't feel her hurt ankle at all. Was her ankle hurt? That must've been a dream. Was that blood on her arm? Surely not—she was just dancing and dancing. Something in her snapped into place, like a clock's gears turning. Yes, this was right.

Weren't the lights all around her lovely?

Wasn't the dance elegant and dreamy?

Chloe would keep dancing always. It felt good to move in harmony with so many other happy souls. Her steps were buoyant; her head empty of everything except the music.

The Mountain King spun her again, and her gaze went upward, tracking the bobbing bits of light that floated up to the chandelier—the beautiful, lovely, glittering chandelier.

How perfect to be part of this dance. How lovely. How very—

Fight it, Brave One, Coffee said into her head. *You must fight it. You're hobbling through that dance on a hurt ankle, forced into it against your will. Remember who you are! Fight!*

Chloe's attention wrenched away from the dance and back to the cavernous ballroom. Pain flared up her ankle. That was Coffee's voice in her head.

Where was Coffee? From very far away, like she was watching a play in her own mind, she remembered the king shoving the tiny dragon into a cage. A gilded cage. Somewhere in the ballroom.

Where was it? As she twirled with the other dances, her ankle now throbbing with each step, Chloe glanced around, trying to find the tiny dragon.

He wasn't among the dancers. Nor by the door where they'd come in. Not with the guards.

There he was. He strained against the bars of a gilded birdcage beside the throne. Chloe's heart broke to see him trapped again, like he'd been in the redcap's stall.

She had to save him.

She would save him!

The king spun her again, and another set of hands found hers. In a blur of faces, music, and steps, she was passed from one dancer to the next.

What a lovely, lovely dance. Her feet swept over the ground, one stride following the next, her pain disappearing with the graceful movements of the Endless Ball.

Fight it! Coffee shouted in her head. *I need you! Hyacinth needs you!*

Where was Hyacinth? Chloe would like very much to dance with her. Was she here?

The guards took her to the deepest dungeon, Coffee said into her head. *You need to fight this dance. Don't get lost in it, Brave One.*

Yes! Chloe had to fight this dance, even though half of her wanted nothing more than to eat cake and spin endlessly with the others.

No. She couldn't do that. If she did that, she'd never be able to help Hyacinth. She'd never free Coffee. She'd never find a way home.

"You're thinking about your friend," the Mountain King said, taking Chloe's hand again and leering at her with broken teeth. "I can tell. She's a High Fae, you know. She won't want to see you again now that she knows you're a human."

Was that true?

Maybe it was and Chloe should keep dancing. If she did that, then she wouldn't be lying to anyone or disappointing them. She wouldn't have to worry about her sister.

No.

Yes.

Fight him!

Chloe tried to wrench her hand away from the Mountain King, but he grabbed her even more tightly.

"Bring me my goblet!" the Mountain King shouted to his guards. One of them rushed forward with a cup filled to the brim with silvery substance.

Chloe knew what that was, didn't she?

Her head spun like the dancers all around her as she tried to place it.

The king drank deeply.

"What is that, Your Majesty?" Chloe asked through the cloud in her mind.

He raised his glass to her. "Starlight, of course. Fresh. I'm sure yours will taste delicious as well."

Chloe's feet stopped moving. Dancers collided with her, and her mind cleared as the king's words scythed through the fog from the enchanted cake.

Starlight.

It all came back to her in a rush along with the pain from her injuries.

Chloe had known it was starlight in the chandelier the minute Larissa had led them into the ballroom. She'd hoped to never see that awful silver-blue glow again, but here it was, pulsing above her.

The Mountain King was harvesting starlight from the humans in the Endless Ball. This was worse than the human queen who'd trapped Chloe and Anya, and his treachery was on a scale that made Chloe's skin crawl. How old was the Mountain King? How long had the Endless Ball been going on? How many humans had given up their starlight to the king?

Chloe knew more about magic and humans than she'd told anyone since getting stuck in the Fae world. She knew humans had starlight in their bones. She knew this could be harvested by moonshadow snakes and crafted into starlight lace. She knew how it felt to have her bones stripped of their essential starlight. But she didn't know exactly how the Mountain King was extracting it from the humans on the dance floor. Was it something in the movements? In the food? Something else? Could she free them or herself?

The king finished his goblet of starlight and dragged Chloe back into the dance again, sweeping all thoughts from her head. "Dance, dance, little human!" he said. "You're so young, you'll be able to give me years of your life."

Fight it.

Step, twirl, flow with the others.

Fight it.

If she was swept up into the Endless Ball, she might forget herself totally. The king would take her starlight, and she'd die.

"Anya," she muttered. "Hyacinth. Coffee." She said the names, but their faces swam in her memory.

The king twirled her again. Other people surged around her, dizzying in their number. Their hands reached out for a dance, and they pulled at her clothing and body.

Fight this.

There was only one way to do so that Chloe knew of.

Slowly, like she was moving against a great current, Chloe's hand went to her sword. She wouldn't get trapped in this never-ending dance. She would fight. With effort, she drew her sword, holding it up. "You won't make me part of your interminable ball! You won't take my starlight!"

The king cackled in delight. "Spirited, this one! I like that! Let's do something different. Clear the way, everyone! A fight's as good as a dance!"

The dancers made a wide circle, and the music stopped, replaced by drumbeats.

"Bring her some armor too!" the king called out.

What had Chloe gotten herself into?

Two goblins came forward, flinging some chainmail and pauldrons to the ground. Chloe didn't want armor. She wanted to get out of here. She wanted to keep dancing. No, she didn't. She wanted to free Coffee and Hyacinth. She wanted to fight, but not like this! She wanted to fight her way out of here.

Bramble and marsh, why was her head so muddled?

"Put the armor on!" the king said. "Let's have some entertainment!"

She would not be entertainment!

Only once had Chloe fought for entertainment, when she was fifteen and Anya was sick and needed medicine that the orphanage hadn't been willing to provide. Desperate for money, Chloe took her anger to the fighting pits. She'd been beaten bloody, but she'd won. Barely.

That was one reason why she'd started taking sword lessons, though: so she had a blade between herself and her opponent.

She wasn't sure how much good that would do her now with her injuries and the enchanted cake still in her body.

One of the goblins forced the chainmail shirt over Chloe's head, wrenching her out of her memories. The other strapped on a breastplate and pauldrons. She clanked a bit when she walked, but at least she was more protected.

If only her head were clearer, her ankle steadier. No matter. She would fight. She would win.

The tusked goblin guard stepped into the ring.

"Time to dance, human," the goblin growled. "The king wants your starlight, and once you're dead, I'll take that blade of yours."

He would not. Chloe dropped into the stance Wendell had taught her. If she was going to die here, she would go down fighting.

Chapter Fifteen
Hyacinth

"You'll never escape if you sit here crying," Hyacinth muttered, wiping her eyes and taking a long shuddering breath. She looked around the narrow cell and touched the potions at her hip for comfort.

Flickering torchlight seeped in from the grate in the cell door, casting shadows on the stone walls around her. Fetid shallow puddles covered the floor. The air smelled like mildew, and a dripping noise *plinked* somewhere nearby. Far above where she sat, a wide hole in the ceiling let in the barest hints of moonlight. It was hundreds of feet up, though, and the rock walls here were smooth, probably from many hands who'd tried to climb them before.

What cruelty to put a way out in view, but make it impossible to reach. If only her wings really worked.

Hyacinth gazed up at the nearly full moon shining in the sky. Was it nighttime already? It'd been morning when they fled the Wild

Root Inn, no more than noon when they'd fallen into the Mountain King's trapdoor. How long had it taken them to walk to the ballroom? Did time somehow work differently below the mountain, or had they been watching the dance much longer than it seemed?

Hyacinth didn't know. There was so much she didn't know! Where were Chloe and Coffee? Were they alright? What was the Mountain King planning for them?

One question nearly strangled her: Why had Chloe lied about being human?

Wouldn't you lie about being human too if you were one?

Hyacinth had never given being human much thought. She'd seen humans in the Moonshadow Kingdom, of course. She'd glanced a few at the Solstice Market in Keldale and a few in Mushroom Town last night. Sometimes, High Fae nobles brought them before her mother for punishment, and she supposed some of them worked in the palace or the stables, but she'd never paid them any mind.

Why hadn't she paid them more mind?

Because she'd never had a reason to. At least not until those two human girls, Esme and Sybil, came through a door into this world a few months ago. They were the first humans Hyacinth had been around for more than a moment.

Well, that wasn't entirely true, was it? Chloe was a human, and Hyacinth had spent so much time near her. She'd even kissed her.

She'd kissed a human! What would her mother or half sisters say about that?

She wasn't sure she cared.

But why had Chloe hidden her secret for so long? Who were her parents? Where was her sister? Had she come through a door like

Esme and Sybil, or had she been born here like some of the other humans in this world?

It didn't matter, did it? Being a human in the Fae world was always dangerous, no matter how you got here.

A pang of sympathy went through Hyacinth. What had Chloe endured throughout her life? A vision of the many humans twirling in the Endless Ball upstairs followed the thought. Those humans were miserable, drained of some vital force by the Mountain King, and they were clearly in trouble. If Hyacinth thought about it, she could come up with hundreds of other times she'd seen humans beaten, tormented, or just generally run-down in her life, not that she'd done anything about it.

Why hadn't she done something about it?

Hyacinth surged to her feet as her thoughts churned. She paced her cell.

She would've hidden too if she'd been human. A glamour token was the least she would've done. She wouldn't have told anyone—not even her friends, for all the trouble it would bring.

Now Chloe was in even worse trouble. Could Hyacinth help her?

She had to try, at least. Hyacinth turned to the cell door and rattled the handle. It didn't budge. She shoved her shoulder against the door, irrationally hoping to break it open, which only made pain spike up her arm.

Think! What do you have to open this door?

Juniper heart for illusion. A moon-drenched secret for levitation. Bitterroot berry for healing—well, no, phoenix balm really. Dragonheart ashes for fire and ruin.

Could she use the moon-drenched secret for levitation? She glanced upward again. The hole in the cell's ceiling seemed wide enough for her to squeeze through, but if she did that, how would she get back to Chloe?

All at once, a sharp stinging shot up the back of her neck. It felt like she was being pinched by a dozen tiny hands all at once.

"Bramble and marsh!" she swore, spinning around.

Something pulled at her hair.

"Who's there?" Hyacinth swatted at her neck. Something tumbled to the ground.

"Hey! What did you do that for?" A shrill voice shouted up at Hyacinth. She peered down to where a fairy no bigger than Hyacinth's pinkie stood at her feet. The creature wore a plum-colored dress, and her midnight-blue skin was speckled with stars. Gossamer dragonfly wings stood out from her back.

"Who are you?" Hyacinth squatted down to see her better.

"Hellebore!" said the little fairy. "I'm a—"

"A Nightpine fairy," Hyacinth interrupted, remembering her lessons about the many creatures in her mother's kingdom. Nightpine fairies were tree spirits of sorts, inhabiting the tallest, most ancient pines. "I've read about you, but never met any before! What are you doing down here?"

Hellebore scowled. "We were *tricked* into entering the Mountain King's domain, and then we got locked in a cell. My whole family has been here for weeks!"

"Why haven't you flown away?" Hyacinth asked, looking from the fairy's wings to the hole in the ceiling.

"Why haven't you flown away?" Hellebore mocked, nodding at the wings on Hyacinth's back. "Don't you think we've tried that? The whole place is ensorcelled! No innate Fae magic can work down here, under the mountain. We can't fly out of here. That's the meanness of this cell!"

"But I saw the Mountain King doing some kind of magic up there."

"Nasty, vicious magic," Hellebore spat out. "He's pulling starlight from those humans' bones and then drinking it to stay alive."

Hyacinth's mouth fell open. "What do you mean? How do you know that?"

"Well, I wasn't born just this morning!" Hellebore glared at Hyacinth. "Don't you know anything about the Mountain King? Are you one of those Fae working for him?"

"No! My friend and I fell into the mountain through a trapdoor. What's he doing up there? Why has he locked me away and kept her up there? She's a human, but—"

Hellebore hissed. "Not a bit of good luck for her, that's for certain."

"Can you tell me more about him?"

Hellebore shrugged. "Not much to tell, really. He was a bad man, but a clever one who got trapped in the Fae world. He talked his way under the mountain, where an ancient High Fae king ruled a kingdom of humans, trapped in the Endless Ball. He bargained with the king that if he could do three impossible tasks, he could ask for anything. The king agreed, and somehow the man managed to do them."

"What were the tasks?"

Hellebore shrugged. "Who can remember? This was more than five hundred years ago."

Hyacinth's mouth fell open again. The High Fae had long lives—her still-youthful mother was nearly eighty—but she'd never heard of a human living for centuries. "But I've seen him! He looks like a middle-aged man, not one who's hundreds of years old."

"That's the magic," Hellebore said. "Somehow, he did the impossible tasks, and then he asked for the king's throne and kingdom. The High Fae had to honor his bargain, and the human man killed him and took over the Endless Ball. He's been harvesting starlight from humans ever since. It's a potent magic, which is why the goblins serve him. They can't stay away from it."

Hyacinth's mind whirled with this new information. "But he was eating cake? Where does he get that?"

Hellebore scowled. "The ancient king's kitchens still produce the enchanted foods he used to trap humans here so long ago. Now any human who finds their way under the mountain is fed cake and made to dance. The cake keeps them compliant and addicted, always wanting more. Something in the magic of the dance strips them of their starlight until they're nothing more than bones. Any Fae who fall into the Mountain King's realm are given the choice to serve him or rot in these cells until they die."

Horror filled Hyacinth. All those people up there were literally dancing their lives away. Chloe was up there too, thrust into the dance!

"Can we help them?" Hyacinth asked.

Hellebore shook her head. "We can't even help ourselves. All our innate magic is useless, so we can't fly or enchant ourselves out of here."

An idea was forming in Hyacinth's mind. She might not have innate magic, but she had her potions.

"Does *all* magic not work down here or only innate magic?"

"If you had a magical item, it would work," Hellebore said. "The king needed that loophole in the enchantment so he could keep his harvesting chandelier and his other creature comforts working. But the guards are always careful to check anyone who falls through for magical items."

Except they hadn't been. In all the commotion, they'd failed to take her potion belt.

"I have a levitation potion." She pulled it from her belt. "We can try it."

Hellebore's eyes widened. "You have a levitation potion! Brilliant!" She whistled, and the walls seemed to come alive with other Nightpine fairies.

Hyacinth looked around the cell. "How many of you are there?"

"Barely two dozen anymore," Hellebore replied desolately. "If you help us out of here, we'll grant you one wish."

"Can you do that?" Hyacinth asked, her voice eager.

"'Course we can!"

A loud clattering from somewhere outside the cell made Hyacinth jump. It sounded like someone walking toward their cell. Probably the guards, coming back to confiscate the items they'd left her with.

"I'll take you," she said hastily. "Let's get going before the guards get back."

The Nightpine fairies, of whom there were actually at least six dozen, clambered onto her shoulders, her skirts, and along her wings. She plucked the levitation potion from her belt and tipped it into her mouth. It hit her belly with an effervescent sensation, and then, all at once, she felt lighter. She floated a foot off the ground, then shot toward the hole in the ceiling like an arrow loosed.

Bramble and marsh, she hadn't thought this through. What if the hole in the ceiling was too small for her? What if she went through it and the levitation spell worked too well and she floated into the night sky, never to be seen again?

The ceiling approached at an alarming rate. Far below them, the cell door clanged open, and the goblin guards shoved in. "Hey! Get back here!" one of them yelled.

It was too late. Hyacinth was already popping like a cork out of the hole in the ceiling. As soon as she hit the night air, she kept rising, but many tiny hands grabbed her, holding her in place.

Hellebore called out a charm, and suddenly, weight returned to Hyacinth's body. Her feet hit the ground, and she tumbled forward, landing on her stomach at the base of an enormous pine tree. Beyond the tree, other mountains rolled in the distance, like the spine of a great beast.

Thank the Sisters. Hyacinth hugged the tree roots.

"You did it, you enormous winged girl!" Hellebore shouted. She planted a kiss on the end of Hyacinth's nose. "Now, what is your wish? Want a magical chariot to race across the sky? A bed made of pine sap that will preserve your rest for a century? You name it, we Nightpines will give it to you."

Hyacinth sat up, breathing in the night air. It was so good to be out from under the mountain. Too bad she had to go back in immediately. "I wish for your help in freeing my friend who's stuck at the Endless Ball."

Hellebore groaned beside her. "Are you sure?"

Hyacinth wasn't, but she couldn't leave Chloe there. She nodded.

"Follow me," Hellebore said with a pained sigh. "I'll help you find your friend."

Hyacinth didn't like the sound of that sigh, but she stood up and followed Hellebore, who fluttered in front of her.

✦

Hyacinth shivered as she looked up.

A rock wall rose in front of her and Hellebore, towering hundreds of feet in the air. They were midway up the mountain. Thick mist coiled at their feet, and ravens cawed at them from the tops of pine trees farther up the slope. The peak stretched around them in every direction, vast and impassable. A green wooden door was set inside the rock, painted with moonlight.

Here goes nothing, Hyacinth thought, wanting nothing more than to hide or find a carriage back to her comfortable bedroom. Instead, she pulled on the handle, and the door swung open. A long torchlit cavern stretched in front of them.

"This leads to the ballroom," Hellebore said. "Many humans and Fae find it, open it, and are lured into the Endless Ball. Are you sure about wanting to go back?"

Hyacinth really, really wasn't, but she had to go forward. For Chloe. For Coffee. For herself. Who would she be if she just let her friends perish under the mountain?

Not someone she'd like very much.

"I'm sure. We'll use my compass to get to the ballroom." She pulled her enchanted compass out. The last thing she needed was to get lost in the vast tunnels and never find Chloe—or their way out—again. Hyacinth leaned over the compass and whispered the words to activate it: "Wayward finds a way. Wayward finds a path. Spin you needle, and show me the route to Chloe. Please and thank you."

The compass needle spun before pointing to the left. Hyacinth stepped through the door, and, as it had when they'd fallen into the trapdoor, a bell rang three times, letting someone know that they'd crossed into the Mountain King's realm. Who would be coming to get them? Larissa again? Hyacinth didn't want to get caught by her. A plan was forming in her mind, and she needed the element of surprise to make it work. The needle on the compass swung around and then pointed right.

"This way," she said, turning down a tunnel in that direction.

She ran with Hellebore clinging to her shoulder, as the tunnels turned left and right and left again. At each fork, she paused to mark a long arrow on the wall with her enchanted ink pen. "Mark the way out of here, and stay for always," she whispered.

The pen marks glittered bright blue on the wall, showing the path to escape the mountain. At one point, Hyacinth ducked into a shadowy alcove as Larissa hurried past, muttering to herself, "The westerly door! Must get guests for the king. He'll be happy, happy. I know he will."

A pang of sympathy went through Hyacinth as Larissa passed—how long had she been under the mountain? Was there any way to help her as well?

Maybe. If Hyacinth's plan worked, she might help all the trapped humans. Though it was a big if and relied on many things outside Hyacinth's control. Still, she had to try.

Even running, it took too long to get back. Hyacinth gasped for air as she and Hellebore stopped in an alcove about a hundred feet from the ballroom. The goblins guarding the door were facing the dancers, not the tunnels. The music had stopped, and loud cheering and grunting filled the air.

Hyacinth pulled the bottle of juniper heart from her belt and held it out to Hellebore. "This is a plan in three parts," she whispered to the fairy. "I'll take the illusion potion and go get Chloe. You take the levitation potion and get the tiny dragon. He's locked in a cage by the throne," Hyacinth said. "Then, once you have him, take this other potion, and use it to destroy the chandelier."

Hyacinth handed Hellebore the two bottles, which were nearly as big as she was.

"What's in this one?" she asked, nodding at the shimmering orange potion.

"Dragonheart ashes for fire and ruin. We're going to finally break up the Endless Ball."

Hellebore grinned her understanding. "I like it. Meet you back at the mountain door."

"Good luck."

Hellebore winked at her and hurried into the ballroom, darting through the goblin guards' legs with the potion bottles under her arms. She skirted the edges of the crowd, and when she got to the king's throne, she waved to Hyacinth.

It was time.

Hyacinth drank the illusion potion in one gulp. "Make me into a goblin guard," she asked the magic. "A very large, mean-looking one."

An illusion shimmered in the air. Hyacinth couldn't see it, but she felt heftier somehow, taller and stronger.

"Let me through," she said, her voice booming across the arena.

Bramble and marsh, she must've taken too much. Everyone in the ballroom—except for Hellebore, who was working at the lock on Coffee's cage—turned to her.

Hyacinth glimpsed the dancers in a ring, still shuffling their feet, as they kept up the endless dance. They surrounded the Mountain King and Chloe.

Oh Chloe. Hyacinth's heart ached to see her.

The stablehand wore makeshift armor and gripped her sword with one hand. Blood covered her arm, and a purple bruise bloomed across her cheek. The enormous tusk-faced goblin they'd seen earlier stood across from Chloe, his knuckles painted with her blood.

"Who are you?" the Mountain King said in surprise, turning toward Hyacinth.

"New guard," Hyacinth said. "Here to help you manage these . . . erm . . . humans."

The king's face lit up. "You're a big one too, very good! Come over here by me. This human fighter's about to die. You can finish her!"

Hyacinth's stomach flipped as she strode toward Chloe, putting as much goblin shamble into the walk as she could.

Chloe cast Hyacinth an exhausted look, clearly not recognizing her through the illusion. She looked so beaten and broken, Hyacinth wanted to give her a hug. But there was no time because Chloe let loose a loud cry and charged forward, her sword pointed at Hyacinth's chest.

Chapter Sixteen
Chloe

Chloe swore under her breath. This new goblin fighter was a monster. Twice as tall and three times as wide as the one she'd been fighting.

Where had he come from? Had he been waiting in the wings of the ballroom? Or was he just some goblin who'd found his way into the tunnels and the Mountain King was going to let him fight her?

None of it mattered, she supposed. Now that he was here, she had to deal with him. Everything in her hurt, from her wounds to her struggle to remember Hyacinth and Coffee, but she had to fight her way out of here. Drawing in a deep breath and clearing her head as much as the enchanted cake would allow, she charged the fighter.

He . . . darted out of the way?

What in the world?

She lunged forward with her sword, and the goblin stepped aside again. Chloe's sprained ankle gave out from her momentum, and she fell to the ground, landing on her belly.

The goblin was on her in a moment. He grabbed her around the back and lifted her upward. His enormous, hairy, muscled arm wrapped around her chest, pulling her close. Chloe fought against the monstrous goblin, but to no avail. All around her, the other goblins and the Mountain King cheered for her death.

Chloe lifted her sword, swinging it as widely as she could while being held by the goblin.

"*Stop* trying to kill me!" A familiar voice hissed into Chloe's ear.

"Hyacinth?" Chloe muttered, looking around. Where was she? Was Chloe hearing things now? Was that a side effect of the enchanted cake too?

"It's me!" Hyacinth said. "*I'm* the goblin you're fighting. It's an illusion spell." The goblin spun her around so they were face-to-face.

An illusion spell? Chloe strained to see any part of the High Fae princess in the warty, reeking goblin. Her sword was still pointed at the goblin's belly, though she wasn't entirely sure it would go through the muscled surface.

"Kill the human fighter!" the Mountain King bellowed to the goblin. "What's wrong with you?"

The goblin held up his hands, as if in surrender, and took a step back. Chloe's mind raced. Was that really Hyacinth?

"Tell me something only Hyacinth would know!" she demanded.

The goblin grinned, showing Chloe a mouthful of stumpy black teeth. "I kissed summer wine off your lips in Queen Mab's garden in the early hours of the solstice a few days ago."

Heat rushed into Chloe's cheeks. Bramble and marsh, that *was* Hyacinth.

"I believe you," Chloe croaked.

"Pretend to fight me," Hyacinth said. "Strike out with your sword."

Chloe did as she was told, getting near enough that Hyacinth could grab her and pull her close again as if she were choking her. Chloe fake-strained against Hyacinth's grip.

"How did you get out of the dungeons? What's your plan for getting us out of here?" Chloe murmured.

"Look by the throne," not-goblin Hyacinth said.

Chloe glanced that way just in time to see the door of Coffee's cage swing open. A tiny fairy poured a bit of potion into his mouth, and then she climbed onto his back. She held another potion bottle. Coffee rose all at once, flapping his wings like a bird learning to fly.

"What are they doing?" Chloe watched them bob and weave toward a stalagmite column.

"It's a levitation potion and then dragonheart ashes for wrath and ruin," Hyacinth said, as she lightly shoved Chloe. Chloe stumbled away in an exaggerated manner, feeling every step in her hurt ankle.

"Finish her!" the Mountain King roared. "You're a brute, end it!"

Chloe backed up a step as one of the other goblin fighters thrust a sword into Hyacinth's hands. If it weren't so dangerous and they weren't fake fighting under the mountain, Chloe might have laughed. The not-goblin who was Hyacinth blinked down at the sword. It looked like a matchstick compared to the illusion of her bulk. She gave it a tentative swing, making it look more like a tennis racquet than a weapon.

Chloe raised her own sword and lunged in close so she could talk to Hyacinth. "Why a levitation potion and dragonheart ashes?"

Every word was punctuated with a sword thrust or a step away as they fake fought for the Mountain King's entertainment. He roared his approval.

"Innate magic doesn't work here. And I wasn't sure if Coffee could carry the potions and the fairy without the levitation potion," Hyacinth said, as she stepped in close again to stab with her own sword.

The blow glanced off Chloe's armor, but just barely. Chloe wasn't as fast as usual with her injuries and the enchanted cake in her system. If she wasn't careful, Hyacinth might accidentally stab her while trying to save her.

"Why does it matter if innate magic doesn't work here?" Chloe said as loudly as she dared while she ducked one of Hyacinth's blows. What she didn't say was *You don't have any innate magic, and neither do I, so what are you planning?*

Hyacinth seemed to hear the unspoken question, and she glanced up at the chandelier. Even through Chloe's brain fog and the ache of her injuries, Hyacinth's plan became clear. Chloe watched Coffee and the little fairy hover around the chandelier, dipping and weaving as the fairy dripped dragonheart ashes along its arms. They were so far up and the chandelier was so vast, Coffee looked like a hummingbird darting around a mighty oak.

Something didn't make sense, though.

The goblin who was Hyacinth knocked Chloe's sword away. She stepped closer, gripping Chloe's arm. "If this dragonheart potion works, we should have about—"

Chloe didn't hear how long they'd have to see if the potion worked because at that moment, the chandelier above them exploded.

Absolute chaos descended upon the Mountain King's ballroom. Crystal globes shattered, and trapped starlight whizzed out of them like water rushing from a dam. The starlight flew around the ballroom, wriggling like eels in a too-small pot. Shards of glass rained down. Plumes of green smoke rose from the skeleton of the chandelier. The enchanted humans screamed and ran in every direction. The Mountain King screeched for his own guards and also leaped up, grabbing at wisps of starlight. Chloe saw Hyacinth reach out toward him and snatch the enchanted glasses from around his neck. Then Chloe's attention was drawn upward.

"Coffee!" Chloe yelled, looking through the falling glass for the tiny dragon.

"This way!" the tiny fairy riding Coffee shouted, directing them toward a tunnel entrance nearby.

"Come on," the goblin who was Hyacinth said. "We've got to get out of here."

Chloe bent down and grabbed her sword before following Hyacinth and Coffee through the heaving crowd.

The goblin guards pushed at the human dancers who surged around them. Some of them caught flickers of starlight and wrapped it around themselves. Others gobbled it up. Others just stood there, cuts from the falling glass bleeding down their faces and arms.

"Who did this? Get back here, all of you! The Endless Ball isn't over!" the Mountain King shouted.

Chloe glanced over her shoulder, and her eyes widened. The humans who'd been trapped in the Endless Ball seemed to grow in strength. They turned as a unit and faced the Mountain King.

"What are you doing?" he called as they surrounded him. "Leave me alone! I'm your king!"

Before they could tear him to pieces, the king screamed and sunk to the ground. His spine seemed to collapse in on itself, and he screamed again.

"All his years are catching up to him!" the tiny fairy on Coffee's back explained. "Without the starlight magic feeding him, he will become his true age."

Chloe watched with grotesque fascination as the king's skin puckered around his bones. In seconds, it dropped from him in long sheets, exposing his muscles and the viscera underneath them. Soon, he was only bones, and then dust.

The humans who'd been trapped in the Endless Ball seemed stunned for a moment as their tormentor disappeared before their eyes. Then they pushed forward, pulling down the throne of bones.

"Come on, let's go before those goblin guards decide to hunt us or the tunnels collapse," Hyacinth said, tugging Chloe's arm. "This illusion spell will be gone soon."

It was already fading; Chloe could see Hyacinth's outline more clearly now. Hyacinth slung an arm under Chloe's shoulder, and together they hurried through the tunnels, following the inked arrows Hyacinth explained she'd left and letting Coffee and the tiny fairy fly in front of them. Chloe had never been so tired, but immense gratitude for Hyacinth—who'd come back for her!— overwhelmed her. She looked over at the princess, who still had the glimmer of the goblin brute on her and who was sweating and biting her lip as they navigated the tunnels. She'd never looked so lovely before in all the time Chloe had known her.

Chapter Seventeen
Hyacinth

Hyacinth and Chloe stumbled free from the door in the mountain and landed in the soft grass of an alpine meadow. Above them majestic pines swayed in the breeze, and stars studded the night sky. For a long moment, Hyacinth lay beside Chloe. Relief flooded her body. The metal of Chloe's armor bit into Hyacinth's shoulder as both of them heaved in breaths. A giddy laugh broke free from Hyacinth, wild as the night air around them.

"I can't believe that worked," she said, utterly overwhelmed by how unlikely it had all been. "I can't believe it actually worked."

She couldn't keep the note of triumph from her voice, and she turned to Chloe. "Are you alright?" Concern for Chloe quickly replaced Hyacinth's euphoria. Yes, her plan had worked, but was it too late? How much cake had Chloe eaten? How injured was she?

"You saved me," Chloe said, her voice full of dazed wonder. She turned toward Hyacinth with a lopsided smile on her face. "You didn't leave me, Princess."

A great lump rose in Hyacinth's throat, followed by a choked-out sob. "I would *never* leave you there. Though, once again, I'd like to say how sorry I am for getting us into this mess."

"You don't have anything to be sorry for. I'm sorry for lying about who I am." Chloe leaned closer, and one of her hands cupped Hyacinth's cheek.

A spark lit within Hyacinth at the touch. It would be so incredibly easy to inch forward and kiss Chloe. Everything in Hyacinth screamed at her to do that; everything in her told her Chloe would like that too. But she was so tired, and they'd been through so much already.

"I'll try to be less sorry," she muttered, wrenching her eyes away from Chloe. "Do you see Hellebore—she's the Nightpine fairy who helped me—or Coffee anywhere?"

This question broke the moment between them, and Hyacinth sat up.

Chloe followed, clutching her wounded arm and looking around. "I don't see them. Coffee's over there—"

The tiny dragon ran to Chloe, who scooped him up with a happy exclamation.

"I'm right here!" Hellebore called out. It was coming from the tree above their heads. "And so are all my friends you saved! We've come to celebrate with you!"

Hyacinth looked into the shadowy boughs of the pine tree, where dozens of tiny Nightpine fairies had alighted. Some of them were sprawled on branches, others flitted about, some just hugged the tree happily.

"Thank you for destroying that vile chandelier," Chloe said to Hellebore. She stood up, adjusting her sword and the armor she'd taken from the Mountain King's arena, and offered the Nightpine fairy a bow.

In the moonlight, Chloe looked like a magical knight, ferocious and beautiful. Something in Hyacinth's belly tightened as she took Chloe in.

"Thank your friend for getting us out of that hole!" Hellebore spat in the direction of the Mountain King's door.

"What will happen to the humans down there?" Hyacinth asked.

Hellebore shrugged. "Hopefully they'll find their way out. The goblins might keep them there, but now that the Mountain King's spell is broken, I suspect many goblins will die. They've been drinking his foul magic for a long time too, and when it goes away, their natural age will claim them."

Hyacinth hoped that's what would happen. She hated to think of leaving all those other humans under the mountain. Perhaps they'd find their way out using the arrows she'd marked on the wall.

"Should we go back for them?" she asked Chloe.

To go under the mountain a third time might break her, but it felt like the right thing to do.

Chloe shook her head. "I can't go anywhere tonight. I need to rest." She turned to Hellebore. "Is this safe? Will the goblins find us here?"

Hellebore smiled. "We'll create a circle of protection around you, so even if they come looking, they won't discover you."

"Can you heal my friend?" Hyacinth asked, looking at Chloe's bloody face, arm, and swollen ankle.

Hellebore looked pained. "Healing isn't one of our magics, unfortunately. She needs human medicine, I think. Take her to the witch in the Hyacinth Cottage at the edge of the swamp."

The words rang familiar in Hyacinth's head. She'd seen that place on her father's map. She dug in her belt pouch for her book.

"Is this witch friendly?" Chloe asked, suspicion lacing her voice.

Hyacinth wondered the same thing. Perhaps her father had mentioned that in his notes? Worth a look.

Hellebore shrugged. "I don't know her disposition. Just know she's the one to see about injuries of the body and spirit if you're a human. Now rest. We'll celebrate midsummer and make a ring of protection for you. You may eat with us."

Chloe shook her head violently. "No more Fae food. I had enough of that cake."

Hyacinth desperately wished she had something, anything, that she could give Chloe to eat that was wholesome and healing. The rolls she'd taken from the Wild Root Inn had fallen from her pocket somewhere between the dungeons and the tunnels.

"No, no," Hellebore said gently. "We offer Fae food, yes, but freely given in friendship and with the intention to strengthen and protect you. Now, please, rest. The feast will start soon."

"I think it will be okay," Hyacinth said to Chloe, squeezing her hand reassuringly. "They've been very good to me so far, and they helped me find you."

Chloe blew out a breath. "I hope you're right, but I'm not sure who to trust right now, and I'm too tired to fight any more."

The cloud of Nightpine fairies flitted about Chloe and Hyacinth, conjuring a ring of glowing orbs out of nowhere. There was a swooping noise, and troops of other fairies poured from the trees surrounding the pine.

"Are you sure this will keep us safe?" Hyacinth called out.

"Absolutely," Hellebore said. "Our magic is strongest at this time of summer, and when we're all together like this, nothing can hurt you within the circle."

She flitted around them, swirling until she stopped suddenly in front Hyacinth to greet a palm-sized fairy in a yellow dress with glittering wings.

"Solvia? Is that you?" Hellebore sounded delighted.

The fairy in the yellow dress turned and gasped loudly. "Hellebore! Where have you been?"

They embraced, tears streaming down their tiny faces.

"It's a terrible story," Hellebore said. "We were on a rescue mission to help those poor souls in the Mountain King's ballroom, but he trapped us until the tall winged one saved us."

The other fairies welcomed the lost Nightpine fairy clan enthusiastically, spinning them around, calling greetings, and dancing. They also cheered as Hyacinth and Chloe were introduced. Soon, they had placed more golden lanterns around the circle.

The fairies flitted around Chloe, encouraging her to place her sword in a nook in the tree and remove the armor as well. Much to Hyacinth's surprise, she did. A smile tugged at Chloe's lips.

"Look at Coffee!" Chloe called, pulling Hyacinth's attention out of her own thoughts.

Hyacinth's gaze dropped to Chloe's shirt pocket, where Coffee peeked out, watching all the fairies in the ring warily. There were so many of them, it made Hyacinth's head spin. They moved about in a flutter. Some set platters made from acorn caps on a rock in the center of the ring. Others brought berries, mushrooms, baked goods, and other plants. Hellebore and the fairy in the yellow dress darted up to bop Coffee on the nose. He squeaked in outrage and then dove back into Chloe's shirt pocket.

One of the fairies offered a goblet made from a tulip to Hyacinth. Raspberry-colored wine glittered inside, smelling fresh and lovely. Another fairy held out a plate of strawberries.

Hyacinth's stomach grumbled. It had been so long since they'd eaten last night at the Wild Root Inn. She took the goblet and downed the wine before popping two berries into her mouth. Lively fiddle music started up, and some of the fairies danced at one side of the ring. Even Coffee now wore a flower crown, and he swayed to the music.

Hyacinth turned to offer Chloe some of the berries, but she paused with the plate outstretched. Chloe leaned against the tree's trunk, her eyelids drooping.

Hyacinth wanted to talk to Chloe about being human. But she also knew the stablehand needed her sleep.

Hyacinth popped a few more berries in her mouth and then leaned back against the tree as well. Eventually, Coffee crawled into Chloe's arms, and all around them, the fairies reveled in their midsummer celebration.

It was like a dream itself, and a sense of cozy warmth and safety flooded through Hyacinth. There was clearly deep magic here, and for the first time in days, Hyacinth drifted off to sleep, happy, content, and feeling safe at last.

CHAPTER EIGHTEEN
Chloe

When Chloe woke up, it was all gone. The fairy ring, the glowing lights, the dancing Nightpine fairies, the music, and the food. It was early morning, and ribbons of orange and pink light filled the eastern sky. Hyacinth and Coffee were curled among the roots of a tree, still sleeping.

Where were they? With her cuts and her sprained ankle still throbbing, Chloe extricated herself from Hyacinth's arms and took in their surroundings.

Although her head was still fuzzy from the Endless Ball and her deep sleep in the fairy ring afterward, she knew they weren't under the mountain pines from before. Somehow, they were in a vast forest at the edge of a swamp. Red maples and yellow birches stretched around them in every direction. Small islands—really lumpy hillocks of wet ground and swamp grasses—dotted the landscape beyond the trees. Dense gray fog hung over the water, and from a nearby tree, a crow cried menacingly. Footprints lined the swamp's muddy shore, but Chloe didn't see anyone besides them.

A small note was tucked under a rock beside Coffee's head.

> *We wanted to leave you closer to the witch's cottage. Good luck and thanks again. You'll always have a friend in the Nightpines.*
>
> *-Hellebore*

Wow. That was powerful magic to move them many miles to the swamp. Chloe was immensely grateful she wouldn't have to traverse those miles on her injured ankle, though she still felt deeply unsettled from what had happened in the Mountain King's ballroom.

She had been so very close to losing herself. To having her starlight sucked away and her years given to the Mountain King. She could've died there, and her sister never would've known what had happened to her. She would've died there, were it not for Hyacinth.

Chloe glanced over at the princess, who snored softly with her head pillowed on her arms. Warmth bloomed in Chloe's chest as she watched Hyacinth's breath rise and fall, sending one of her curls floating. It was more than fondness. More than the spark of attraction she'd felt when they'd kissed in the garden. A deep admiration for Hyacinth rolled through Chloe.

Hyacinth had *saved* her.

Usually it was Chloe who did the saving, but Hyacinth had escaped a dungeon and then braved the mountain to rescue Chloe.

She might have been an unmagical High Fae princess, but she was also brave and kind. There was so much more to her than Chloe could've expected.

Bramble and marsh, it would hurt so much to leave Hyacinth behind when Chloe finally found a door home. Even now, just imagining it sent a stab of regret through her belly.

You can't regret what hasn't happened yet.

Maybe not, but she could admit that she was torn about the prospect of leaving.

Should she tell Hyacinth now about her quest for a portal home? If they were being honest with each other, she should tell Hyacinth everything. But what good would that do if there was no door waiting for Chloe? Wouldn't that just cause more strain between them? Besides, they had so much to sort through, telling Hyacinth about the portal and Chloe's plan to leave would only distract them.

Chloe's stomach growled, reminding her how long it'd been since she'd eaten a full meal. To distract herself from her hunger and untangle thoughts of home and portals that might or might not exist, she retrieved her journal from her bag.

She hadn't had time to write Anya since the evening of the solstice, before they'd flown to Keldale. Gods, that felt like a year ago. So much had happened since then, and Chloe needed to think through it all to make sense of what she should do next. Pulling a pencil from her bag, she scrawled out a hasty letter.

DEAR ANYA,

LAST NIGHT, I DANCED IN THE ENDLESS BALL, AND I THOUGHT I'D BE TRAPPED THERE FOREVER. WHICH WAS FINE! I WAS VERY BRAVE AND—

No.

She crossed all that out. What would she say to her sister if she were *actually* being honest with her? This was a good place to practice for being honest with Hyacinth. Chloe started her letter again:

DEAR ANYA,

LAST NIGHT, I THOUGHT I WAS GOING TO DIE. A WICKED HUMAN WHO'D LIVED FOR CENTURIES TRAPPED ME AND TRIED TO PULL ALL THE STARLIGHT FROM MY BONES. I'M SURE YOU STILL REMEMBER HOW THAT FEELS. TODAY, I'M NOT MYSELF. REMEMBER HOW WEAK IT MADE US? HOW MUCH WE HATED IT?

Chloe shivered to remember the dazed feeling of eating the cake and spinning on the dance floor. The wretched sensation of her starlight being sucked from her bones overwhelmed her all at once, and she slammed her journal closed. She couldn't talk about it. Not yet. Once her thoughts were in order and her feelings were clearer—

"What are you writing?" Hyacinth said sleepily, sitting up.

Chloe swallowed the lump of fear that thinking about the Mountain King's Endless Ball inspired in her. "Nothing."

"More letters to your sister?"

Chloe let out a breath. What should she say? Hyacinth already knew she was a human, with a sister she hadn't seen in a long time. She deserved to know more about Chloe. But Chloe would start out small and build from there. She could be honest about this at least. "Yes. I've been writing her letters in this book for over a year."

Hyacinth stretched. "Where is she? You said she's far away. Is she in the Starlight Kingdom? Or the Solstice Kingdom? Do you ever go back and see her? Do . . . do humans have it as bad in those other kingdoms as I've heard?"

Those were good questions. If Chloe were being fully honest, this was the moment to let all her secrets tumble loose.

But before Chloe could say anything else, a loud croaking reverberated around them. A shape moved through the mist. Where was her sword? She grabbed for it, but then . . .

Out of the mist stepped a frog.

Well, not exactly a frog. It was more of an older gentleman with a frog's body, complete with a mud-colored waistcoat, green velvet pants, and a top hat. He came up to Chloe's waist, and he carried a lantern. Inside the lantern, lights bobbed and weaved like fireflies. He looked like a less refined version of Lord Helston.

"Hello," Chloe said cautiously. The last thing they needed was to run into someone connected to Lord Helston. She put a hand on her sword's pommel.

"Oh! Hello," the frog said, his voice laced with surprise. He swept his top hat off his head and bowed. "Didn't expect to see anyone out so early. Especially not charming ladies with swords."

"Who are you?" Chloe demanded.

That was rather rude, she knew, but she was hungry, dirty, and ready to reach this witch's cottage. Perhaps there she could be honest with Hyacinth at last.

"Hello, sir," Hyacinth replied quickly, making a small curtsy. "We're surprised to find ourselves here as well. In fact, I confess, we're not even quite sure where here is."

"Why, you're in the Swamplands!" the frog gentleman said with a laugh, as if that explained it all. "I've lived here my whole life, and they're the most beautiful place in the world."

Chloe scoffed. The bubbling, smelly swamp was not her idea of a beautiful place.

"Do you know how to get *through* them?" Chloe demanded. "We're hoping to get to a witch's cottage that's supposed to be here."

"The Hyacinth Cottage," Hyacinth added with another curtsy.

"That, I can do! For a small fee of course."

Of course. Because nothing in the Fae world ever came for free. What did he want, some of their teeth? Years of their life? Chloe had very little left to give at this point, and she was so tired of trading bits of herself for small boons.

"We can't pay you," Hyacinth said. "But perhaps you can help us out of the kindness—"

"What's that on your belt?" the frog asked. He pointed to the enchanted compass Hyacinth had used to find the Wild Root Inn.

Chloe stepped closer to her protectively. This frog was not going to rob them; she'd see to that at least.

Hyacinth held a hand over the compass. "It's an enchanted compass, but it's got only one finding left. Surely you don't want that. Perhaps we can just use it to find—"

"I'll take it," the frog declared. "If you use it to find your way, you could still run into all sorts of danger in the swamp. There's rapidly sinking sand, the bog hag's hunting grounds, fanged monsters in the mist, and so much more. But trade me your compass, and my will-o'-the-wisps will get you to the witch's cottage safely."

Chloe was too tired and wounded to battle any monsters or swamp hags. "Just give it to him," she said to Hyacinth. "That's the easiest way."

"What if we need it in the Labyrinth?"

Chloe shrugged. That sounded like a problem for another day. "Right now we need to get to this witch's cottage as fast as possible. I'm not fit for getting lost."

It pained her to admit that, but it was true. She could barely stand, much less wander the marshes.

Hyacinth looked like she wanted to argue, but the frog was already reaching for the compass. "Fine, take it," she muttered.

"Very good, very good!" He opened the door of his lantern, and two glowing fairies the size of beetles zipped out of it to land on the frog's hand. He leaned down and whispered something to them, and then they flew upward again.

"Follow their lights," he said. "They'll take you to the witch's cottage, where you might find some rest." Then he bowed and hurried away.

Chloe hoped this witch wouldn't be another version of the horrible Mountain King. Was it too much to hope that they might find someone helpful out here in the wilds of the Moonshadow Kingdom? The Nightpine fairies seemed to believe going to the witch was a good idea, but Chloe would keep her sword ready, just in case. She also put on the armor from the Mountain King's court. Part of her hated to wear what had been so brutally forced upon her, but another, more sensible side appreciated the protection it could offer.

Chloe's eyes met Hyacinth's. "Should we follow them?" she asked. On her shoulder, Coffee eyed the bobbing lights like they were a snack.

"Every story I've ever heard says it's certain death to follow bobbing lights into a swamp, but I don't see what choice we have." Hyacinth shrugged. "Better than getting lost?"

"I'm keeping my sword out, though." Chloe shifted her sword from one hand to the other.

"That's an excellent choice."

The tiny fairies zoomed around them, flying through Chloe's hair and past Coffee's head. "Hurry, hurry," they whispered in chiming voices. "The witch is this way!"

"I'll go first this time," Hyacinth said, as the glowing fairies moved into mist. "So we don't lose them."

"And I'll try to keep up," Chloe muttered, putting weight on her injured ankle. Pain shot up her leg, but she bit back her cry. She would make it through this swamp if it killed her.

The fairies led them for what felt like many miles. They skirted fallen logs, squishy grass mounds, and enormous boulders. With every step, Chloe's ankle ached and her belly grumbled with hunger.

"Almost there," the fairies urged. "This way."

They turned toward the gray expanse of water that lapped at the shore. Dense mist stretched in every direction. The fairies had led them to a dead end. Perfect.

"We can't walk over the water," Chloe spit out more viciously than she'd intended. She glared at the swamp and the fairies bobbing around in front of her.

What were they supposed to do now? She was in no shape to turn around, and she desperately needed the healing the cottage witch might offer if she wanted a chance at getting through the Labyrinth and possibly finding a door there.

Did she still want to find a door there?

Not a thought for right now.

"Follow the path!" the fairies urged. They darted toward the water, their tiny golden lights breaking up the fog to reveal a trail of small stones beneath the surface. "Follow the stones to the cottage!"

Well. That was something at least. Chloe could manage a few stones. At least, she hoped she could. She took one stumbling step forward, tripped, and barreled into Hyacinth.

"Are you alright?" Hyacinth's brow furrowed in concern as she caught Chloe.

Chloe drew in a long breath and sighed. She was so tired, and all her wounds seemed to ache at once. "Fine, fine. Let's just go."

Keep going, Brave One, Coffee whispered. *You can do this.*

"I'm fine," Chloe lied, trying again.

Her foot snagged on another root, and her head spun. Then she was falling. The murky waters of the swamp rushed toward her with alarming speed. She fell face forward with a splash.

CHAPTER NINETEEN
Hyacinth

"You are *clearly* not fine." Hyacinth slung Chloe's arm over her shoulder and hauled her out of the murky water. Chloe's armor dripped, and her breastplate clanked against Hyacinth's nearly empty belt. All she had left were the magical glasses she'd taken from the Mountain King, her enchanted pen, her father's book, and a tiny measure of phoenix balm. None of which would help Chloe.

What was wrong with Chloe? Was she worn out from her wounds and all their walking? Was it aftereffects of the Endless Ball and the enchanted cake? Was it something more worrying, to do with her stolen starlight?

"Don't fret so much, Princess," Chloe slurred sleepily. "I'm only lightheaded."

Hyacinth bit her tongue to hold back her worries and instead focused on helping them over the stone pathway through the swamp.

"Careful, hurry, hurry," urged the will-o'-the-wisp fairies. "The cottage is close!"

"Who lives in the cottage?" Hyacinth called out, as Chloe stumbled again and Hyacinth barely caught her. She'd love to know what to expect from this witch, but the fairies made no reply.

At the end of the path, a small island shaped from the tangled roots of the largest willow tree Hyacinth had ever seen rose from the water. Each of the roots was thicker than Hyacinth was tall, and they twisted together almost like a basket. Among them grew swaths of emerald moss, other small trees, mushrooms—and a whole carpet of blue, pink, and purple hyacinths.

Hyacinth's breath caught in her throat as the smell of the flowers wrapped around her. It was overpowering, but also comforting, like she was back in the palace with a bunch of the fresh hyacinths her mother gave her every year for her birthday.

A pang of longing for her mother and her home went through her. What did Queen Mab think had happened to Hyacinth? Would they ever see each other again? Was Maurelle still on their trail, or had she returned to the palace?

Did Hyacinth really want to go back, or was she just missing the easy life she'd had there?

"Look," Chloe murmured, her voice barely a whisper. She nodded toward the tree's trunk.

Hyacinth abandoned her questions to consider the cottage situated in the willow. Set within the enormous trunk were several round windows and an arched blue door. Wooden boxes sat beneath the windows, all filled with more hyacinths.

The Hyacinth Cottage, indeed.

The will-o'-the-wisp fairies zipped around Hyacinth's head.

"*This way, this way*," their synchronous whispers hummed.

Anxiety choked Hyacinth, making it hard to breathe for a moment. The cottage was inviting enough, but she had no idea who might be waiting for them inside. Still, what choice did they have?

"Can you make it up the stairs?" Hyacinth asked Chloe. They both considered the twisting root staircase that curved up from the shore of the swamp to the cottage's front door.

"I'll try if you'll help me."

Chloe's shaking fingers gripped Hyacinth's shoulder hard, making pain shoot along Hyacinth's arm. But, she stood tall, supporting Chloe as they ascended. The tricky thing was that the roots were placed at irregular intervals, and Hyacinth had to haul Chloe up some of them.

By the time they reached the front door, Hyacinth was exhausted. Mud covered her boots, and her dress was soaked with sweat.

"I hope whoever lives here is friendly," she said.

"I just hope we can rest a bit." Chloe's face was pale, and sweat drenched her brow. She slumped against the doorframe.

This entire adventure had been such a terrible idea. If Chloe died out here, it would be Hyacinth's fault. She'd never forgive herself if, in trying to find her father, she lost her friend.

Stop being so dramatic. Knock on the door and help her. You can do that.

Inhaling a shaky breath, Hyacinth banged on the cottage door. It swung open, revealing a darkened room. The smell of flowers, baked bread, and books filled the air.

That was encouraging at least.

Tears filled Hyacinth's eyes, unbidden. It reminded her of home. Of her mother's library. Of safety and comfort all at once. Was it too much to imagine they might've found a refuge in the middle of this swamp? What a relief it would be to sit beside a fire with a book and a cup of tea.

"Go in, go in," urged the will-o'-the-wisp fairies. They darted around Hyacinth's head and shoulders, nudging her toward the door.

Everything in Hyacinth wanted to step across the threshold, but also everything they'd been through since leaving the castle made her pause. What if the charming cottage was a trap? What if the witch was power-hungry and corrupted by ambition and magic, like the Mountain King had been?

"This witch had better be able to heal me or at least have a comfortable place to sleep," Chloe said, stumbling across the threshold.

"Chloe, wait!" Hyacinth called, remembering too late that there might be hospitality traps set for them. Things that would ensnare them and keep them there.

"Silly girl," one of the will-o'-the-wisps said. "The witch is on her way. She said you can make yourself at home."

That was something at least.

Hyacinth followed Chloe into the living room, then helped her remove her armor. The gray light coming in from outside illuminated the room enough for her to make out a small table covered in plants and teacups and a sofa beside the fire. A clock on the fireplace mantel showed it was almost noon.

She settled Chloe on the sofa—her clothes were wet from falling in the swamp, but she wasn't going to make it on her feet much longer—but before she could say more, a shape filled the cottage door.

"Oh, there you are!" a cheerful voice said from the doorway. "The fairies told me you were on your way, but I didn't think you'd be here so soon. Welcome!"

Chapter Twenty
Chloe

Chloe struggled to sit up at the sound of the voice. It was merry enough, but she wasn't taking any chances after the Mountain King. According to Hester and Fellmi, terrible things usually happened to girls who were lured into Fae cottages. She had to get up; she had to get moving; she had to protect Hyacinth. How would Chloe ever see Anya again if she got eaten by a witch in the middle of the woods?

Mind reeling with awful possibilities—witches who carved human bones into flutes or made potions from the dreams they siphoned from those trapped in their cottages—Chloe staggered to her feet. Where was her sword? Why had she agreed to come here? It could only be because of how addled she was from the Endless Ball.

She looked around, and the world spun, tilting like she was on a ship caught in a storm. For a quick moment, she glimpsed Hyacinth standing beside a plump, middle-aged human woman with curling brown hair holding a basket of mushrooms. They seemed to twirl away as the world revolved.

"Stay away from her." Chloe wasn't sure if she was warning Hyacinth or the woman. She picked up her sword and drew in a ragged breath. "Hyacinth, don't—"

Before she could finish the sentence, she'd collapsed back onto the sofa. Coffee jumped onto an armrest, chirping in concern. Chloe needed to help Hyacinth, but she simply couldn't move any farther.

Her head fell back on the sofa cushions, and her eyes closed. Soft hands cupped her cheeks.

"Sleep," said the cheerful woman. "You can find respite here, I promise."

"Will she be okay?" Hyacinth asked, concern making each word brittle. "She's injured and has had some starlight stripped from her bones. Can you heal her?"

Chloe was so very tired, but she forced her eyes open. She reached out and gripped Hyacinth's hand.

Another hand covered Chloe's arm. Warmth that felt like sunshine or a cup of hot cider on an autumn day filled her. "I can heal her, don't either of you worry. I'll make soup. You stay with her, rest yourself. There's room on that couch for both of you."

"Oh!" Hyacinth sounded startled, which made Chloe smile despite her throbbing wounds and empty stomach. "I couldn't rest," Hyacinth said. "Not while she sleeps. She'd keep watch for me. I'll sit in this chair." She settled herself into an armchair by the fire.

Chloe wanted to protest. Perhaps they shouldn't be so trusting—what if the woman in the cottage had ill intent? She was a witch, after all. But she was a witch who was currently cutting carrots and potatoes and humming to herself. It was tremendously cozy, and Chloe had been on her guard for so long. Surely, she could just rest here? For a moment? The sofa seemed to say, *Yes, rest. Stay here. You're safe.*

She couldn't rest, though. That wasn't her job.

"I'll stay awake, Princess." Chloe promised. "Just to keep an eye on things . . ."

✦

She didn't stay awake.

Rather, Chloe woke several hours later, if the clock on the mantel was correct, to the smell of soup filling the cottage. It was garlicky and rich. Her stomach rumbled. Hyacinth was no longer in the room, a loss that Chloe felt immediately. With her head still spinning, Chloe got to her feet.

"Hyacinth?" she croaked. She should've used Hyacinth's fake name, but she remembered that too late.

Hyacinth strode into the room, a cup of something steaming and honey-fragranced in hand. "Ah, you're awake." Her relieved smile sent a flutter through Chloe's heart. "Drink this. It's tea." Hyacinth offered her the cup. "Perfectly safe, I've had three cups already."

"I'm not sure I should. . . ."

Of course she wanted to, but she was still so wary of eating anything after the Mountain King's Hall.

"Drink it, Chloe," the woman insisted, coming into the room behind Hyacinth. "You're guests in my home, and I promise it will make you feel better. I've also got some salve for your wounds and a potion for that ankle mixed into the tea."

Chloe was out of energy to resist. She wanted to argue with the woman and demand more information about where they were and who she was, but the warm smell of honey and herbs soothed her. Plus, by the rules of Fae hospitality and by the binding power of the woman's words, they were guests in her home. This was food and drink offered in friendship, meaning it wouldn't harm Chloe.

Thank goodness, because she was ravenous and desperate for her wounds to stop hurting.

She wrapped her hands around the cup and sipped tentatively. The tea was delicious. As comforting as the hot beverages she once drank with her family. A small surprised noise escaped her lips, and she drank more. "It's making me feel more awake—it's better than coffee!"

At this, the tiny dragon snorted and gave her an offended look. He nestled deeper into a pile of blankets on the sofa.

"Not you, sweeting," Chloe amended, stroking his head. "The beverage, I promise."

He chirruped and then closed his eyes.

She finished the drink and stood. The room didn't spin, and her ankle didn't hurt as much. What an absolute miracle.

"Come, come. This way," the woman said, handing her a small jar. "First a bath, then you can put this salve on your cuts. It should have them healed by morning. I'll answer all your questions after the bath as well. Hyacinth, show her where to wash up, will you?"

Hyacinth smiled at Chloe. "You won't believe the bath Elora—that's the cottage witch's name—has here."

They went up a twisting staircase that curved along the trunk of the tree. At the top, set into the boughs, was a room roofed with woven branches. A copper tub full of steaming water sat in the middle of the space, and a cake of purple soap rested on its rim. Thick towels hung from a rack in one corner, and lush green plants filled the room. A round window looked out over the flower-filled cottage yard, and another cup of tea waited on the windowsill.

"Oh my gods, I've never seen a more inviting place," Chloe murmured. She could weep.

Hyacinth grinned. "It's lovely, trust me. I lingered in the bath for so long, Elora had to check on me."

A sudden thought of Hyacinth in the bath filled Chloe's mind. She swallowed hard. Her eyes flicked to Hyacinth's lips, and for one agonizing moment, she thought about leaning forward to kiss her.

"I'll leave you here," Hyacinth said, holding Chloe's gaze a beat too long.

Stay, Chloe almost said. *Please, wash my back. Tell me everything is going to be okay. Kiss me again. . . .*

She said none of these things, and Hyacinth turned and shut the door to the bathroom. Which was probably for the best. If all went to plan, in a few days, they'd be through the Labyrinth and Chloe would be on her way back to her world.

She sighed, pushing the thought away again. Stripping, Chloe sunk into the tub, grateful for the heat of the water. Dirt sloughed off her as she scrubbed her skin with the sweet-smelling soap.

When she was fully clean and her bones felt liquid, she got out of the tub. Somehow, her clothing had already been laundered.

"Thank you, magical cottage," she murmured, as she belted her sword back on. She glanced in the mirror that hung on one branch. Dark circles rimmed her eyes, making her look older than eighteen. She felt like she'd aged a decade in the Mountain King's ballroom, but at least her ankle didn't hurt so much.

She recalled how Hyacinth had barged into the ballroom, disguised as a goblin, and saved Chloe.

Was she really prepared to walk through a portal and never see Hyacinth again? No. But could she really give up her sister for Hyacinth? Also no.

Chloe slicked her short red hair back with one hand and turned from the mirror.

The princess didn't need the stablehand in her life forever. They were traveling companions, nothing more. Hyacinth would forget Chloe before the trees shed their leaves in autumn. All would go back to how it'd been before they knew each other, and Chloe would be home and happy again.

But if that was the case, why did her insides twist at the thought of leaving? Of never hearing Hyacinth's laugh again?

Her stomach hurt because she was hungry. That was all. There was only one path forward, and Chloe had to take it, no matter who she left behind.

With that resolve, she smeared salve on her cuts and went downstairs. The smell of baking bread and soup called to her, and she emerged into the kitchen with a small flourish.

"Better?" Hyacinth stood by the window overlooking the yard. She offered Chole a smile.

"Much. How are you?"

Before Hyacinth could reply, the witch—Elora, Chloe reminded herself—came through the front door. A bundle of purple hyacinths rested in a basket on her arm. She placed them in a glass jar on the kitchen table.

Elora beamed at them. "Ah, everyone's cleaned up, and we have flowers. Let's eat."

They sat down to soup and bread. The first few moments were spent eating, but then Elora broke the silence. "So, you already know I'm a human witch who lives here in the Swamplands. Tell me, please, where have you come from, and where are you headed, travelers?"

Chloe looked over at Hyacinth. How much should they reveal?

Hyacinth shrugged.

Chloe took a long sip of a fresh cup of tea—which really was making her feel much better—and said, "We've come across the Moonshadow Kingdom, and we're headed to the Labyrinth."

Elora choked on her spoonful of soup. She coughed and sputtered, and Chloe stood to whack her on the back once.

"Thank you," Elora managed to say, as she found her voice again. She took a sip of her own tea. "Did you say you're going to the Labyrinth?"

Chloe nodded, and Hyacinth took out her father's book. She flipped to the map. "Yes, we're headed here. We've come a long way but—"

She stopped as Elora placed a hand over her mouth. She gaped at the book. "Where did you get that?" she whispered, her voice suddenly thick with emotion.

Chloe looked up from her soup, watching the woman.

"What do you mean?" Across from Chloe, Hyacinth raised an eyebrow. "Do you know this book? It's a very famous guide to the Moonshadow Kingdom. Do you have a copy too?"

Elora held out a hand. "May I see it?"

Chloe shook her head slightly, but Hyacinth was handing the book over. "It's from a bookshop in Keldale. It belonged to—"

Elora opened to a page and then looked up at Chloe and Hyacinth, "My brother," she said, at the exact moment that Hyacinth said, "My father."

Silence consumed the kitchen, broken only by the ticking clock. Chloe felt like she had fallen headfirst into someone else's story and was watching it unfold.

"Your brother is Evan Bramblefen?" Hyacinth asked. Fragile hope glimmered in Hyacinth's voice.

Like every orphan, Chloe knew that hope. It spoke of home, of family you'd lost, of somehow finding out there were more of your people in the world than you'd ever imagined.

Elora nodded. "He is—or he was—I don't know anymore."

Hyacinth's mouth fell open and then closed over what she was going to say. She tried again, but still no words came out.

"Evan went to the Labyrinth," Chloe jumped in. "We know that much, though we're not sure if he's still there. But, we aim to find out."

Understanding lit Elora's features. "Oh girls, no. You can't go to the Labyrinth."

"Why not?" Chloe asked stubbornly.

"We've been through more than you can possibly imagine since leaving my home," Hyacinth added.

"Since leaving your mother's castle?" Elora asked gently.

"Yes, since leaving my mother's castle," Hyacinth snapped. "If you know about my mother, why have I never heard of you?"

It was a good question. Chloe snaked a hand under the table and squeezed Hyacinth's hand in what she hoped was a comforting way.

Hyacinth shot her a small, grateful smile.

"I suppose I better start from the beginning." Elora turned to Hyacinth. "There's so much to tell you and so much I'm sure you don't know."

Underneath the table, Chloe gave Hyacinth's hand another squeeze, just to say, *I'm here with you. We'll figure this out, together.*

Hyacinth squeezed back, which made Chloe yearn to tell her about portals and where she came from, but she could save that. One family story at a time. Right now, they were in the middle of Hyacinth's. There would be time for Chloe's. Soon enough, there would be time.

Chapter Twenty-One
Hyacinth

Elora smiled fondly at Hyacinth. "I know it's a shock to learn I'm your aunt, since you were raised in the castle, but it's true."

Hyacinth released Chloe's hand as she struggled to make sense of all Elora had said. She was Hyacinth's father's sister? How was that possible? What was her aunt doing out here in the Swamplands and why had no one told Hyacinth about her?

It wasn't just that, though. If Elora was her aunt, what did it mean about Hyacinth's father? Was he human too? Did that mean *she* was half-human? How in the world had her father made it to the Crescent Atheneum, the magical college for the High Fae and some very bright common Fae? Why had her mother never told her any of these things? Why had she never met her aunt before?

Hyacinth's head spun with questions.

Elora walked over to a carved wooden chest in the corner of the room. From it, she pulled a small framed photo. It showed a teen boy with a mischievous grin and a head of dark curls. He was clearly laughing at something. Beside him stood a girl with Elora's serious eyebrows and curving half smile. Another girl, shorter than them both, with long brown braids, beamed up at the two of them.

"This is me and your father and our younger sister when we were growing up. Our father was a photographer who stumbled into Fae and fell in love with a human herbalist here. He took our pictures only a few times before his equipment stopped working, but these photos were his cherished possessions."

Hyacinth ran a finger along the photo, tracing her father's younger face. If both her paternal grandparents had been humans, then that meant she *was* half-human. The knowledge didn't make her feel differently, but it was still a shock after a lifetime of thinking of herself as a High Fae princess. Bramble and marsh, what would her half sisters say about her if they knew?

"Don't you think Evan looks like you?" Elora asked.

"A lot," Chloe said, peering over Hyacinth's shoulder.

And he did. This picture had been taken years before the portrait in the castle was painted, and her father's face was so much like her own, minus the pointy ears, which she clearly got from her mother.

"What was he like?" Hyacinth asked, giving voice to the question that had haunted her for years.

Elora sighed. "He was wonderful. Such a kind, funny, curious boy. Hyacinths were his favorite flower—maybe you knew that?"

Hyacinth shook her head.

Elora picked up one of the hyacinths on the table, sniffing it for a moment before she continued. "They were my mother's favorite flower too, which is why the cottage abounds in them. Evan wanted to study at the Crescent Atheneum. He was always exploring, reading every book he could get his hands on. He was desperately curious about the Moonshadow Kingdom."

"And what about your younger sister?" Hyacinth asked. "Does she live with you here too? Or is she somewhere nearby?" Hyacinth was still trying to wrap her mind around having more family. It would be delightful to discover another new aunt today as well.

Elora's eyebrows drew together. "Larissa . . . is gone." Her voice hitched.

"Larissa?" Hyacinth echoed.

Her eyes met Chloe's across the table for a moment. Chloe's eyebrows flew upward, and she shrugged. They'd met a Larissa in the Mountain King's realm. Surely, that was just a coincidence, though it wasn't a terribly common name.

"I'm so sorry your sister is gone," Chloe murmured, her voice breaking slightly.

The tone made Hyacinth pause. Chloe had told her a little bit about her sister, Anya, but she hadn't really said much about where she was now. Hyacinth bumped her knee against Chloe's under the table. It was small comfort if Anya was gone too, but it was all she could offer.

Elora sniffed back a sob. "Thank you. It's been so long since we lost Larissa, but it was a tragic thing."

"Do you want to tell us what happened?" Hyacinth asked gently.

Elora traced a finger over her sister's face in the photo. "It's the oldest story in Fae, I think. But, still, it hurts when it happens to your family. Although Larissa was only a year younger than Evan, she was always different. A little wilder, a little more restless. From her earliest days, she raced beyond the cottage, making friends with the Fae creatures. By the time she was a teen, she snuck out to their parties. None of us could stop her, and slowly, she changed. We knew she was stealing Fae food, drinking their wines, always chasing that next bit of magic. We didn't know where she was getting it or the things she was doing for it."

Elora paused, her voice laced with sorrow. "She left home at fifteen—disappeared with a couple of magic-seeking human wanderers who'd come this way. By then, my parents had tried everything to keep her here, but she wasn't having it. When she came home a year later, she was a shell of herself. The magic had desolated her. Your father searched his books for ways to help her; my mother and I crafted every remedy we could think of; my father tried to learn more about what she'd eaten and what the magic was doing to her, but none of us could figure it out. It was some vicious piece of magic that really did her in. She wanted this enchanted substance—cake, she called it—more than anything else in the world. She craved it. She chased it through waking and sleep, always talking about dancing in an Endless Ball and eating more cake. She disappeared on midsummer that same year. That was twenty years ago yesterday."

Hyacinth's heart hammered in her chest. It *had* to be the same Larissa they'd met. It had to! But should they tell Elora? What if it wasn't the same person and they just brought up heartbreaking memories all over again?

All at once, Hyacinth understood why her mother didn't like to talk about her missing husband, Hyacinth's father. It really was like reopening a wound, but it wasn't good to forget them either.

Elora wiped away her tears and kept talking. "My parents faded away soon after Larissa disappeared. They were never the same. Evan became obsessed with scholarship, and he finagled a way into the Crescent Atheneum. I stayed here, helping whoever I could—especially humans—with remedies and healing."

"You don't do magic, though?" Hyacinth asked, finally giving voice to the other question that had been bugging her this whole time. "There's not some way you've learned magic?"

If her aunt could learn it, perhaps she could too, even if she was half-human. Maybe some of her High Fae gifts could still come in, or there was another way to access innate magic.

Elora shook her head. "Not as such, and not in the way the Fae do. I practice human healing—along with using some potions I get from the Fae, but that was never enough to save Larissa. Your father was the one looking for a more permanent cure. He was desperate to uncover all the ways magic worked here. To better understand it so he could help other humans avoid Larissa's fate. He wanted to know if humans could have innate magic of their own, and he thought the answer might lie in the Labyrinth, built by the three Celestial Sisters. . . ."

So many things clicked into place for Hyacinth. What her father had been looking for. What was important enough that he abandoned her and Queen Mab. What might have compelled him to seek out the three Sisters—the source of all magic.

"He was looking for ways to make the Fae world better for humans?" Chloe asked.

Elora nodded. "Since he couldn't save Larissa, that was the next best thing. He was a natural scholar, always curious. I imagine that's what got him into trouble."

"We're going to go look for him in the Labyrinth," Hyacinth blurted. "No matter what you say, we have to do it!"

Elora's eyes widened. She put her teacup down forcefully and shook her head. "Hyacinth, no. You *can't* go into the Labyrinth. Not even if Evan is in there."

Her aunt didn't understand. This wasn't something Hyacinth wanted to do. She had to do it.

"We need to," Hyacinth said.

"You don't."

"What if he's still alive?" Hyacinth cried out. "Everyone else has abandoned him to his fate! But I won't."

"*You* aren't the one to rescue him!" Elora protested. "Not even Queen Mab's bravest soldiers could make it through the Labyrinth."

Hot anger bloomed in Hyacinth. Everyone was always underestimating her, but look how far she'd come already.

"Is it really so bad?" Chloe asked.

Hyacinth was grateful for the interruption so she could have a moment to compose herself. Getting angry at Elora wouldn't do any good.

Elora blew out a breath and picked up her teacup again. She took a long sip. "If the stories Evan told me are correct, then it's treacherous."

"Have you been there?" Hyacinth frowned. What did her aunt know if she'd only heard stories, but never experienced it for herself?

"Of course I've never been! One doesn't simply stroll into the Labyrinth. No one comes out alive. I tried to tell Evan that long ago, but he wouldn't listen."

"Please," Chloe said. "What's waiting for us there, according to your brother?"

Elora looked conflicted, a frown deepening the lines at the edges of her mouth. "I'll humor you, fine. Just to scare some sense into you. According to Evan, who found tales of the Labyrinth in his books and who traveled the kingdom, gathering stories about it, there are three guardians set by the Celestial Sisters. Their job is to stop you from getting to the tree in the center. Some accounts say there's also deep magic, flowing from the Sisters and their tree, throughout the Labyrinth. Supposedly, any creatures within its walls can be influenced by it. It might make a mouse the size of a dragon or make a fire salamander think it's a wild boar and try to charge you. Nothing but death and danger await you there, believe me."

Hyacinth did believe her aunt, not that it mattered. Now, more than ever, she knew she had to try to help her father.

She took a deep breath and then looked at Chloe. She mouthed, "Larissa?"

Chloe nodded slightly, so Hyacinth pushed on.

"Elora," Hyacinth said. Maybe she should call her *Aunt Elora*, but that would take some getting used to. "We have something else to tell you."

The soup grew cold as Hyacinth and Chloe took turns telling Elora about the Mountain King's realm, the Endless Ball, the starlight he'd been harvesting, and the Larissa they'd met.

"That has to be her," Elora choked out through her tears as they finished. "I can't believe she's still alive."

Hyacinth fidgeted with the pair of rose-colored glasses she'd taken from the Mountain King that hung from her belt. "I hope that's still true. We blew up his chandelier and destroyed the magic trapping the humans there, but I'm not sure what happened to them."

Hope lit Elora's face. "I'll find out! I'll leave first thing in the morning and search for her. I might have lost Evan, but I can still find Larissa! You can both stay here until I get back, and then we can all heal together."

That sounded wonderful, but Hyacinth wanted her father to be part of the reunion too. Which was why they had to find him. They'd leave first thing in the morning.

✦

Many hours later, a hand landed on Hyacinth's shoulder. In the moonlight streaming in through the cottage window, she saw Chloe bending over her pillow.

"Let's go," Chloe whispered. Her sword was strapped at her side, and she wore the armor from the Mountain King's ballroom.

Hyacinth's brain was still fuzzy with sleep. She'd been dreaming of having tea with her aunts and her father, while her mother watched with a knife clutched in her hand and her half sisters danced all around them. It had been both awful and vaguely wonderful to have all her family together in one place. Clearly, Hyacinth's mind was still catching up to all the new things she'd learned about herself over the last few days. "Where are we going?"

"The Labyrinth," Chloe said, exasperated.

"Now?"

"Yes, before Elora wakes up."

"But I want to thank her."

"We will, someday. For now, let's get moving. I don't want her to try to stop us with some sort of charm that binds us to this house until she gets back or something like that." Chloe moved away very carefully, so she didn't clank too much.

A pang of sadness overtook Hyacinth as she got up, dressed, and then tiptoed to the door. So much of her family's story had happened in this cottage, but it still felt empty. Perhaps she'd come back with her father someday and sit at this table with him and her aunts, just like in her dream. They could tell her more stories of Hyacinth's grandparents, and Hyacinth's mother might even join them.

The thought of Queen Mab, ever-glorious monarch of the Moonshadow Kingdom, having tea in the cottage was absurd, but it made Hyacinth smile. Which lifted some of her gloom and worry. That vision of her family, ridiculous though it seemed at the moment, was worth fighting her way through a Labyrinth.

Shutting the cottage door very softly, Hyacinth followed Chloe into the misty morning. Elora's boat was tied to a wooden dock at the back of the house. Beyond it, the wide expanse of the swamp stretched in every direction.

"It's no royal barge," Hyacinth said, as she eyed the small boat. It had two narrow planks for seats, a pair of oars that were fuzzed with age and moss, and a small lantern hanging from its prow. Golden light cast a circle into the mist.

"We'll manage." Chloe stepped into the dinghy, which wobbled beneath her feet.

Hyacinth clambered in. The boat nearly capsized at the movement, tipping to the side. Hyacinth fell into Chloe's lap.

Chloe sucked in a breath as she caught her. "Careful, Princess."

"Sorry, sorry," Hyacinth said, extricating herself from Chloe. Bramble and marsh, how Hyacinth hated her fake wings.

"No problem. Let's just not fall into the swamp this morning."

"Agreed. Though I'm certain you'd rescue me," Hyacinth declared, smiling at Chloe like it was the easiest thing in the world to believe.

"Or perhaps you'd rescue me, Princess," Chloe said. "Like you did at the Endless Ball."

Hyacinth shuddered. She was no hero. Though perhaps that was always the way with heroes. They rarely wanted to run into danger, but they found themselves rising to it. "Let's hope Elora's reports of the Labyrinth are greatly exaggerated." She pulled out her book and flipped to the map, studying it. All she knew was the Labyrinth was southeast of the cottage, and there was nothing else in that direction. If they headed that way, they should run into it eventually. "I wish I hadn't traded my enchanted compass to that frog."

"He did help us find your aunt, and I'm entirely healed now," Chloe said, lifting her sleeve to show Hyacinth the smooth skin of her once-wounded arm. "I took some of your aunt's salve too, in case anything else wants to slice us open."

A fair point and a smart move. "Worth it, then," Hyacinth agreed. She pointed in the direction she hoped was southeast. "Let's head that way and hope we run into the Labyrinth."

Chloe grinned and shoved off from the dock, digging the oars into the water with powerful strokes. "Sounds like all our other plans, which have gotten us this far. Let's go for it."

Hyacinth gripped her book and stared into the mist. *We're coming, Father. I just hope you're there for us to find.*

Chapter Twenty-Two
Chloe

As Chloe rowed across the swamp, the eastern horizon began to glow orange and pink with the whisper of sunrise. Coffee slept in her pocket, and her thoughts lingered on their time in the cottage. She thought about lost sisters and lost parents and home—a place she hadn't had since she'd left Anya in their world—and finding it again. She thought about the Labyrinth and what waited for them there. And she thought about Hyacinth learning her father was a human.

That couldn't have been an easy revelation, though the princess was handling it well.

Chloe glanced over at Hyacinth, who was studying her father's book. Unsaid things tangled between them, needing to be unraveled. But where should Chloe start? Yes, Hyacinth now knew Chloe was human, but that wasn't her only secret. Could she tell Hyacinth the rest now? About Anya and how Chloe had gotten to this world and why she had to leave?

She had to try. They hadn't really had more than a moment alone over the last few days when Chloe wasn't feeling miserable or recovering from the ordeal in the Mountain King's ballroom. If she didn't say something now, before they got to the Labyrinth, she might not get a chance.

"Hyacinth?"

She felt Hyacinth's eyes on her. "What is it?"

Shoving her doubts to the side, Chloe plunged right into the conversation she'd been avoiding, fighting against herself in an effort at full honesty for once in her life. "How are you doing . . . with it all? Finding out I'm human and you're half-human?"

Hyacinth swallowed visibly, her hands fluttering to her belt, where her potion bottles usually rested. "I'm . . . not sure yet, to be honest. I'm definitely still getting used to how you look now that I know you're a human."

Ah. Chloe had been wondering if her appearance might change for Hyacinth now that the glamour token was gone. "Is it really so different?"

"No," Hyacinth said. She scooted closer on her seat, until her knees brushed Chloe's. "Your hair is still a bold cherry's skin, your face is still sharp angles when you scowl, your lips are still . . . well."

Her eyes flicked to Chloe's lips, and heat flared through Chloe. She liked that Hyacinth was thinking about her lips. That was another thing they needed to talk about: their kiss in the garden and what it meant. They'd get there. First, they had to get through all the lies and revelations.

A blush colored Hyacinth's cheeks as well. "It's all mostly the same, but your eyes are grayer now, your ears are different, and there's an altered aspect to you. I can't put my finger on it, but you feel sharper, more present in a way I didn't even know was missing."

The attention Hyacinth paid her made Chloe's insides do funny things. She stopped rowing for a moment to look at Hyacinth. "I'm sorry for tricking you."

And she was, even if it's what she'd had to do. Just like she'd be sorry to leave if there was really a portal home waiting for her in the Labyrinth.

Hyacinth blew out a long breath. "I was hurt and surprised when I first found out because I thought we were going to be honest with each other."

Chloe started rowing again, just to have something to do with her hands. Being honest was harder than she'd thought. "We were! It's just . . . how was I supposed to tell you that I was human? Humans are treated so badly here and—" she shut her mouth, not sure whether to keep defending herself or not.

"And you did what you had to," Hyacinth finished, taking the words out of Chloe's mouth. She stared at the water and fidgeted with the enchanted spectacles. Chloe hated to see anything from the Mountain King still on Hyacinth's person, but she fought the urge to fling the wretched things into the swamp.

"I did what I had to do," Chloe agreed, "but I'm still sorry." She could be sorry and know she'd make the same choice again for her own safety.

Regret and relief tangled through her. Was this how she'd feel once she got back home and remembered her time with Hyacinth? Sorry to have lost it, but certain she would've always chosen to return to her world?

She didn't know.

Hyacinth dropped the spectacles and put a hand on Chloe's knee, bringing her back to the moment. "I had some time to think about it too in the dungeons, and since then, especially after I found out I'm half-human. I'm not sure what I would've done had I known that sooner. Would I have still tried to act like a High Fae princess? Would my half sisters treat me badly if they knew? I mean, my mother clearly knows—she fell in love with a human!—but her court is so vicious toward those who are different. Believe me. I know."

Behind those words lurked pain and stories Chloe longed to ask Hyacinth about. Had she seen humans mistreated in the Moonshadow Palace? Had she ever done anything to help them?

Before Chloe could ask any of these things, though, their boat hit a wide beach with a soft *thump*, driving all other thoughts from Chloe's head. She'd been mostly honest at least, and that felt good. She hadn't told Hyacinth about the portal she hoped to find, but that could wait until she knew it was really there.

She leaned forward slightly. "Thank you for understanding, Princess," she said softly. "And, for what it's worth, I'm sure your sisters wouldn't treat you differently if they knew you were half-human. You're still the incredible person you've always been. Now you just know a bit more about yourself."

Hyacinth swallowed a sob and shrugged at the same time. "I hope you're right. Maybe if the truth comes out, I'll be able to stop pretending with these wretched wings."

Chloe touched one of them lightly. "They are looking a little worse for the wear after our journey here, but you're still lovely, Princess."

Hyacinth stared at her for a long moment. Water lapped at the boat, Their foreheads were so close together, and Chloe fought everything in her that screamed to lean forward and kiss Hyacinth.

"Thank you," Hyacinth murmured at last. "Now let's go find my father."

Chloe pulled away at the words. It was for the best, truly. She would most likely be leaving soon, and getting even more entangled with Hyacinth would only make it harder to leave.

She couldn't convince her heart to believe that, but she hopped out of the boat anyway. Her boots sunk into gloopy mud as she and Hyacinth shoved their boat farther up the beach. She grabbed the lantern, and they stumbled up a narrow strip of sand. A dense tangle of blackberry bushes, high as a three-story house, stretched forebodingly in every direction.

Hyacinth had her father's book open. "According to my father's notes, the Labyrinth is on the other side of these bushes."

The bramble's branches arched like intercrossed fingers. Thorns peeked through the snarl, and clusters of berries hung within the bushes. The air was thick with mist, but silent. Really, too quiet. Trepidation slithered up Chloe's spine as she stood there.

"What now?" Hyacinth plucked a blackberry off the bush and offered it to Chloe.

Chloe shook her head. "I suppose we do the only thing we can: Keep moving forward."

Hyacinth scoffed. "How? I don't like the thought of being torn to ribbons by bramble, and I doubt your sword can hack through this."

That would need to be tested.

Chloe drew her sword and slashed at the closest branches. They shivered at the movement, the smallest ones snapping. Chloe hacked at them again. This time, a branch as thick as her wrist and dense with thorns seized Chloe's blade.

"Hey!" Chloe yelled. "Give that back!"

The bramble whipped the weapon, but Chloe held on to the pommel, grunting with the effort of holding the sword.

"Help me, Princess!" she yelled.

Hyacinth wrapped her arms around Chloe's waist and pulled. The bramble branch was strong, and it felt like they were playing tug-of-war with a goblin warrior.

"Pull!" Chloe yelled. "I can't lose my sword!"

She dug her heels into the sand, tugging as hard as she could.

A snapping sound filled the air as the bramble released the sword. Hyacinth and Chloe fell backward upon the beach. The bramble thrashed a few skinny, thorn-covered arms at them, as if in rebuke. Then it pelted them with berries.

Chloe covered her head as the small fruits rained down.

"We don't want your berries, you nightmare of a shrubbery!" Chloe yelled, flinging them back. A long scratch throbbed across her cheekbone from the bramble's thorns, and she gripped her sword with two hands.

"So hacking our way through is out," Hyacinth said, getting to her feet. She opened her book and ran a finger along a handwritten passage near the middle.

"Clearly." Chloe opened the pot of salve from Elora and swiped a bit on her cheek. Instantly the scratch there felt better. She would miss the healing power of magic when she was back in her world. She could admit that at least.

"Hmmmm . . ." Hyacinth said. "My father's notes speculate—from a song children sing in the Swamplands—that we can get through if we eat exactly ten berries. . . ." Hyacinth bent down and offered Chloe a handful of blackberries.

Eat ten berries? That was it? "I don't suppose you could've said that before I was attacked by a bush?"

Hyacinth snorted at Chloe. "I've only just found that among his notes. It also says we have to ask the hedge for permission to go through. Do you want me to sing you the song? There's a bit of it here."

Ridiculous magic with its rules and manners. Chloe sighed. "We can skip the song, but the rest is worth a try, I suppose." Brushing sand off the berries, she shoved ten into her mouth.

As with the berries she'd eaten what felt like ages ago in Queen Mab's garden during the solstice party, these berries filled her mouth with sweetness, a touch of bitterness, and something earthy. But as she swallowed the last one, a green bubble of light spread from the tips of her toes. It crept upward, coating her almost entirely. She glowed like she was encased in an emerald lantern.

"Bramble and marsh!" Chloe cried out. What was happening to her now? Had she poisoned herself somehow? It didn't hurt, but she felt entirely unsettled. "Get it off me!"

"Maybe it's supposed to do that," Hyacinth said, through a mouthful of her own berries. A green glow quickly encased her too, and she moved toward the tangle of blackberry bushes.

Chloe didn't like it one bit. She put her hand on her sword as Hyacinth approached the hedge and gave it a formal, courtly bow, which was ridiculous. Even more absurd, she asked, "Will you please let me pass?"

There was a long pause.

"I think I'm going to have to fight it again," Chloe called out, resigned and certain she'd lose at least a hand to the hedge before they made it through. Her arm glowed green as she lifted her sword.

"Wait." Hyacinth held out an arm to stop her. "I have a good feeling about this. Let's just watch for a moment."

As she said it, the branches began rearranging themselves. In short order, they formed a thorny tunnel, so low that the girls could barely stand. Chloe held up the lantern, trying to make out what was ahead. Was that really the Labyrinth through there? From her pocket, Coffee peered out. All Chloe could see was shadowy foliage, lit up by the lantern and the green glow surrounding them. It was eerie, and Chloe had the strongest desire to turn around and row their boat back to the cottage.

But she'd never find her portal home if she did that.

Hyacinth took a step forward, into the tunnel.

"Wait, I'm coming with you!" Chloe reached out to her, but the hedge shot a thorny branch across the entrance, blocking her way.

"You have to ask permission to come through," Hyacinth reminded Chloe. "Like my father noted in his book."

Chloe blew out a long breath. Of course, she had to ask the hedge permission. This was the Fae world. Where even the bramble had a point of view. Ridiculous. She stood up straighter and inclined her head at the towering tangle of blackberry bushes. "Oh, most magnificent shrubbery, may I please walk through this tunnel and into the Labyrinth?"

The bramble branch tapped her sword twice, as if admonishing her.

"I think it wants you to put your sword away."

"Absolutely not."

"Chloe! Put it away! This is our only path through."

Chloe scowled. "Fine." She slid the blade back into its sheath. "Happy now?" she said to the branches.

They waved her forward, and she gave a mocking bow.

Then she was beside Hyacinth. Her hand reached out to grab the princess's.

"What are you doing?" Hyacinth said, turning to Chloe.

"Keeping you close," Chloe said. "The last thing we need is to get separated."

✦

The moment the bramble tunnel closed behind them, the green glow faded from their skin. The lantern Chloe held lit a small circle around them, and the rest of the Labyrinth stretched in shadowy corridors to their right and left. A loud snuffling filled the air, coming closer.

"What is that?" Chloe asked, failing to keep the fear from her voice. Now that they were officially in the Labyrinth, deep dread settled in her stomach.

"I don't know," Hyacinth muttered. "One of the guardians?"

"Gods, I hope not," Chloe replied. "We just got here, and I have no idea which direction leads to the center or away from such things."

She held up her lantern and glanced around. There were towering bushes on one side and ivy-covered stone walls on the other.

The snorting grew louder, and panic gripped Chloe's heart. "Let's go that way," she called out, pointing to their left, where it seemed the noise wasn't coming from. They ran down one lane and turned right at the next fork—stopping short when a giant wild boar rounded the corner. It was twice as big as the ones that pulled Lord Heston's coach, and its tusks gleamed in the lantern light. For a moment, it looked as surprised to see them as they were to see it. Then it pawed the ground, preparing to charge.

No way could they survive a goring by a furious wild boar, especially one of this size. Chloe still wore the armor from the Mountain King's fighting pit, but it covered only part of her body. Hyacinth had no protection.

"Stay behind me, Princess," Chloe said, putting herself between Hyacinth and the boar. On Chloe's shoulder, Coffee brandished his little needle teeth.

"I don't think you'll be able to stop this beast, Little One," Chloe muttered, wishing for the first time since she'd found him that Coffee were about a hundred times larger.

The massive animal rushed forward. Chloe slashed with her sword, cutting the creature's nose. Surprised, it backed up a few steps and then charged again, knocking Chloe backward into a wall. Stone fragments rained down around her.

Hyacinth picked up a piece of stone and flung it at the boar.

"Run!" Chloe said. "Get out of here! Take Coffee with you!" She tossed the small dragon to Hyacinth, who plucked him out of the air.

"You're coming with us!"

Chloe would like nothing better, but if she did that, who would stop this creature? The beast charged a third time, and Chloe sliced again as it moved around them. It evaded her weapon and stabbed a huge tusk into Chloe's shoulder where her armor didn't cover.

She screamed and fell to the ground. Bright, blooming pain radiated down her arm as the tusk shredded her skin.

The boar roared, shaking its head back and forth. Every movement sent more pain through Chloe, but she was pinned between the beast and the stone wall.

"Leave her alone!" Hyacinth cried, whacking the boar with a stick. The beast turned at the same time as Hyacinth thrust the stick forward again. Somehow, the stick found its eye socket, sinking in with a sickening squelch. Blood poured down the boar's face.

Gods, this girl was brave. Foolish, yes, but also brave. Chloe adored her.

The boar roared and wrenched backward, freeing its tusk from Chloe's shoulder. Pain lanced through her, but they wouldn't get another chance. "We have to get out of here, Hyacinth! Go! Now!"

The boar wailed behind them, but Chloe didn't look back as she and Hyacinth ran down one long corridor of foliage and then another. They twisted left, then right, then left again. The beast followed behind them at every step, its heavy feet pounding into the ground. They turned right again, and Chloe swore.

In front of them was a dead end. There was nothing but a huge stone wall. Before they could find a different route, the enraged boar turned into the corridor, blocking their exit.

Chloe lifted her sword again. "Stay behind me. I'll distract it. You try to climb." She stepped in front of Hyacinth protectively.

"Don't be silly. I won't let it kill you!" Hyacinth cried out. She was running her hands over the wall behind them, as if searching for something. "In stories, dead ends in a maze always have a hidden way out! I know this is a Labyrinth, not a maze, but—"

Hyacinth kept talking, but Chloe tuned her out to focus on the boar. Her wounded shoulder throbbed, and she let out a long, slow exhale.

A letter she would never write to her sister flicked through her mind: *Dear Anya, remember when we were in the orphanage and the girls would play that game, where they tried to make up increasingly outrageous deaths the others might die? Truly macabre, now that I look back on it, but no one ever guessed I'd die as breakfast for an outraged pig in a labyrinth. Please know that I love you, and I'm sorry I won't get to worry you anymore. . . .*

Anya would be so annoyed if she died here. Chloe would be annoyed about it too! The thought emboldened her, and Chloe braced herself for the beast's attack. It stepped forward, drool dripping from its lips.

And then Hyacinth pulled Chloe right through the wall of the Labyrinth.

Chapter Twenty-Three
Hyacinth

Hyacinth had been desperately running her fingers over the wall, shoving and kicking it while Coffee screeched on her shoulder. He ran his tiny claws along the stone as well. Behind her, Chloe—the brave fool!—wedged herself between Hyacinth and the boar. She was going to get herself killed unless Hyacinth did something. The boar's fierce snuffling and rotten breath filled the space.

"Why aren't you a door?" Hyacinth shouted, pounding on the wall. Desperately, she wished for a potion or magical item or some other way to make a door where there was none.

Coffee battered his head against the wall, and then, all of a sudden, the stones shifted, resolving themselves into an arch with a wooden door beneath. Hyacinth flung it open.

"This way!" she yelled, dragging Chloe through the entrance after her.

Behind them, the boar squealed. Hyacinth slammed the door shut. The terrible pounding of the boar's head against wood sounded on the other side, but luckily it held. Eventually, after several agonizing moments, the boar moved on.

They'd made it!

It was a small comfort, but relief flooded Hyacinth. She collapsed against the stone wall beside the door to steady herself.

Beside her, Chloe hauled in breaths. She slumped against the wall as well, applying pressure to a wound on her shoulder.

"What was that?" Hyacinth managed. Her pulse fluttered wildly in her chest.

"One of the guardians?" Chloe still had her sword out, and she held it in her good arm.

Hyacinth shook her head. "I don't think so. That thing just wanted to eat us. It was probably one of the wild creatures that got stuck in here and grew huge from the magic, like Elora mentioned."

Chloe scowled beside her. "Great, so we have ordinary creatures turned into monsters *and* guardians to deal with."

"Just another beautiful morning in the Moonshadow Kingdom," Hyacinth said glibly.

There was a pause, and then Chloe started laughing. It was brittle at first, the laughter of someone who'd barely escaped death a few too many times, but then it became a deep belly laugh. The sound undid the knot that had tangled within Hyacinth, made from worry about her father, stress from their journey, all the lies they'd told, and the truths they'd hidden from each other. She began laughing too, letting herself feel the release that came from the absurdity of it all. They stayed like that, racked with entirely disproportionate laughter, for a few moments. Hyacinth wiped tears from her eyes and struggled to catch her breath.

"Just another *beautiful* morning in the Moonshadow Kingdom, indeed," Chloe repeated. "Where you have to bow to the hedgerows and you're the breakfast."

Hyacinth snorted. "Who knows what we'll find ourselves doing by midday." She turned to look at Chloe, taking in her new human appearance. Appreciating the way the morning light caught her eyes and noticing a smattering of freckles she'd never seen across her nose. Gently, Hyacinth brushed a lock of red hair off Chloe's cheek. Chloe froze at her touch, her eyes meeting Hyacinth's.

"What are you doing, Princess?" she rasped.

What was Hyacinth doing? She wasn't sure, but all of her yearned to lean forward, to cup Chloe's cheek. To kiss her and kiss her and kiss her.

Instead, she swallowed hard. "Just making sure you don't have any other injuries. How's your shoulder?"

Chloe grimaced and lifted her hand. "It's been better."

Blood soaked Chloe's shirt. The cut was deep, and flaps of skin hung off the edges.

"Bramble and marsh, you just got healed by Elora. Give me that salve."

Chloe handed it over, and Hyacinth smeared a handful on Chloe's wound. The bleeding stopped, and the skin knitted together in front of her eyes. "Try not to get stabbed again, okay?"

Chloe grinned. "I'll do my best, Princess. Any idea where we are in relation to the center of the Labyrinth?"

At this, Hyacinth looked around, taking in their surroundings. They were clearly still within the Labyrinth, and tall stone walls stretched in every direction. The corridors were narrow enough that they couldn't walk beside each other. Far above the walls, clouds hung low in the sky, showing glimpses of morning light. Fog crept along the ground, and an eerie stillness filled the air, weighing it down. Lichen and moss covered the stone wall now at their back. The door they'd come through had vanished.

"I have no idea," Hyacinth said. Her laughter quieted, and awestruck dread took its place. She really was out of her depth here in this magical Labyrinth.

Focus on your father. He came this way. You can do it too.

Could she, though? He was a scholar, skilled in survival after growing up as a human in the Moonshadow Kingdom. She had—here she checked her belt again—a tiny measure of phoenix balm potion in case Coffee needed it, the Mountain King's spectacles, and an enchanted pen. Hardly enough, but it would have to do.

"Which way do you want to try?" Chloe asked, adjusting her armor so it now covered her healing shoulder.

Hyacinth considered the right and the left, both equally unappealing. "Right, I suppose?"

Chloe nodded. "I'll lead the way."

"You don't have to," Hyacinth called, pushing off the wall.

"It's fine," Chloe said, shooting Hyacinth a small smile. "I'm sure we have many miles to go yet. Lots of time for us to trade places." Coffee settled on her shoulder, and she started forward, down the path.

With a sigh, Hyacinth followed. Stone corridor after corridor stretched before them. They turned left, right, and kept making right turns. Dead ends arose every few paces, and they had to retrace their steps.

Hyacinth lost track of how many ways they turned, of how long they'd been walking. Of where they were going and where they had been.

Then, all at once, there was another door in the wall facing them. It was a round one, made of smooth white stone.

"That way?" Hyacinth asked warily.

Chloe nodded. "Seems like what the Labyrinth wants us to do." She pushed it open and walked through into a wide circular courtyard. As soon as they were through, the door slammed shut behind them.

"Bramble and marsh," Chloe swore, spinning around. She tried to push the door open, but it was locked.

"This is . . . not what I was expecting," Hyacinth admitted, looking around.

Statues filled the courtyard. There were horses rendered in exacting detail, High Fae carved with delicate stone wings, a pair of peacocks with their feather fans extended. There were fox Fae, brownies, goblins, and even a large giant's face set into the wall. Its eyes bulged and its mouth hung open like a threshold. All the statues were frozen in different poses, like they'd been captured there or carved from life.

Ivy grew along some of the creatures, hanging down in long tresses. Moss filled the cracks in others, giving them texture.

A low wind rustled through the grove, making the ivy dance.

Hyacinth ran her hand along letters carved into the stone wall beside the door.

"The Garden of Beginnings," she read softly. "This is Celestine's garden, I think."

"The Goddess of Beginnings? From the stories?"

Hyacinth nodded, walking over to a pair of faun statues holding a stone basket between them. "I wonder where all these sculptures came from? Who made them?"

"I wonder how we get through here." Chloe brushed some moss off one of the fauns. "I don't see a guardian to fight, just a bunch of statues. . . ."

Before Hyacinth could reply, a loud crunching filled the air.

One of the fauns turned its head. The stone on its neck and shoulders cracked and chipped off its body like crust breaking from around ice.

That was not what Hyacinth had been expecting. She lurched backward.

Chloe drew her sword. The faun shook off more chips—though it was still made of stone, it moved more like a living person—and turned toward them. It bowed.

"Greetings, travelers." Its voice was granite, rattling out of its chest. "To pass through the Garden of Beginnings, you must first best Celestine's guardian."

Hyacinth looked around. "Is that you?"

Chloe scoffed beside her. "We can fight you any day."

The faun grinned. "Oh no, travelers. You don't understand. I'm merely the messenger. That's Celestine's champion."

Hyacinth's heart sunk as something she'd taken to be a large boulder in the corner shook itself, raining more gravel and moss around them. It stretched colossal arms and legs, then stood up.

It was a troll. Twice as tall as the walls around them.

"For bramble's sake," Hyacinth muttered.

With ambling steps that shook the entire garden, the troll blocked the open mouth carved into the wall. Several of the smaller statues toppled into one another.

"Time for a fight!" the troll rumbled.

Chapter Twenty-Four
Chloe

Of course, navigating a Labyrinth couldn't be as easy as fighting vicious, oversized ordinary monsters. No, there had to be a giant stone troll as well.

Chloe sighed. Despite the healing salve, her sword arm throbbed from her run-in with the boar's tusk, and she was weary from walking. Still, she dropped into a fighting stance and faced the troll.

The guardian swung out a hand, smashing several statues. As one, the other statues began to move, grumbling and tumbling to escape the troll's club. The peacocks shrieked, their voices rending the air. The goblins and brownies spread out in front of the opening in the wall, as if they were blocking it too.

"Why are there so many of them?" Hyacinth shouted. "I thought there was supposed to be only one guardian! Elora said my father told her there'd be three guardians in total!"

Perhaps your father didn't know everything, Chloe thought as she dodged a blow from the troll. The other statues charged at them, picking up stones and sticks and flinging them in their direction. Bramble and marsh, was there nothing Chloe wouldn't have to fight? At least in her own world, there were no violent statues that came to life.

There was also no Hyacinth.

A handful of pebbles thunked off Chloe's armor, jerking her mind back to the problem at hand. Packs of apparently murderous statues.

"Get to the mouth in the wall," she called out to Hyacinth. "We'll flee through there."

The troll's stone fist swung through the air, whipping ivy and leaves with it. It pummeled Chloe to the ground, knocking the wind out of her.

Pain razored through her, and she was slow as she rolled away from the troll's next punch. Barely gaining her feet, she slashed out with her sword. Her healing shoulder ached with every move, but she had to keep fighting!

Hyacinth, on the other hand, stood stock-still. She looked like she was in shock. Of all the things they'd seen and fought so far, the fleet of statues had made her pause.

"Princess!" Chloe shouted. "Move!"

Hyacinth's eyes refocused, almost like she was coming back to herself. Just in time, she dodged two goblin statues who reached for her.

Chloe's sword did nothing to stop the statues. Coffee growled from her shoulder, his claws digging into her skin. She gripped Hyacinth's hand, pulling her close. "Stay with me! Let's run for the opening in the mouth!"

The troll smashed another fist into the wall behind Chloe and Hyacinth. Chips of stone rained down upon them.

The fauns with the basket surged forward. "You cannot defeat stone with blade or brawn!"

"Not helpful!" Chloe shouted back.

The enormous stone troll stepped forward. It grabbed Hyacinth around her waist and plucked her into the air.

"Princess!"

Hyacinth screamed and battered the stone troll's hand with her fists.

What was Chloe supposed to do now? How could she help Hyacinth?

Above her, Hyacinth yelled again. The stone troll plucked at one of her wings, holding her in the air like she was a butterfly.

Chloe looked around frantically.

And then the troll let go of Hyacinth's wing. Hyacinth plummeted to the ground, twisting in the air.

"Hyacinth!" Chloe ran to catch her.

"Don't worry about me!" Hyacinth shouted.

Chloe looked up to see Hyacinth—who had proven again and again how much more competent she was than she seemed—dangling from a long fringe of ivy that hung from the stone troll's arm. Relief filled Chloe. She had to stop underestimating Hyacinth.

In one quick move, Hyacinth slid down the ivy and landed on her feet. Chloe ran to her and grabbed her hand. "Let's go!"

Dodging and weaving, they sprinted to the mouth of the enormous face in the wall. The troll roared behind them. They had to shove two High Fae statues away and avoid a brownie's arrows, but they stepped through the mouth.

Chloe had never been so happy to see the stretching passageways of the Labyrinth in front of them. She glanced once over her shoulder, surprised to see all the stone statues behind them frozen in midaction, like the clockwork toys Chloe had seen in shops as a child. The troll's club was raised. The fauns ran toward the mouth in the wall, and one of the horses was mid-leap, balancing on only one foot. But they weren't moving or giving chase.

Would they stay like that forever? Or until another traveler braved the Labyrinth? Or—worse still—would Chloe and Hyacinth have to fight their way past them again on the way out?

You won't if you find a door back to your world.

Did that mean Hyacinth would have to fight her way through the Garden of Beginnings alone? Chloe almost couldn't bear that thought. She swallowed a lump of emotion.

They'd be fine. They'd figure it out.

"Well, one guardian down," Chloe said, forcing all other thoughts from her mind. "Let's keep walking."

Chapter Twenty-Five
Hyacinth

Hyacinth's ribs hurt from where the stone giant had picked her up, and one of her wings fluttered in the breeze, a rip in the gossamer near the top. Which was fine. Perhaps something else in here could fully tear the fake wings from her back.

All around them, the moss-covered stone of the labyrinth walls rose into razor-sharp spires. Monsters or worse could wait around every turn. It was enough to make Hyacinth's heartbeat spike.

"I need a moment," she told Chloe. Her breath sputtered out of her chest, and she struggled to fill her lungs as cold panic overtook her.

"Are you ill?" Chloe bent over her, forehead creased.

Hyacinth shook her head. She wanted to go home. She needed to go forward. She wasn't sure she could take another step, but they weren't turning around. How was she supposed to help her father in this state?

"Give me just a moment," she said. "Please."

Chloe glanced around, and Hyacinth followed her gaze. The rock walls seemed to narrow around them, leaning in as if they were listening.

"Just a moment, Princess. Then we keep moving," Chloe said. "I don't like it here."

A laugh burst out of Hyacinth at that. "No one likes it here, I suspect." Hyacinth hugged her ribs as more laughter bubbled forth, making her bruises ache. She clamped a hand over her mouth to hold back a sob.

"Hey," Chloe whispered. Gently, she removed Hyacinth's hand and folded her into a hug. "It's going to be alright, Princess. We're going to reach the tree in the center of this Labyrinth. We're going to find your father."

"That might be what scares me most," Hyacinth confessed. "What if he's not like I've imagined? Or what if something else has happened to him?"

Chloe held her, and Hyacinth relaxed in the embrace for a moment. If they were anywhere but inside a deadly Labyrinth, she might actually feel rested. She might let herself linger in her growing feelings for Chloe. Instead, her nerves were fire-laced.

Exhaling sharply, Hyacinth pulled away. "Let me check my book. Maybe my father has some advice for us about the second guardian or what else to expect."

"Good idea."

As she flipped through the book, Hyacinth touched the many notes her father had scrawled in the margins. There were thoughts on the kingdom's politics, notes on the Swamplands' monsters, and the Labyrinth, but nothing specifically about the second guardian.

All at once, a loud noise, like stones being ground against each other, startled her from her search through the book. She looked up. "What's happening?" she asked Chloe in alarm.

Hyacinth watched as three of the walls before them shifted, changing the direction of the paths they were following.

"It's almost like the Labyrinth is directing us," Chloe said, nodding toward the passageway ahead, where more walls were moving.

Hyacinth didn't like it. Was the Labyrinth listening to them? Was it taking them closer to where they wanted to go, or farther from it?

The wall behind them shifted suddenly with a horrible wrenching noise. Hyacinth leaped up before the wall put up a barrier between her and Chloe.

More urgently now, led on by the shifting walls, they strode forward through the Labyrinth. It felt like they were retracing their steps.

"I think we've already been this way?" Hyacinth said after they walked past a familiar clump of ferns growing out of the wall. It was maddening. Every time she thought they'd made progress, the walls shifted, disorienting her totally.

Another section of the wall shifted in front of them, blocking the way ahead. Hyacinth swore loudly.

"We definitely *have* been this way," Chloe agreed, spinning in a circle to look around. On her shoulder, Coffee made a loud frustrated noise.

"Here we go again," Hyacinth ground out. This was worse than the time she'd gotten lost in the maze in her mother's garden when she was eight. Her half sisters Tansy and Maeve had been playing hide-and-seek, but Hyacinth had turned down an unfamiliar path and ended up deep in a part of the maze she'd never seen. Her frantic screaming had brought her sisters running, and now she could feel a scream climbing her throat. But there was no one to come rescue them.

Blowing out an exhausted breath, Hyacinth started again down the path where the walls were directing them. They kept walking. The sun rose higher above them, meaning it had to be close to noon. They ate the food Chloe had brought from Elora's house and shared the last few sips of water. They kept walking. Another hour, or maybe two—who knew anymore?—passed. Hyacinth's throat dried out, and her lips burned.

Then, all at once, the wall in front of them shifted, and the most welcome sound filled the air: water. Not a trickle, but a great rush. Hyacinth exhaled in relief.

"Oh, thank the Sisters," she said.

Chloe shot her a look.

Right, maybe they shouldn't be thanking the Sisters. Celestine, Millicent, and Aria were the reasons Hyacinth and Chloe were in this mess of a Labyrinth. One of their guardians could be waiting at any turn. But at least there was water they could drink. That had to count for something.

Hyacinth rounded a corner and then gasped. To their right rose a sheer cliff, and to their left, the ground sloped sharply downward. In front of them, a huge waterfall frothed down a rock face, looking like a lacy veil. Hundreds of feet below, at the base of the falls, was a churning plunge pool surrounded by enormous rocks. Leading up to the falls and then slipping behind it was an emerald-green moss-slicked trail. It was terrifically inviting, and Hyacinth longed to rest behind the waterfall for a few hours.

A loud rumbling sounded behind them. Hyacinth turned back toward the path they'd come from, but the walls had already blocked them in. So much for going that way even if they'd wanted to.

"I guess we go forward," Hyacinth said.

"We go forward." Chloe affirmed. She started up the mossy trail.

The roar of water pounding into the pool grew louder with every step. Spray misted around them. The water was glorious on Hyacinth's cheeks, and she licked it off her lips. When they stood behind the curtain of the falls, the water thundered so loudly, Hyacinth could feel it in her chest. She had to shout to speak to Chloe.

"What's that?" she yelled.

"What's what?" Chloe yelled back.

Hyacinth pointed to a narrow opening in the cliff face behind the falls. Was it a cave? A tunnel? Something else? Would it lead them to the next guardian? Or take them to the center of the Labyrinth?

She didn't want to explore it, but that's how she'd felt all afternoon.

You have to do this. Your father might be here. Keep going. Leave no stone unturned.

But what if he isn't here? What if this entire adventure is for nothing?

Would it still be worth it? She glanced to Chloe, who had slipped into the crack in the cliff face.

Yes. It would've been worth it to do this with Chloe. No matter what.

Hyacinth stepped into the narrow hollow. Immediately dread surged through her. Was there a beast waiting in this cave, ready to fight them? Could they actually defeat such a thing?

Hands out, she stumbled forward. Only cold, damp stone met her palms. Beside her, Chloe ran her hands over the stone as well. Coffee glowed silver in the darkness, illuminating a narrow space, but no hidden cave or passageway.

"Did you find anything?" Hyacinth shouted.

Chloe smacked the wall in frustration. "Nothing!"

Hyacinth retraced her hands along the stone, searching the entire rock face, but the cavern stopped. There were no secret exits, no hidden tunnels. Light shone through the fissure they'd come from, and the waterfall's roar filled the bowl of rock.

She stepped out of the small opening behind the falls and looked around. Did the Labyrinth want them to stay here? Was this where it had been steering them?

Almost as if reading her mind, the rock walls surrounding the waterfall moved forward, pressing them in even more tightly. They were very clearly trapped behind the falls.

Which left them nowhere to go.

"What do we do now?" Hyacinth asked.

Chloe let out a frustrated growl. "I don't know! We can't go forward in either direction. This cave goes nowhere. There must be something we can do!"

Hyacinth had a terrible idea of what the Labyrinth wanted them to do, but she didn't want to voice it.

"I think we need to jump," Chloe said, looking over the edge of the falls.

That, in fact, was exactly what Hyacinth feared they were supposed to do. She just really, really didn't want to.

"We can't jump!" Hyacinth cried out. "We'll die!"

Chloe threw up her hands. "We can't turn around either. What else should we do?"

The falls pounded the rocks below. They would drown beneath all that water if they didn't break their necks first.

What Hyacinth wouldn't give for more of her levitation potion. Or for wings that actually worked. Terror filled her. How could they possibly survive this fall? Maybe they wouldn't, but this seemed like the only way forward. Maybe her father had passed this obstacle too.

She swallowed hard and held out her hand. "I don't want to do it alone."

Chloe took her hand. "You won't be alone. On the count of three, we'll go over together, okay?"

It was most definitely not okay, but Hyacinth nodded. She squeezed Chloe's hand.

"One, two, three!" Chloe shouted.

Hyacinth gripped Chloe's hand and rushed forward with her. They leaped into the relentless falls, and Chloe's hand was ripped from hers.

A long scream tore from Hyacinth as she fell. Spray smashed into her body, pounding her like a hundred stone trolls' fists. She tumbled upside down over and over again. She had the barest moment to hope she wouldn't be shattered on the rocks. Then she hit the surface of the plunge pool. Pain gripped her. Water swallowed her head, dragging her down. It filled her nose and ears. She sunk like a stone to the bottom of the pool.

Chloe was nowhere in sight, and murky darkness overtook Hyacinth.

Bramble and marsh, what a bad idea this had been.

Chapter Twenty-Six
Chloe

Chloe sunk into the frothing pool beneath the waterfall, her heavy armor pulling her into the depths. Where was Hyacinth? Where was Coffee? She had been so foolish to think this was the right plan. A lot of good those thoughts did now that she was stuck at the bottom of a thundering waterfall.

She spun around in the water, desperately searching for anything that would help orient her to the surface. Her lungs burned, and she wrestled for a moment with the armor, but she couldn't get it off. *Forget it.* She had to breach the surface before she ran out of air. She kicked her legs, propelling herself toward a light that glowed pale green in the churning water.

Maybe that was something? Adrenaline clouded her mind, and her body ached. Still, Chloe kicked toward the light. Something smashed into her as she swam. It was a tangle of wings and girl and skin.

Hyacinth. The princess's eyes were enormous, and foamy shadows from the roiling waterfall flitted across her face. She opened her mouth, and bubbles poured out of it.

Chloe grabbed her shoulders, trying to calm her. She'd drown them both if she kept struggling. Chloe pointed toward the glowing light. Clamping her mouth shut, Hyacinth nodded.

They kicked and swam, fighting a wicked current. Long fingers of weeds entangled them, and the spectral shapes of fish blurred past them. Chloe kicked harder, her armor slowing her down. At her side, Hyacinth flopped and pushed through the water.

The glow grew brighter in front of them. It looked like a bubble. Or a green glass dome on a rooftop. Or the curve of a greenhouse, protecting something inside. Or was it something else?

Chloe didn't care what it was as long as it saved them from the ceaseless battering of the waterfall. She kicked once more, shoving her hands toward the light.

Then, suddenly, she landed on her stomach in the grass.

Grass? Here? At the bottom of the pool that had seemed deeper than anything she'd ever experienced? How did that make sense?

Of course it didn't make sense. They were in the Celestial Sisters' Labyrinth, which was transforming at every turn. She sucked in a breath, which was another unlikely thing about being in the dome. She could breathe. That was certainly an improvement in fortunes.

Beside her, Hyacinth sat up. "Where are we?"

It was the question they'd asked each other so many times on this adventure. As usual, Chloe had no idea. She tried to speak, hoping to say something reassuring, but spat out water and a bit of grass. "I don't know," she croaked at last.

A small wriggling inside her shirt pocket made her heart flip. "Coffee? You're alive!"

No thanks to either of you. Next time a bit of warning before we go for a swim?

"I can do that," she murmured, holding him close. He nipped at her fingers, and she put him down on the grass so he could shake out his wings.

Hyacinth produced her father's book from her bodice. "I can't believe that worked."

Chloe touched the book. It was dry—which was impossible, since Hyacinth's dress and Chloe's clothing were utterly soaked.

Something in the center of the bubble snagged Chloe's attention. Had that been there before? Shimmering in front of them was a cottage. Or was it a castle? Or a manor home? Or just a hut? It seemed to shift with every flicker of the bubble, and then it resolved into the shape of a shop in a city like she'd find in her world. Chloe looked over at Hyacinth.

"Tell me you see that too," she said.

"I see it, though it keeps changing. I think it's a castle? What do you see?"

Before Chloe could say anything, the door of the cottage opened, and a gnomish woman with a broad smile, round belly, yellow braids, and a pointed red hat stepped out. She beamed at them.

"Oh, you've made it!" she called out. "I'm so glad to see you. Please come in. Get comfortable at my table!" Something about her was as wavering and watery as the cottage itself.

Chloe blinked.

But the woman was still there.

"Onward we go," she muttered, helping Hyacinth stand up. "Stay close."

"Always," Hyacinth said, shoving her father's book back in her belt pouch.

Chloe walked into the cottage, a step ahead of Hyacinth, and her breath caught in her throat.

"What is this?" she said, looking around.

She knew exactly what it was. A coffee shop. Like the one she and Anya had seen a few times while living at the orphanage. The ones they'd dreamed of visiting. Velvet curtains hung from the mullioned windows. The walls were painted deep green. Golden-framed portraits of flowers and fairies hung on them. Small tables with chairs around them filled the room, and a yellow sofa sat near a cozy fireplace.

A steaming cup of coffee sat on a table near the door. But that wasn't all.

Chloe blinked and stared. No. It couldn't be.

Her sister's favorite blue jacket hung on the back of the chair.

"How did you get this? Is Anya here? Where are you keeping her?" Chloe spun around, her heart racing.

But the gnomish woman was no longer beside her. Nor was Hyacinth. Chloe touched her sister's jacket and held it to her nose. It smelled like Anya, right down to the lemony-mint perfume Anya rubbed behind her ears and on her wrists each day.

"Anya? Are you here?" Chloe called out, hope surging in her.

It didn't make sense. She knew it didn't. How could her sister be in this Fae world? But Chloe was here, and that was strange, so perhaps Anya had made it into this world too. Maybe she'd come through a door and been waiting in this coffee shop for Chloe all this time. Perhaps the best thing to do was sit down and hope Anya returned.

Which was exactly what Chloe did.

✦

Hyacinth

Hyacinth followed Chloe into the cottage, but a surprised gasp left her lips as she crossed the threshold. Chloe vanished, as did the gnomish woman. The room she stepped into was so much bigger than she'd expected from the outside.

She held a hand over her mouth, trying to take it all in. *Bramble and marsh*, it was her mother's sitting room in the castle. Tall windows showed a view of the garden and stables, and her father sat in an armchair with a book open in front of him. What was he doing here? Her mother sat next to him, reading her own book. Their hands were entwined, and a sense of peace filled the space.

Evan Bramblefen looked up as Hyacinth walked in. "Hello, Hyacinth. I've waited so long to meet you."

He looked just like the portrait she'd studied so many times before, and there were also echoes of him from the photo Hyacinth had seen. Tears rose in her eyes.

Queen Mab smiled at her, the expression gentle and kind. "Join us, please. Tea has just been sent up, and we have your favorite books. Your aunts are on their way too."

She waved a hand, and a tea tray filled with delicate cakes, steaming cups of fragrant tea, and little sandwiches appeared. There was a pile of books, all with familiar names along the spines.

A plush armchair appeared beside her father's. His eyes sparkled as he said, "Now let's relax like a family should."

Hyacinth sunk into the armchair, happiness suffusing her. She reached for a cup of tea and slice of cake, then pulled one of the books off the stack—a green one, with gold lettering on the spine. It was *A Willow's Journey: Life Along the Banks of the Mossley River*, a memoir full of romance and peril written by a very famous dryad. Hyacinth knew it well.

A wisp of thought bothered at the back of Hyacinth's mind as she ran her hands over the green book. Was there another book here? Something else with a green cover? Something else she should remember?

"Drink your tea, darling," Queen Mab said. "We want you to know your father and I are so very proud of you."

Hyacinth let the wisp of thought escape her grasp and took a long sip of tea, bliss suffusing her at her mother's praise.

✦

Chloe

Chloe held her sister's jacket close and looked down at the coffee shop table. She drew in a sharp breath, trying to steel her beating heart. Some part of her knew she should look for Hyacinth, but she couldn't help it. This shop, this world, was all so familiar.

Home.

It felt like home.

It felt like her and Anya laughing together or teasing each other about the silliest things.

It felt like the days when her dreams had been smaller and hadn't involved Fae creatures and dragons. Or unmagical princesses.

Another cup of coffee appeared on the table, and a heady giddiness filled her as she wrapped her hands around it, breathing in its delicious warm scent.

Coffee . . . her mind whispered. *You're forgetting coffee. . . .*

That was silly. How could she forget coffee when she had a cup of it in hand?

She took a long sip. A smile pulled at her lips as a soft humming from the other room caught her attention. She'd know that song anywhere: "The Traveler's Lullaby."

Her mother had sung to her and Anya before bed every night. Once her parents were gone, Chloe had sung it to Anya again and again during those long nights in the orphanage. Who was singing it now? Was her sister really here?

It was too much to hope for. Yet Chloe hoped. It was all she wanted. She stood up.

"Anya? Are you here?" Anticipation laced her voice, and Chloe fought against the tears that filled her eyes. She opened her bag, taking out the small journal. Somehow, like Hyacinth's book, it too wasn't soaked and ruined. She put the journal on the table and opened it.

"Anya, I've been writing you letters! I have so much to tell you, and I'm so sorry I went away. Are you here?" She ran her hands over the fabric of Anya's blue jacket. It felt substantial enough, and small stitched flowers covered the collar. Chloe remembered when Anya had made those stitches, so long ago in the orphanage.

Chloe stood, peering around the room. As she did so, the small coffee shop expanded. A long hallway with rooms branching off it stretched into the distance. The lullaby repeated, the humming lilting on the air. Her sister had to be here somewhere! Chloe grabbed the journal from the table and strode down the hallway. With every step, the singing grew louder.

Sweet, familiar, and melancholy, it wrapped around Chloe. Her sister was down that hallway! Chloe knew it. She knew it more clearly than she had ever known anything in her life. All she had to do was reach Anya.

Chloe ran down the hallway, which seemed to elongate as she moved. A door appeared on her right, and she opened it. Nothing. The lullaby swelled. She opened the next door and the next, only to find more empty rooms.

Still, the lullaby filled the air. Another door appeared, swinging open of its own accord.

A small joyful noise escaped Chloe's lips.

Because there, with her back to Chloe, silhouetted in front of a window that glowed with green wavering light, was Anya. Her blonde hair was shorter, her shoulders more upright somehow. But it was her. It was her sister. At last.

Chloe rushed into the room. She'd waited so long to hug her sister, and here she was.

"Anya!" A sob broke Chloe's voice. The door slammed shut behind her.

Anya turned around.

"Chloe," she said. "I'm so glad to see you."

Chloe ran forward to hug her sister.

✦

Hyacinth

Lamps flickered in Queen Mab's sitting room, their green glow almost like water in a glass vase. Hyacinth basked in the space, but a question nagged at her.

She reached over and took her father's hand. He looked so much like the painting in the library, it had to be him. "I'm so happy to see you, Father, but what are you doing here?"

Evan Bramblefen offered her a small smile and shrugged. He returned to his book. Hyacinth wanted to say more, to ask how he'd gotten home, why he'd been gone so long . . . but maybe it was enough to just sit with her parents and read a book. To enjoy time together as a family.

As she shifted in her chair, a green book fell from her bag. She picked it up, running her fingers across the gem on its cover. It sparked something in her memory. A girl with red hair and a tiny dragon. A bubble of green light beckoning to her. "I think I was supposed to come find you in a different library?" Hyacinth murmured.

The words were out before she could stop them. Her father's eyebrows flew up as he took in the book. But he didn't say anything. Her mother didn't either.

Hyacinth flipped through the book, her finger flying over blank pages where she knew something had been, but it wasn't there anymore. What was it? How had she forgotten? Perhaps it was important?

Again, a feeling that she was missing something niggled at the back of her mind. But she pressed on, flipping through more pages until her finger stopped on the map.

Then, with terrible certainty, she knew where she was.

This wasn't real.

She was still in the Labyrinth.

Her father wasn't sitting in front of her. Her mother wasn't here either. This vision of home she'd yearned for was an illusion.

"It's the second guardian!" She said the words aloud, and they echoed around her. "This is Millicent's challenge."

Her words broke the room into pieces. Her mother and father melted away, as did all the furniture, the tea set, and the books.

Hyacinth sat in an uncomfortable chair in the middle of a small room, facing a rickety window. Outside the window, she could see a green glasslike dome with water outside it. Coffee waited at Hyacinth's feet, making insistent worried noises.

Hyacinth bent down to scoop up the tiny dragon. "What is it?" she asked. "Where's Chloe?"

Coffee nodded to the other side of the room, and Hyacinth spun around. Chloe sat opposite her, in another rough-made chair at a small table. She was all alone at the table, but was lifting her hand, pantomiming drinking something. She was also talking to someone excitedly, but nothing came out of her mouth. It was almost like she was trying to speak underwater.

Still a bit hazy from the illusion of her family and losing them so suddenly, Hyacinth went over to Chloe. What was she seeing in this shack? Was it a vision like Hyacinth's had been? Something with her own family?

Hyacinth touched Chloe's shoulder, light enough not to startle her too much but still firmly. Chloe continued her conversation with the invisible partner, gesturing and laughing. Hyacinth felt a nudge at her side. Coffee was pulling on the Mountain King's spectacles. Ah, the ones he used to see through magic and illusions. Hyacinth slipped the glasses on, and this time, when she looked across the table from Chloe, she saw a smiling blonde girl who shared Chloe's nose and freckles. Coffee and pastries sat on the table between Chloe and the girl. Through the window just beyond the table looked to be a street filled with carriages, gas lamps, and humans in fine clothing. It wasn't like the Fae world at all . . . which was strange.

She glanced again at Chloe, who was holding out a small journal to her sister. Now, with the spectacles on, Hyacinth could hear what Chloe was saying.

"Anya, I've missed you so much! I've been stuck here in the Fae world a year, but I'm trying to find a way back to our world! But now you're here! I can't believe it!" Chloe shoved the journal across the table, and her sister picked it up. "I've been writing you letters—I've seen so much, you wouldn't believe it. My friend Hyacinth—"

Here, Chloe paused, as if remembering Hyacinth all of a sudden. Hyacinth's heart pounded in her chest. Would Chloe remember her and break out of the illusion on her own? What did she mean about trying to find a way back to her and Anya's world? She was a human, yes, but Hyacinth had always assumed she was from the Fae realm. What if that assumption was wrong?

Hyacinth knew in her bones all at once that it was. Why else had Chloe been so eager to help the two humans who'd come through the door? Why had she been so cagey about discussing her sister?

She'd always been trying to get back to her own world. She was going to leave Hyacinth.

Knife-sharp betrayal stabbed her. She tore off the spectacles, not wanting to see or hear any more. So much for Chloe being honest with her. How could Hyacinth possibly trust her when she had been lying about where she came from?

Hyacinth watched Chloe's movements as she kept talking to her sister. Now, without the spectacles on, they were ghostly and grotesque. She was playacting at being reunited with her sister, and she looked so happy.

Hyacinth couldn't leave her like that. Not here, in this hut. Trapped forever in a fake world. If she was going home, that was fine, but she should have the choice. At least Hyacinth knew now what Chloe intended. She still needed help to find her father.

She had to break Chloe out of the illusion.

Roughly, Hyacinth shook Chloe's shoulder. Nothing happened. Chloe laughed at something in the imaginary conversation she was having.

Hyacinth shook her harder.

Still nothing.

"Bite her," she commanded Coffee. He shot her an indignant look. "Not too hard! Just enough to snap her out of it."

Coffee obliged, nibbling on Chloe's finger, but nothing happened. Chloe was still lost in the illusion.

So, despite her maelstrom of hurt and betrayal, Hyacinth did the only thing she could think of to do.

She pressed her lips to Chloe's and kissed her.

✦

Chloe

In the midst of a lovely conversation with Anya, a featherlight touch brushed Chloe's lips. It stirred something deep within her. The scent of summer wine, sweet and delicious, filled her memory. She blinked once and then Anya disappeared. Where had she gone? Chloe looked all around for her sister, but she wasn't there. She was in a run-down shack, and Hyacinth stood in front of her, so close that Chloe's forehead pressed against hers.

"Princess," Chloe gasped. "What are you doing here?"

"Helping you remember where you are," Hyacinth whispered against her lips.

Head swimming with confusion, but delighted to be kissing Hyacinth, Chloe started to lean into the kiss, just for a moment. Hyacinth pulled away quickly.

"I'm glad you're alright," Hyacinth said, her voice sharp. "I wasn't sure how else to get you out of that illusion." As if kissing her had been only a solution, not something she wanted. Very well. Chloe shouldn't be kissing her anyway. Not when she might be headed home soon.

She looked around again. Gone was the coffee shop. Her sister's sweater. The sweet sense of finally being at home where she belonged.

Had any of it been real? Chloe let out a long shaky breath. "What happened?"

"Don't you remember anything about where we are?"

Chloe shook her head.

Hyacinth frowned. "We're at the bottom of the waterfall, and this place is showing us illusions. I think that gnome woman we saw is the second guardian. My illusion showed me my family and a scene of home—exactly what I wanted to see. What about you? What did you see?" Hyacinth twisted the Mountain King's spectacles as she looked at Chloe.

Coffee sat on Hyacinth's shoulder, and Chloe smiled to see him. She held out her hand. He scrambled into her arms, and Chloe nuzzled his nose.

No more separating from each other, Brave Ones. The tiny dragon's voice carried annoyance and concern, and he clearly was speaking to both of them.

"I promise," she said to Coffee.

Hyacinth scoffed at her words, but she nodded at Coffee. "We'll stick together, I promise too."

Chloe searched the hut again, gathering her thoughts. She didn't want to tell Hyacinth about finding her sister and having coffee with her. It felt too intimate and too much her own at this moment. But she owed Hyacinth at least some explanation, if for no other reason than that she had saved Chloe again from a Fae trick.

And so she flipped through the book of letters, as if that would help her explain. "I saw my twin sister, Anya, who is somewhere in another realm. . . ."

"Another *realm*?" Hyacinth's eyebrows shot up skeptically.

What did she mean by that?

"Yes. Another realm." Chloe waved a hand vaguely, as if to indicate somewhere in the Fae world. She still wasn't ready to tell Hyacinth about the human world and the door she was hoping to find at the center of the Labyrinth. So she let loose a string of other truths. "It was only us for our entire lives except for a very short time when we were small. Then I lost her. And I want to see her again. I thought I saw her here . . . but then, when you kissed me, she disappeared. . . ."

It wasn't everything, but it would have to be enough. At least for now.

Hyacinth swallowed hard, and Chloe could practically hear the questions she wanted to ask.

But before either one of them could say anything, a lilting voice called out: "Welcome to the Place of Middles, the goddess Millicent's home. Here our stories stretch in so many directions. Neither beginning nor end, just all possibilities. Stay, and you may have your dearest vision of home."

The gnome woman who'd invited them into the cottage stood in the center of the room.

"That's the second guardian," Hyacinth whispered.

Obviously.

The woman studied them. She looked at Chloe. "Are you sure you don't want to stay?"

A breath shuddered out of Chloe, tinged with regret. She didn't want this fake version of Anya. She wanted her real sister and her real home, even if it meant she never got them. She nodded. "I'm sure."

"And you?" The woman turned to Hyacinth.

"I also want to go," Hyacinth said.

"Very good," the gnome woman said. "You may go."

The woman waved her hand, and a new door appeared behind her. Chloe turned the knob, not wanting to stay in this dreadful place a moment longer. She wanted to reach the center of the Labyrinth and the portal that hopefully waited there.

She pushed through the door and stopped in her tracks. Hyacinth slammed into her back.

"Bramble and marsh, this place is astonishing," Chloe said.

They were no longer under the green dome. No longer in a bubble at the bottom of a fathomless pool. Now they were back in the Labyrinth, the door behind them tucked underneath a stone arch. In front of them, a dense pine forest stretched in every direction.

"Yes, everything is full of surprises," Hyacinth said behind her, a note of bitterness in her voice. Or maybe that was exhaustion. They'd come so far already, and who knew how long they had yet to go. Chloe was tired too, but she could be encouraging for Hyacinth.

Chloe turned and offered her a smile. "C'mon, Princess. We're getting closer. I can feel it."

Chapter Twenty-Seven
Hyacinth

Hyacinth was in a foul mood. She stood on the other side of the second guardian's door, watching Chloe stride toward the pines and trying not to recall the illusion of Chloe's most-desired happiness.

The truth of it wouldn't leave her alone, though. Chloe wanted to return to her world and be with her sister. *That's* what would make her happy.

The thought of it broke Hyacinth's heart.

She wanted to be the one who made Chloe happy, she realized now.

Bramble and marsh, what a miserable thing to suddenly understand about herself. Chloe was her friend, but they couldn't have a future together. Not even if Chloe stayed in this world. Hyacinth's mother would never let her spend the rest of her days with a human stablehand.

Which wasn't fair at all, really, since her mother had married a human scholar. But when had her mother ever been fair?

Hyacinth huffed and pulled the Mountain King's spectacles off her belt. She glared at them. They were hateful things. What good had they ever done?

Some reasonable part of her whispered gently in her mind: *Perhaps you're blowing things slightly out of proportion?*

After all, Chloe had told her about her sister before the illusions and the second guardians, even if she hadn't said exactly where her sister was. Maybe Chloe wasn't really looking for a door back to the human world. Maybe her sister actually was in another part of the Fae realm and Chloe had told her the entire truth at last. Maybe Hyacinth should stop focusing on Chloe and mind her own goals. She was here to find her father; that's what really mattered.

Bitter frustration washed through Hyacinth. She was so tired. Tired of being lied to. Tired of lying. Tired of hoping things were what they seemed.

Maybe she didn't want to see things as they really were. Maybe it was enough to leave things as they were and go forward from there.

Yes, that's what she'd do.

Hyacinth dropped the Mountain King's spectacles on a flat rock, and stepped on them so they shattered. Then she followed Chloe into the pines, trying to keep up.

Hyacinth scowled as she looked around the forest. Carpets of moss and feathery ferns coiled around hundreds of tree roots. The trees were sentinels, watching Hyacinth and Chloe. The air was thick with the scent of pine sap, and small creatures scratched in the undergrowth. Cold menace rolled off the trees, deep as the shadows beneath them. The trees stood so close together, Hyacinth wasn't sure she could slip between them with her hateful fake wings.

Coffee growled in the direction of the forest, and Chloe whispered to him soothingly.

Hyacinth caught up with Chloe, then paused. She ran a hand over her dress, which was still wet from the plunge into the falls. What were they supposed to do now? Would getting through here lead them to the center of the Labyrinth? Wasn't a labyrinth different from a maze and supposed to have one clear path to its middle?

Perhaps that's what a labyrinth was in Hyacinth's books, but the Celestial Sisters' Labyrinth was one of tangled brambles, shifting walls, gardens of stone statues that came to life, and waterfalls with cottages full of illusions in their plunge pools, so why not also include an endless pine forest?

Hyacinth shuddered. Her feelings for Chloe were as complicated as the Labyrinth. Chloe was her friend, but she'd lied to Hyacinth. Chloe was a human, maybe one who was trying to leave this world. She was always putting herself in danger for Hyacinth. She was a person who needed someone to look out for her, after a lifetime of being the one who looked out for everyone else. She was brave and foolish and lovely and infuriating, and Hyacinth didn't know what to do about her!

Every time she thought she might've figured her feelings for Chloe out, a wall arose, or some new twist and turn surprised her. It was all tremendously confusing, and Hyacinth wished she had some guide for those too.

Yes, she'd been the one to kiss Chloe in the second guardian's cottage. But that didn't mean anything. It was meant only to bring Chloe back to herself.

Surely that's all it had been.

Hyacinth knew that wasn't the truth, and her head spun as she tried to work out her real feelings for Chloe outside of any illusions or magical quests.

"Let's keep moving," Chloe said, squeezing Hyacinth's elbow gently. "I don't want to be caught out here after dark."

Hyacinth looked over at Chloe. Her eyebrows were drawn, and worry carved lines into her forehead. Chloe had her own problems—a sister she had lost. A whole life and memories that had nothing to do with Hyacinth. She wasn't thinking about kisses or romance. She was trying to survive this adventure so she could move on to her own story.

Hyacinth sighed and tried to suppress her frustration. Once they got back to Queen Mab's castle, she could send out scouts to help Chloe find her sister. Or use her mother's influence in some other way.

There will be time to figure this out later, when you're free from this place. When you've found your father.

The image of her father and mother in the sitting room reading together rose in Hyacinth's mind. Yes, it had been an illusion, but it was also an aspiration. Something to work toward.

She had to find her father. That's what mattered right now. The only labyrinth she needed to concern herself with was the one in front of them.

"I also do *not* want to go through this forest," Chloe muttered. Her clothes were wet like Hyacinth's, and she'd lost one of her pauldrons after jumping off the waterfall.

"Me neither," Hyacinth agreed. "But I'm not sure we have a choice. We can't go back."

"That's true." Chloe said. Her mouth was a grim line and resolve hardened her features. "Even if we could get back through this door, how would we climb the waterfall? I have no idea how to navigate the Labyrinth in reverse."

What that meant for them escaping once they'd found Hyacinth's father or at least reached the Labyrinth's center, she didn't know. "I don't want to go back either," Hyacinth admitted. Her voice shook as she said it. There was no way to go but forward, regardless of what awaited them there.

Chloe nodded. "So we keep going. I'm sure your father still needs us."

Hyacinth nodded. "Let's stay together in these pines. There's supposed to be a third guardian somewhere out here. And we promised Coffee we wouldn't get separated again." She started to walk forward, but Chloe's hand snaked around her wrist. Surprise made her pause.

"Princess, wait."

"What is it?"

"I . . . well, thank you."

"For what?" Hyacinth waited, leaning toward Chloe even though she told herself to keep her distance.

"For helping me back there, with the second guardian. You didn't have to."

"Of course I did. We're friends. And maybe . . ."

"Maybe what?"

Hyacinth shrugged, trying to sound as casual as possible. "I was happy to help you because you're helping me. And we're much stronger together, don't you think?"

They were.

That didn't mean she didn't want to kiss Chloe again. That she didn't want to talk about her feelings and that night in the garden during the solstice and everything else that had happened since then, but Chloe was already moving into the pines.

Shoving all her restless thoughts aside, Hyacinth followed Chloe into the forest's gloom.

✦

Hyacinth hated pine trees. At least these pine trees. Her wings, already torn by the stone troll and then battered by her leap into the waterfall, kept getting caught in the narrow space between branches. These wings were her curse, her endless, sap-sticky nightmare.

"Can you help me?" she growled in frustration for what felt like the fiftieth time in ten minutes.

Her wings were snagged again on a pair of low-hanging branches. She yanked them, but nothing happened. Her annoyance built, and she let out a long breath to keep from crying.

Chloe turned, a half smile on her face. "I really do wish you'd let me cut those away." She brandished her sword, and on her shoulder, Coffee growled at the offending branch.

"I'd like nothing better, but I suspect my mother's spell makes that impossible, and you'd end up slicing me apart."

"We could narrow them a bit?"

Hyacinth shook her head. "Just free me, please."

With a quick slash, Chloe removed the branches trapping Hyacinth. Relief instantly coursed through her now that she was unsnarled.

Slowly, Hyacinth threaded her way through the pines, keeping Chloe in her sight. Her thoughts still churned. *Imagine if I find my father and he rejects me.* The thought stung, even in a hypothetical situation. She had to stop thinking that way. It was just the forest's melancholy and her cursed wings weighing her down.

"Agh! Can you free me again, please?" she shouted to Chloe as her wings caught once more upon pine branches.

Chloe shot her a sympathetic smile and hacked at the branches.

They kept walking. The pines narrowed, now barely a sliver between them. Chloe had to turn sideways to pass, and Hyacinth heaved her way through one branch at a time.

"What do you think this next guardian will be?" Hyacinth called out, wrangling another branch out of the way. Sap clung to her fingers, and needles stuck in her hair and dress. The last thing they needed while in these woods was to face the third guardian. What if it was a wraith? Or a pine tree come to life? How could they even fight in such tight confines? If only she hadn't used up all her potions, then she'd have *something* to fight with.

Chloe held back another branch for Hyacinth to pass through. "Who knows? I just hope it's possible to kill." She tried to draw her sword from its sheath, but there was barely space between the pines to do that. "If the guardian comes upon us now, I don't think I'll be able to fight it."

Coffee rumbled on Chloe's shoulder. Not for the first time, Hyacinth wondered what the little dragon was thinking. Was this adventure terrifying for him or exhilarating? Why was he so small? Her mother's baby dragons were bigger than Coffee from birth, so what was he?

It was an academic question, merely a curiosity, but Hyacinth kept turning it over. At least it was something to think about besides her worry over her father, or her feelings for Chloe, or the way the pines seemed to draw even closer.

Were the pines getting closer?

Panic crept up Hyacinth's throat. She couldn't see through the wall of trunks now, and the undergrowth was dense and tangled among their roots. Even light could barely make its way through, and she could no longer tell the time of day.

A few steps ahead of her, Chloe stopped walking. "I'm not sure how we'll push through this." She gestured ahead a few inches to an impenetrable snarl of pine branches.

Stuck again. Fantastic.

Hyacinth sighed and looked upward. Above her head, the branches splayed in every direction, making a jagged ladder. Maybe that was something?

"We had to jump down the waterfall," she mused out loud. "What if we need to climb up here?"

Chloe shot her a surprised look, and then a smile broke out on her face. "Oh, you're brilliant! That's exactly what we need to do, I bet. Do you think you can climb with those wings?"

Hyacinth shrugged. "I'm not sure I have a choice, but if I get stuck, please come rescue me."

"Always," Chloe promised, almost reverently. "And I'll go first."

Embarrassing though her earnestness was, the tone of Chloe's voice made Hyacinth's stomach flip. It was too serious for what lay between them. She was determined to ignore it entirely and focus on climbing the tree.

Chloe climbed ahead of her, agile and quick. Hyacinth wrapped her hands around the lowest boughs and hoisted herself up. Rough pine bark scraped her hands, and her wings got caught over and again, though she was able to wiggle out of the branches' grips most times without Chloe's help. Eventually, they reached the top of the tree.

"Wow," Hyacinth breathed, taking in the view. Well, this might have been worth it. The horizon stretched on all sides. Behind them she could see the rise of the waterfall and the stone walls of the Labyrinth they'd come through already. Far in the distance, the mountains they'd passed rose against the sky, snowcapped even in summer. The gray expanse of the Swamplands bordered the Labyrinth, and forest filled the rest of the landscape. Somewhere out there was her mother's castle, far to the west. It was like the map in her father's book made real.

The day had passed while they were beneath the pines, and twilight painted the horizon peach and orange. Above them the first few stars glittered against a navy sky. It was beautiful. Peace settled over Hyacinth for the first time since they'd entered the Labyrinth.

Of course it didn't last. A gust of wind billowed around them, sending the pine she clung to swaying.

"Hold on!" Chloe shouted from a few branches higher.

Hyacinth clung to the trunk, pushing her cheek into the rough, sticky bark. Pine needles rained onto her body, and a loud clattering broke up the whisper of the branches. What was that? She spotted a rickety wooden bridge connecting their tree to another. The bridge was made of rope and a handful of planks, and it swayed in the wind like a ribbon flung about in a child's hand. As Hyacinth watched the bridge move, she noticed dozens more making a path through the treetops.

She'd been right! They were supposed to climb to go forward.

"Look!" Chloe called triumphantly. She pointed beyond the dark mass of pine trees. "There's the center of the Labyrinth!"

It was. Hyacinth could've leaped for joy. If she weren't clinging to the tree for dear life, she might have. "At least we know where we're going," Hyacinth said. "Even if we have to cross those bridges to get there."

Chloe grinned. "Let's hope the third guardian doesn't appear while we're crossing." She secured Coffee in her pocket and took a tentative step onto the first swinging wooden bridge.

"We can hope." Hyacinth shoved away the image of having to battle a monster while navigating the unstable bridges. They'd surely plummet to their deaths. Chloe ran across the bridge, nimble as a cat on a rooftop, and then secured herself in the branches of a pine tree about a hundred yards away.

"C'mon!" Chloe urged. "You can do it."

Hyacinth swallowed hard and looked down. Bramble and marsh, it was a long way to the ground. The boards strung between the ropes were rotted in places, and the bridge itself danced with every gust of wind. She took a deep, calming breath and then stepped onto the bridge.

Her foot immediately broke through one board, and she screamed.

"Hyacinth!" Chloe shouted.

"I'm fine." Hyacinth's voice shook as she steadied herself on the bridge. She was not.

"Keep your eyes on me! You can do it."

Hyacinth could. She knew it, and she had to cross this bridge. For her father, and herself. She was not going to get trapped on this accursed bridge.

You wouldn't be stuck here if you had real wings, whispered a treacherous voice in her head that could've been her own or her mother's or Chloe's or her half sisters'. It was the voice of all her doubts and fears.

Not helpful.

She was the girl who'd broken out of a dungeon, rescued her friend, and gotten this far. She could cross a damn bridge.

Hyacinth stepped forward, eyes on Chloe. With every passing minute, the sun sank lower on the horizon, making each step more treacherous as night blanketed them. Hyacinth's wings caught the wind every few feet, lifting her slightly. She clung to the rope railings. Forcing her feet forward, Hyacinth stumbled over the bridge, desperate to reach Chloe on the other side.

A long sob broke out of her when she finally did.

"One down," Chloe said, as she grabbed Hyacinth's hand and pulled her off the bridge. "Only a dozen or so more to go."

"Hooray," Hyacinth said weakly, still a little dizzy from the swaying bridge. She hugged the tree trunk. "Let's get it over with, shall we?"

Chloe squeezed her hand and hurried over the next one.

Hyacinth followed. Together, they slipped, slid, and stumbled across the warren of bridges. Each new treetop was a triumph. In front of her, Chloe moved over the bridges with the grace of a fighter. Coffee peeked out of her pocket, nervous little growls and chirps leaving his mouth.

After what felt like forever, they crossed the last of the bridges. They'd made it. They were so close. Hyacinth's heart raced as she looked toward the center of the Labyrinth.

"All we need to do is get to that wall." Chloe pointed to a crumbling stone wall below their final tree. The pines stopped there, and on the other side of the wall were a few twists and turns of the Labyrinth, and then a wide stone ring marked the center. Inside that circle stood the largest oak tree Hyacinth had ever seen.

"Down we go, then, I suppose," she said.

"And no third guardian in sight," Chloe added. "I'd say our luck is about to change, Princess."

Hyacinth dearly hoped Chloe was right—though she had her doubts.

Chapter Twenty-Eight
Chloe

Chloe kept her sword ready. Every shadow on the wall made her jump, and it was nearly full dark. She knew the center of the Labyrinth was close—at least it had seemed close when they were in the pines.

They turned again, walking down a long stone alley until they turned right again. Suddenly, all at once, they were at the center.

They'd made it. Chloe's breath snagged in her chest.

A sprawling oak tree dominated the space. She'd seen it from the pines, but up close, it boggled the mind. It was the size of a castle tower, bigger perhaps, its trunk twisted, its many branches thicker than she was tall. Silver lights and lanterns hung from its mossy branches, casting an ethereal glow. The oak's crown was gloriously dense, and its leaves rustled in the wind. Among its many forks and valleys, bundles of light-green fungus, ferns, and mushrooms grew. Woodland creatures roosted in its branches. Roots tangled beneath the tree, rising like archways in some spots and twisting together like entwined fingers in others.

Set in the trunk of the tree was a blue wooden door.

It was the door they were looking for. If the stories were correct, it would lead them to the Sisters' magical library and maybe Hyacinth's father. Perhaps even to Chloe's way home.

She was so close to going home.

Chloe almost didn't believe it.

She glanced over at Hyacinth, whose eyes were wide as she took in the tree. Her wings hung raggedly off her back, and she gripped her green book so tightly, her knuckles stood out like pebbles.

Hyacinth met Chloe's gaze and smiled, all wonder and happiness. The look made a sparrow of panic flutter through Chloe's chest. How was she going to tell Hyacinth she was leaving? How could she actually leave Hyacinth? A memory of their most recent kiss filled her mind.

A hard truth rose alongside the memory: She didn't want to leave Hyacinth. Hyacinth was brave and kind and funny. Chloe wasn't sure she wanted to go home.

No. That couldn't be true. Of course she wanted to go home! She had to go home. Anya needed her. Chloe belonged in her own world, with her sister.

But if that was true, why did it feel so wrong?

"Where's the third guardian?" Hyacinth asked, looking around warily.

That was a good question. Chloe surveyed the space as well. She fully expected something to charge at them or leap out of the tree to devour them. Her hand hovered over her sword's pommel.

But there was nothing.

"I don't know," she said. "Let's get inside before it decides to appear."

Coffee made a sharp growl as Chloe approached the door. "Hush, Little One," she soothed. "We have to go inside."

Coffee didn't reply in her mind, so Chloe ran a hand over the wooden surface of the door. Stars, moons, and suns were carved into the grain along with three letters: *C*, *M*, *A*.

"Celestine, Millicent, and Aria," she whispered, tracing the letters. The goddesses who'd created this world and built the Labyrinth. This was their door and their library. Chloe shivered as the feel of very old magic wrapped around her.

Coffee growled again and then whispered into her mind: *Steady on, Brave One. I feel like I've been here before, but I can't remember why.*

"We'll be fine," Chloe whispered back, reassuring herself as much as Coffee.

"Is there a key?" she called over her shoulder. "Did your father say how to actually get into the library?"

Hyacinth walked up to the door and turned the knob.

The door at the heart of the tree swung inward, revealing a shadowy hall beyond. The smell of paper and moss floated out of the doorway.

"This is too easy," Chloe murmured. "There's no third guardian. The door is just unlocked? It doesn't make any sense."

Dread snaked through her as she peered into the darkness of the oak tree.

"Come in, come in," whispered a soft, ancient voice. It could've been wind through the oak leaves, but it wasn't. It sounded welcoming and terrifying all at once.

Hyacinth crossed the threshold, but Chloe grabbed her arm. "Don't go in there."

Hyacinth tensed under her grip. "What do you mean, '*don't go in*'? We've come all this way! This is what it's all been for. My father could be in there. We have to find him!"

Chloe shook her head, trying to clear the fog from it. Something about the tree reminded her of the Mountain King's ballroom. Was it the magic she felt? Something else? "There's something bad in there. I don't know what, but it feels dangerous."

"Come in, come in. I've been waiting for you," whispered the ancient voice again.

Chloe shuddered.

"I'm going. Are you coming?" Hyacinth shook off Chloe's hand and stepped into the tree.

Everything in Chloe screamed to run away. To pull Hyacinth back and slam the door. But they had come this far. If there was a portal back to her world, Chloe had to find it. Drawing her sword and securing Coffee in her pocket, she followed Hyacinth through the doorway.

Shadows filled the space, thick with the scent of paper, dust, stone, and the earthy smell of things growing.

"I'm so glad you made it," whispered the voice. Then the door slammed shut behind them.

Chapter Twenty-Nine
Hyacinth

The library door banged closed, the noise ringing out in the vast space. Hyacinth spun around in surprise.

"Welcome to the Celestial Sisters' Library." A lilting voice whispered all around them.

"Who said that?" Hyacinth called out. A small whimper left her lips, and she spun around. "Chloe?"

Chloe stood behind her, Coffee glowing silver on her shoulder. His light did almost nothing to diminish the vast darkness of the library, meaning it must be bigger even than the cave beneath the mountain. "It wasn't me," Chloe said. "Though I heard it too. Do you think it's the third guardian?"

Hyacinth had no idea. Maybe Chloe had been right and they shouldn't have entered the library, but Hyacinth could hardly give up now, not when her father might be here. Still, her heart raced.

"We could use some more light," Hyacinth grumbled.

A light flared, just a flickering candle in a glass globe. Then dozens of others illuminated the room.

"How did you do that?" Chloe asked. "Something from your belt?"

Hyacinth wished. She had only the enchanted pen left in her belt and a very small measure of phoenix balm, which would help Coffee if he needed it, but not anyone else. "I didn't do that. It feels like the library is listening to us."

"In that case, I'd like a cup of hot chocolate and a pastry," Chloe said.

A surprised laugh burst out of Hyacinth. "And I'd like to find my father and get out of here."

Neither the snacks nor her father materialized. Hyacinth sighed. "What do we do now?" She looked around, considering her own question. The library was enormous. In front of them rose an immense cylindrical space, many times wider than all the first floor of Queen Mab's palace. Bookshelves lined its walls, rising to heights Hyacinth couldn't fathom. A staircase coiled like a snake around the edge of the walls. Balconies encircled the tree at every level, where hundreds of archways led to branching corridors.

Directly before them were several long tables and empty wooden chairs. Books were piled on the tables, almost like a scholar's library. An enormous tapestry covered the wall. It had been slashed to ribbons, as if it'd been clawed apart. From its bedraggled threads, Hyacinth could barely make out the faces of three women. Was this the work of the third guardian? If so, was it going to jump out at them anytime?

"Bramble and marsh," Chloe muttered at her side. "How are we ever going to find your father?"

Hyacinth was asking herself the same question. She turned to the closest shelf. Books bound in every color filled it. Names and titles sparkled on their spines, and Hyacinth ran her fingers along the closest shelf, disturbing the dust and cobwebs.

What stories did they contain? Who had written them? How had they gotten here? She pulled the closest book from the shelf, bringing a cloud of dust with it.

"Princess," Chloe said, before Hyacinth could investigate the random book. "Let's get moving. I think the faster we're through this place, the better. I still don't think we should linger here."

Hyacinth shoved the book back on the shelf. Chloe was right, but her words annoyed Hyacinth deeply. Shouldn't they look around a bit? One book wouldn't take up that much time; why shouldn't they linger as they figured out what to do?

More questions chased those, ushering in a heap of doubts. Was her father really here? He might not have even made it this far. Had she really expected him to be waiting right here to greet her? Bitter despair filled her stomach as she appraised the towering library.

They were never going to find him. They might as well turn around.

No. She had come this far. She could take action. She cupped her hands around her mouth and shouted, "Father!" Her voice echoed in the enormous space. "We're here! We've come to rescue you! Where are you?"

Chloe's fingers dug into Hyacinth's arm, hard enough to hurt. "What are you doing?" she demanded. "There's someone or something else here, or have you forgotten the mysterious voice? Let's not announce ourselves so boldly. That's a great way to get killed."

Hyacinth yanked her arm away, annoyance flaring. How dare Chloe speak to her like she was a child! "We're in a *library*. No one's going to kill us. I'm looking for my father. That's why we're here after all, or have you forgotten?"

Chloe scowled. "We can't just go about shouting for him. Have you learned nothing on all our adventures?"

Are you going to let her talk to you like that? someone or something whispered to Hyacinth.

Hyacinth's annoyance turned to fury so fast, her head spun. "As I recall, *I* saved you on more than one occasion on our journey. So, yes, I think I've learned *something*."

"Well, then show it!" Chloe snapped. "Stop running around like a child and think!"

Hyacinth's mouth dropped open. This! From the girl who ran into danger like it was calling to her.

"I am thinking!" she spat. "I don't see why *you're* the one who always has to make the plans!"

Chloe's eyebrows flew upward. "I'm not always making the plans, Princess!"

"Don't call me 'Princess'!"

Good, that's good, urged the voice on the wind. *Fight her. She doesn't respect you. End this.*

"Are you hearing that?" Hyacinth barked.

"Hearing what?" Chloe looked around, her sword ready. "What are you talking about?" Her tone was dismissive, like Hyacinth was making things up.

Hyacinth wanted to punch Chloe, the impulse immediate and imperative. Her fingers curled into fists at her side, and she fought against herself to unclench them.

Don't punch her. You don't want to punch her.

That was true, wasn't it?

Still, Chloe's comment had burrowed under Hyacinth's skin like a splinter. They'd survived these adventures together. Hyacinth wasn't the same coddled princess she'd been when they left the palace. "We'll *never* find him if we don't make an effort."

"Fine. Let's start looking. Where would you like to go, Princess?" Chloe's tone was mocking and unkind.

Hyacinth's fingernails dug into her palms. "I think we should split up," she ground out. If she wasn't around Chloe, then she wouldn't want to punch her. Then this blazing, irrational, all-encompassing frustration with her might dissipate.

"That's a terrible idea."

Hyacinth scowled and threw her hands up in exasperation. "What would you do, then? *Your* brilliant idea was to wait outside! If we'd done that, we'd never find my father!"

Why was Hyacinth fighting with Chloe? The words didn't feel like her own, but something in the air encouraged her, as if enjoying their discontent.

She let all her worry, exhaustion, and stress from the last few days roil inside her. "Why don't *you* go outside and wait? I know you don't want to hang out with someone unmagical. Well, maybe I'm not so proud to know you! Princesses don't kiss stablehands, after all. Especially not human ones!"

Why had she said that? She hadn't meant to bring any of that up.

Very good. End it. This story of yours is nearly over, whispered the disembodied voice.

Hyacinth spun around, looking for who was speaking. Whatever it was had to be the thing making her feel so angry. She couldn't take the words she'd flung at Chloe back, but, bramble and marsh, how she wanted to.

Chloe's knuckles whitened around the pommel of her sword. "Yes, *Princess*," she hissed. "You've made it *very* clear, I'm a mere human. Unfit for your royal presence, half-human though you are. Don't worry, I'll be out of your life soon enough."

Oh no. She really was going to leave this world and go back to her own. Hyacinth didn't want that! She really didn't, but no words of reconciliation left her lips. She just glared at Chloe.

"Fine," Chloe relented. "We'll follow your *brilliant* idea and split up."

"Fine," Hyacinth growled, voice trembling with rage. "I'll take that corridor." She pointed to a hallway that twisted to the right. "Let's meet back here. Then we can search the other rooms."

Chloe made a deep mocking bow. "I hope Your Highness can stay safe without your *human* companion around. And keep an eye out for who or what has been whispering at us."

Without another word, she marched down the nearest tunnel. Hyacinth almost called after her. To apologize, or perhaps say something hateful again. She didn't know, and she swiped at her sudden tears.

They'd fought so hard to stay together throughout the Labyrinth, but now it was all broken!

Which was Hyacinth's fault, though Chloe certainly wasn't blameless.

Who did she think she was, keeping things from Hyacinth after all they'd been through?

Hyacinth might've been unmagical, but she was brave too. She'd seen that again and again over the last few days. She didn't need Chloe. She'd find her father on her own, no matter what she encountered in this library.

You ended that so well, the air whispered all around her.

Hyacinth wanted to shake whoever had been egging her on, but she couldn't grab hold of air. Instead, she gulped in a few deep breaths, trying to calm her anger. Then she stormed in the opposite direction Chloe had taken, braving the massive library on her own.

Chapter Thirty
Chloe

Tears filled Chloe's eyes as she left Hyacinth. She turned down one branching hallway filled with books and into another. As she hurried along, she sucked in a ragged breath.

Her head pounded. Hyacinth's words echoed in her mind: *Maybe I'm not so proud to know you! Princesses don't kiss stablehands, after all. Especially not human ones!*

It was a knife to the chest, carving out Chloe's hopes and heart. Of course, she'd said terrible things back. But still.

Where had that anger come from? Why had she fought with Hyacinth? She hadn't meant to, but her feelings were a mess and her body was exhausted from their journey. She yearned to go home, and she wanted to stay here. Not that it seemed like her staying would please Hyacinth.

Grief and loss battered at Chloe as she walked, and her tears fell faster. Coffee nipped at her chin lightly.

"I'm fine, Little One," she whispered as a sob filled her throat.

She wasn't fine at all. She was wrung out like a dishrag and wanted nothing more than to curl up in a corner and cry. She wanted to hug her sister. She wanted to go after Hyacinth. She wanted to find something to stab and unleash her anger on.

Chloe wanted so many things, but none of them would help her get home. None of them would undo the things she'd said to Hyacinth.

I don't think it's a good idea to separate from Hyacinth, Coffee whispered into her mind. *You two are safer together, even if you exchanged harsh words.*

Chloe took a shuddering breath, trying to get her bearings in the endless library corridors. Twinkling golden lights spread a magical glow every few paces, but she had no idea where the central room with the door they'd come through was. Bramble and marsh, was she lost already?

Maybe Coffee was right. No matter what Chloe or Hyacinth had said to each other in anger, they were better off together.

"You were here as a protector," she whispered to herself. "Now go find her and apologize."

Exactly right, Coffee agreed. *That's the best path, Brave One, even though this is hard.*

How she loved this little dragon. She caressed Coffee's head and turned to retrace her steps. She walked down one passage, then the next. Some narrowed to points like the branches of the oak might, while others just diverged endlessly.

At last, she found her way back to the central room of the library. The lights were still on, but there was no sign of Hyacinth.

"Princess?" she called out. Her voice echoed in the space. "Hyacinth? Where are you?"

There was no answer. Of course not. Hyacinth was probably off fuming. Well. Chloe would just have to find her. She'd search every room in the library if she had to.

She climbed to the second floor and was entering another long hallway when a voice whispering from below stopped her in her tracks. It was the same leaf-rustling ancient voice she'd heard outside: "This way, Chloe Wreckersfind. This way. I've been waiting to meet you. I have a door to your world. . . ."

Chloe's heart pounded against her ribs. Something slithered beneath the voice, but how could she ignore it? If there was a chance of a door back to her world, she had to take it.

"Hurry, Chloe Wreckersfind," murmured the voice. "Hurry, hurry . . ."

Chloe paused, trying to pinpoint which hallway the voice had come from. The sound of leaves rustling, or maybe pages turning, to her right nudged her forward. She took a step toward the corridor.

With a flash of silver, Coffee darted out of her pocket. He hovered in the air for a moment, flapping his little wings like a hummingbird before he chomped down on her hand.

"Coffee!" she cried out, glaring at the tiny dragon, who appeared a little larger. Was he growing? No, that was just a trick of the flickering light. Blood welled under his teeth. "What did you do that for?"

The tiny little dragon looked up at her, his eyes wide. *Don't go down there, Brave One*, he whispered into her mind. *I don't know what awaits you, but it's nothing good.*

"Chloe, this way," the voice goaded. "How will you get back home without my help?"

Stay here, Coffee begged. *Please!*

Chloe ignored him as she raced down the hallway, speeding toward the voice and the promise of a way back home.

Her heart shattered to hear Coffee's desperate roar, a sound almost lost to the vast space of the library. If she got home, she'd never see him again.

Which had to be worth it, right?

He fluttered a few paces behind her as she followed the voice.

Chapter Thirty-One
Hyacinth

Hyacinth explored the library, part of her utterly in awe at the number of books, part of her still shocked they'd reached the center of the Labyrinth, and the rest of her absolutely devastated over the cruelties she and Chloe had exchanged.

What an absolute mess Hyacinth had made of it all.

Why had they fought like that? There was no reason for it besides stress, disappointment, and worry. Plus, that awful voice had been pressing her to argue and celebrating the fallout. Who—what—had that been?

As usual, she had no idea.

A headache bloomed behind her eyes. She paused to massage her temples, which did nothing for her pain.

She needed to focus on what was really important right now: finding her father. That's why they were here. There would be time to fix things with Chloe later.

Hyacinth breathed in the scent of old books, dust, paper, and the leafy smell of the tree itself. Magic floated in the air like dust motes. Hyacinth reached out a hand, letting silver particles flutter around her fingers. How had the Celestial Sisters made this library?

She chose a hallway to her right. It curved upward along one of the oak's enormous branches. Countless other hallways filled with more books, tables, lamps, and chairs, twisted off the sides. One passage to her left seemed to glow with a soft light. Ivy leaves grew around the doorway, all of them glittering with silvered magic.

"Father?" she called out. "Are you here?"

Something nudged her in that direction. Just a hint of a whisper. Should she follow it? Or would it lead her astray as the voice had done earlier?

There were thousands of branches in the library, twists and turns along every level. She had to pick something. At a loss for what else to do, Hyacinth followed her instinct and turned down the corridor.

"Father?" she called again. "Evan Bramblefen, are you here?"

The end of the hall loomed, and Hyacinth ran forward, desperately hoping her father would be there waiting for her.

He was not. It was just a sitting room with more bookshelves and an empty armchair.

Hot tears spilled down her cheeks. Brushing them away, she stomped along a different path. Then another one. And one more.

Truly, the tree was a labyrinth with more and more arteries splitting off in every direction. Bramble and marsh, she hated labyrinths so much.

Hyacinth blew out a frustrated breath and headed back toward the center of the tree. Where was Chloe now? What was she doing?

Trudging up the steps that encircled the central area, Hyacinth spiraled up to the next level of the trunk. She looked up to see hundreds more levels and corridors above her head.

She would never find her father. It was hopeless.

But she had to keep going.

She went up one level, then the next.

"Father!" she called out as she ran down yet another book-lined hallway. "Evan Bramblefen! Where are you?"

To her absolute shock, this time a voice answered her. "Who's there? Please, help me!"

Hyacinth stopped abruptly, tripping over her feet and falling to her knees. She scrambled up. Her father was here! "Keep talking so I can find you!"

"This way! Please . . . !" The voice snagged, giving way to a vicious coughing fit.

What was wrong with her father?

Desperately racing in the direction of the hacking coughs, Hyacinth ran through more dizzying turns of the library—and then she found her father.

Oh no.

No, no, no.

He looked nothing like the portrait in her mother's library or the illusion of him she'd seen under the waterfall.

"Father," Hyacinth whispered in astonished horror. "What's happened to you?"

Evan Bramblefen sat at a table beneath a window that looked out of the tree, so if he turned, he could see into the Labyrinth beyond. His thin frame hunched over a desk, and the bones of his face glowed starkly in the lamplight. Roots and vines climbed his legs and his arms, like the tree was devouring him. His hair was bone white, and another cough rattled his narrow chest. An inkwell with dregs of a glowing substance inside, a silver fountain pen, and a book sat on the table in front of him.

He looked up, meeting Hyacinth's gaze with haunted red-rimmed eyes. Deep-purple circles stood out underneath. and his skin stretched taut over his skull. "Who are you?" he managed between coughs.

Hurt stung Hyacinth, but that wasn't reasonable. She knew it. Her father hadn't seen her since she was two. Very gently, she said, "I'm your daughter, Hyacinth Bramblefen."

He blinked at her, not understanding. "But Hyacinth's just a toddler," he whispered. "Mab kept her at the castle. If you're my daughter, you must be—well, I don't know. I have no idea how long I've been here. It feels like only a few weeks, but also a century."

"I'm seventeen," Hyacinth said quietly. "You've been gone for fifteen years."

Shock crossed her father's features. His eyes widened as he searched her face. "Fifteen years! Hyacinth? Oh yes, I can see the resemblance to me and Mab now. My sweet girl, you shouldn't be here."

Hyacinth rushed toward him, clasping his hands. It was only then that she noticed the constellation of bruises and cuts on his sapling-thin arms. "But I am here. What's happened to you, Father? Who has done this?" She pulled at the roots and vines, snapping some of them even as more grew in their place. She needed Chloe's sword. Chloe's strength. Chloe's clear thinking to help her make sense of this.

Her father picked up the ink pen and scratched out some sentences along a page.

"What are you writing?" Hyacinth asked.

"The story of the Celestial Sisters," he said. "I have to change it. I can't leave this desk until I do."

Hyacinth wrenched the pen from his hand. "What do you mean? Surely I can free you from these vines! I'm taking you home."

Her father shook his head. "She'll never let me go."

"Who won't?"

"Aria." Her father's tone was bleak.

Hyacinth's mind reeled. "Aria?

"The Goddess of Endings." Her father grabbed the pen back and kept writing. "I'm certain we read a story about her when you were smaller."

They had, but that had been just a story, wasn't it?

"That doesn't make any sense," Hyacinth blurted.

Her father nodded, fixing her again with his empty stare. "None of it makes sense, I know."

Hyacinth struggled for breath as her mind raced. Her father resumed scratching words into the blank page in front of him.

How could she possibly help him? Was he enchanted? Was that why he kept writing? She put her hand gently over his, making his pen slip and drag a long mark across the paper.

"Father, please, start from the beginning. How did you get to the library, and why are you sitting here, letting the tree overtake you?" Hyacinth snapped a strand of ivy that curled around her father's wrist like ropes, but another grew in its place. "Why don't you leave?"

Her father's eyes clouded for a moment, as if he was searching for the right words. "I don't remember much of it, really . . . One moment, I was with you and Mab, saying goodbye, and then I was in the Labyrinth. . . . I don't know, Hyacinth. I have flashes of clarity, and then they go away. Aria's been feeding me Fae food for years, and she harvests my starlight to use as ink."

"Your starlight!" Hyacinth covered her mouth with her hand. A horrible vision of the Mountain King and the Endless Ball rose in her mind. If Aria had been siphoning her father's starlight for fifteen years . . .

Her father shuddered and tapped a finger against the nearly empty inkwell. "I've given so much of myself away, I don't know how much is left. . . ."

"How did you make it through the Labyrinth?" Hyacinth asked as her mind churned. There had to be some way to free him!

Her father shook his head. "I don't remember my entire journey, but I fought the stone guardian—"

"We ran into him too."

"Tough one to get past." Hyacinth's father nodded. "I wish I could remember more. . . ." His voice got wistful. "I do remember I carried so many potions and magical items with me then. Feathers and rings and stones and a dozen other things strung about my clothing." A rueful smile crossed his lips. "I clinked everywhere I walked. Mab used to tease me."

Hyacinth answered with her own bittersweet smile. Maybe that's one reason her mother hated her potion belt as well. She touched it once now, wishing she had more potions to offer her father that might help.

"What about you?" her father asked, his eyes brightening for a moment, like sunlight peeking through cloud cover. "Do you have a measure of Mab's magic? I see your wings came in at least."

Hyacinth shook her head, hating her fake wings all over again. "None. These wings are imitations, made by my mother to impress her courtiers during the solstice season. I can't do any of the High Fae or common Fae magics."

Her father winced. "Ah, well I'm sorry I gifted that to you, but you might be able to do another kind. That's why I came to this library, after all. I remember that at least! It was the question I chased for so long, the one I left you and your mother for: Can humans do a different type of magic than the Fae? I wanted to help my sister too. I wouldn't forget that."

Hyacinth would tell him about meeting Larissa and Elora once they were out of here.

He went on. "I've discovered there's more than one kind of magic in this world. But the greatest of all comes back to stories. That's how the Sisters created the world. All magic begins in starlight and stories."

"But that's just something people say at parties."

Her father cast her a knowing smile. "Sometimes, the greatest truths float around like common sayings. Now, perhaps it is just something people throw about at parties, but for Aria, Millicent, and Celestine, it was their guiding principle. In the human world, they wove peoples' lives together with stories, making a grand tapestry. Then they built the Fae world, word by word, infusing it with magic. All the stories of the Fae are in this library—everyone who's ever lived and every moment of their life is written in these books, along with much more."

Realization dawned on Hyacinth. "You mean *all* the stories of the people in our world are here?"

Her father nodded. "Somewhere in here, there's a book of your story so far." He gestured to the book in front of him. "This book here is Aria's story, along with her sisters'. She . . . made a mistake along the way, and she wants me to rewrite it for her."

"Can you do that?"

Her father shook his head.

"But why would she keep you here, then, if—"

A loud shredding sound interrupted Hyacinth's question, and the tapestry on the wall behind her father was ripped away.

Standing on the other side of it, in a vast room, were Chloe and a small woman holding a stack of books with a very dangerous-looking smile on her face.

Chapter Thirty-Two
Chloe

"H*urry, Chloe, this way.*" The ancient voice had whispered, urging Chloe onward. As Chloe followed, she tried not to think of Coffee's warnings that the voice meant danger. She tried not to think of Hyacinth.

Just put one foot in front of the other. That's all she had to do. Listen to the voice and she'd go home.

Was she doing the right thing, though? Was it fair to Hyacinth to just leave like this? How would she get home?

She shoved the questions away.

"*Hurry, Chloe, you're almost there. . . .*"

Chloe turned down a hallway to the right and found herself in a spellbinding room. Three-story bookshelves encircled the expansive walls. A vaulted ceiling towered above a stone floor inlaid with stars, moons, and flowers. In the center of the ceiling, a round window showed the night sky. Branches and leaves hung down, like veils. Tables and chairs filled the room, and an enormous arch covered the back wall, making an alcove. In the center of the niche stood three marble thrones. Stone statues of women sat in two, but the third was empty.

Chloe approached the stone women. "Who are you?" she murmured. She had an idea, of course . . . but if these were the three Celestial Sisters, why had the artist carved only two of them?

One of the stone women was short, plump, and had pointed ears. Her cheeks were dimpled, her mouth open in a slight O. She held a stone basket full of flowers in her lap that reminded Chloe of the figures in the Labyrinth's statue garden. A plaque at the base of the throne said CELESTINE.

The other stone woman was willowy, with long hair draping her shoulders. She had a pair of wings on her back and a teacup balanced on her lap. Her eyes were cast to the side, her eyebrows raised in surprise. "Millicent," Chloe whispered, reading the name carved into the stone.

"I see you've met my sisters," an ancient voice rasped behind her—the one Chloe had been hearing since they first reached the oak tree.

Chloe spun around, her hand flying to her sword. All her training and instincts told her to run or fight, but there was only a tiny woman standing behind her. A stack of books rested in her arms, and her flyaway salt-and-pepper hair sat in a loose bun on top of her head. One of her ink-stained fingers tapped her lip as she studied Chloe. Her faded green velvet dress hung from her thin frame, and her huge eyes blinked deep blue from behind thick spectacles.

"Hello, Chloe Wreckersfind," the woman said. "I'm so glad you made it to my library. My inkwell is running dry, and I have need of you."

She pointed to an inkpot on a table that glowed silver blue, just like the Mountain King's chandelier.

Starlight.

Chloe recoiled, dread gripping her bones. "Who are you?"

"But don't you know?"

Dumping her books on the nearest table, the woman walked over to the empty third throne and settled herself into it. "Must you see me and my sisters together to understand? Everyone always did think of us as a group. Three sides of the same coin." She nodded toward the plaque at the bottom of her throne.

"Aria?" Chloe breathed.

"Goddess of Endings," the woman said, melancholy lacing her voice. "I'm the one who snips the thread, forces the end. Makes a story stop." She reached for the statue of Millicent and ran a finger over her stone arm. "It's such a terrible thing to lose a sister, isn't it?"

Chloe nodded through her confusion about the sudden topic change. Best to try to keep Aria happy and talking so Chloe could make sense of what was happening here. Was this woman really a goddess? Perhaps that didn't matter so much, not if there was a portal here that could take Chloe home. Aria would certainly know about that, so Chloe played along with her.

"It is a terrible thing to lose a sister," she agreed. "What do you mean lose them, though? Aren't your sisters somewhere in this library?"

Aria's eyes met Chloe's, and this time a ferocious light burned within them, a flame of rage and despair. "These statues *are* my sisters, Chloe Wreckersfind. Both Celestine and Millicent turned to stone and abandoned me here."

Chloe flinched at the words. "What happened to them?"

Aria moved from Millicent to Celestine, smoothing a stone tendril of hair as if it were real. "You want my story?" she said softly. "I haven't told it in so long, but I suppose it's a fair trade. One sister story for all you're going to give me."

That was ominous. Chloe didn't dare move as the goddess pinned her in place with a look. "Please, tell me what happened. I've heard stories of how you and your sisters built this world, but I've never heard anything about your sisters turning to stone."

Aria shook her head. "You wouldn't have heard that part. I made very sure to keep our secret safe. What do they say about us, I wonder, out there in the world? Probably something like, 'Many ages ago, the three sisters built this world for their children the Fae . . .' Is that right?"

"Something like that," Chloe agreed. "And they say 'all magic begins in stories.'"

Aria laughed, a bitter, brittle noise. "Of course they do. As if it were that simple to build a world. As if my sisters and I were so easy to capture in words. The truth is, although we were sisters, we were always our own people. Not long after we built this world, we began fighting. We wanted different things for this place and its people. Celestine wanted to grow things and make this world a paradise for her children. She wanted to make everyone equal and share our gifts among them. Millicent was always building things. She's the one who created the three Fae kingdoms and who started the Crescent Atheneum as a place of learning."

"And you?" Chloe ventured.

Aria's hand fluttered to her spectacles, which had slipped down her nose. "I told you. My job is ending stories. That's always been my place—to take a life when it's time—but Celestine and Millicent didn't like that. They insisted we give the Fae much longer lives. That wasn't my way, but I went along with it. Every fifteen years, my sisters and I returned to this library to renew our magic, to meet and talk, to share our own stories, and to strengthen the bonds that hold this world together. Then we'd all return to our own tasks. Each time Celestine and Millicent left, it broke my heart to see them go. Time passed, and they changed even more. They became distant from me, too concerned with tending their gardens or accepting Fae offerings. But, oh, how I missed them and who we once were! You have a sister—you know this! We were girls together, long, long ago! We shared all our secrets, all our hopes. We had a whole world, but we grew apart, and before I knew it, it was too late. They were different, I was different, and we couldn't go back."

The words were knives in Chloe's core. Could she and Anya ever go back to the way they had been? Time moved on and people changed. The feeling that her sister was changing without her there to see it was agony.

"What did you do to get your sisters back?" Chloe said, very softly through the tears lodged in her throat.

"What I had to!" Aria pounded a fist against Celestine's throne. "I ended their stories to keep them here with me! Where they belong!"

Horror filled Chloe. She could see from Celestine's and Millicent's stone faces that they'd been stunned by Aria's trap. "*You* did this to your sisters?"

Would Chloe make the same choices to keep her sister the same always, no matter what the cost?

She wouldn't. She wanted Anya to grow and change and become someone new, even if that meant they were no longer close.

Aria's shoulders slumped. "I needed my sisters near me. No one understood me as well as they did! I was so alone. But I knew as soon as I performed the spell, I'd made a mistake."

A sob snagged in Chloe's throat. She knew that loneliness and desperation to be near her sister. Knew it so well.

"Can you bring them back?"

Aria paced. "I've been trying for nearly fifteen years. I just want to go back to the beginning! To who we were before. That's why I'm here in this library. This tree and its stories are the heart of our world. If I can change our story, I can undo the spell and free my sisters. I can bring them back, and we can start over again, but I'm running out of starlight ink."

Aria's eyes were wild with her plans, and the hungry look that passed over her face made Chloe tremble with fear. She was a much more dangerous, more powerful version of the Mountain King. Chloe longed to flee the room.

Steady, Brave One, Coffee whispered from her pocket. He'd dove in there at the first sight of Aria, but now his head peeked out.

"What, or who, have you been using for ink?" Chloe had a terrible sinking feeling that she knew. If Hyacinth's father had made it this far fifteen years ago . . . if he had somehow gotten caught up in Aria's scheming . . .

The goddess grinned.

Aria waved her hand, and silver light filled the space. It blinded Chloe for a moment, and then the tapestry on the back wall ripped away, revealing a small room. Inside the room was a man hunched over a table, covered in vines. And Hyacinth.

"Hyacinth, run!" Chloe shouted.

But it was too late, Aria waved her hand again, and one set of vines snaked around Chloe, binding her to a chair. The other tendril captured Hyacinth and flung her at the goddess's feet.

"Let me go!" Hyacinth protested, fighting the vine.

"Aria, please," the man cried out. "Let my daughter and her friend leave. Take me. Finish me, end this, but don't hurt them."

Ah, so that was Hyacinth's father! They had found him, but he was in terrible shape. Chloe glanced around, frantic. How would they get out of here?

Aria scoffed. "I've gotten everything I need from you, scholar. Your starlight is nearly gone. But your daughter might make a wonderful inkwell. She's half-human and half-Fae. Her starlight might be exactly what I need to rewrite my story. We've certainly never tried that before!"

He flinched at the words, his posture deflating.

Aria couldn't have Hyacinth. Chloe wouldn't let her. A fierce protectiveness rose within Chloe. Her eyes met Hyacinth's, and she tried to say everything she hadn't been able to. *I'm sorry for lying. And for saying awful things to you.*

Hyacinth looked away, still battling the vines that trapped her.

"Let her go!" Chloe yelled. "Please, you can have me instead."

Aria ignored her and unsheathed Chloe's sword. Then she wrenched Hyacinth's head back by the hair and put the sword to her neck. A drop of blood rose beneath the sword's point. "I will pull blood and starlight from you, Princess. We will rewrite the story of the Celestial Sisters and—"

Chloe struggled against the vines that held her. "Please! Aria! I'll do anything you ask!"

Aria's eyes flicked to Chloe. "Anything?"

Chloe nodded.

Aria whispered another word, and one of the bookshelves swung open. On the other side, there was a flash of silver light, and then noise filled the library. City noise.

Familiar noise.

Carriages clattering over cobblestones. Vendors calling out. The smells of roasted meats, baked goods, and woodsmoke drifted into the room. A small bright blue shop, its cozy windows filled with dresses, sat directly across from the door.

"Anya and Ruby's Dress Emporium," Chloe read out loud.

Tears sprung to her eyes. The vines holding her loosened, and she stumbled forward. It was Anya's shop. Her sister was so close. Through the shop window, Chloe could see a blonde girl wearing a fashionable blue dress. She was laughing about something, and her smile made Chloe's heart lurch.

There was Anya. Just a few steps away.

"All you have to do is leave, Chloe," Aria said. "Choose to end your story here, and step through the door. You'll be home. You'll have your sister back, and I'll have mine returned to me too. You won't have to think of this world ever again."

Chloe watched Anya bring a dress to a customer. Anya's girlfriend, Ruby, walked over and rested a hand on Anya's shoulder. They looked so happy, so at ease. Chloe yearned to join them with every fiber of her being.

It would be so simple. A few steps, and she'd cross through the door. All this would be over. She'd be back home.

She glanced over at Hyacinth, who stood stock-still. The princess's hair tangled around her shoulders; her shredded fake wings were barely hanging on. Still, her chin jutted out proudly. Something in her had changed on this journey, and her gaze burned into Chloe's.

She was beautiful and ferocious.

She was Chloe's beginning, middle, and end.

She was home.

With one last longing look at her sister, Chloe grabbed the bookcase door and slammed it shut.

"You shouldn't have done that, Chloe Wreckersfind," Aria snarled. "Now you'll die like everyone else."

Chloe had eyes only for Hyacinth. "I think that's worth it," she murmured.

Tears sparkled in Hyacinth's eyes. "Thank you," she mouthed.

"Enough," Aria shouted. She dragged Hyacinth over to the stone statues of her sisters and forced her to kneel before Celestine. "Her blood and starlight will bring them back! We will be together again."

Aria stabbed the blade toward Hyacinth's neck, but the princess twisted away at the last moment. In one quick move, Chloe grabbed for the sword, but she missed it as Hyacinth twisted in Aria's grasp.

"You can't escape me." Aria grabbed Hyacinth again.

Then Aria sliced the sword across Hyacinth's back. A scream ripped free from the princess.

"Stop it!" Chloe yelled. "You're hurting her."

"I'm *killing* her," Aria corrected. "I'm giving her life to my sisters." She smeared some of Hyacinth's blood along Celestine's hands and Millicent's cheeks.

Chloe didn't have a sword, but she grabbed the closest thing at hand: the starlight-filled inkwell on the table next to her. She flung it at Aria, but it shattered on the statue of Celestine. Silver tendrils of magic rose from the broken bottle, covering Celestine and Millicent.

That is enough of this nonsense! A rockslide of a voice rang out through the room. Chloe spun around to see Coffee, who'd leaped out of her pocket, growing in size at a tremendous rate. He was the size of a dog, then a horse, then an elephant, and then he was nearly as tall as the library itself. All at once was he an enormous dragon with glimmering pearlescent scales and sharp teeth.

"Little One?" Chloe said in disbelief.

I remembered who I am, Brave One, he whispered into her mind. *I'm Ora, the dragon of the Celestial Sisters and the third guardian. I'm Aria's champion. A few months ago, she made Evan transform me into a teacup-sized dragon to see if it was possible to rewrite a story. It was, but I escaped the library and the Labyrinth, hoping to get help for the trapped scholar.*

He sounded vengeful, furious. He lumbered toward Aria.

"Stay away from me!" Aria shouted. "If you kill me, dragon, the library will go, and this entire world will fall apart!"

That's a risk I'm willing to take, Coffee snarled. *May I eat her, Brave One?*

"You're your own dragon," Chloe said, stepping out of the way. "Please do as you will."

Chapter Thirty-Three
Hyacinth

The cut across Hyacinth's back throbbed. One of her wings dangled off her shoulder, hanging on by the barest thread of a spell, but she couldn't look away from Coffee, who was suddenly as big as Runa or any other dragon in Queen Mab's stable.

"I'll make you small again!" Aria shouted, darting away from Coffee. "I'll make you nothing! I'll end you."

"Being small isn't nothing," a placid voice said from behind them.

Hyacinth was weakened from her injuries, but she turned at the sound. Her mouth fell open in shock.

Celestine, the Goddess of Beginnings—who had been trapped in stone with a basket of flowers on her lap—blinked as she put the basket aside and stood. Stone chips fell from her shoulders as she stretched, shaking off whatever spell had calcified her. She glowed lavender as she transformed into a living, breathing person again. "You've always gotten that wrong, Aria. You gave High Fae the most power, but there is great power in the small ones *and* the large ones, and it should be shared equally and given freely."

The Goddess of Beginnings turned to her other sister, Millicent, and touched her forehead, undoing the spell Aria had wrought. Millicent shook off the stone too and yawned, as if she'd been asleep. "Hello, Sister," she murmured.

Celestine kissed her sister's forehead. As she did so, Hyacinth stepped away from the goddesses' reunion.

Chloe rushed to her side, slipping an arm around her waist. "What will we do now that there are three of them?" she asked.

"Well, we have a dragon," Hyacinth said.

Chloe shot her a grin and then looked up at Coffee. "That's certainly true. Let's try to get out of here?"

Hyacinth nodded, and they slunk toward her father, who was still bound to the table in the library, eyes wide from all that had happened. He looked like he was about to faint.

Coffee growled down at Aria, who only had eyes for her two restored sisters.

"Celestine, Millicent, my dear ones," Aria said. Relief filled her voice. "I'm so happy to see you!"

The Goddess of Beginnings and the Goddess of Middles shed the remaining stone and then stepped toward their sister. They clasped their arms around her.

"We have been waiting a long time to see you too, Aria." Celestine's voice was blistering. "You stole my stone-crafting spell and cast it on us."

Millicent glared at Aria. "And you tricked us into a world of illusions using my magic. Do you know how long we stumbled around in there, trying to get out?"

A skittish, fragile laugh escaped Aria's mouth. "Well, that may be, but I had to keep you here somehow! We were becoming so different. I had to keep us together."

"By casting us in stone? By not letting us change or grow? That is not the right way, Aria!" Celestine snapped.

"It *was*!" Aria shot back. "You both have always been so united. So together in your plans for this world. Never listening to me! Well, listen now, Sisters. I know how to do it. Now that we're together, we can strip this world down to its roots and start over! We can weave all the stories again and truly be united in our vision for them."

A frantic note rang out in Aria's voice as she unspooled her plan.

"We can't do that, Sister," Millicent said. "We don't want to tear this world apart. We love it and all our children here."

"But they don't love you back!" Aria shouted. "They use magic for themselves and don't remember us."

Hyacinth couldn't help herself. "That's simply not true!" she blurted. "We remember you at every feast, every gathering, every holiday. We tell the story of the three Sisters, and we use your words—'All magic begins in stories'—often. It's almost an incantation! If we don't know the full truth of you three, that's hardly our fault. You've hidden yourselves away for so long, how could we understand more?"

Celestine's eyes met hers, and she nodded. "We know that, and we appreciate it."

"It's all lies!" Aria shouted. "This miserable half-human princess isn't even magical. She's useful only as a conduit for my great work in bringing you back. Now that you're here, I don't need her anymore! Dragon! Ora! Eat this princess."

Coffee puffed out smoke and stepped between Hyacinth, Chloe, and Aria. *I will not.* His voice boomed in their minds.

Chloe laughed and patted Coffee's leg. "Thank you, Little One."

Aria screeched in rage. "None of you are leaving here! I am going to break the world! We are going to start over!"

There was a great flash of silver, and then silence fell over the library.

Hyacinth gripped Chloe's hand and peered around Coffee's bulk.

Celestine and Millicent stood beside Aria, who was now a statue, frozen with her mouth open in a scream of rage.

"We hate to do that to her," Celestine said. "But perhaps a few hundred years as a statue will give her the rest she so clearly needs."

"Come forward, please," Millicent called out. "We won't hurt you."

Was that it, then? Was it over?

Chloe reached for Hyacinth's hand, and they stepped forward.

"You too, scholar," Millicent said to Hyacinth's father. She waved her hand, and the vines holding him to the desk released him.

He lurched forward unsteadily, and the three of them stood before the goddesses who had built their world.

"We are so sorry about Aria," Celestine said. "She was always getting things wrong, putting people into artificial hierarchies, and ending things too soon, though we loved her."

"We did love her," Millicent agreed. "But sometimes you have to let people go and hope they might change."

"What will you do now?" Hyacinth asked.

Celestine appraised the mess in the library. Books littered the floor, and a crack had split the tree on one side. "Repair this, for a start."

"Then I think we should open the Labyrinth," Millicent said. "Make a path so anyone who wants to can come here and study with us. This tree contains all the stories of the Fae and their world, yes, but it also has many more besides. We always intended to make it a place of learning."

Hyacinth's heart leaped at the words. "Could unmagical half-human princesses learn here?"

Celestine's eyes twinkled. "They certainly could. We have all sorts of magic to teach you."

A happy noise left Hyacinth's lips.

"Give us a few weeks to put things in order," Millicent said. "Then we'll send for you."

"I would love that," Hyacinth said. Suddenly, her future and her story stretched before her more incredibly than she'd expected.

"As for you, scholar," Millicent said. "We can't give you back the years Aria stole from you, but we can return some of the starlight she took. At least in part. Step forward, please."

Celestine and Millicent placed their hands on him, and silvery light flowed from them and back into his body. He seemed to grow taller, shake off the decrepitude that had bent his back and his spirit.

Relief washed through Hyacinth to see it. Her father would be okay. She had found him and helped save him.

"Thank you," he murmured with a bow.

As one, Celestine and Millicent nodded. "Tell the kingdoms our story, scholar. Help us make things better and fairer for everyone in this world."

Hyacinth's father nodded back. "I will. Though I may not visit this library for a long time." He shuddered as he said it. "Or ever again."

"We understand," Celestine said.

Then they turned to Chloe. "As for you, traveler from another realm, what can we give you?"

Hyacinth turned to Chloe, who bit her lip as she considered. Would she leave this world and go back to her sister? Stay here and always regret the chance?

Chloe released Hyacinth's hand and approached the goddesses. She leaned over and whispered to them.

Celestine's eyebrows shot up, but she smiled. "We'll see what we can do."

Chloe nodded happily and walked back to Hyacinth.

"What did you ask for?" Hyacinth whispered.

"You'll see," Chloe said with a smile.

Lastly, the goddesses turned to Coffee, who still towered over them all.

"And you, dragon and guardian? What would you like?"

A rumbling filled the air, and then Coffee's smooth-as-velvet voice rolled through the room: *Release me from my obligation as a guardian, and give me freedom to be who I want.*

"Absolutely," Millicent said. "What Aria made the scholar do was fundamentally rewrite your story, so you were stuck as a tiny dragon with no memory of who you were or how you'd gotten that way. We'll give you a bit of our shape-shifting magic and a bit of our illusion magic so you can change your size to whatever suits you at the time."

Magnificent, Coffee thundered.

Celestine and Millicent chanted some words, and a net of silver threads rose above Coffee. The threads slipped over him like a cloak and then disappeared.

He let out one more puff of smoke—which clouded the air and sent books tumbling to the ground—then he shifted to the teacup size he'd been.

He fluttered onto Chloe's hand, and she let out a delighted laugh. "I missed you, Little One," she said.

And I've gotten used to riding around your pocket, Coffee said, once again letting everyone hear his words.

"Now go on your way," Celestine said. "But come back whenever you'd like."

With a word, she transported them to the main library door.

"Ready for the rest of our story?" Chloe asked, squeezing Hyacinth's hand.

She was. She was so ready for all of it.

She stepped through the door—and her heart skipped a beat.

Queen Mab glowered at the oak tree. Her dragon Runa stood behind her, enormous and scowling as well.

✦

The queen's face shifted to wonder as she beheld Hyacinth.

"Hyacinth?" she gasped, surging forward to pull her into a tight hug. "I had a feeling you were here, but I couldn't get inside. I was so worried about you!" She squeezed Hyacinth.

"Mother, I'm fine."

"You're not. What happened to your wings? Where have you been? I'm so sorry for—"

The queen's words stopped as she saw Hyacinth's father stagger out of the tree. She released Hyacinth. "Evan? Is that you?" Her voice was ragged with hope.

"Mab," he replied on the edge of a sob. "My love, it's me. I'm sorry to have been gone so long."

With a cry, Queen Mab, ever-glorious monarch of the Moonshadow Kingdom, ran forward into Evan Bramblefen's arms. They clung to each other, whispering words Hyacinth couldn't hear. She was so happy, she didn't know what to say.

"You did it, Princess," Chloe said, wrapping an arm around her waist and tugging her behind a particularly enormous oak root so they were hidden from Hyacinth's parents. Coffee fluttered off Chloe's shoulder and over to Runa to say hello.

"*We* did it," Hyacinth replied, turning to Chloe. "I can't believe how this all worked out."

"It's like something out of a story." Chloe smirked.

"Beginning, middle, and end," Hyacinth whispered, leaning in close.

"Beginning, middle, and end," Chloe replied against her lips. "Now kiss me?"

Hyacinth could think of nothing she'd rather do.

Epilogue
Chloe
Four Months Later

The dragon dipped on a wind current, making Chloe's breath catch in her throat. She let out an exuberant shout as he spread his enormous wings and spirited her over the treetops.

"You're doing amazing, Little One," she called out.

You better hang on, Brave One, Coffee whispered in her head.

Although he could change sizes at will and was often not little at all, the nickname had stuck. Over the last few months, Chloe and Coffee had trained and traveled the Moonshadow Kingdom together, delivering messages for Queen Mab, taking Evan Bramblefen far and wide to spread the Sisters' stories, and ferrying Hyacinth back and forth to the library in the oak tree.

They were on their way to pick up Hyacinth now, and they had to hurry. They had a very special evening planned, and they couldn't be late.

They soared above the Swamplands, passing over the flowery abundance of the Hyacinth Cottage, where Elora and Larissa, who was recovering slowly from her years under the mountain, always kept a kettle on for a visit from their brother, their niece, or even just Chloe sometimes. Then they were above the Labyrinth, a long straight path now leading right to the center. Chloe still liked to fly past the former stone garden. (Celestine had released all the statues—who turned out to be Fae who'd begged to live forever long ago and had been turned to statues so they would never fade away—from their binding, and they now wandered the Labyrinth, setting up homes, strolling together, and getting on with their own stories.) Chloe and Coffee also loved to fly through the sparkling waterfall and atop the pines.

After all that, they landed with a flutter of wings outside the enormous oak tree. Hyacinth waited there on a bench made of roots.

As they landed, Hyacinth looked up from the book she was reading and waved. "Hello!"

Chloe slid off Coffee's back and strode over. She pulled Hyacinth close for a long kiss. "I've missed you, Princess."

"And I you, dragon rider."

In truth it had only been a few days since they'd last seen each other, but even that was too long.

"You know you could stay here and study with me," Hyacinth said.

Chloe shuddered at the thought. After Celestine had granted her request and she'd become a dragon rider, there had been nothing she wanted to do more than see the kingdom from Coffee's back.

Well. That and come home to Hyacinth.

"Are you ready?" Chloe asked. There was just one piece missing from her story, and if all went to plan tonight, that would slip into place. Nervousness shivered through her. She so hoped it would all work out.

Hyacinth shoved her books into her satchel, and Chloe glimpsed Evan's green book among them. She and Chloe were adding notes to it as Chloe traveled more and Hyacinth studied in the library.

"I'm ready."

"Let's fly, then, Princess."

✦

Their home was on the far side of Keldale, by the western bend of the river. It was busy on market days, but this evening it was quiet. Two windows, filled with purple, blue, and pink glass diamonds, flanked a door painted bright green. Candlelight spilled from the shop, speckling the cobblestones with gems of light. A wooden sign hung above the door. COFFEE'S SHOP, said the sign, and below the letters was a painted picture of Coffee curled on top of a pile of books with a warm beverage nearby.

Home.

Chloe loved it here so much.

A few hours after they'd settled back in, Chloe returned from the bakery, holding a large box in her hand. Coffee had transformed back to teacup size as soon as they landed outside the city, and he now napped in her pocket.

Her boots crunched through the fresh snow that had fallen that evening, sugaring Keldale's rooftops and softening the world. She loved walking up to her and Hyacinth's home. She loved their coffee and tea shop, where her sword hung behind the counter. She still used it: carrying it on every flight with Coffee, giving Hyacinth late-night sword-fighting lessons on the rooftop, or strapping it on when they did their monthly trip back to the Moonshadow Palace via dragon to see Hyacinth's family.

She paused outside one of the windows. From her coat pocket, Coffee gave a small contented snore. Chloe stroked Coffee's head and watched as Hyacinth sat down at a desk and picked up a pen.

Hyacinth had been busy studying magic and writing up their adventures these last few months, and tonight was the night she'd promised Chloe could read them.

It was her birthday, after all.

Chloe shifted the box in her arms. Nervousness filled her as she thought about what was written on the cake.

Happy 19th Birthday,
Anya and Chloe!

Would her sister really show up, though? Celestine and Millicent had promised a door and the shop in Keldale, and Queen Mab had agreed to both, much to both Chloe's and Hyacinth's immense relief. It had taken the Sisters a few months to untangle the magical mess that Aria had left in her wake, but they'd sent invitations through the worlds to the party. Tonight, the door to Chloe's world would finally open, and Hyacinth would meet Chloe's friends and family.

If everything worked out.

Everything had to work out.

Chloe strode into the shop, too excited and worried to dwell on it much longer.

"Hi there," Hyacinth said, looking up from her book. "I'm so glad you're here. I'm about to write the two most important words."

Chloe set the cake box down and approached the desk. She leaned over Hyacinth's shoulder as Hyacinth wrote *The End* with a flourish.

"Of course, it's not the end of our story," Hyacinth said, facing Chloe. "But it feels so good to retell our adventure."

Chloe put a finger under Hyacinth's chin and tilted it upward gently for a kiss. "Have you thought of a title yet? Because I have one. What about *The Hyacinth Labyrinth*?"

Hyacinth kissed her back and then laughed. "That's a little much, don't you think?"

"It's not! It's perfect and speaks across many levels to both our adventure and how complicated you are, Princess!"

Hyacinth kissed Chloe again before closing her book. "It's called *The Princess and The Swordswoman*, but that's a temporary title. We'll keep working on it." She handed Chloe the book. "Happy birthday, love."

Chloe accepted the leather-bound book and hugged it to her chest. "This is the best present I've ever gotten."

And it was. Her life with Hyacinth, the small coziness of their days, *and* the wild adventures they went on were everything she wanted. She couldn't wait to share it with Anya.

Speaking of which . . .

She kissed Hyacinth once more, then pulled away. "We should get ready. Our guests will be here soon."

✦

Their guests arrived through the magical door on the rooftop of Coffee's Shop. This was the first night the portal was open, a birthday present from Queen Mab, to show her thanks for Hyacinth and Chloe finding her long-lost husband. Tonight, it would allow guests to come through to Fae, though Chloe had been able to send invitations via a spell Hyacinth and her father had whipped up with the help of Celestine and Millicent.

First came Chloe's friends from the stables, Hester and Fellmi, and then some friends from her world, Quinta and Twain, arrived carrying two packages wrapped in red paper. Chloe was certain the packages contained something strange and magical from their enchanted curiosity shop, the Vermilion Emporium.

Then the girls they'd met last year, Esme and Sybil, entered holding a small gray cat, a bunch of flowers, and a bottle of absinthe. "We're so glad you're okay," Sybil said, hugging Chloe fiercely. "We were so worried. We tried for months to find another door so we could help you!"

After Esme and Sybil, Wendell, the retired Fae stablemaster Chloe considered family, arrived, holding a tray of fresh-baked cookies. Then Marcel, the realm mapper Chloe had apprenticed under, stepped through the door. Tonight, he hugged Chloe, shook Hyacinth's hand, offered Coffee a dapper bow, and then handed Chloe a wrapped present. "It's a book of realm maps I've been working on," he said with a wink. "In case you decide to leave this world and seek out others again."

Chloe accepted it with a smile as Hyacinth studied the book curiously.

Then Chloe and Hyacinth gathered all their friends around the long table they'd set out under the stars. Magical fires, another birthday gift from Queen Mab, burned blue in braziers around the roof. The flames created a warm bubble around them, even as more snow fell.

Minutes passed. Chloe paced the rooftop, watching the magical door.

Hyacinth stood and looped an arm through Chloe's. "She's coming, don't worry."

Chloe was trying not to worry, but she couldn't help it.

Before she could voice her doubts, there was another knock on the door. She ran to open it—and there, on the other side, was her sister.

"Anya!" she screeched, a delighted, giddy laugh raising her voice. "I'm so glad you got my invitation!"

Her sister made a joyous sound and stepped through the doorway, hand in hand with her girlfriend, Ruby.

Chloe clutched her twin sister, hugging her so fiercely. "Happy birthday," she whispered.

"Happy birthday," Anya said, hugging her back. "Now, what is this place?"

Chloe grinned. "I have so many stories to tell you and hundreds of letters to share, but first, come meet my Hyacinth and everyone else."

"I'd like nothing better," Anya said, wiping tears from her own eyes.

Chloe hugged her sister again, and then they went to greet the family Chloe had lost and found in this strange world and through so many adventures.

A Note from the Author
on Fae Stories and Where This One Came From

Researching Fae stories is one of my favorite pastimes, and I've fallen down many rabbit holes as I seek them out. That's the thing about stories: The more you look into them, the stranger they become.

There are Fae stories in so many different cultures and from so many parts of the world. Some of them likely would be very familiar to you, and others are wildly unexpected or surprising. Some of these Fae legends grew up on their own, and they are unique to the people who told them, but many of them influenced one another, as stories so often do when they move from one person or place to another. In general, Fae stories are an absolutely tangled web that's a delight to unravel, but it's a web that avoids easy characterization. (How I wish sometimes to be a Fae scholar like Emily Wilde from one of my favorite adult novels about the Fae world, *Emily Wilde's Encyclopedia of Faeries,* by Heather Fawcett. If you haven't read it, and you like Fae lore and stories, I highly recommend this series!)

It was while I was researching Fae stories that I stumbled across a bit of etymology that directly impacted the world in *The Hyacinth Labyrinth*.

Let me tell you what I found: Although there's still debate about this, it's supposed that the French word *fae*, which originated around the twelfth or thirteenth century, comes from the Latin word *fata*, which means Fates.

Is that true? Is it verifiable?

I'm not sure, honestly. It may not matter, in the most exact sense.

But that whisper of an etymological connection, along with the fact that the word *solstice* has *sistere* (a Latin word that means *to stop* but sounds like *sister*) as one of its roots, got me thinking about sisters and the Fates and the Fae all at once.

Now, lumping all these things together is a bit of a stretch if you're a scholar, but I've always held that story lives in the stretched-thin places and overlooked corners of history.

Stories are magic, after all. This is my guiding belief, one that I made quite literal in this book.

So, once I simmered all those bits of story, etymology, and imagination in my head, this idea emerged. The Greek Fates and the Roman ones after them were three sister storytellers, each of them twining, weaving, and cutting the stories of human lives. In my world, these sisters got tired and decided to build a whole world for their retirement. They wove some more stories, and from those, the Fae as we know them came into being.

As you can tell from this book, that was just the beginning. The middle and end were far different than anyone, including the three sisters, could've imagined. Which is probably how it is with all stories, Fae or otherwise.

Acknowledgments

This story was a labyrinth from the start.

I have wanted to write Chloe's story since I first introduced her in *The Vermilion Emporium*, and I have wanted to write a book set in a Fae world long before that, but it's stressful to write the third standalone in a world you've already built but not entirely planned because you weren't sure this would ever become a book! I had no idea what I was getting myself into!

While writing *The Hyacinth Labyrinth*, I hit dead ends; I had to double back; I changed course (and the plot) more times than I can count; there were turns I didn't see coming and real-life perils that knocked me down. Everything got so twisted at one point, I despaired of ever finishing. Through it all, I held on to a vision of Chloe and Hyacinth riding a dragon together and the two of them finding a magical library inside an oak tree. (Let's face it, few things are more spectacular than magical libraries or ancient oak trees.)

Through this bookish labyrinth, I had my stalwart editor, Ashley Hearn, legendary international sword girl, at my side. She set me back on course. Asked the right questions. Encouraged me. Got me this stunning cover, and was generally just the magical Fae godmother I needed on this journey. Huge, endless thanks to you, my friend!

Thanks also to my agent, Kate Testerman, another excellent companion on all bookish journeys. Cheers to many more books together, Kate!

Thank you to the incredible Peachtree team! Kade Dishmon, thank you for the line edit that helped this story flow so much better, and thank you for all the cheering, gasps, and delight over Coffee. (Also, there are far fewer breaths being hauled in thanks to your keen eyes and smart notes.) Thanks also to Lily Steele for the beautiful design; Manu Velasco for the excellent copy edit; Jamie Evans in managing editorial; editorial intern Anya Ricketson; and Melanie McMahon Ives in production. Thanks as well to the publicity and marketing team, who have done so much for my books at Peachtree!

Thank as well to my amazing cover illustrator, Andie Lugtu, who also did the gorgeous cover for *The Absinthe Underground*! They've captured my vision for both these books entirely. You can learn more about their art here: @levantwinds on Instagram.

Thank you to Gabriela Carrasco Solar, illustrating as Feycompass Cartography, for the spectacular map of the Moonshadow Kingdom. As a long-time fan of the LOTR maps, to have one like this in my book is an author's dream come true!

Thank you to my fellow authors and dear friends, who keep me laughing, motivated, and moving forward through all of it: M. K. England, Becca Podos, Noelle Salazar, Rosiee Thor, Cindy Baldwin,

Ashley Martin, Autumn Krause, Katy J. Schroeder, Roselle Lim, Clare Edge, Maria Mora, and many others.

Thank you to my dear friend Cheryl, for all the heart chats as we both faced so much these last few years and our stories changed in so many unexpected ways.

Thank you to bestie Ashleigh B. What a weird few years it's been for both of us and what a journey!

Thank you to my sister Kim, my brother Mark, and my sister Renee, who remain steadfast and true amongst the storms. I love you all so much.

Thank you to all the readers, librarians, booksellers, bookstagrammers, booktokers, and everyone who's ever sent me a note about my books or shared them with their friends. Your enthusiasm is a light on this path. I appreciate you all so much. (Special thanks to excellent librarian pal Megan Nigh, who messaged me about the sneak peek of this book in the back of *The Absinthe Underground* when I was in the midst of a grueling fourth revision. You are the best!)

And, lastly, thank you to my sweet family, who I would move worlds for and who are my home.

Thank you to Liam, who will always have a place in my heart and my books. I miss you and I love you, Little One.

Thank you to Marcy, for cheering me on, offering helpful teen-reader suggestions, getting me through the moments when I didn't think I'd finish ("Just write a messy draft, Mom!"), and for generally being the most awesome kid I know. I love you.

Finally, thank you to Adam. For taking care of me while I wrote a lot of this book in bed after two surgeries, and for being with me in gardens, on dark roads, and within labyrinths since the beginning. I love you.

About the Author

Jamie Pacton is a bestselling, award-winning author who grew up minutes away from the International Storytelling Center in the mountains of East Tennessee. She has a BA and MA in English literature, and she currently teaches English at the college level. Her YA fantasy novels include *The Absinthe Underground*, an instant national bestseller. Her YA contemporary books include *Furious*, *Lucky Girl*, and *The Life and (Medieval) Times of Kit Sweetly*. Her adult fantasy romance debut, *Homegrown Magic*, published in 2025.

Find her online at JamiePacton.com
and @JamiePacton.